I0643356

Fortuné Du Boisgobey

A Fight for a Fortune

Fortuné Du Boisgobey

A Fight for a Fortune

ISBN/EAN: 9783337149079

Printed in Europe, USA, Canada, Australia, Japan

Cover: Foto ©Andreas Hilbeck / pixelio.de

More available books at **www.hansebooks.com**

ROWLAND'S MACASSAR OIL

is the ... and safest preserver and beautifier of fair hair, and contains no lead or mineral ingredients; it ... also be had in a *golden colour* for and buy old ... dren. Avoid cheap rancid oils, 10/6, and 21/-. WLAND'S MACASSAR OIL. 3,6, 7/-,

ROWLAND'S ODONTO

is the best tooth powder, and contains no gritty or acid substances which ruin the enamel; it whitens the teeth, polishes and preserves the enamel, prevents decay, and gives a pleasing fragrance to the breath; it is the original and only genuine Odonto.

ROW KA...

... and is perfectly ... skin; it eradicates ness, redness, chap... the effects of cold w... it soft, smooth and

...ND'S ...IA

...wder in three tints, ...rranted free from ...ients; 2/6 per box. ... for ROWLAND'S ...London, and avoid ...lar names.

55th Th...

S... ...O.

PARIS ... ...NERS.

...LLING.

ROBERT W. WOODRUFF LIBRARY

SPECIAL COLLECTIONS

EMORY UNIVERSITY

III

The **ONLY UNA**... ...DAUDET's deeply interesting St... ...ity Pages more than any other.

Be particular to ask for VIZETELLY & Co.'s *Edition.*

ZOLA'S POWERFUL REALISTIC NOVELS.

With numerous Page Engravings by French Artists, 6s. ; or without the Illustrations, 5s.

HIS MASTERPIECE? (L'Œuvre).

THE LADIES' PARADISE. (The Sequel to Piping Hot!)

THERESE RAQUIN.

GERMINAL; or Master and Man.

RUSH FOR THE SPOIL (La Curée).

PIPING HOT! (Pot-Bouille.)

THE "ASSOMMOIR."

NANA. (Sequel to the Assommoir.)

" After reading Zola's novels it seems as if in all others, even in the truest, there were a veil between the reader and the things described, and there is present to our minds the same difference as exists between the representations of human faces on canvas and the reflection of the same faces in a mirror. It is like finding truth for the first time."—*Signor De Amicis.*

(A.)

VIZETELLY'S SIXPENNY SERIES OF AMUSING BOOKS.

In picture cover, with many Engravings, price 6d.

MATRIMONY BY ADVERTISEMENT;

AND OTHER ADVENTURES OF A JOURNALIST.

BY CHARLES G. PAYNE.

Contains the Author's experiences in a Madhouse as an "Amateur Lunatic," and on a hansom as an "Amateur Cabby," as well as the details of a other amusing ded search for a wife through the agency of the Matrimonial Journals, and amusing articles.

Uniform with the above, and by the same Author.

VOTE FOR POTTLEBECK!

THE STORY OF A POLITICIAN IN LOVE.

Illustrated with a Frontispiece and numerous other Engravings.

CECILE'S FORTUNE.

BY F. DU BOISGOBEY.

THE THREE-CORNERED HAT.

BY P. A. DE ALARCON.

THE GREAT HOGGARTY DIAMOND.

BY W. M. THACKERAY.

THE STEEL NECKLACE.

BY F. DU BOISGOBEY.

THE BLACK CROSS MYSTERY.

BY HENRIETTE CORKRAN.

CAPTAIN SPITFIRE, AND THE UNLUCKY TREASURE.

BY P. A. DE ALARCON.

YOUNG WIDOWS.

BY E. C. GRENVILLE-MURRAY.

Profusely Illustrated.

A SHABBY GENTEEL STORY.

BY W. M. THACKERAY.

NEW ONE VOLUME NOVELS.

6s. each.

⌐RAMA IN MUSLIN. A REALISTIC NOVEL. By GEORGE
DISE⌐ORRE, Author of "A Mummer's Wife," "A Modern Lover," &c.

⌐SHANTMENT By F. MABEL ROBINSON, Author of
"utler's Ward."

INJURY
DOSTOIÐ INSULT A RUSSIAN REALISTIC NOVEL. By FEDOR
Athenæum toKY, Author of "Crime and Punishment," pronounced by the
"The most moving of all modern Novels."

A BOOK FOR TH₁ PRESENT CRISIS. *SECOND EDITION.*

In ↗un 8vo, price 1s.

IRISH HISTORY FO₁ ENGLISH R₁ADERS

By WILLIAM STEPH₁NSON GREGG₁.

"The history is one that every Englishman *ought* to r₁d. As an outline to be filled up b,
wider reading it is an admirable little book."—*Literary World.*

In crown 8vo, with folding frontispiece, limp cover, price 2s. 6d.

MY FIRST CRIME.

BY G. MACÉ, FORMER "CHEF DE LA SÛRETÉ" OF THE PARIS POLICE.

"An account by a real Lecoq of a real crime is a novelty among the mass of criminal novel
with which the world has been favoured since the death of the great originator Gaboriau. It i
to M. Macé, who has had to deal with real *juges d'instruction*, real *agents de la sûreté*, and rea
murderers, that we are indebted for this really interesting addition to a species of literature whic
has of late begun to pall."—*Saturday Review.*

THE BOULEVARD NOVELS.

Pictures of Paris Morals and Manners.

In small 8vo, attractively bound, price 2s. 6d. each.

NANA'S DAUGHTER. BY A. SIRVEN AND H. LEVERDIER.

THE YOUNG GUARD. BY VAST-RICOUARD.

THE WOMAN OF FIRE. BY ADOLPHE BELOT.

ODETTE'S MARRIAGE. BY ALPHONSE DELPIT.

BEAUTIFUL JULIE AND THE VIRGIN WIDOW.
BY A. MATTHEY.

A FIGHT FOR A FORTUNE.

THE GABORIAU & DU BOISGOBEY
SENSATIONAL NOVELS.

UNIFORM WITH THE PRESENT VOLUME.

THE STANDARD says :—" The romances of Gaboriau and Du Boisgobey picture the marvellous Lecoq and other wonders of shrewdness, who piece together the elaborate details of the most complicated crimes, as Professor Owen, with the smallest bone as a foundation, could re-construct the most extraordinary animals."

The following Volumes are already Published :

IN PERIL OF HIS LIFE.

THE LEROUGE CASE.

LECOQ, THE DETECTIVE.   2 Vols.

THE GILDED CLIQUE.

OTHER PEOPLE'S MONEY.

THE SLAVES OF PARIS.   2 Vols.

DOSSIER, NO. 113.

THE MYSTERY OF ORCIVAL.

THE COUNT'S MILLIONS.   2 Vols.

THE LITTLE OLD MAN OF BATIGNOLLES.

THE OLD AGE OF LECOQ, THE DETECTIVE.   2 Vols.

INTRIGUES OF A POISONER.

THE CATASTROPHE.   2 Vols.

IN THE SERPENTS' COILS.

THE DAY OF RECKONING.   2 Vols.

THE SEVERED HAND.

BERTHA'S SECRET.

WHO DIED LAST ?

THE CRIME OF THE OPERA HOUSE.   2 Vols.

THE MATAPAN AFFAIR.

A FIGHT FOR A FORTUNE.

THE GOLDEN PIG.   2 Vols.

THE THUMB STROKE.

PRETTY BABIOLE.

To be followed by :

THIEVING FINGERS.

THE CORAL PIN.   2 Vols.

THE NAMELESS MAN.

HIS GREAT REVENGE.   2 Vols.

DU BOISGOBEY'S SENSATIONAL NOVELS.

IX.

A FIGHT FOR A FORTUNE.

BY FORTUNÉ DU BOISGOBEY.

FIFTEENTH THOUSAND.

LONDON:

VIZETELLY & CO., 42 *CATHERINE STREET*, *STRAND.*

1886.

A FIGHT FOR A FORTUNE.

I.

"I say, Hingant, do you think that a man has a right to dispose of his property as he pleases?"

"That is a rather difficult question to answer on the spur of the moment. In the first place, the law makes a distinction between heirs expectant and—"

"Yes, yes, I know the code and am aware that you are well versed in it, but that isn't what I asked."

"Then, my dear Léridan, explain yourself more clearly, if you desire me to answer in a pertinent fashion—'ad rem,' as we say in court."

"Good! more Latin and big words. You will never throw that cargo overboard then, old lawyer that you are! What I wish to know is whether, in your opinion, a man conscientiously has a right to leave his property to whom he pleases?"

"Very good. That is a subject for philosophical controversy. I would gladly inform you, my friend; but, alas! I must confess that on this point the moralist is as much at a loss as the law-maker."

"Indeed? Well, then, to the deuce with your moralists and law-makers; and now let us talk of something else."

After disposing of the matter with this abrupt conclusion, the questioner began to whistle, keeping time by tapping his fingers on his knees. His companion shrugged his shoulders slightly, and produced his tinder box to relight his pipe, which had gone out. The conversation ceased entirely.

It must be admitted that the place inclined one to reverie. The two men were seated on a wooden bench near the edge of a narrow terrace, overlooking the Bay of Cancale; and below them, at the base of a precipitous cliff, the sea broke over rocks covered with golden-hued seaweed. In front, as far as the eye could reach, stretched an immense bay, in the centre of which Mount Saint Michel rose up, like a huge pyramid. The Normandy coast covered with verdure extended to the horizon opposite, and on the left projected the Groin—that bare and rocky cape which seems to have been stationed as a sort of sentinel by sad old Brittany.

This excellent observatory, the terrace, was connected with an unpretentious but peculiarly constructed house, built of dark granite. There were only three windows on the land side, and it presented to the sea a lofty, narrow, pointed gable of dazzling whiteness. Seen from a distance, this gable strongly resembled a column planted on the verge of a precipice; and the fishermen of the district, who had long been familiar with it, utilized it as a sort of beacon, not only during the daytime but also during the night, for every evening at sunset a light appeared in the one garret window of the gable, and was only extinguished at dawn. However, more than one captain, less familiar with the dangers of the coast, had reason to curse this unauthorized lighthouse, for shipwrecks were frequent between the little port of La Houlle and the cape. So the house was in rather bad repute in that part of the country ; in fact, it was commonly called the Pignon Maudit.*

Apart from the magnificent view one enjoyed from the terrace, the dwelling had no attractions. Standing alone at the end of a sterile moor without a flower or tree near it, it was fully exposed to the terrible tempests so frequent on this coast. There were no neighbours. It was necessary to walk considerably more than a mile to reach the first houses of the village of Cancale. From a distance one was inclined to take this granite building, so strangely situated between the lonely moor and the wild sea, for a Druidical monument.

Assuredly it could only be occupied by a misanthrope, or an eccentric person, and indeed both of these terms applied to Mériadec Léridan, who had built it and resided in it. However, he possessed a sufficient amount of worldly goods for his countrymen to be more than willing to overlook any faults of disposition. Mériadec Léridan was simply the richest landowner in the parishes of Cancale, Saint Coulomb, Saint Méloire-des-Ondes, and other neighbouring places. He was old, very old, and more than thirty years had elapsed since he had left home ; but in his youth he had ploughed every sea of the globe, and visited the four quarters of the world, as a privateersman.

Indeed, it was to this dangerous calling that he owed his fortune, for he was the fifth son of a poor sailor of Paramé, and in the second year of the Republic he had commenced earning his living as a cabin-boy on board a ship called the *Rights of Man*. In time, the cabin-boy became maintopman, then master, and finally, under the first Napoleon's consulate, after retiring from the State service, he was able, thanks to his prize-money, to purchase an interest in a fine brig, with ten guns, for which a merchant of Saint Malo had just obtained letters of marque—that is to say, permission to prey upon English ships of commerce. In 1809, after five or six fortunate cruises, he purchased the brig altogether, and commanded her with wonderful success until 1814. When the peace was signed he sold his vessel, realised his profits, and started for Paris.

What did he mean to do there ? No one knew, not even his four sisters who were living in comparative poverty ; but this much is certain : during the following year he returned to Cancale, purchased several fine farms in the neighbourhood, and having built his eagle-nest, took up his abode there with a sole companion—an old seaman known to everybody in the neighbourhood by the nickname of Porpoise, but who really rejoiced in the cognomen of Mathurin Callec.

The ex-privateersman's relatives did not forget him on his return to Cancale, and his presumptive heirs neglected no opportunity to win his favour and gain an entrance into the abode in which he had, so to say, entrenched himself. They laid positive siege to his fortress ; but all their labour was wasted, and not a single heir succeeded in crossing the threshold of the Pignon Maudit. Weary of the contest, they finally retreated, and at the date when this story begins they had long since left the retired sea-

* "The Cursed Gable."

wolf quiet. They had resigned themselves to waiting until it pleased Providence to consign him to the tomb. In the meantime a romantic legend
had become current in the neighbourhood. It was said that Léridan's visit
to Paris in 1815 had been connected with a project of marriage, which had
failed, and that disappointment in love had caused him although wealthy
and still young to condemn himself to an owl-like existence. It was also
reported that avarice had gradually usurped the place of love in his heart,
and that he had secreted tons of gold in his house, and was spending his
life in watching over his treasure as he would have watched over an adored
wife. Porpoise was the Cerberus, charged with guarding the treasure,
which was probably concealed in some cellar excavated in the rock upon
which the house had been built. Others declared—but what was not asserted of an evening around the tables of the Café Français, the favourite
resort of Houlle—others declared that the barrels full of English guineas
and quadruples were, on the contrary, secreted on some desert island of the
Chausey or Minquiers archipelago.

If one could have believed these well-informed persons, this was the cause
of the frequent sailing trips upon which the captain's one servant embarked;
and the signal-light which appeared at night-time in the garret window
was to show the old sailor exactly where to steer on moonless nights. For M.
Léridan owned a pretty sloop rigged in first-rate style and a remarkably
safe craft as well as a swift sailor. It was generally moored in a small
cove at the foot of some steps hewn in the cliff below the house. The old
privateersman had named it the Goëland in remembrance of the brig
which with its ten guns had so enriched him in former years. However he
never set foot on board it, for the very good reason that he had the gout,
and was unable to descend to the place of embarkation.

Was there any truth in these reports of the ex-privateersman's hidden
wealth? Various things certainly seemed to confirm the conjectures of
those who believed he possessed millions. Country people have good
memories, at least in regard to anything connected with money matters,
and the old people of the part recollected perfectly well the amount of
prize-money which the fortunate captain of the Goëland had deposited with
various Saint Malo bankers in 1814. This sum alone greatly exceeded the
amounts paid for the estates that the privateersman had purchased, and
for the house erected upon the cliff. What had become of the residue—to
say nothing of the old man's savings, for he did not spend a tenth part of
his income?

There was but one person in the neighbourhood who perhaps knew what
to think on this subject, for he alone enjoyed the enviable privilege of
visiting the ex-privateersmau, and of holding long and familiar conversa-
tions with him almost every day. This person was none other than M.
Jean-Marie Hingant, justice of the peace for the canton, and the very
person who sat chatting with Mériadec, on the terrace, on the chilly March
evening already spoken of.

M. Hingant, more familiarly styled M. Jean-Marie by his many acquain-
tances, was a philosopher. The only son of a well-to-do farmer, who had
been bent upon giving that son a good education, he had first studied at a
small seminary at Rennes. Then came a course of law, the legal profession being almost universally regarded by well-to-do peasants as a sort of
emancipation for the scion of a family long bent over the plough. Jean-
Marie's parents wanted a notary, a solicitor, or at least an advocate in the
family; and he became a solicitor. When the young fellow's law studies

wcre completed, and he had passed a very creditable examination, his
father purchased a practice for him. He conducted this honourably and
profitably for some time ; but litigation had very few delights for him.   In
fact, he was afflicted with an inclination to effect an amicable adjustment
of all differences, and this was not only extremely detrimental to his private
interests, but it also elicited expostulations from his brother lawyers.
Accordingly, as soon as he had amassed a modest competence, he sold his
practice, and through the influence of some judges who held him in high
esteem, he secured the position of justice of the peace, in the canton in
which his family property was situated.

This property came into his possession much sooner than he wished, and
brought him an income of about ten thousand francs.   This was enough
to live on anywhere : at Cancale it meant opulence.

M. Hingant made good use of it, and devoted himself to his duties in a
manner as commendable as it was uncommon.   He was not merely just
and sagacious, but he hated quarrelling ; and his natural instincts made
him endeavour to reconcile all disputants.   It may be said that he was a
born peacemaker.   He therefore almost invariably succeeded in arranging
the most complicated disputes, only sometimes it cost him dear ; for very
often when he had to deal with litigants who proved deaf to all entreaties,
he himself settled the claim of the plaintiff, who in exchange gave him a
promise not to continue the prosecution, without the opponent ever knowing
that this result was due to good M. Jean-Marie's generosity.

It was one of these acts of conciliation on the part of the worthy magistrate that had gained him the confidence of the fierce owner of the Pignon
Maudit.   The old privateersman was in the habit of amusing himself by
shooting from his terrace at the sea-gulls which sometimes lighted on the
rocks below.   Although he was an excellent shot, it chanced one day that
a fisherman, who was hauling in his nets below the cliff, was hit by several
grains of lead, and for this he modestly demanded three thousand francs
damages.

it is needless to say that Mériadec Léridan absolutely refused to pay
such a sum.   He did even more, he showed the door to the over zealous
justice of the peace who had thought it his duty to call and advise him to
pay a slight indemnity.   Jean-Marie did not insist, but sent for the
wounded man and gave him five hundred francs out of his own pocket, on
conditions that he would allow the matter to drop.

Unfortunately, the fisherman told everything to Porpoise who immediately
repeated the story to his master, and the next morning the peacemaker received a formal challenge in which the infuriated commandant summoned
him to fight with pistols at a distance of five paces on his terrace.

Worthy Hingant kept the appointment, but no blood flowed.   The
peacemaker found a means of pacifying even the bellicose mind of the
captain, and of making him a friend on the spot, but he was obliged to
consent to a re-imbursement of the amount he had expended, under penalty
of engaging in the proposed duel.

From that day forth their sudden friendship waxed stronger and firmer,
and twenty-four hours seldom elapsed without the old magistrate spending
a few hours at the Pignon Mandit.   At first, the intimacy caused a great
amount of comment at Cancale and La Houlle, and the frequenters of the Café
Français would have given a deal to know what was said at these daily
interviews.   But M. Jean-Marie was extremely prudent, and even the
most cunning soon had to relinquish the idea of obtaining any information

from him. Moreover, they would have been greatly astonished had they been present during the visits paid by the justice of the peace to Léridan, for most of the time was spent by the friends in playing backgammon or in chatting on unimportant matters, while they smoked their pipes.

The conversation rarely went beyond generalities, for the two men were equally reserved. Léridan did not seem at all inclined to make any confidential disclosures, and nothing would have induced Hingant to encourage him to do so. The result was that they usually discussed morality, politics, and religion, three points upon which they disputed incessantly, although they perhaps secretly agreed with each other.

The old privateersman believed in natural morality, that which depends solely upon the conscience, and cares but little for social laws. In politics, he advocated a firm rule, and would not admit that France could be governed in any other manner than that in which he had formerly ruled his crew. His religion was that of a sailor, simple, unquestioning, unreasoning. He believed what his mother had taught him to believe.

The magistrate on his side had an idol, an ideal—virtue. He asserted, that if every person in the world would practise it, civil codes and governments would become unnecessary. He did not go so far as to renounce the faith of his childhood, by any means ; but he was inclined to mingle with it certain theories borrowed from the stoics, who maintained that one should do good merely for the sake of doing good, and not with any hope of reward. The excellent magistrate believed also, that all men were naturally good at heart : Léridan declared the contrary ; and this was an inexhaustible topic of discussion.

They sometimes finished by losing their tempers, but their sulks did not last long. True, it was almost always the good-natured magistrate who first made overtures of peace ; but we must add that the commandant did not long resist them.

On this particular evening, that of March 13th, 1848, the course of events was in conformity with the usual programme. After the outburst of ill-humour in which Léridan had just indulged, already regretting his vivacity, he suddenly raised a spyglass which was lying on his lap, and applying it to his eye, possibly to conceal a desire for reconciliation, kept it persistently levelled at the open sea in the direction of the Groin. The magistrate, after puffing away silently for awhile, at last emerged from the cloud of smoke in which he had taken refuge to preserve his dignity, and softly inquired : " It's Mathurin Callec whom you are waiting for with so much impatience, is it not ? "

" Whom else do you suppose it could be ? " rejoined the privateersman, in a milder tone. " You know very well that he is the only human being in whom I take the slightest interest."

" The only one ? " asked Jean-Marie, smiling.

" Yourself excepted, of course, though you are sometimes almost unendurable with your philanthropical attacks. But you are very comfortable here, while my poor Porpoise has been at sea for thirty-six hours in an equinoctial gale."

" It was foolish to send the Goëland out in such weather. Your nephew, Le Planchais said so to me last evening—"

" My nephew ! " exclaimed the commandant, turning round in a passion. " What business has he to meddle with my affairs ? So he watches me, it seems. Look here, Hingant, never mention his name in my presence if you wish to continue sailing in the same boat with me."

"Bnt, my friend, it isn't merely Le Planchais who makes remarks about the trips of the *Goëland*, it is the whole neighbourhood, and I assure you—"

"Indeed!" M. Léridan interrupted, with apparent surprise, "so these good oystermen take the trouble to concern themselves about me, my servant, and my sloop? And what do they say, if you please?"

"A great deal of nonsense which you can undoubtedly guess, and which I don't care to repeat to you. I only allnded to this gossip in order to show you, my dear Mériadec, that you are sometimes unjust towards your family."

"My family! I have none. I want none."

"You can't help yourself in the matter; your sisters left you three nephews and a niece."

"I disown them, as I disowned their mothers when they made up their minds to take husbands from Normandy, instead of marrying worthy Bretons like you and me."

"That, as you must admit, is a rather singular cause of offence in this age of progress."

"Bah! don't talk to me about your progress, I don't care a fig for progress."

"Perhaps not. But confess that it isn't the fault of your heirs if—"

"My heirs, my heirs! it is your foolish civil code which makes them that; but it also says that a man can bequeath his property as he likes, and my conscience in nowise troubles me about availing myself of this permission to disinherit them if I choose."

"Are you quite sure of that? It seems to me some scruples still re- main, for only a few moments ago you were consulting me—"

"But I no longer do so."

"And I haven't any desire to give advice unasked."

There was another pause, and the commandant again raised his glass. But the hopeful magistrate did not consider himself beaten yet. "In short, what do you reproach these poor people with? Are they not earn- ing their living honestly?"

"Honestly!" roared the old privateersman. "What do you call the professions which that coxcomb, Charles, and that stuck-up doll, Mathilde, have chosen?"

"But it seems to me that business—"

"Pretty business, indeed! The girl does dnty as a cashier at the Café Militaire at Saint Malo, instead of marrying a brave sailor: the other scratches away all day in a broker's office, and spends his Sundays at the promenade, instead of sailing about like a man."

"But, what else could yon expect? Charles isn't strong enough for a seaman's life, and Mathilde has been petted too much. But your nephew, François, the school-teacher—"

"The school-teacher! an underhand scamp who spends his days over a desk; a coward, who prefers flogging little children to serving in the navy!"

"Yon forget that the poor fellow is near-sighted. And Le Planchais, the son of yonr elder sister? I hope you have nothing to say against this nephew, who is a registered sailor of the port of Cancale?"

If M. Hingant had fancied he was reserving his best card for the last, be was terribly mistaken, for the commandant, on hearing this praise of his fourth heir, was seized with such an attack of anger that he rose up, and resting one hand on the back of the wooden bench, while with the other he brandished his spyglass as if it had been a sabre, he cried out in a voice husky with passion : " He a seaman ! You call him a seaman because his name is inscribed upon the marine register, and he goes out every evening in his old boat to set lines in the bay. He's as much a sailor as I'm a soldier. The others are only idlers and simpletons ; he's a scoun-drel ! Mathurin told me that he came one night and stole some lobsters out of our traps. One of these days he will kill somebody, and I shouldn't be surprised if it were me, for he is so often seen wandering about among the rocks, and on the day before yesterday I surprised him perched on the cliff only a short distance below the terrace. He had better not come again, or I'll shoot him. He is, perhaps, lurking about here still," con-tinued the captain, advancing towards a wooden platform which projected balcony-like beyond the terrace.

However, his friend detained him by catching hold of his arm and ex-claiming : " Don't step upon those boards. You know very well that they are not safe."

"That's true, besides I don't care much about finding the ugly bird. But for heaven's sake, never speak to me again of any member of the tribe."

The magistrate said no more, but he sighed heavily.

" Why are you blowing like a whale ? " curtly inquired the old privateers-man.

" Because I think it is unfortunate to die without ever having had any affection for anyone, and—"

" How do you know that I never loved ? " interrupted M. Léridan with singular vivacity.

Jean-Marie, surprised by this remark, was trying to find some persuasive words which might induce his friend to open his heart to him without re-serve, when he heard him exclaim : " This time I am not mistaken ! It *is* the *Goëland* I see rounding the point. I recognize her rigging. But we can see her better from here."

And before the justice of the peace had time to prevent it, the owner of the Pignon Maudit hopped on one leg on to the platform hanging over the cliff. He had scarcely set foot upon it when the boards gave way be-neath his weight, and dragged him with them in their fall to the bottom of the precipice.

II.

A WEEK had passed. A week—an eternity to the four heirs who had been so suddenly raised from poverty to affluence. For the poor commandant was dead—really dead. A perpendicular fall of one hundred and fifty feet, upon jagged rocks, is certain death to anyone, and thus an accident had put a sudden end to a life which had resisted twenty years of warfare, and thirty years of idleness. The privateersman's vigorous frame, which one might have supposed to be cased with metal like the *Goëland* herself, had been shattered like glass on the hard granite ; and he had not even the con-solation of a grave in the sea, for his mangled remains lay on a pointed rock at the foot of the precipice. It was there that the terrified justice of the peace collected his mutilated remains. Le Planchais, who happened to be fishing near the cliff, assisted him in the mournful task, and the remains were transported to La Houlle in the nephew's skiff.

When Porpoise, whose reappearance with the *Goëland* had been the innocent cause of his master's death, reached home and heard the terrible
news, he did not shed a tear, but relapsed into a gloomy silence which contrasted strangely with the demonstrative grief of Jacques Le Planchais, who,
however, must have already begun to realize the consolation that his share
of his uncle's property might afford him.

As for M. Hingant, it is needless to say that his sorrow was sincere and
deep.   He had lost a firm and devoted friend—a man whom he greatly esteemed ; and, what is perhaps even more painful when one lives in comparative solitude and is no longer young, he had lost his favourite companion.   To prevent himself from sinking into a state of positive despair, he
was obliged to summon up all his professed stoicism.   But he only half
succeeded, and he had to admit that he found less consolation in the finest
pages of Marcus Aurelius than in the truly Christian hope of again meeting
his dear Mériadec Léridan in heaven.

Fortunately, his duties as a magistrate served to divert his attention a
little.   It was necessary for him to at once affix the Government seals to
the doors, drawers, cupboards, &c., in the Pignon Maudit, to inform the
absent heirs (whom it was scarcely necessary to warn, as public rumour had
already done this with the rapidity of the electric telegraph), and to draw
up an official statement of the circumstances and probable causes of this
strange demise.   Finally, in the capacity of a friend, he felt it his duty to
see that the obsequies of the ex-privateersman were suitably solemnized,
and that the officials of the neighbourhood were invited to attend them.
These various duties engrossed most of his time during the first few days,
and no unexpected incident occurred.   The seals were affixed with the consent and almost at the request of nephew Le Planchais, the only member of the
family present.   Porpoise had no right to object to the accomplishment of
this legal formality, but the justice of the peace, a trifle impressed in spite
of himself by all the stories of wealth concealed in the house, almost expected to see him display some discontent on finding himself thus excluded
from his master's abode.

However, Porpoise did not even frown.   On the contrary, he assiduously
helped the magistrate in all the investigations started for the purpose of
discovering how this frightful accident could have occurred, and he seemed to
take the greatest interest in the matter.   Still, the investigations revealed nothing new.   The platform which had given way under the commandant's weight
had been constructed more than thirty years before by his orders.   He had
formerly used it for fishing, and with the aid of a long line, he could thus
catch barbel, mullet, and mackerel without leaving his own grounds.   Indeed, it was his servant, Mathurin Callec, who had constructed the platform
with his own hands.   It was built of heavy oak timber, secured at one end
to the stonework of the terrace, and supported at the other by solid beams,
strongly riveted to the cliff itself, and so it had been at first sufficiently
substantial to satisfy the most apprehensive person.

But time, with the west wind and the rain, had so shaken and rotted the
timbers that the whole structure had threatened to fall to pieces, and M.
Léridan, although not naturally a prudent man, had abstained from using
it for several years past ; however, as he had given up fishing, he neglected
to have it repaired, despite the fact that his friend, Jean-Marie, had several
times urged him to do so.   Besides, Mathurin Callec, perhaps by reason of
a builder's vanity, had declared that the platform was still strong enough
to bear one, or even two persons.   During the investigation he still main-

tained that such had been the case, and, indeed, this was the only point upon which he ventured to speak.

The accident had, unfortunately, proved that he was mistaken, unless one admitted that the supporting timbers had been mischievously sawed through, during the past few days. The justice of the peace called Mathurin's attention to this fact, but instead of replying he shook his head, and relapsed into silence. Any verification of the matter had, moreover, become impossible, for the beams, which had gone down with the unfortunate commandant had fallen into the sea, which had swept them away, or scattered them among the rocks; at least they could not be found.

M. Hingant accordingly drew up a report, in which he stated in all sincerity of belief that the death had been accidental; and he then gave his attention to the preparations for his friend's funeral. This took place a couple of days afterwards and was attended by an immense crowd, for after all, Mériadec Léridan had no enemies, and, in spite of his eccentricities, his compatriots honoured him as a man who had acquired wealth by dint of courage and perseverance. The nephews acted as chief mourners, and wept in a manner which surprised many of the spectators, and touched some few of them. Beside the grave they even sobbed so vehemently as to greatly interfere with the eloquence of the sub-commissioner of the navy, who had bestowed much time and thought on an interminable discourse in which the late M. Léridan was highly praised, and even compared to a soldier-farmer. This comparison, however, would have irritated him beyond measure had he been able to hear it, for he had all a sailor's dislike for a soldier.

To the great astonishment of the people present, including the justice of the peace, who walked directly behind the relatives, Mathurin Callec was not in the funeral procession. The old fellow had for thirty-six hours watched over his master's body, but when the pall-bearers entered the house to remove the coffin, he knelt down, said a short prayer, then rose with a resolute air, and saw the mournful procession start for the cemetery of Cancale without shedding a tear. He followed it for some time with his eyes, as it slowly wended its way along, and then returned to sleep on the doorstep of the Pignon Maudit, like a faithful dog guarding the abode of an absent master.

When the day to remove the seals came, he was still there. This was an eventful day for the offspring of the deceased privateersman's sisters. The niece and the nephews arrived at daybreak with composed faces, though their hearts were agitated by mingled fear and hope. A few lines on a scrap of paper might dispel all their dreams of wealth, and it was quite likely that the old privateersman had written them. Had he not all his life refused to see his relatives, or even to hear them mentioned? So it was likely that they would still feel the effects of this antipathy even when he was in the grave. He had, it is true, no other relatives on earth, but nothing need have prevented him from bequeathing his property to his friend Jean-Marie, or to some charitable institution, such as a sailor's home, for instance. The will, in case there was one, must be in the house, for no one knew of his having employed any notary, so the heirs-at-law felt a great deal of anxiety during the search, which was made in their presence.

More than once, the justice of the peace could not repress a smile on seeing all four of them turn pale at the sight of a scrap of paper, discovered in some drawer. But their apprehensions were not realised. They not only found no will, but, what seemed much more extraordinary, they only found a very insignificant sum of money. The absence of a will was a set-off against this disappointment, however, and all that now remained to be done was to divide the landed property, which was worth at least eight hundred thousand francs ; no trivial amount to persons who were not the joint possessors of fifty pounds. In addition to this there was the Pignon Maudit, not a valuable piece of property by any means, but which would serve as a meeting place until the division had been effected. So they stayed there from morning till night, and, in order to be able to talk with freedom, they politely requested Mathurin Callec to take up his abode elsewhere, and the old sailor had no difficulty in finding shelter at the residence of the worthy justice of the peace.

Thus placed in possession of the house and the fortune, the heirs congratulated each other, and exchanged protestations of eternal friendship. There was even a bit of a feast, and for three days all went merry as a marriage bell. On the fourth day, however, the subject of dividing the property was broached for the first time. Each heir took a seat at the table in the drawing-room, and François Dolley, the schoolmaster, made solemn preparations to draw up a scheme for dividing the property. This village schoolmaster was a man about thirty years of age, with a pale, pleasant face framed by red whiskers, and with grey eyes screened by spectacles. He had the reputation of being a ready speaker ; moreover, he was the eldest of the party, and so he opened the conversation. "My dear cousins," he said, in a most insinuating voice, "our much-regretted uncle left four estates of almost equal value ; so there can be no difficulty in coming to a satisfactory understanding. As for this shanty, I am about the only one of you who could make any use of it, since I reside in the neighbourhood, and I am very willing to take it, at its value of course."

"But I also live in the neighbourhood," interrupted Jacques Le Planchais, sulkily, "and the house suits me ; I claim it myself."

"I also should like to have the house, to arrange it as a shooting box and entertain some friends I mean to invite from Paris," said Charles Dugenêt, the handsome clerk.

"And I," simpered Mathilde, "think of spending the coming summer at the seaside, and should like to secure the house myself."

There came a spell of silence, and glances of no very friendly character were exchanged. The heirs had very much the air of duellists observing each other before crossing swords. Le Planchais, who had a sanguine temperament, opened fire the first. "Shall I tell you the truth ?" he exclaimed, dealing the table a formidable blow with his fist. "It isn't the old man's shanty that you are after : it is his money."

This pointed declaration caused an immense sensation. The schoolmaster adjusted his spectacles, the clerk twirled his budding moustache, and Mathilde began to smooth her blonde curls. All three were evidently trying to conceal their embarrassment. "Come," resumed Le Planchais, coarsely, "admit that each one of you wishes to secure the hoarded wealth without sharing it with the others. Do you think you can fool me with your tricks ? Do you fancy you can make me swallow such absurd reasons as you have just invented ? They may deceive an old simpleton like Hingant, but I know well enough what you are after. It is uncle Mériadec's treasure."

"And what if that were the case ?" asked the schoolmaster, with a cold glance at his cousin.

This question was the signal for a general revolt. "Yes ; and what if that were the case ?" repeated the clerk, with an insolent air.

"Yes; what have you to say about it?" added Mathilde.

"Nothing, except that I want my share of the money, as well as the rest of you," growled Le Planchais, after some hesitation.

"All right! On that point we certainly agree with you," rejoined Dolley, quietly. "But to begin with, you speak with great assurance. What makes you suppose there is any money concealed here?"

"There must be some either here or somewhere else. The old man possessed nearly two millions in 1815. Since then they must have increased, and the landed property is worth scarcely a single million. Where is the rest of the money?"

"Somewhere, that's certain," replied the schoolmaster, "the question is to discover it."

"I suggest that we all unite in searching for it," said cousin Charles.

"A very good idea; but how shall we begin? We cannot demolish the cliff, and overturn the moor."

"That's true," replied Mathilde. "We must at least have some clue."

"And there is only one man who can probably give or sell it to us," insinuated François, suavely.

"And who is that?" inquired Le Planchais, in a sulky tone. "It can't be the justice of the peace, for he has such a tender conscience that he would long since have told the rightful heirs the hiding-place."

"That is admirable reasoning; but I don't refer to him."

"To whom then?"

"To a man who knows more about this matter than all the rest of the world together, and whom you drove from the house like a dog."

"Old Porpoise!" exclaimed all the other cousins in concert.

"Yes, Porpoise; and I am surprised that you haven't thought of purchasing him before this."

"And I suspect that if you didn't, it was because you wished to secure him for your sole use and benefit," retorted the terrible Le Planchais.

"But you see such isn't the case, as I suggest the matter now."

"That's true," muttered Charles and Mathilde.

Strengthened by their approval, the schoolmaster thought the moment had come for a display of his eloquence. "My friends," he began with a deliberate air, "we shall gain nothing by bickering. On the contrary, 'in union there is strength.' That is the motto on the new five franc pieces, and we should do well to adopt it."

"To the point!" exclaimed Jacques, who was not fond of preambles.

"My advice," continued the schoolmaster, "is for all four of us to remain joint owners of the house, and to allow the gratuitous use of it to Mathurin Callec for six months."

"Are you mad? Do you wish him to steal the money from us?"

"No, I only wish to be able to watch him without his suspecting it, and thus discover the treasure."

"I don't understand you," growled Jacques.

"You will if you listen to me. One of two things is certain. Either there is some money concealed somewhere, or there is none. If there is, Mathurin, who knows where it is, won't fail to disinter it some fine night; and as we shall mount guard by turns in a little hiding-place I know of, we will detect him in the act. If there is no gold, we shall only have to send the fellow away at the end of the six months."

"Charming, charming!" sneered the handsome Charles. "We should use him as our truffle hunter."

Le Planchais said nothing, but by the contraction of his features and the knittiug of his brows, it was easy to see that he was deeply meditating. " Why not?" he murmured, after some moments' reflection. " It is perhaps the only means. Only there must be no foul play. I don't hesitate to say that I will certainly break the head of any one who attempts to defraud us."

" And you would be quite right; but nothing of that kind is possible. One can't carry off a ton of gold in a single night; besides, we can follow Mathurin and see where he goes. Cancale isn't Paris, by any means, and hereabouts one knows all that is going on each hour of the day."

" Paris," repeated Mademoiselle Mathilde, almost unconsciously.

" Yes, my girl," said François, smiling. " You know very well that it is of Paris you are dreaming."

" And I also," muttered the handsome clerk, straightening the knot of his cravat.

" Ah, well, a little patience, my children. You shall go there in six mouths, at the beginning of the winter. That is a good time, folks say, to enjoy the pleasures of the capital. And who knows but what I may do the same, for you may rest assured that when the estate is once wound up, I sha'n't amuse myself by remaining here to teach fishermen's brats to spell. We are entering upon a period in which an intelligent man may reasonably expect to make his way in the great Babylon."

" I have good strong fists to make mine," growled Jacques.

" Ah, I see we shall all find ourselves there during the ensuing year," said the schoolmaster, " but now, what is your decision ? Is my proposal adopted?"

" I vote for it," exclaimed Mathilde. " It will give me time to send for some dresses before leaving."

" And it will give me time to get rid of that little fool, Yvonne, the haberdasher's girl, whom I promised to marry," muttered Charles between his teeth. " I consent to the plan."

" I also consent, but on one condition," said Jacques, in his turn.

" What condition ? " inquired the schoolmaster, already uneasy.

" That we make old Porpoise a present of my uncle's sloop. When people begin to be generous there must be no half way work. We will give Mathurin a home. That is proper. But by giving him the *Goëland*, we should furnish him with the means of earning a livelihood; it will make us popular in the neighbourhood, an advantage that shouldn't be overlooked."

Charles snapped his fingers, and Mathilde shrugged her shoulders to indicate that they attached no more value to a quarter interest in the *Goëland* than to the consideration of their compatriots. But François Dolley acted differently. His eyes glittered ominously, his lips became compressed, and he began to gaze fixedly at this cousin who had suddenly become so generous. Le Planchais sustained Dolley's piercing gaze unflinchingly. He knew that his motives were understood, but he thought that the schoolmaster would not dare to reveal his secret thoughts in the presence of Charles and Mathilde.

Nor was he mistaken. François Dolley perfectly understood the motive that had prompted Jacques' suggestion. If the treasure were concealed on one of the deserted channel islands, Mathurin, on becoming master of the *Goëland*, would not fail to pay a nocturnal visit to the gold which he himself must have concealed. Le Planchais, a seaman by profession, intended to follow him, take him by surprise, and, perhaps, even murder him to obtain possession of the gold. More than once already during his uncle's life he had attempted to carry all or a part of this fine scheme into execution, but the wretched craft he owned was in no condition to follow the swift-sailing *Goëland*, and he had invariably lost sight of Porpoise. Now, however, there was nothing to prevent him from purchasing a fine yacht at Saint Servan, and managing in such a way as to watch and overtake Porpoise on his next trip.

The schoolmaster himself was no professional sailor, but like all dwellers on the coast, he knew how to hold a tiller with one hand, and slacken a sail with the other, so there was nothing to prevent him from playing the same game as his cousin. It was better to risk this than to take Mathilde and the clerk into confidence, for they, having always resided at Saint Malo, were not acquainted with all the gossip of Cancale, and really believed that it was merely a question of giving Mathurin a boat for which they cared little or nothing. "The worst that can happen is that I may be compelled to share with Le Planchais," thought Dolley, "and I would much rather do that than take merely a fourth or nothing—" "Well," he said aloud, "I see no objection whatever to giving this worthy man a memento of his master."

"Then it is decided?" inquired Jacques, eagerly.

"It is decided, as there is no opposition. To-morrow we will send for Mathurin, transfer the boat to him by deed and let him remain in the house. He can take possession at once, if he chooses, and to-night we will shut the place up and leave the key at Monsieur Hingant's, so that there will be no cause for jealousy."

"Bravo!" exclaimed Charles, "in that case I can spend the evening playing pool at the Café Français."

"That will suit me also," cried Mathilde, "for the wife of the commander of the coastguard has invited me to spend the evening with her."

Le Planchais said nothing, but his mind was full of such thoughts as these : "The notary will be quite willing to advance me, on my share of the property, enough money to purchase a boat now for sale at Saint Servan, and the next time the *Goëland* goes out to sea, I shall be as sure of overtaking Mathurin as I am that the million isn't concealed here."

"I know what you are plotting," Dolley thought, "but I am as sharp as you are, and you will have to divide the spoil with me."

He had just risen to give the signal for departure, when the door gently opened, and the genial face of the justice of the peace appeared. "How do you do, young people?" said M. Jean-Marie pleasantly, "may I come in?"

There was a general outcry :—"Why, certainly. Monsieur Jean-Marie!"

"You would honour us by doing so, sir."

"I hope you will condescend to take some refreshment with us. Our poor uncle had some excellent rum, and I will—"

"Thank you, thank you, but I am not thirsty—"

"Still it is a long walk from Cancale, and you seem to have walked very rapidly," remarked Dolley, with a shade of anxiety in his manner. He was still so unaccustomed to his wealth that he was in constant fear of seeing it crumble before him like a house of cards, and the slightest incident seemed to forebode evil tidings.

"Yes," said M. Hingant, quietly, "I did hurry a little, as I wished to reach here before night. Since the unfortunate death of my poor friend, I have not had courage to come here, and yet it seemed to me it would do me good to revisit the house in which we spent so many pleasant hours together."

"It is at your service, and we also, Monsieur Jean-Marie," replied the schoolmaster obsequiously.

"I knew I should find you all assembled here, and that was what decided me to come."

"Have you anything to say to us?" inquired François, eagerly.

"Nothing, my friends—at least nothing new." There were several sighs of relief. "Only I wish to profit by the opportunity to tell you how glad I am that your uncle has left you his property. Do you know that I was really very uneasy? Léridan had such strange ideas. But Providence didn't allow such a handsome fortune to pass out of the family, and I sincerely rejoice with you. There is only one thing I regret," added M. Hingant, " that your uncle neglected to make any provision for his old servant—"

"Mathurin?" exclaimed Dolley. "That's true; but we have been thinking about it, and have just decided to give him the *Goéland*, and permission to reside here for six months."

"Oh, my dear children!" exclaimed the justice of the peace, with sincere emotion, "I might have expected this from worthy people like yourselves; but I must still say it is kind, very kind of you. And now I may as well admit that my object in coming here was in a measure to ask you to think of this poor sailor, who has suddenly found himself destitute of all resources. I would not have deserted him, of course; but it is far better for him to be indebted to you than to me."

"Have no fears, Monsieur Jean-Marie, he will be taken care of," said Le Planchais, brusquely.

"And if you will tell him this very evening what we have decided to do for him, we shall be greatly obliged to you," added Dolley. "The worthy fellow's happiness must not be any longer deferred."

"You may be sure that I shall not fail to do so. Now let us talk a little about yourselves. I suppose you have come to a friendly arrangement as to the division of the property."

"Yes, it's all settled, sir. Each of us takes a farm, and, out of respect to our uncle's memory, we retain a joint interest in his house, which is equally dear to all of us."

"That is an arrangement of which I fully approve. I also think, I can guess your other plans."

Intense astonishment, mingled with uneasiness, was depicted on every countenance, for the heirs fancied that the magistrate had guessed the scheme upon which they had just decided for the recovery of the treasure. "You, my dear child," resumed the artless justice of the peace, addressing Mathilde, "will soon marry a merchant captain, or—who knows?—the son of a ship builder."

"Oh, I am in no haste to marry, sir," replied Mademoiselle Pelchat, quickly; "besides, I don't propose to reside at Saint Malo. In Paris suitable opportunities are not wanting, and it is my intention—".

"In Paris!" repeated M. Hingant, in great astonishment. "You certainly don't think of establishing yourself there alone, I hope. It would be extremely imprudent for a young person of your age—"

"The wife of the commander of the coastguard has promised to accompany me," murmured Mathilde, blushing.

Léridan's old friend dared not insist any further, but turning to the young clerk, he said gaily : "Your future, my dear Charles, is clearly marked out for you. You will purchase your employer's business, and in ten years—"

"I !" interrupted the young fellow, "I'm not so foolish as to bury myself in a shop in a little town, when I can buy an interest in a stockbroker's business in Paris."

"Ah !" sighed the magistrate, "I see we shall only be able to keep with us Jacques and François."

"Pooh ! there is nothing much to be done here by any intellectual man," replied the schoolmaster.

"Or by a man of energy," added Le Planchais.

"While in the great city," resumed Dolley, "and especially in an age of social reform—"

"Well, well, my friends, " said Hingant, evidently disappointed, "I will not attempt to interfere with your plans. Besides, perhaps you are right. Nowadays, one desires above all else to make one's way, and country life does not suit everybody. Besides, I am quite sure that wherever you may reside, you will always be an honour to our province."

"Oh, you need feel no anxiety on that score, Monsieur Jean-Marie," protested all the heirs, at the same moment.

"However, it is growing late. and you are about to return to Cancale or La Houlle, and I must not detain you any longer. I will call again some other day—"

"By no means, by no means," exclaimed the amiable schoolmaster. "We had just decided to intrust the keys of the house to you until Mathurin takes possession of it, and you could not have come at a better moment. We will leave the keys with you and retire. Pray make yourself entirely at home and remain as long as you please."

"Ah, well, my friends, I will accept your offer," replied M. Hingant. "I am glad of an opportunity to spend an hour or two alone here, thinking of my old friend. It seems to me that the very walls will speak of him, and ——" He paused, for the tears had risen to his eyes, and emotion choked his utterance ; the heirs, who had no desire to weep, profited by his passing emotion to make their escape.

Charles and Mathilde were greatly afraid of losing their evening's enjoyment, and Jacques and François felt that they had no time to lose to prepare their important plans. However, Jacques cast a suspicious glance at the magistrate on crossing the threshold. "Simpleton !" the schoolmaster whispered in his ear, "you know very well that if Mousieur Hingant should by any chance discover the treasure, he would rather come to awake us up at midnight than retain the responsibility of such a find until to-morrow."

Le Planchais did not insist, and his silence was a tacit tribute to M. Jean-Marie's undisputed honesty.

The old magistrate's eyes were still wet as he watched the heirs depart. "Kind-hearted creatures !" he muttered. "How touching, how praiseworthy was their conduct in providing for Mathurin even before I asked them to do so ! In this one recognizes the Breton blood that flowed in the veins of my poor Léridan and which flows in theirs, though he maintained the contrary. How fortunate it is that he did not have time to disinherit them, for he thought of doing so. I guessed it by the questions that he put to me not an hour before the accident. And, now, here I am almost congratulating myself on his untimely death!" exclaimed M. Hingant, suddenly perceiving that his enthusiastic admiration for the generosity of the heirs was carrying him too far. To prevent this, he went out and sat down on the bench where but a few days before he had talked for the last time with his old comrade.

III.

THE sun was setting, but the atmosphere was clear and the sea calm. It was a magnificent spring evening—a rarity on the coast of France in the month of March. However, the wonderful panorama visible from the terrace made no impression upon the magistrate. He was entirely absorbed in sorrowful recollections of the catastrophe which had occurred there under his very eyes. In thought he again beheld the privateersman seated beside him, with his strong features, rapid gestures, and clear, frank gaze. Again he heard his rather harsh but sonorous voice, and he recalled each word of the singular conversation which had been interrupted in such a shocking manner. Gradually his mind reverted to the trip made by Mathurin Callec with the *Goëland* whose impatiently awaited re-appearance had been the cause of a terrible catastrophe. Then he began to think of the rumours which had so long prevailed respecting the old sailor's nocturnal expeditions and his master's tons of gold.

"Ridiculous stories," he murmured. "Mériadec was no miser. What object could he have had in hoarding money? People say that his estates do not represent the fortune he possessed when he gave up his seafaring life. But what does that prove? Simply that he led a gay life during his stay in Paris in 1815. He was the very man to spend several hundred thousand francs in a few months. My father has often told me that in those days gold slipped through his fingers. Since that time Mériadec may have secretly given away large sums in charity. No, it is certain that he had no property except his farms."

Perhaps M. Hingant was less convinced of the truth of this last assertion than he would admit even to himself, for a moment afterwards he resumed : "Still, it would be as well for me to question Porpoise about his nocturnal expeditions. I shall have a deal of trouble in getting anything out of him, he is so very taciturn, but I shall try, all the same."

Night was now fast approaching, and the magistrate wished to visit the house before he returned home. Accordingly he now repaired to the drawing-room, where he found a lighted lamp upon the table—a delicate attention that François Dolley had paid him before his departure.

Taking this lamp, M. Hingant ascended to the first floor and entered the dead man's chamber, not without emotion. Everything was still arranged as in Léridan's lifetime. It seemed as if the old privateersman were only absent for a moment. Affected to tears the magistrate did not tarry there long. On the second floor there was a large room in which Léridan had spent a good deal of his time in bad weather, and where he had collected all his glasses, compasses, sextants, and other articles pertaining to his former calling. On entering this room, as the magistrate's emotion overcame him more and more, and his limbs tottered, he was obliged to set down the lamp and seat himself in a large bamboo chair that happened to be near him. He was a great smoker, and on such occasions as these, he seldom failed to have recourse to his favourite sedative—his old pipe which never left him. He drew it from his pocket and filled it, but he could not find his tinder box, and suddenly he recollected that he had left it at home. He then glanced about him for a scrap of paper which he might light at the lamp; but he saw none on the table or elsewhere—for the old sea-dog seldom wrote. However, on the hearth, among the ashes, M. Hingant at last espied a crumpled fragment, yellow with age. He picked it up and was about to present it to the flame of the lamp, when he fancied he saw two or three lines of Léridan's writing upon it. He then looked at it more carefully, and in his surprise almost tumbled from his chair. He had just read the very words with which most wills begin: "I give and bequeath—"

At first, M. Hingant fancied his eyes were deceiving him. How was it possible that the deceased had written his last wishes upon this paltry scrap of paper? At the most he could only have traced upon it some informal project, abandoned almost as soon as conceived. Nothing, however, could be easier than to satisfy himself on this point, as he had only to unfold the crumpled scrap and read the writing to the end; but although he realized the necessity of ascertaining the truth, yet as he unrolled the paper his hand trembled and a mist obscured his vision. The fact was he realised that this soiled fragment of paper, half destroyed by time, might mean the ruin of those generous heirs who had just entered upon their new life by making such a noble use of their freshly acquired wealth in assuring the welfare of their uncle's old servant. He also had a presentiment of the weighty responsibilities that might devolve upon him, and he was tempted to rid himself of them by throwing the paper back into the ashes from which he had rescued it: however, the promptings of duty stayed his hand.

He cautiously unfolded the paper, approached the lamp and read: "I give and bequeath all my property, real and personal, to Mademoiselle Marie Bréhal.

"Paris, July twenty-nine, eighteen hundred and fifteen." Then came the signature, firmly written like the lines that preceded it, in a clear round hand,

"MÉRIADEC LÉRIDAN,
"Commandant of the privateer brig, the
"Goëland of Saint Malo."

All further doubt was impossible. It was a will, signed, dated, and written in the hand of the testator, and consequently as valid as if it had been drawn up and deposited in a notary's office. The date, too, was given in full, as if the old salt had attached particular importance to this formality. M. Hingant, stupefied, overcome, thunderstruck, allowed the terrible bit of paper which condemned the privateersman's interesting relatives to endless poverty to drop upon the table. When he partially regained his self-possession, his feeling was one of regret that he had picked up the paper at all, and above all that he had examined it. When he remembered that there had been nothing to necessitate his remaining in the house that evening, he actually cursed himself for his imprudence. However, his regret and his recriminations had no power to change the situation, and, peculiar as was the manner in which the will had been discovered, it was with all its pitiless consequences, an unquestionable fact. It was upon him, Hingant, that fell the painful duty of hurling all these poor people from the height of their newly attained prosperity, and of again reducing them to the life of poverty to which the inexplicable caprice of a millionaire uncle condemned them for always.

Worthy Jean-Marie pictured the scene which awaited him. He saw the pale faces, the compressed lips, and tearful eyes ; he heard the sobs, imprecations, and reproaches, as well as the accusing words, pronounced by the four disinherited relatives : "Had it not been for you, we should be rich ; had it not been for you, the abominable act of injustice which despoils us would never have been discovered." Leaning on the table, he buried his face in his hands, and muttered : "No, I shall never have the courage to tell them this frightful news ! "

He remained for a long time absorbed in thought, seeking some solution, but finding none, and losing himself in interminable reflections. The light of the lamp fell full upon the fatal scrap of writing before him, and each line, standing out clearly, had very much the effect of a death-warrant, which stern necessity compelled him to read to a condemned man. Suddenly an idea occurred to him. Had not the writer of this document really meant to destroy it by thus throwing it into the ashes ? M. Hingant remembered that Léridan had received him in this room but a short time before, and that he had had a fire lighted there on that occasion. As the will was found intact, it must have been thrown on the hearth only a few days before. "No doubt Mériadec," thought the magistrate, " recollected that he had made this absurd disposal of his property in former times, and, seized with remorse, he searched for the accursed paper in some drawer in which it had been mouldering for more than thirty years, and when he found it, he threw it there, expecting that it would be destroyed in the first fire Porpoise kindled. So he must have changed his intentions, and have decided not to deprive his nephews of an inheritance which belonged to them ; in that case this scrawl is of no importance, and I can—" Here the worthy man suddenly paused, for he again remembered his last conversation with the privateersman. "And yet," he muttered, with a discomfited air, "I must admit that he had a prejudice which I could not overcome against his relatives. I ought really to say an antipathy ; and he expressed himself in bitter, even violent, terms on that fatal evening of the 13th of March, only a few moments before—"

Overcome by this sorrowful recollection, M. Hingant paused, and again relapsed into a state of perplexity ; but soon he struck his forehead as if a flash of light had suddenly burst upon his mind. "I recollect," he said, joyfully, " that before complaining of his nephews, he asked me if a man had a right to dispose of his property as he chose. As he consulted me, he could not have finally decided to disinherit them."

The worthy man's face brightened. He took up the will which he had not found courage enough to touch since he had allowed it to fall on the table, and began to re-peruse it attentively. "Marie Bréhal," he muttered. "I am not acquainted with any one of that name in this neighbourhood. Who is this sole legatee, whose residence is not even mentioned ? An imaginary being, perhaps. Mériadec may have wished to impress upon his mind the proper formula to be used in such cases, and have made use of the first name that occurred to him. Hum ! that is rather improbable," resumed the old magistrate, after a short pause, "but let us see. The document was written in the year 1815, and in Paris—in Paris, where he made a long sojourn about that time, without any one knowing the reason why. Ah, I have it now : this young lady—he calls her ' mademoiselle '— must have been a person with whom he fancied himself in love. He was very warm-hearted and impulsive then, and the damsel could not have found it difficult to turn his head. In some enthusiastic transport he

must have thought of giving her everything, then he changed his mind and
returned to Cancale. Unfortunately, however, he neglected to burn this
stupid will. But I should be mad to look upon such a whim, seriously, and
I will destroy all trace of it if only out of respect for Mériadec's memory."

Coming to this conclusion M. Hingant crumpled the paper in his hand,
but instead of tearing it up, he rose to his feet and began walking up and
down the room, resuming his soliloquy. "And yet if I were mistaken,"
he said to himself. "If this Marie wasn't what I take her for. But
then she would have given some sign of life, Mériadec would have mentioned
her to me ; and besides is she even alive ? During the last thirty-three
years she has had time to disappear from the world altogether and then the
will would be valueless ! Even if she had any heirs they would have no
claim, for by the terms of the law one can only bequeath what one possesses
during one's lifetime. Moreover, admitting that she exists, how could she
be found ? Is she in Paris, or even in France ? The search would be
difficult, all but impracticable, probably fruitless, very long in any case, and
then what a situation for my poor friends. Their uncle's property taken
out of their hands to be managed by a trustee until this woman be found !
They would relapse into misery besides becoming the laughing-stock of all
the country side. Come, come, my scruples are really ridiculous and I'm
sure that by burning this wretched paper I shall act as an honest man."

Abruptly approaching the table, as if he wished to deprive himself of
further time for reflection, he then stretched out his hand to ignite the paper
which was already rolled like a spill, at the flame of the lamp. However
before the writing took fire, his arm was suddenly lowered again. "I might
act like an honest man," he muttered disconsolately, "but certainly I
shouldn't behave like a magistrate, and I am a justice of the peace. How
could I for one moment have forgotten it ! Ah ! if I were simply poor Léridan's
friend ! I should only be accountable to my conscience in that case and I
could take upon myself to suppress a document which he certainly intended
to destroy. When a man is a magistrate, however, the case is different.
Burn a will ! the deuce ! the deuce ! that would be a bad finish to a career
of thirty years, honourably employed I'm proud to say. Jean-Marie," he
added, addressing himself, "before being a friend you are a magistrate, and
you mustn't evade the law even when the law seems unjust to you."

Thereupon, and no doubt to avoid exposing himself to fresh temptation,
he hastily produced his pocket book, placed the fatal paper inside ; and returned the whole to his pocket. "And so," he sighed, "it was written that
these young people should have but a brief season of enjoyment. How can
they be apprized of this fatal discovery ? I would rather decamp than announce it to them myself."

M. Hingant was trying to think of some one to whom he could confide
this unpleasant mission, when a loud knock at the front door made him
start. He did not expect anyone, and his first idea was that one of the heirs
had returned to speak to him in private. He was moreover rather glad to
be disturbed, for his reflections were peculiarly unpleasant ones. Accordingly he hurried to the front door, and on opening it he perceived
Mathurin Callec standing outside. "What, is it you ?" the magistrate
muttered looking at the old seaman, who merely nodded by way of reply.
"Have you anything important to say to me ?"

Porpoise did not speak even this time, but drew a large square envelope
from his pocket and handed it to the magistrate. The latter at once saw
that it was an official envelope, and concluded that it contained some minis-

terial circular such as he had often received since the establishment of the Republic. "And so it was to bring me this that you came as far as here?" he said to Mathurin.

"I thought it was important as it was brought by a mounted gendarme. Your old servant, Brigitte, couldn't walk a league and a half, so I undertook to deliver it."

"Oh! there's probably nothing of any great moment inside, but thank you all the same. Come in, you must rest awhile and we will go back to Cancale together."

"Enter this house—no, never more!"

"How's that? what do you mean?"

"I've sworn not to cross the threshold of the Pignon Maudit as long as—"

"As long as what?"

"No matter; it's an idea of mine, Monsieur Jean-Marie."

"It lacks common-sense, my good fellow, and you will please relinquish it this very evening. I want to speak to you, and we can't talk on the doorstep."

However Mathurin, instead of complying with his protector's request, drew back and said in a low voice: "It's impossible, Monsieur Jean-Marie. We'll have a talk at your house if you like, but not here."

"But, you obstinate fellow, you are going to live here and that's just what I have to tell you on behalf of the commandant's nephews. They will allow you the use of the house and furniture for six months, and what's more, they make you a present of the *Goëland*, in memory of their uncle, to whom you were so attached. You can't make a difficulty about accepting such a present, I hope." Mathurin said nothing, but his face expressed the emotion he felt. "Come, admit that you judged the young people wrongly," resumed M. Hingant who fancied he had touched the right chord. "Thanks to their generosity, you will now be almost rich. I needn't tell you that my house will always be open to you and my purse as well, but surely you wouldn't grieve our poor friend's relatives by refusing their gifts."

"Thank you, Monsieur Jean-Marie, thank you," said Porpoise in a husky voice, "I could accept anything from you but nothing from them."

"That's very wrong, Mathurin; very wrong indeed, and I won't hide from you that if you persist in refusing the offers of these worthy young people, you will grieve me as much as if you refused mine." While speaking the magistrate held his lamp to the seaman's face and saw two large tears trickling down his cheeks. "Come in, my good fellow," he said gaily, "or you will make me catch cold."

"No, no!" cried Porpoise, "I can't,—still I don't want to pain you. Tell them I accept—"

"That's right."

"That I accept the *Goëland*; but I only do so because the commandant gave it to me during his lifetime. I don't need a lodging on shore as I shall sleep on board—still if you like you can let them think I shall stay in their house—though to tell the truth I shall never enter it." Thereupon, without waiting for any fresh remonstrances on M. Hingant's part, Mathurin Callec took to his legs and hurried away.

"He's mad, stark mad," said the magistrate shutting the door again. "His master's death has turned his brain. However, I've prevailed on him not to wound the young people by a refusal, and that's something at all events." Thus soliloquising, M. Hingant entered the sittingroom on the ground floor and prepared to resume his meditations. "After all, if any one is mad it's I," he suddenly exclaimed, "I press him to profit by the kindness of those poor fellows, and I forget that I have a will depriving them of their inheritance, in my pocket. Nothing here belongs to them, and they can no more give Mathurin the *Goëland* than the use of the house. A fine idea I had in talking to him about all that! as if it wasn't enough to have to console four outcast heirs to-morrow—and now my folly will bring poor Mathurin his share of deception as well. Cursed will, cursed pipe, as if I needed to smoke and pick up that very bit of paper for a light! Besides, if I hadn't read it I should have burnt it, and my mind would have been at ease."

This soliloquy was not calculated to calm the magistrate. He paused, threw the letter which Mathurin had brought him on the table, leant on his elbows and began to reflect anew. But however much he turned and twisted the problem, he failed to arrive at any satisfactory solution of it. His position as a magistrate troubled him more than aught else for he had contrived to persuade himself that as a private citizen he might, without acting contrary to his duty as an honest man, make proper inquiries about the legatee before producing the will. He even went so far as to believe that in the event of this stranger being found and proving unworthy of the privateersman's legacy, it would be allowable for him to destroy this iniquitous document. If, however, he ascertained that Mademoiselle Bréhal was really deserving of Léridan's generosity, and that there were no improper reasons for this strange legacy, nothing would prevent him from producing the scrap of paper that enriched her and exhorting her to share the property with the legal heirs. Such a cause was calculated to please kind-hearted Jean-Marie, and he felt strong enough to carry out this really providential mission. He need only keep the will in his pocket and institute a search for the heiress. "Yes," he said slowly, "it would be a noble task, and I would willingly devote the rest of my days to it. I have money enough to live on, my old frend Mériadec is dead, his nephews won't remain in the province. So nothing keeps me here, nothing except my functions— still they suffice to retain me especially as we have just passed through a revolution,* and a day doesn't elapse without my receiving some despatches from the new authorities. In proof of it, Mathurin just brought me one and I must read it, although I'm hardly in the mood to attend to official matters. In point of fact, however, it may change my thoughts."

So saying he carelessly tore the envelope open and began to read. Scarcely had he glanced however at the ministerial communication than he turned as red as a cherry and let the missive fall on the table. "Dismissed!" he muttered. "Oh! I didn't expect that—I couldn't expect it, for since I have been a magistrate I have never failed in my duty, and since I have been in the world I have always tried to do what was right."

Although M. Hingant was nearly sixty he had lost none of the illusions of youth; a young man fresh to life might have spoken as he had just done. "Well, so be it," he exclaimed drawing himself up, much as a spirited horse rears at an undeserved prick of the spurs. "My services are ignored, I am discharged as if I were guilty of something dishonourable. But I won't protest or even complain. For now I am free, free to devote myself to a task which will amply suffice for the years that may be left to me. I am my own master now, I need only render an account of my actions to myself, and I can follow the inspirations of my heart. It sha'n't be said that Mériadec Léridan's intentions were not carried out for lack of an

* The revolution of 1848 by which King Louis-Philippe was overthrown.—*Trans.*

honest man bent on discovering the truth. He cannot have seriously meant to leave his fortune to a stranger ; but, I swear by the friendship that united us, that if I find he really wished to give this woman everything I will ensure the execution of his will, even if I have to abandon my own property to indemnify his nephews."

Thereupon, without further delaying himself by useless talk, the dis-charged magistrate placed the ministerial letter in his pocket-book beside his friend's will and hastily left the house. "Three weeks to wait for my successor's arrival and settle my affairs," he muttered, striding over the moor. "In a month's time I can be in Paris, and I will take Mathurin Callec with me. Who knows but what he will enable me to find Mademoiselle Marie Bréhal ? "

IV.

INCIDENTS of importance seldom occur at Cancale, and the question of the Léridan property supplied the idlers and gossips of the community with abundant matter for talk. So much attention was paid to it that politics were forgotten for the time being, and the dismissal of the justice of the peace passed almost unnoticed. Worthy Jean-Marie had sworn that he would not complain, and he kept his word. The ingratitude of the villagers did not draw a single bitter remark from him, and he gave his successor as cordial a greeting as if he had not been superseded. A few folks came to condole with him, more or less sincerely ; but he simply said that he was growing old, that he was very well off and had no need of a salary, so there was nothing for him to regret, and, indeed, he wasn't sorry to recover his liberty and travel for a time. Nobody believed, however, in this surprising resignation ; for in the French provinces a man clings to his functions as he would cling to life itself, and a dismissal had caused more than one suicide. The fact is, every one firmly believed that M. Hingant was only going to Paris to interview the minister and try to recover his post.

Jean-Marie let the gossips chatter and quietly made his preparations for departure. By the end of March he had already settled everything in view of a somewhat prolonged absence. Old Brigitte, who had served him faithfully for thirty years, was to remain behind to attend to the house and receive the rents from the farmers. M. Hingant did not lack money, for he did not live up to his income, and he always kept a handsome sum in his desk. Accordingly, nothing prevented him from starting, nothing except that Mathurin Callec did not appear over eager to accompany him. The old tar had not declined the proposal to go to Paris with his master's friend, only he had asked M. Hingant to allow him a few days to take the Goëland to Granville, where he wished to place her in charge of a comrade, the only person in whom he had any confidence. The magistrate had will-ingly humoured the old seaman's fancy, although it seemed a rather singular one. However, he was so pleased that Mathurin had agreed to accept the heirs' present that he did not care to put him out. Porpoise, who seemed delighted, now barely left his boat, saying that he was only waiting for a good wind to cross the bay, and promising to return within three days' time from his departure. However, the favourable breeze did not spring up.

Meanwhile, the four heirs did not lose their time. The great affair of dividing the property had been promptly settled ; an understanding had been arrived at on all points, even on the one which had at first caused such an explosion. By one accord, the privateersman's house was not in-cluded in the lots ; and as Mathurin Callce declined to live in it, it was offered, rent free, to a gendarme who had retired from the service. This worthy man and his wife were quite incapable of appropriating the treasure, supposing one were found, and quite competent to protect it against any thieves. This was a precaution which each heir took against the other three, a kind of mutual insurance as it were. Besides, the heirs cunningly related that their uncle had not secreted anything whatever, and François Dolley jocularly poked fun at the people who still believed in such a fantastical story.

Even Mathilde managed to hold her tongue, although she was not remark-able for reticence. It is true, however, that she had no great belief in the existence of any treasure, and besides, for the time being, her mind was fully occupied with other matters. She was bent upon betaking herself to the Paris of her dreams, and this although three former admirers, who frequented the Café Militaire, had recently proposed for her hand. More-over, she had hastily returned to Saint Malo, in view of discussing the fashions with the local dressmakers.

Charles also had returned there, and barely left his tailor's establishment, so intent he was upon procuring a stylish outfit. The schoolmaster and Jacques Le Planchais alone had remained at La Houlle and gave no signs of meaning to leave the neighbourhood. They saw but little of each other, as Dolley spent his time settling business matters with his farmers, while the seaman occupied his leisure hours in cruising about in a pretty boat which he had obtained at St. Servan. The pair only met on the wharf or at the café, when by chance the grave-looking schoolmaster deigned to go in and play a hundred points at piquet. Le Planchais, however, was an old frequenter of the establishment, and betook himself there regularly every evening, remaining until closing time.

And yet one evening, when cousin François had not embellished the gathering by his presence, Jacques declared with a yawn that he felt tired, for he had been rowing about all day, and so he meant to go to bed, al-though he had merely swallowed three glasses of rum. His friends wanted to detain him, but he resisted their entreaties, and would not even play an enticing game at billiards with the local tax collector. He put out his pipe, donned his hooded overcoat and his glazed hat, settled his score and walked out. People retire early at La Houlle, and on the wharf he only perceived a coastguard strolling gloomily along. Le Planchais took care to avoid this fellow by keeping in the shadow of the houses, and soon turned into a path leading to the summit of the cliff. It was a steep, stony, difficult ascent, but there was no other route when the tide was high and one wished to follow the coast.

For a quarter of an hour or so the sea had been at its highest ; it would soon run out ; but for the time being the beach could not be crossed, and Jacques, who no doubt had business in the neighbourhood of the Groin, proceeded by the shortest road. He must have been well acquainted with it, to follow it thus at dead of night, for it overlooked dangerous precipices, and the moon, now in her last quarter, not having risen, one could barely see where to set one's feet. However, the bold fellow did not spend more than a quarter of an hour in climbing to the summit of a promontory stretching out from the main coast line just in front of the islands and the fort of Les Rimains, from which indeed it was merely separated by a narrow channel. Here Jacques stopped to draw breath and to look in front of him and below him. At a few hundred yards further on, beyond a deep cove, the Pignon Maudit stood out like a huge block of stone against the dark sky. No light could be seen in the windows, for the ex-gendarme and his wife habitually went to roost at the same time as their fowls. At the feet of the nocturnal watcher, the sea sparkled every now and then in the dim light of the stars. It might have been likened to a vast sheet of lead speckled here and there with silver. Le Planchais gave but little heed to the marvellous sight of the clouds racing across the sky and the waves breaking over the rocks. All his attention was centred on one point, a black object, invisible to every one but himself. This object was softly rocked by the water below the cape which Léridan's house surmounted.

"I guessed right," muttered Le Planchais between his teeth. "The old shark has already got the *Goëland* beyond the rocks of the point. He's on board, and only waits for the breeze from shore and the running out of the tide to raise the anchor. So it really is for to-night, and I have only just time to go aboard, if I don't want to miss him, as has often happened before." Thereupon, without losing time in useless reflections, Jacques resolutely began to descend a kind of staircase hewn out in the rocky cliff, and, thanks to his dexterity, he accomplished the perilous descent in less than ten minutes. There was here a kind of cavity or fissure in the cliff into which the sea poured each time the tide was high, and which was admirably adapted for the shelter or even concealment of a boat of small tonnage. It was there, indeed, that for a week past Le Planchais had anchored the skiff he had purchased at St. Servan. The spot was well chosen to watch the doings of old Porpoise, who still kept the *Goëland* moored just below the Pignon Maudit. The prudent heir had been careful to watch every night, but so far Mathurin Callec had not put out to sea, perhaps on account of the dead calm which had followed the equinoctial gale. Jacques had thus begun to grow impatient, but it seemed as if there would be work for him that night. The wind had freshened considerably during the day, and it was blowing from the south. Porpoise had inspected the rigging and the hull of his sloop during the afternoon, and Le Planchais evidently had no time to lose.

Before making the needful preparations, however, he wished to get a sight of his enemy's manœuvres once more, so he climbed on to a rock sheltering the creek, and from this point of vantage he obtained a more distinct view of the *Goëland*, which now seemed to him rather farther from the shore. "Mathurin is quite capable of standing off gently with the ebb tide and rowing till he catches the breeze," muttered Jacques, feeling rather alarmed. "It's time for me to do the same, to prevent him from getting too much of a start."

In three bounds he reached the prow of his boat and leant down to pull up the grapnel; but the next minute he rose erect as if a serpent had stung him. Some one had just tapped him on the shoulder and was whispering in his ear: "A capital idea, a fine sea, a good breeze! We shall catch Porpoise to-night, that's certain. Only we must share alike."

Some people pretend that the first thought is always the best. The one that occurred to Le Planchais was to send the intruder into a better world, for he caught up a boat-hook and raised it with the intention of felling the meddler to the ground. But the new-comer nimbly sprang aside and levelled a pistol, saying: "Have a care, cousin; if you touch me I shall blow your brains out, and then it won't be a question of dividing—everything will go to one of us, and that one will be me!"

"François!" exclaimed Le Planchais, recognising the schoolmaster's unctuous voice. "I ought to have guessed it."

"I don't say the contrary, my fine fellow, for if you had reflected ever so little you would easily have understood that I shouldn't let you go alone after the *Goëland* and dig up the treasure without inviting your nearest relative to share the spoil."

"You will share nothing at all, for I simply came here to pull up my lines, and in an hour's time I shall be in bed at La Houlle. All the same, if you will lend a hand, you shall have some fish, providing the haul's a good one."

"Jacques, my boy," said Dolley, shrugging his shoulders, "you are only a simpleton, for you waste precious time telling me lies which a child wouldn't believe. Porpoise is leaving his anchorage by now; you know it as well as I do, and even better; for do you imagine I didn't see you on the look-out on that pebble yonder, before you came here to get ready? In ten minutes' time the *Goëland* will have wind in her sails and be running the north-east tack, while we shall still be here disputing."

"I hope a thunderbolt will sink her and you as well!" growled Le Planchais, who could barely restrain his rage.

"Well," resumed François, quietly, "according to all appearance this will be Mathurin's last trip, for he is going to Paris with old Hingant, so if we miss the opportunity of pocketing our dear uncle's gold to-night, we probably sha'n't have another chance."

"And it will be your fault, you cur," cried Jacques, casting dissimulation aside. "If you hadn't played me this trick, I should be outside by this time; but now Porpoise has a start, and the fiend might blow my sails without my catching him."

"It isn't a question of catching him; all we want is not to lose sight of him, and, in fact, if we had showed too much haste we should have spoilt our game, for the old chap has good eyes. He would have recognised us and have acted cautiously."

"Good! Well, as you seem to know so much about the business, what are we to do? Just tell me that, Mr. Schoolmaster."

"We must make haste and cut our moorings; that'll be quicker than pulling up the grapnel; then dip two oars, and pull hard to round the Rimains island on the south."

"The south!" repeated Le Planchais, ironically. "'Pon my word, the fellow still fancies himself in his schoolroom. The south! Then you want to let the *Goëland* get a start of a mile or two?"

"No; I want Mathurin to take us for Cancale fishermen leaving La Houlle with the night tide. If we begin the chase in the channel between the fort and the shore, he'll soon guess whom he has to deal with, and will amuse himself by keeping us knocking about in the open sea in front of the Groin till to-morrow morning. All our trouble would be lost. But come, help me instead of chattering," said François, seating himself, and preparing to row on the starboard side.

Le Planchais, conquered by his cousin's cool assurance, and in a measure, perhaps, by the reasons he had given, cut the moorings, swearing in a frightful manner as he did so. Three minutes later he was seated larboard, and the two heirs pulled away in capital time. "You see that we are not too late," said Dolley, as the boat got clear of the rocks sheltering the anchorage; and at the same time he jerked his head so as to designate a white speck which could only be the *Goëland* under sail.

"All right! all right! Keep pulling, you pedagogue!" growled Le Planchais; "we shall know what to think by-and-by." He had not yet digested the lessons which the schoolmaster had ventured to give him, for he did not admit that Dolley was competent as a seaman, and his wounded pride almost made him forget the treasure, half of which he must now abaudon to his hateful cousin. However, he pulled vigorously, and the boat soon rounded the southern coast of the fortified island which protects the entry of the haven of Cancale.

"Now, old fellow, you won't say that my calculation was faulty," said Dolley. "There's the *Goëland* over there, before us, with a couple of knots' start at the most—just what we need to see her without treading on her heels, especially as the moon is showing her horns and the sky is clearing. There are three luggers from La Houlle to starboard and two more astern. Porpoise would need to be a sorcerer to guess that we don't mean trawling like the others."

"Well, what then? Give your orders, as you've appointed yourself captain. What have we got to do now, Mr. Admiral?" asked Jacques with a sneer.

"Why, put our oars by and hoist canvas; for the breeze is beginning to blow westward, and we must catch it now if we don't want to get wind-bound in the bay. Just you hold the rudder; I'll see to the canvas, and it won't prevent me from having an eye on the capstan."

Le Planchais mechanically obeyed, yielding in spite of himself to the schoolmaster's influence; only, while lending a hand, he muttered between his teeth: "The fiend must have taught him all this."

He was not a devout believer in the fiend by any means; in fact, he prided himself on being a free thinker; but anger troubled him, and besides, the frequenters of the Café Français were not at hand to hear him. Dolley's orders were carefully carried out, and the boat began rapidly making way towards the north-east. "Your craft sails well," said the pedagogue suddenly. "It was a splendid idea of yours to buy her. Do you know that I myself went to look at her at St. Servan; but when I heard that you had made an offer for her, I guessed your motive, and said to myself that it wasn't worth while making a higher bid, for you would surely offer me a seat aboard when you started on your intended trip."

By way of response, Le Planchais gave a growl and let the rudder slip, so that the boat slightly swerved in her course. "Mind what you are about, Jacques," cried François. "You must steer properly, if you don't want us to lose our advantage. And, by-the-way, do you know two men are not too many to manage a boat like this. Without me you might have been greatly bothered."

"Porpoise manages the *Goëland* alone, and I could very well have done without you," retorted Le Planchais.

"Who knows? In the first place, Porpoise has his reasons for not taking anyone with him, and then, although he is old, he's a first-rate seaman—besides, your boat isn't the *Goëland*."

"No, she's a better one."

"In a swell, perhaps, for she's more solidly built; but she must tack less easily; and I would bet that she draws a couple of feet more water than old Léridan's craft. I know the *Goëland*; I saw her hauled-up. She could go anywhere. The old man had her built expressly for sailing about in shallow water and among rocks."

"Oh! do shut up! You don't know anything about it, and you had much better keep a look-out ahead."

"Be easy; I can see Mathurin as well as if he were only three cable lengths off, and besides, I know where he's going."

"Yes, just like I know what's happening up there in the moon."

"He's already far out from the Groin," resumed the schoolmaster, imperturbably. "With the sou'-wester freshening as it is, he would already have to tack if he wanted to skirt the coast and reach Cape Fréhel; but you see he's skimming, wind astern, and that means he's heading for Chausey."

"Or Jersey, or England, or the polar star."

"There's no danger of his going so far. Our dear uncle didn't like the English well enough to trust his treasure to their keeping."

Le Planchais, having exhausted his arguments, thought proper to remain silent; Dolley's talk came to an end, and the heirs went on their way without any immediate incident of note. Their boat behaved well, and kept her distance. The sky had cleared, and in all probability the *Goëland* would remain in view all night. Moreover, both the pursuer and the pursued, impelled onward by a stiff breeze, made way so speedily that the finish of the drama could not be long deferred. Thus everything progressed as favourably as could be desired; only, the nearer the finish seemed, the fiercer became the rage which swelled Le Planchais' heart. Dolley, however, was transported with delight at having devised such a capital scheme. He had at first thought of acting alone; but the difficulty of managing a boat without assistance had made him change his mind. He lacked his cousin's strength and seafaring experience, although, theoretically, he was the more able man of the two. He had thus decided to associate himself with Jacques, without asking permission to do so, and thus far he had been most successful. However, the decisive moment seemed at hand, for the countless islets which form the little Chausey archipelago were becoming very distinct, and the *Goëland* did not swerve from her course.

V.

THERE were certain points remaining to be settled between the two cousins, and François thought that it was time to deal with them. "I say, Jacques," he calmly began, "how shall we proceed, on shore, when we have found the spot where the treasure is?"

"Why, we shall divide it. That's understood," said Le Planchais, bitterly.

"It's understood, of course; but one of two things may happen. Porpoise has either come to see if the hoard is still in its place, and then we shall only have to let him re-embark, and when he has gone, remove the money; or it may be that the old fellow has come to take a full cargo of gold, and make off with the *Goëland*, laden like a galleon. Heaven only knows where he might go, and that's why, in that case—"

"Well, in that case, we'll kill him," interrupted Jacques.

"I've brought everything needful for that," said the unctuous François, without evincing the slightest emotion.

"Really now, it can be seen that you are a cautious man."

"Well, yes, I provided myself with a brace of pistols so as to be ready for any emergency."

"Any emergency!" repeated Le Planchais, ironically. "That, no doubt,

means that you would have tried their effect on me if I had refused to let
you come with me."

"What a bad-tempered fellow you are ! You forget that it was you
who wanted to fell me when we met. I put myself on defence, that was
all. But it won't do to dispute when we more than ever need to come to
an understanding. Let us rather decide what we shall do when Porpoise
lands."

"Oh ! there's no hurry. My idea is that he'll keep us sailing about like
this all night."

"Well, I feel sure that he won't. Do you see him over there, rather to
larboard. He has already passed the *Great Island*, and steers as if he
wanted to make for the north-east. I bet he'll land on one of the less
frequented rocks, the 'Lizard,' the 'Mill stone,' or 'La Foraine,' or else
'Aneret.' There are some fine spots there to bury a ton of gold without
fear of anyone routing it out."

"Perhaps so, and admitting that you are not mistaken, how shall we
manage to watch him without his noticing it ? He is as cunning as a fox ;
if we follow him too closely, he'll guess what's up and make for the open."

"Yes, but I'm as cunning as he is, and I promise you he won't suspect
us, providing we steer properly. The question is to guess where he's going
and I will take charge of that matter. As soon as we have made sure,
we'll tack, and put her head on Granville. He won't bother about us,
even supposing he has already noticed us ; he'll simply go to his hiding-
place. We'll allow him time to moor the *Goëland*, land and begin his work,
and then we'll softly come back, steering skilfully past the rocks, and land on
the other side of the same island. We will jump ashore, creep up stealthily,
and just as old Mathurin least expects us we'll ask him what he's up to.
If things don't go smoothly I've my pistols to fall back upon, and you
can take the boat-hook you brandished over my head.

"No need of that, I have all I want about me," said Le Planchais,
coldly.

"Ah !" ejaculated the schoolmaster, whose face clouded. Perhaps he
regretted his companion's forethought, at all events he turned his back on
him, and again began watching the *Goëland*.

The miniature archipelago which the two boats were approaching comprises fifty-two islands of various sizes, scattered over a considerable area,
and all forming part of a chain of rocks, some of which rise up out of the
sea, and constitute the Chausey and Minquiers groups, while the others are
below the water line, and offer great dangers to navigation. Some of them
emerge from the sea every day at low water, and others are only seen
during the equinoctial tides. Large vessels carefully avoid the archipelago,
which is mainly frequented by Norman, Breton, and Jersey fishermen.
Even they have to take every precaution with their boats, for at low tide
many of the channels are not deep enough for the passage of a lugger.
This is not the case, however, with the Beauchamp channel, through
which an iron-clad fleet might pass at any time, and which divides the
Chausey islands into two sections. The least important one, that nearer
France, comprises a number of rugged, uninhabited rocks called the
Huguenans. François Dolley, who knew them well, was now looking at
them eagerly, as they grew larger and larger in the nocturnal obscurity.
Did the *Goëland* mean to double them and steer for Jersey, or would she
enter the Beauchamp pass ? The success of the cousins, enterprise depended on this point. If Mathurin passed the *Huguenans* without tacking,

he might mean to steer straight for England, and the heirs were not prepared for so long a trip; but if he entered the channel he must be bound for some central point of the archipelago, and then no doubt François' predictions would be realised. It was the moment or never to steer carefully, for the slightest blunder might compromise everything. However, Le Planchais was at the helm, and with his experience one might hope that everything would progress favourably.

"Let her go a bit to starboard," suddenly said the schoolmaster. "Porpoise is in front of the channel, and to rid him of any fear of being followed we had better change our course."

Jacques complied without even growling, for he realised all the necessity of this ruse. So the boat tacked as if to leave Chausey to larboard; but she had scarcely headed north-eastwards for ten minutes when François exclaimed with restrained delight: "The helm to windward—That's enough dodging—Mathurin isn't paying any attention to us now. He is going straight into the Beauchamp channel." And the schoolmaster rubbing his hands, added complacently: "The millions are ours, old fellow."

"You don't hold them yet," growled Le Planchais between his teeth.

The schoolmaster did not hear this rejoinder. He was too occupied in watching the movements of old Porpoise who was steering into the channel. The question now seemed to be decided, for this route could only lead the old seaman to one of the islets that the ingenious pedagogue had spoken of. The heirs' boat speedily resumed the chase, and on doubling the point which concealed the entrance of the pass, François was delighted to see the *Goëland* speeding along under press of canvas. "Let us keep near in shore, Jacques," he said hastily. "The shadow of the rocks will hide us."

"All right, only the sea has run out a good deal since we started. We mustn't get into shallow water—"

"We have no choice in the matter. Mathurin would see us if we took the middle of the channel."

"Oh, he isn't thinking about us. If he were he wouldn't be in the channel at all."

"All the same a little prudence isn't amiss. Take us in near shore; if I see any rocks ahead I'll warn you."

Le Planchais once more complied. The *Goëland* was still skimming onward, and Dolley soon perceived that in her turn she made for the shore. "We are getting near, getting near." he muttered joyfully. "You are caught, Mathurin; I can guess what you mean to do! When you have passed through the channel you'll port your helm, and I know a little corner where we shall be able to hide and watch your goings on." Then addressing his companion Dolley exclaimed: "Keep her close to shore, cousin. We must almost graze the point which Mathurin will round in a moment. You must steer as straight as the postilion of the Rennes coach does when he passes under the dyke-gateway to enter Saint Malo." The schoolmaster felt so delighted that he became facetious.

"I tell you we shall run a-ground if we steer like that," growled Jacques.

"Run a-ground! Pooh! See the *Goëland* has passed on all right."

"The *Goëland* draws two feet less water than we do. You said it yourself a little while ago."

"Pooh, we shall have at least three feet under our keel."

B

"You know nothing about it—the tide is running out fast and I'm better acquainted with the channel than you are."

"But, dash it all!" cried Dolley, "don't you understand that if you send us to starboard you'll make us lose at least five minutes, and Mathurin doesn't need more than that to escape us. Keep close in, Jacques, close in."

"All right," muttered Le Planchais. "Only remember that if we run a-ground it will be your fault."

The instructions of the improvised captain were carried out to the letter, and the boat rounded the point of the island, close to the shore. The *Goëland* was proceeding in the direction that Dolley had prophesied, and no doubt remained as to Porpoise's intentions. He evidently meant to land on one of the rocks forming the north-eastern section of the archipelago. "We hold him! We hold him!" sang Dolley who had seen "Robert the Devil" performed at Rennes, and he added in a more serious tone, "Only it's the moment to keep one's eyes open."

Unfortunately he did not add example to precept, and the last words had barely left his mouth when a violent shock brought the boat to a stand-still, and made her lurch on one side. "A thousand thunder-bolts!" shouted Le Planchais. "We've struck on a rock."

"No, no, it's perhaps a sandbank," stammered François. "Put the helm under, and let us try to get off."

"Get off indeed! Why our prow's stove in, and we have shipped two feet of water already. Ah! you scoundrel, you miserable beggar, it's your fault if we are here; and when I think that I was fool enough to listen to an outsider like you!"

"Big words are of no use, Jacques; we had better think of saving our skins," muttered the schoolmaster who had lost all his assurance.

"Oh! you'll save that precious skin of yours all right, providing I don't send a bullet through it as I feel half inclined to do. Don't you see, you coward, that we are not three cable lengths from shore, and that the tide is still running out? In less than an hour we shall be able to land without even wetting our feet."

"That's true. I didn't think of it. Come, there's nothing lost."

"Oh! no," said Jacques, scornfully—"nothing but the treasure."

"But it won't fly off to-night, and Porpoise will come again. We shall only have to make another try—that's all."

These consolations thoroughly exasperated Le Planchais, who was about to fire off a volley of abuse, when a distant but distinct call resounded in his ears : "Ship ahoy!" cried someone through a speaking trumpet.

They both shuddered, wondering who thus hailed them in this deserted archipelago ; for they did not imagine that the call came from the man whom they had been pursuing, but gazed around them with frightened eyes. "It's perhaps some Cancale fisherman who was casting his nets near the *Huguenans,* and who saw us run a-ground," muttered the schoolmaster. "So much the better, he'll help us off."

"Still your sanguine ideas," growled Jacques, climbing on to the side of the boat and clutching hold of the stays. He was beginning to lose his head altogether, and his dear cousin's mind was not much more lucid than his own. It was a curious sight—these two scoundrels, forgetting the gold they coveted, forgetting even their somewhat perilous situation to try and dis cover whence came the call which had so startled them. Suddenly, how ever, they perceived a boat coming straight down the channel, in their direction. François was the first to recognise it. "It's the *Goëland*," he exclaimed in a husky voice, "Mathurin has put her about."

"And he's coming to sink us, the old blackguard!" cried Jacques. "François, you must make ready to board him when he comes up with us, and mind you break his ribs. We shall lose the coin, but we'll fling his carcass into the water for the fish to feed off. I've my knife, and you, get your pistols ready."

"The priming has got wet," muttered Dolley, piteously.

"'Pon my word, you are an arrant coward, cousin; and when I've settled with Mathurin I shall send you after him," said Le Planchais, gnashing his teeth.

The moment for putting his threats into execution was drawing nigh, for the *Goëland* came along at full speed. If the heirs had been in a condition to reflect they would easily have realised that Porpoise did not mean to try and sink them. His boat was not strong enough for such a venture, and besides, she would have been shattered by the very same rock which had wrecked the cousins. The old seaman accordingly took good care not to try such a hazardous game. Steering clear of Le Planchais' boat, he passed down the channel, bawling : "So there you are, you pair of thieves!"

"He has recognised us, and is deriding us," muttered Dolley.

"Thunder!" shouted Le Planchais. "If he'd only come within reach of my boat-hook—"

"You'd murder me, eh, Jacques? Just like you murdered your uncle," resumed old Porpoise.

"You lie, you brigand! Just come near if you have any pluck left in you. Come near and I'll settle you—"

"Hum! So Jacques killed old Léridan," said François to himself, "that is worth knowing."

"However, you won't murder anyone else," continued Mathurin. "Do you hear me, Jacques? You won't even kill me, for I'm going away, and shall never return."

"The scoundrel is decamping with the treasure," growled Le Planchais.

"No, he can't have had time to remove it," was Dolley's response.

Meanwhile the *Goëland* was scudding along, and Porpoise's words soon grew less distinct. However, the two cousins heard this phrase which fell upon them like a thunderbolt: "The birds have flown. It isn't worth your while looking further, my boys." And then just as the *Goëland's* sail was lost to view in the darkness, there came the mocking farewell: "Good luck to you, you scamps!"

On the morrow the two cousins returned, crestfallen, to Cancale. At daybreak, a fishing boat had rescued them from the rock, where they had been able to land at low water. They took good care not to boast of their expedition, preferring to relate that they had simply gone to cast their nets near Chausey, and had been unlucky enough to strike upon a rock ; which story was generally believed. However, after this adventure, they lost all hope of setting their hands upon their uncle's treasure, for they felt certain that Mathurin had spoken the truth and that he would never more be seen in the neighbourhood ; so they turned their minds to other matters. François Dolley, who intended to realise his landed property, hoped to turn the proceeds to good account in Paris ; Jacques Le Planchais reflected that bold men make their way in revolutionary times, and he was tempted to fling himself into the political struggle, after a fashion of

his own. When Léridan had been dead a month, all four of the heirs had
started for the city, where they hoped to realise their dreams. M.
Hingant had previously arrived there, unattended, for Mathurin Callec
had never returned to Cancale. In vain did the ex-magistrate make inquiries on all sides ; he could obtain no information as to the fate of the
Goëland, or her master. And yet no wreck had been reported along the
coast. Poor Jean-Marie came to look upon Porpoise's disappearance as an
act of ingratitude, and determined to leave the province to which no ties
now bound him. He repaired to Rennes, where he took the diligence for
Paris. His heart was heavy as he climbed into the vehicle, and more than
once during the long journey, he muttered to himself : "Ah ! if my mind
were only at rest respecting that fatal will ! "

VI.

BRIGHT sunlight was streaming over the streets and boulevards of Paris,
the delightful city that the privateersman's heirs had so often dreamt of.
It was one of those splendid June mornings which tempt everyone out of
doors to inhale the open air—the time of day when busy folks usually hurry
here and there through the metropolis, which seems like a giant ant hill.
And yet the thoroughfares were deserted, the houses silent, their windows
closed. You might have fancied yourself in an old Andalusian city at the
hour of the siesta. Instead of the rumble of vehicles going at full speed
over the pavement, instead of the buzz of the crowd, and the characteristic
cries of the street-hawkers, only strange and ominous sounds were heard—
a clang of metal, a continuous bass rumbling, with at times the rub-a-dub
of a drum calling the National Guard to arms, and the loud challenge of
some invisible sentinel. Then came silence, silence as ominous as the calm
preceding a storm. The south wind sped by, raising a cloud of dust and
wafting a smell of powder through the city.*
    The boulevards especially had an alarming aspect, with their broad road-
way quite deserted, and their shops closed like the gates of a fortress about
to be assaulted. At the end of the Boulevard Bonne Nouvelle, and close to
the Porte St. Denis, there rose a huge barricade manned with defenders,
whose muskets were levelled in the direction of the Madeleine. It was the
outpost, so to say, of a formidable mass of improvised fortifications thrown
up on all the open spaces along a line which, cutting Paris atwain from
north to south, stretched from La Villette to the Faubourg St. Jacques.
Facing this line there extended the Paris of the middle and upper classes,
who, still dumb with astonishment, were counting their forces and hesitating as to whether they should employ them. Within the line insurgent
Paris, feverish and excited, was encamped, loading its guns, collecting its
paving stones, and waving its red flags. It was June 22nd, 1848.
    In front of the loopholed wall near the Porte St. Denis the Boulevard
Bonne Nouvelle stretched away, silent and deserted. The houses, in close
proximity to the barricade, seemed to be almost untenanted, for it was only
at long intervals that a Venetian blind was timidly raised and that one saw
a pale face, with anxious eyes, a mother's eyes, perhaps, peering into the
distance. Then the blind was lowered again, and the sun only beamed on

* The incidents which M. du Boisgobey describes in this chapter are supposed to take
place during the rising of the Red Republicans in June, 1848, which General Cavaignac so
promptly and effectually quelled.—*Trans.*

a lofty, silent, inanimate house-front, which might have been likened to the escarpment of a bastion. And yet behind this protecting wall how many hearts palpitated with anguish at the thought that the horrible struggle would perhaps begin there, before those peaceful thresholds, under those trees the early foliage of which had, only the day before, shaded playful children. And perhaps some of the buildings which overlooked the barricade sheltered insurgent sharpshooters, for at times a bayonet or a gun barrel gleamed furtively at a garret window. These suspicious gleams were mainly visible in the old buildings at the corners of the Rue de la Lune, for in the handsome new houses on the northern side of the boulevard there was barely a sign of life. The masculine tenants had no doubt joined their battalion of the National Guard, and their wives and daughters did not venture to approach the windows.

In a large and somewhat stylishly furnished room, on the first floor of one of these new houses, a young girl, clad in mourning garb, was weeping and praying on her knees before a crucifix. She was tall, slender, and fair-haired. Her large blue eyes and her delicate regular features had an expression of resigned grief. Her figure was that of budding womanhood, and it could be seen that she was not twenty years of age. She was praying with that passionate ardour which only imminent peril or deep love can inspire, and yet one could divine that her thoughts constantly reverted to earthly things. Every now and then her lips ceased to move, she closed her eyes, and half turning her pretty head, listened with feverish attention.

Suddenly she no doubt fancied that she heard some sound betokening the advent of the struggle which she dreaded, for, rising up, she took a few steps across the room, and then, pausing, pale and trembling, she again began to listen. She looked charming as she stood there, with her figure inclined forward, her eyelids lowered, her snowy neck outstretched, her hands uplifted—hands as slender and as delicate as those of the Duchess of Ferrara in the Titian's picture at the Louvre. A Greek sculptor would certainly have selected her as the model for a statue of anxiety. "Nothing," she muttered at last, brushing back the long fair curls which fell in disorder over her forehead—"nothing yet—I was mistaken—I thought—" Then a flush of colour came over her cheeks, and clinging as it were to the slightest hope she resumed : "No, this horrible battle will not take place ; they won't kill each other under the eyes of their wives, their children—their sweethearts. But alas ! do they even think of them ? " she added, clasping her hands. "When I begged my father on my knees not to take part in this frightful conflict he repulsed me, spoke to me of duty, of the peril that threatened society—but what do I know about all that ? I only know one thing, that he has gone, and that Paul also is about to risk his life."

She stopped short, half stifled by her sobs, which at first prevented her from distinguishing a dull regular sound which rapidly drew near. But soon she resumed her attentive attitude, and almost at the same moment a cry burst from her lips : "The drum—yes, it is the drum. They are approaching, advancing on the barricade, and Paul told me that his company would march the first." Frantic with alarm she darted to a door, flung it open, then hastened through a large drawing-room and reached a window overlooking the boulevard. Leaning out, she took in the whole situation at a single glance.

On the left rose up the barricade, threatening but silent. One might now have supposed that it was not defended. On the right, marching somewhat irregularly, there came a detachment of the National Guard, preceded by a drummer who was beating a march as placidly as if he had been leading those behind him to a barracks. In the rear marched two companies of foot Chasseurs who had been despatched to support the National Guard in the event of the insurgents engaging in a struggle. The regulars were barely in front of the Gymnase Theatre, while the citizen soldiers had approached to within fifty paces of the window where the young girl stood. "It is he! it is my father!" she suddenly exclaimed. "He is marching alone at their head."

And in fact, in advance of the National Guards there bravely marched a captain whose silver epaulets glittered in the sunshine. With his sword drawn he walked along carrying his head erect. He looked nearly fifty, however; he was somewhat stout and his features indicated a peaceable disposition. It may be that he was not conscious of any danger, or that he believed that the insurgents would give way. One thing is certain, neither he nor his men evinced the slightest sign of fear. His daughter was not so confident, however, and yet she did not leave the window. She was now trying to recognise someone among the Chasseurs in the rear, and her lips parted to murmur: "Paul must be there as well; I cannot see him, but I feel sure of it."

At this moment some of the National Guards, looking up at the houses around them, shouted out, "Close your windows." The young girl sprang back to execute the orders of her father's subordinates, but, ere she did so, she caught sight of a man in ambush behind the shutters of a window below her; he held a gun in his hand. She wished to return to the window and call to her father to warn him of the seeming danger, but her limbs suddenly gave way beneath her, a cloud gathered before her eyes, and she sank on to the floor. Volition speedily returned to her, however, and she tried to rise. Finding herself unable to do so, she dragged herself along on her knees, stretching her hands out towards the window-sill. She had just clutched hold of it and she was again trying to rise, when the sharp report of a gun broke upon the gloomy silence which had for a moment prevailed outside.

As if impelled by an electric battery, the girl now bounded to her feet, and leant out of the window. At that very moment there was a frightful discharge. One might have thought that the shot had been a signal, for well-fed volleys suddenly came from the barricades and the windows of the houses round about the Rue de la Lune; and then a general continuous fire lasted for a minute or two. The shrill whistling of bullets mingled with the shrieks of the wounded; and the smoke of the powder, descending flake-like to the ground, soon enveloped the sanguinary scene. The unfortunate National Guards, taken unawares, attacked by hidden foes, swept round for a moment amid the deadly fire, and then those who had not fallen, killed or wounded, retreated in disorder.

The poor girl barely beheld the boulevard strewn with corpses. On looking for her father, whom she had seen but a moment before marching so proudly at the head of his men, she failed to perceive him. He had disappeared amid the frightful confusion which had followed the fusilade. "Ah!" she murmured, falling backwards, "he is dead! My presentiments did not deceive me." And with these words she sank fainting on the floor beside the window.

Her fair tresses had become unloosened in her fall, and made the deadly pallor of her face all the more apparent. Her clenched hands were pressed to her bosom, as is often the case with those whose hearts are wrung by

sudden and atrocious suffering. You might have thought that a stray
bullet had penetrated to her heart. And yet her swoon was soon followed
by a sort of lucid torpor which, although paralysing her limbs, left her the
power of reflection. She distinctly heard all the noise that was going on
outside. First, there came confused shouts, cheers of triumph and shrieks
of agony ; then a curt command was given in the distance, followed by a
clash of weapons and the clangous notes of a trumpet sounding a charge.
The girl realised that the regulars were advancing, at double-quick, upon
the barricade, and in her terrified mind she fancied she beheld the face of
the officer she loved. It seemed to her as though she could see him fall,
bleeding on the reddened pavement, and she had strength enough to utter
a cry of anguish.

It was lost amid the rattle of a fresh volley, followed by the crackling
of occasional shots. But the firing soon ceased, and all she then heard was
a dull, rumbling sound which gradually died away in the distance. She
divined that the troops had passed on, and that the barricade had been
carried. Then came a moment of lugubrious silence, abruptly disturbed
by the tumultuous stamping of a crowd of men rushing forward in disorder.
Shouts of anger arose from the excited crowd, which seemed to have
gathered just below the window. Had the insurgents, concealed in the
houses, gone down into the street to renew the combat? Such was the
question which the young girl was asking herself in her fright, when
suddenly she thought she could hear somebody hastily climbing the stairs.
The door communicating with the ante-room was open, and from the spot
where she lay extended, she could easily recognise a man's heavy footfall.
" My father perhaps ! " she exclaimed, making an effort to raise herself
on her elbows.

The footfall drew nearer ; whoever it was, was coming up the stairs four
at a time. " Yes, it must be he," muttered the girl. " He must have
caught a glimpse of me at the window, and he has decided to come and
reassure me, to tell me he has escaped unhurt, and that Paul—"

At this moment a loud ring at the hall door of the flat brought her
soliloquy abruptly to a close. Joy promptly restored her strength. She
scrambled to her feet, hastened to the door and threw it open. She was
already stretching out her arms to embrace her father, but it was a
stranger she beheld, a stranger who darted into the ante-room, and hastily
closed the door behind him. His head was bare, his face livid, his eyes
were haggard, his clothes in disorder, and he breathed hard, like some one
who has run a long distance, or has just escaped some great danger. He
stood there, leaning against the wall, trying to regain breath, and only able
to articulate harsh and unintelligible sounds. The girl, overcome with surprise and fright, gazed at him intently, and almost swooned again. " Conceal me," the stranger eventually stammered.

" Who are you ? " asked the girl.

" No matter—I am pursued—they want to kill me."

" Kill you ? "

" Yes, they have entered the house, and have begun searching the floor
below. I only just had time to climb up here ; they will soon follow—"

" Who are you speaking of ? "

" They will come, I tell you—come in here. Show me a closet, a cupboard where I can hide. The chimney will do if there is nothing better.
I can climb up it—only make haste."

" But why are you pursued ? What has happened ? "

" What has happened ? Why, there has been fighting of course. You must have heard the reports of the guns, but I have no time to give you any explanations. Will you hide me, yes or no ? I warn you that if you won't help me I shall remain here, and then so much the worse for you, if any misfortune happens."

The stranger had gradually recovered from his fright, and his eyes now assumed a threatening expression. He was a man of medium height, but of very robust appearance. His features were coarse and stern, and he wore long black whiskers. Savage as he looked, however, the young girl did not evince any alarm. " You can kill me, sir," she said, in a firm voice, " but before doing what you ask of me, I must insist on knowing what crime you are accused of."

" It's no question of crime. Don't you know that Paris is in a state of revolution, and that a man's life is of no more account than a fowl's for the time being ? The insurgents don't stick at trifles."

" Then you are not one of them ? "

" Of course not, since I am on this side of the barricade."

The girl hesitated for a moment longer. Perhaps this man lied, although he certainly looked more like a member of the middle classes than like a barricade defender ; but in any case it might also happen that he had been mixed up in the struggle despite himself, and was innocent of bloodshed. The girl was ignorant of what had taken place on the boulevard since she had left the window. She did not even know which of the two parties had won the day, and the stranger did not seem disposed to give her any information. " Come, sir," she said, suddenly arriving at a decision ; and she rapidly darted into the drawing-room.

The man required no urging to follow her : " Where do you mean to hide me ? " he abruptly asked.

" I'm leading you to a door communicating with a staircase, which will take you into a courtyard at the rear of the house. When you reach the courtyard you will find a passage leading into the Rue de l'Echiquier."

" That will do capitally. I'm quite sure of not meeting them in that direction ; but let us make haste, for they won't stop long downstairs."

Just as he spoke, a noise of voices and footsteps could be heard approaching. " Do you hear ? " cried the fugitive.

The girl, instead of answering him, darted into the room where she had been praying prior to the conflict.

At this moment there came a violent ring at the bell, and the door was shaken by repeated blows with the butt end of a musket. " Open the door or we shall break it down ! " cried several furious voices simultaneously.

" Quick, quick, show me the way out," stammered the fugitive as he pressed close to the girl, who was passing her hands over one of the panels of the wainscoting. She trembled to such a degree that some moments elapsed before she could grasp a little brass knob concealed among the folds of the chintz hangings. She pressed this knob as hard as possible, but the hidden door of which it was the handle failed to open. A cry escaped her : " The secret ! I forgot there was a secret."

" A secret ! What do you mean ? " exclaimed the fugitive.

" Yes, a secret which only my father knows."

The stranger gave vent to a perfect roar, pushed the girl aside, and threw himself against the secret door to try and force it open. Meanwhile the noise on the landing of the flat was increasing, and the men outside were battering the front door so violently that it would evidently soon be shivered to pieces. "I'm lost!" shouted the stranger, realising the futility of his efforts; "lost! caught in a trap, like a rat! for they'll shoot me down on the spot."

One could now hear the panels of the front door cracking and falling to pieces. "You'll be the cause of my death," cried the stranger, turning to the girl; "if you had told me all this instead of chattering, I should perhaps have been able to escape over the roof." And as he spoke he savagely raised his clenched fist.

The girl realised that she was lost, for at that same moment the outer door gave way with a frightful crash. In her terror she darted towards a portrait set in a panel—the portrait of her mother—and with her hands clasped over her forehead, she pressed her lips to it.

Then something very strange occurred—so strange indeed that the girl was barely conscious of it. She suddenly felt that the partition yielded, she saw the stranger spring forward and disappear; and then the secret door, for a moment set ajar, was abruptly closed by a push from the other side. The girl, in kissing her mother's portrait, had, without knowing it, pressed a spring hidden in the frame. The secret door had opened, and the stranger had hastily availed himself of this unexpected chance of escape. It was time he did so, for scarcely had the panel returned to its place than the assailants rushed into the drawing-room, and thence into the adjoining chamber, where the girl still stood in front of the partition, with her head thrown back and her arms outstretched, as if to continue defending the man whom she had so generously saved.

The uproar recalled her to herself, and she hastily abandoned an attitude which was calculated to betray her. She even had courage enough to take a few steps forward, and found herself face to face with a party of armed National Guards. They seemed exasperated, and advanced with lowered bayonets and threatening words. But on finding themselves in presence of a young and beautiful woman, they abruptly stopped short. They had evidently not expected such a meeting, and astonishment at first moderated their anger. Their bayonets were promptly raised and their cries ceased. "What do you desire, gentlemen?" asked the girl, whose voice trembled despite herself.

"We want the man who has taken refuge here," cried the guardsmen in the rear, making the floor resound with the butt ends of their muskets. Those in front remained silent, for the girl's beauty, her soft, gleaming eyes held them spell-bound.

"There is no one here, gentlemen," she said quietly; "no one but myself."

A moment of silence and hesitation followed; and then murmurs arose and hostile exclamations. "Come! That isn't true. He must be hidden somewhere here. The doorkeeper told us he heard him ringing on the landing, and he can't have flown out of the window. We must search the place."

The National Guards were about to proceed from words to acts when a sergeant, who apparently commanded them, restrained the more impatient of the party by a peremptory gesture, and spoke with tolerable calmness as follows: "We regret, madame, that we are obliged to enter your abode in this manner; but fighting is going on, as you are aware. We have been fired upon, and several of our party have been killed. The scoundrel we are pursuing can only be in this house. We have searched the floor below, and now we feel certain that he ascended to this flat. Believe me, don't try to deny it, it would be useless, for we are determined to demolish the whole house rather than let the man escape us."

"Good heavens ! What has he done then, and what do you mean to do to him ? "

" We mean to shoot him ! " cried a dozen furious voices.

" And I swear to you, madame, that he well deserves his fate," added the sergeant.

"Shoot him !" repeated the girl. "Kill him here before my eyes ?— no, no, never !"

"Such is war, alas !—civil war—and if you knew—"

"I do not wish to know anything, sir; this man is not here. I have already told you so ; but even if he were, I would place myself between him and your guns unhesitatingly, and your bullets would strike me before they reached him."

This courageous declaration seemed to make a forcible impression on the sergeant, who looked like a well-bred man. But it produced quite a contrary effect on his subordinates. "Enough of this chattering," said one fellow, while another exclaimed : " Let us search the place, the hussy must be in league with the scamp." These and similar exclamations speedily drowned the voice of the sergeant, who could only just whisper to the imprudent girl : " Have a care, don't say anything more. I am no longer master of my men."

She gave him an expressive look to thank him for the interest he showed in her, and resumed her position in front of the secret door without saying another word. She had merely wished to gain time, and she felt but little concern respecting the search, for she was now convinced that the fugitive had been able to make good his escape.

The National Guards spread through the rooms and began searching every nook and corner. The sergeant did not seem particularly inclined to help them, though he eventually decided to follow them, but not without turning round more than once to see if the girl was not giving way under the terrible emotion she must be a prey to. This sergeant, despite his rank, was not at all a man of warlike appearance ; his age and his peaceful expression indicated that he had only taken up arms from a sense of duty. He looked at least sixty, with his white hair and clean-shaven face ; and the respectability of his appearance and the softness of his eyes somewhat reassured the girl.

But recurring thoughts soon diminished her firmness. For the last quarter of an hour she had been unable to reflect; for on finding herself with a man whose life was threatened, she had only thought of assuring his escape. It seemed to her as if she was offering the fugitive's salvation to Providence in exchange for her father's life. But now, as her excitement subsided, the frightful scene she had witnessed on the boulevard again appeared in all its horror before her mind. The smoke had so enveloped the scene of carnage that she had been unable to recognise those who had fallen. What had become of the two beings to whom she was so attached? "These men must know," she muttered, thinking of the National Guards, who were now busy overturning the furniture, opening the cupboards and wardrobes, and ferreting under the beds with their bayonets. "They were there—they saw everything—perhaps they even know my father's name and will be able to tell me—"

She was on the point of hastening after them to ask them for some information, when, the search being finished in the other rooms, they returned

to the apartment where she stood. They were greatly enraged as they had
so far utterly failed to find the fugitive. The sergeant tried to calm them
but his efforts met with little success.

"There is only this room to be searched now," said one guardsman.

"Oh! she must have hidden him here," rejoined a comrade. "Come,
my beauty, move on and let us have a look."

All that the old sergeant could do was to reply, "Come, come, pray remember that you are in presence of a woman."

But no attention was paid to this appeal, and the men began sounding the
walls with the butt ends of their guns. One of the party soon raised a cry
of triumph for he had discovered a spot where the woodwork gave a hollow
sound. "Here it is, my hearties!" he exclaimed, "I've found the hiding-
place."

The other guardsmen darted forward and set to work with such feverish
ardour that the secret door seemed doomed to speedy destruction. The
girl instinctively drew nearer to the old sergeant, who fancied that he could
read in her eyes an intense dread of witnessing the bloody scene, now close
at hand; for he had no doubt but what the fugitive was crouching behind
the panel. "Come, madame," he said, trying to lead her gently away, "if
you will follow me, and leave the apartment, I promise you I will do all in
my power to induce my men to spare this wretched fellow's life—although,
to tell the truth, he is hardly deserving of your pity. But in Heaven's
name, come quick."

The girl did not seem to hear these words; one would have fancied, indeed, that she was unconscious of what was taking place around her. The
sergeant presumed that she declined to believe in the fugitive's guilt, and
thought that his best course was to convince her of it. "Believe me, my
child," he resumed in a voice tremulous with emotion, "don't take such a
scoundrel under your protection. If he were merely one of the poor mis-
guided fellows who defended the barricade, I would be the first to stand by
him and plead his cause—but this man is a murderer."

"A murderer! what did he do then?"

"Why, he concealed himself like a coward behind the shutters of a window on the floor below, and just as we marched up intending to parley with
the insurgents, he fired and killed our captain—"

A heart-rending shriek interrupted the well-meaning sergeant and the girl
sank into his arms murmuring: "Unfortunate creature that I am! I have
saved the man who murdered my father!"

At that moment the secret door had just yielded to the repeated battering of the guardsmen. When they beheld merely the first step of a wind-
ing staircase built in the wall, they hesitated to descend fearing some snare,
for the modern houses of Paris are not usually provided with mysterious
outlets, like those of the Ducal Palace at Venice. However, they were so
eager to secure the fugitive that they speedily mastered their fears; the
boldest member of the party began the descent, and seeing no one called his
comrades who rushed after him, shouting: "He escaped this way—we
shall find him all right. Fire at him as soon as he shows himself."

The girl and the old sergeant were thus left alone; she, barely conscious,
and he in a state of consternation, at having plunged her in despair—
"Good heavens!" he muttered, "how unfortunate it is that I should have
thought of telling her that!" And at the same time he tried to think of a
means of repairing the evil which his indiscretion had caused. "Madame,
mademoiselle," he stammered, "I may have been mistaken; in the midst

of the frightful confusion my eyes no doubt deceived me—I was so disturbed."

However, his efforts to retract his statement proved unsuccessful. "It
was he, I know it," interrupted the unfortunate girl whom civil war had
deprived of a father's love and care. "It was he, I saw him walking alone
in front of his men—I saw the murderer in ambush, he was holding his gun
in his hand ; and then I lost my head, and when I tried to look again there
were dead and wounded men lying about, and blood, blood everywhere ! "

"Calm yourself, mademoiselle, I entreat you."

"Then that man came and rang here. He told me that he was being
pursued, that he would be shot if I did not hide him—and I believed him
and helped him to escape, without anything warning me that this scoundrel
—ah ! how unfortunate I am ! "

"The punishment that this villain has escaped would not have restored
our poor captain to life again, unfortunately," said the old sergeant. "The
mischief!" he added between his teeth, "here am I talking stupidly again."

"Ah ! I knew very well that my father was dead ! " the girl exclaimed.
"You tried to reassure me out of pity and kindness of heart; but fear
nothing, sir, I know how to bear suffering."

Tears came to the sergeant's eyes and he was only able to stammer by
way of consolation : "You must think of the dear ones that remain to you
—your mother."

"My mother," rejoined the girl, bitterly, "I am in mourning for her."

The worthy sergeant realised that he had again spoken too quickly, and
felt indignant with himself for his blunders. "Forgive me, mademoiselle,"
he timidly remarked, "forgive me for having unknowingly awakened such
sad memories at such a time ; however, if your other relatives reside in a
distant part of Paris, I can at least apprize them of what has taken place,
or even conduct you to them."

"I am now alone in the world," replied the girl, overcome by grief.

"What ! haven't you a relative, a connection, some friend of your childhood ? "

"There is a man I love and whom I was to marry ; but at this very moment he is under fire, and they will no doubt kill him as they have killed
my father."

"No, no, providence will protect him. You will soon see him again, for
this abominable struggle cannot last. If necessary I will go in search of
him. I will bring him to you if you will but give me some particulars—"

"His name is Paul Gilbert. He is a lieutenant in the Ninth Battalion of
Chasseurs."

"I will find him, mademoiselle, even if I have to face twenty fusilades
like the one we were exposed to just now."

A gleam of delight shot from the orphan's eyes, but she speedily lowered
her head as if reproaching herself for having forgotten her loss even for a
moment. "Thank you," she said with an effort, "and now I entreat you
to lead me to the spot where my father fell. I wish to see him again and
embrace him—"

"Don't think of that. Fighting is still going on, along the boulevards ;
can't you hear the bullets whistling ? "

"Do not fear for me. I am brave and strong, since I did not die of grief
when you told me—"

"I have no doubt of your fortitude, but what you ask of me is impracticable. The dead and wounded have already been picked up and removed

to the ambulances, for the troops have remained masters of the field. You would uselessly expose yourself."

"What does that matter? But I am sorry that I forgot that you have other duties. Farewell, sir! My name is Marthe Moulinier, and I shall never forget the kindness you have shown me in the midst of my misfortunes."

This was a formal dismissal for the sergeant, and it seemed as though the only course remaining to him was to follow his men down the secret staircase. Instead of doing so, however, he began looking at the girl compassionately. "Listen to me, mademoiselle," he said, softly, "you do not know me, and I cannot flatter myself that I have inspired you with any great amount of confidence; however, I assure you that I am an honest man—"

"I believe it, sir."

"Well then, listen to me. You cannot remain in this house after what has just occurred. It is too near the scene of conflict. The insurgents may at any moment recapture the barricade and install themselves here to defend its approaches; my own men may return by the secret stairs. A sanguinary struggle would then take place before your eyes—you must not witness it—you must leave the house and come with me."

"Leave the house—why, I asked you to help me to do so, a little while ago, and you advised me to remain."

"Because you talked of venturing upon the boulevard and that would be courting death. What I propose to you is something very different. You must take my arm and allow me to protect you until we reach my residence. It is not far off, but thank heavens, it is beyond the area of the conflict. You will be in safety there, and—" the old sergeant abruptly paused. He has just perceived that the girl was blushing and looking at him with an expression of wounded pride. "Oh! mademoiselle!" he exclaimed, "how can you doubt my intentions? My white hair ought to have prevented such a mistake, but I have not yet told you my name and I ought to have begun by doing so,"

"My father knew all the men of his company, and latterly he often spoke to me of those he relied upon. However—"

"He was not able to speak to you about me, for I have only served for a couple of days. My age exempted me from duty, but when I heard what was taking place I felt that it was only right for me to join the force. I was made a sergeant on the spot, though why, I can hardly say, as I have never had any previous military experience. It may be that willing men were lacking—"

"And so, sir, you had never seen my father before to-day?"

"Excuse me, I met him yesterday at the municipal offices; besides, I knew him by name, and I was aware that he had a high reputation for probity in this neighbourhood."

"And you, sir, what is your profession?" asked Mademoiselle Moulinier somewhat impatiently.

"My name is Jean-Marie Hingant and I was formerly a magistrate, mademoiselle. I lived until recently in Brittany, where I was born, and I have only been in Paris for a couple of months or so. I came here to—to inquire into a matter in which I am interested."

"And you came alone?"

"Yes; I have never been married, and recently I had the misfortune to lose the only friend who remained to me in my part of the country. However, if you are willing to accept the modest refuge which I offer you, you will, I assure you, be perfectly at home. I can easily find other quarters for a few days, and you will be waited upon by a worthy woman who does my housekeeping, that is, unless you should prefer to take—"

"Oh ! our servant left us this morning, when she saw that a barricade had been thrown up so near the house."

"Then you will accept my offer, mademoiselle ? " Jean-Marie eagerly asked.

Marthe looked at him steadily with her large soft eyes. " I accept," she said unhesitatingly, " you would not deceive an orphan."

"Thank you, mademoiselle," exclaimed the old magistrate in a voice that came straight from his heart. " You will never have cause to regret your confidence in Jean-Marie Hingant. But let us make haste and leave while the road is still clear. Where does that secret staircase lead to ? "

"To the Rue de l'Échiquier."

"Nothing could be better ! I live but a few steps off, in the Rue Bergère, and there is no fighting in that neighbourhood."

The girl's mind was fully made up ; she speedily put on her bonnet, threw a shawl over her shoulders and said in a firm voice, " I am ready."

M. Hingant took up his musket which he had deposited in a corner and went on in advance so as to cope with any assailant ; however he reached the Rue de l'Échiquier without mishap, and there he offered the girl his arm. " O God ! watch over Paul ! " she murmured as she listened to the ominous noise of the cannon, now booming in the distance.

VII.

ONE fine July morning, a few days after the occurrence of these terrible scenes, M. Hingant was crossing the Luxembourg garden with Marthe Moulinier on his arm. It is needless to say that he had laid his military toggery aside, and had again donned with lively satisfaction a costume be-fitting an ex-magistrate. A frock-coat suited him far better than a uniform, and a white cravat was the best adjunct to his grave and placid face. Naturally enough Mademoiselle Moulinier was dressed in mourning, and despite the heavy veil which half concealed her features, she looked particularly charming. The few people to be seen in the paths involuntarily turned round to admire her marvellous beauty, and some students did not hesitate to express their admiration aloud.

Marthe lowered her eyes and blushed whenever she heard or noticed this spontaneous homage to her charms, but worthy Jean-Marie smiled complacently, and straightened himself up with all the simple vanity of a father enjoying his daughter's success. The fact is, that since the terrible day when such dramatic events had brought them together, they had become united by ties of true affection. They had only needed to know each other for this result to be obtained, and Marthe's somewhat disdainful reserve had not been proof against M. Hingant's respectful attentions and discreet tokens of friendship. He himself had enthusiastically followed the promptings of his heart so prone to compassionating misfortune. Moreover, it was almost impossible for him to live without loving somebody, and after Mériadec Léridan's tragical demise he had, for lack of an outlet, been compelled to restrain his affectionate instincts. Thus he now had a wealth of tenderness at his command, and eagerly bestowed it upon Marthe.

His lost happiness seemed restored to him, a hundredfold, now that he had become a foster-father, and could note all the delicacy and superiority of mind that characterized the orphan whom Providence had confided to his protection. It was his greatest desire to further Marthe's interests and forestall her slightest wishes, and she, on her side, granted him absolute confidence. Had it not been for the responsibility attaching to the privateersman's will, and the discovery of the unknown legatee, the old magistrate would willingly have devoted the rest of his life to the child whom he already considered as his own. The dream in which he indulged was to marry her to the man she loved, to prevail upon the young pair to settle in Brittany, as near as possible to Cancale, and to bequeath his whole fortune to them when he died. For the time being he was occupied in carrying out the first part of the programme—that concerning the marriage—and it did not prove a very easy task.

Directly the June insurrection was quelled he had succeeded without much trouble in ascertaining that Lieutenant Gilbert had been removed to the military hospital of the Val-de-Grâce, to be treated for a severe wound which he had received in the arm, while gallantly leading his men to the attack of the Faubourg du Temple. M. Moulinier, however, had been shot dead, in front of the Porte St. Denis, and like many other victims of the first day's conflict he had been buried during the ensuing night, so precipitately that his daughter was even denied the consolation of embracing his remains. Hingant had only been able to procure a certificate of his death, and to attend to some other formalities in view of protecting Marthe's rights. He believed that she would inherit a considerable fortune as she was an only child, and her father had been a merchant of position. However he lacked precise information, and did not know either the figure of Moulinier's fortune, or how it was invested. He had not yet ventured to question Marthe who was absorbed in her grief, and he was waiting for a favourable opportunity to ask her for the indispensable particulars. It seemed as though this opportunity would present itself quite naturally, for the girl had announced her intention of returning home; and Jean-Marie meant to escort her to the Boulevard Bonne Nouvelle to assure himself that she could reside there in safety, and under proper circumstances, despite her position as an orphan, and to request her to examine whatever papers her father might have left behind him.

In the meanwhile, he had planned, for the day preceding Marthe's return home, a visit which she ardently wished to make. Without warning her he had procured a permit to see Lieutenant Gilbert, and he had then proposed that she should go with him to the Val-de-Grâce. Marthe, who had not seen her lover since the day when he had left her to join his company, thanked the old magistrate with an eloquent glance and pressure of the hand, and they at once started for the hospital on foot.

It was the first time that the poor girl had been out of doors since the fatal day of her father's death, and she was glad to be able to inhale the pure balmy air of a summer's day. Paris still displayed traces of the terrible conflict, but it had regained all its noisy animation. There was as grand a display as ever in the shops, damaged though they were, and children crowed and laughed at casements, each pane of which had been shattered by bullets. The contrast between reviving life, and the conflict of a few days before, was nowhere more apparent than round about the

Luxembourg palace. The thick foliage of the spreading trees in the public garden furnished a pleasant shade for the quiet frequenters of this agreeable promenade, so dear to old savants and joyous students. Beyond the shrubbery, however, one espied the gleaming bayonets, snowy tents and stacked muskets of a battalion encamped on an open space.

Marthe walked along so briskly that M. Hingant had some difficulty in keeping pace with her. As they reached a path leading to the observatory he drew out his watch and remarked : "We are too early, my dear child. Our pass states that visitors will not be admitted before noon, and it is now but a few minutes past eleven. Suppose we sit down here in the shade, on one of these benches. To tell the truth I feel a trifle tired."

Marthe had no inclination to rest, and the delay annoyed her ; but she acquiesced in the suggestion, to please her friend, who on his side was not merely glad to sit down a bit, but wished to avail himself of this opportunity to have a chat with the young girl. At his rooms he barely saw her save in the presence of his housekeeper, and he had not cared to broach certain subjects before a dependent. "Monsieur Gilbert," he now remarked, as he seated himself on a bench, "will be very surprised and very happy to see you. How sad it is that we shall have to acquaint him with your poor father's death."

"He is already aware of it. I wrote to him," Marthe promptly answered.

"Ah ! I did not know that—"

A somewhat awkward silence ensued, they both perhaps regretted what they had just said.

"Excuse one rather indiscreet question," resumed Jean-Marie, hesitatingly, "but if I am not mistaken you told me that your marriage was decided upon when—"

"My father had promised me his consent," interrupted Marthe blushing, "but he had not yet formally given it."

"I understand—the difference of fortune made him hesitate—he was rich and did not consider Monsieur Gilbert's position to be—"

"I am not sure that my father was rich."

"No doubt—you never paid any attention to the matter. At your age that is only natural. But Monsieur Moulinier was considered to be a man of means, and it will be easy to ascertain what he possessed. I will attend to that, for you could scarcely undertake the duty yourself, and as you have no one—"

"No, no one," repeated Marthe sadly.

"Excepting me, and Monsieur Paul Gilbert," said M. Hingant smiling. "However it would hardly be proper for your betrothed to make such inquiries.' Fortunately I am well versed in these matters, and I shall be able to spare you many needless formalities. Besides, we will visit your rooms to-morrow, and we shall no doubt find some memoranda—"

"I doubt it, sir ; we were to have moved in a few days' time, and I believe that my father, foreseeing the insurrection, had deposited all his papers with a friend."

"However, you know this friend's name and address."

"No, I really don't."

"But you must have seen him sometimes."

"Never, my father received no visitors."

"That's strange ! However, you were acquainted with your father's habits and occupation."

"He went out regularly every morning, and only returned at dinnertime; he also often spent his evenings away from home, but he never told me where he went."

"He must at least have told your mother."

"My mother is dead," murmured Marthe.

"I know it, my child, and I am sorry to have reminded you of it; but what you tell me seems so extraordinary that I shall perhaps be obliged to revert to the sad subject again. I shall have to ascertain the date of your father's marriage. We shall need the contract, your mother's burial certificate, her maiden name—"

"Her name was Marie," replied Marthe, trying to restrain her tears.

"Marie! she was named Marie," repeated M. Hingant; and instead of proceeding with his question he fell into a reverie which Marthe had no inclination to disturb. The ex-magistrate had arrived in Paris with the fixed resolution of discovering the Mademoiselle Marie Bréhal to whom Léridan had bequeathed his fortune, and he had at first spared no efforts to achieve his purpose. However, the June rising had interrupted his search, perforce, and Mademoiselle Moulinier's subsequent claims upon his time had almost made him forget it. However, but little was needed to recall his self-imposed task to mind, and the fact that Marthe's mother had been named Marie, like millions of other women, had sufficed to make him remember the privateersman's mysterious will. Common as the name was, it seemed to him to be a rather strange coincidence, and it was not without emotion that he again questioned the young girl. "Marie isn't a surname," he said, gently, "your mother must have had one which I need to know so as to carry out the legal formalities."

"I never heard any name but that one," said Marthe.

"But that's impossible!" exclaimed Hingant, fairly stupefied. "In addition to one's Christian name one always has—" He paused abruptly when but half-way through his sentence, for he saw that the girl was crying; he then at once guessed the truth, and bitterly regretted his previous thoughtlessness. "Her mother was an illegitimate child," he mused, "and I almost compelled the poor girl to blush for her origin. It seems to be written that I shall do nothing but blunder."

This unexpected revelation partly explained various things which had at first seemed very strange to M. Hingant—Marthe's loneliness, for instance. Her father had, no doubt, fallen in love with some girl brought up in a foundling hospital and had married her; hence it was only natural that the merchant's daughter should have no relatives on her mother's side. At all events the matter was of no import as regards Marthe's right to her father's property, that is providing the certificate of M. Moulinier's marriage was obtained, and this could not be a very difficult task. Wishing to curtail this painful interrogatory Hingant now decided to allude to a more pleasant subject. "Another half hour," he said, "and we shall see our wounded soldier, who is quite out of danger now. I made inquiries about him and the surgeon of his ward gave me a very favourable report. And that isn't everything; I was told that Monsieur Gilbert's name was set down for the cross of the Legion of Honour."

Marthe's face brightened and she ceased crying.

"I wanted to leave him the pleasure of telling you that himself," resumed Jean-Marie, "but I take such an interest in your joys and sorrows that I could not resist the desire to divert your mind from gloomy thoughts."

"Thank you," quietly replied Marthe holding out her hand, which Hingant kissed with the respectful tenderness of an old man acquainted with past century courtesies. "I am proud of Paul's success, and yet each time he is promoted or distinguished for his merit, I realise that he will become more and more attached to the military profession, which frightens me besides being the greatest obstacle in the way of our marriage."

"Oh! I'm sure he wouldn't hesitate between you and a little more embroidery on his uniform," said M. Hingant gaily.

"You don't know him. My father wanted him to resign his commission and go into business, but he refused."

"Perhaps he then feared that he might displease his relatives by engaging in commercial avocations, whereas now—"

"Paul has no relatives ; he is alone in the world like I am."

This time Hingant did not know what to say. Surprise followed surprise, and although he did not in the least regret having befriended Marthe, he couldn't help thinking that all this was more than strange. He, a man of regular methodical habits, had suddenly found himself face to face with the most extraordinary problems and situations, such as his previous life had not prepared him for. Since poor Léridan's death he seemed to have plunged head first into the realm of romance. First had came the terrible trial of the strangely discovered will; and now Providence had entrusted him with the protection of an orphan, whose mother had never borne a surname, and who was engaged to an officer who had never known his parents. It was really enough to make poor Hingant lose his head, and for an instant he regretted having left his house at Cancale, his old servant Brigitte, and the apple trees in his garden.

Marthe no doubt realized what was passing in her protector's mind, for she said to him, with no little emotion : "What I have just told you seems strange ; does it not, sir ? "

Hingant made a gesture of dissent and was about to apologise, but the girl resumed, in a firmer tone : "The story of my life, short as it has been, will perhaps seem stranger still. You have given me sufficient proof of your interest to make it my duty to tell you everything."

"Oh, mademoiselle ! " exclaimed M. Hingant, " I have no claim on your confidence, and I beg of you to reflect—"

But the girl had already begun her story. "I spent the first years of my childhood," she said, "at a farm, where I was nursed by a peasant woman. I retain but a very vague recollection of that time, for I barely knew how to talk when my mother came to fetch me and take me to Paris. I recollect that we then resided in an old house near the central markets, and that I had a deal of trouble in getting accustomed to being shut up in an ill-lighted room, instead of running about in the open air and rolling on the grass. I was seven years old when I was sent to a school in the district of the Marais, and I was left there till I became sixteen."

"But you frequently went home? at holiday time for instance ? "

"Never, sir. My mother came to see me every Sunday and my father sometimes accompanied her, but it was only during the last holidays that I left the school."

"And afterwards ! "

"Afterwards I did not leave the bedside of my poor mother, who was already suffering from the illness which carried her off. I then learnt to know her, and I found out how much she had suffered at being compelled to live apart from me for so long. However, my father had decided that she should not have me to live with her until I had completed my education."

"Poor woman," muttered M. Hingant, deeply moved.

"Yes, poor woman," resumed Marthe sadly, "her life was but one long martyrdom."

"She was at least able to confide her sorrows to you, to speak to you about the past—"

"No, no, though I frequently thought she was about to open her heart to me. Very often when we were alone, she, lying in bed, and I, clasping her burning hand, I fancied I was about to wring from her the secret of the fatal sadness which was gradually wearing her life away; but just as I was waiting for some revelation, she invariably overcame her weakness, and turning the conversation from herself began speaking about me, my future and my happiness—"

"But were you the only person who loved her then? Didn't your father—"

"My father always treated her with a grave affection very like that which he showed me; but he was often absent on business, and whenever we saw him he remained silent like a man who has worrying troubles. He asked after my mother's health, gave orders that she should want for nothing, absently asked me a few questions, apologised for having to leave us, and then returned to his business. I remarked that after his visits my mother always became sadder and more affectionate towards me. She often drew me to her, pressed me in her arms, and said : "Promise me, Marthe, that you will marry the man you love ?"

"She knew Mousieur Gilbert, then? she approved of your marriage?" asked Jean-Marie, eagerly.

"It was her dearest wish to see us united, and before dying she obtained from my father a promise that he would not oppose our marriage. She had long been acquainted with Paul, for she met him every week in the waiting room of the school, where I was educated, and where he came to see his sister, my best, my only friend."

"And it was there that you fell in love with one another ? " said the ex-magistrate smiling. " But in that case Monsieur Gilbert is not altogether alone in the world ? "

"His sister died a month before my mother," interrupted the young girl.

M. Hingant lowered his head and said no more. This sad story had touched him deeply. He did not dare to ask for further information, for fear of rendering the poor girl's sufferings still more acute. He rather longed to be able to alleviate her grief, and he vowed that he would do his utmost to ensure her happiness. First of all, however, he must see the young officer, and the visiting hour being now at hand he was about to tell Marthe that it was time to start, when she suddenly clutched hold of his arm and pressed close beside him with a gesture of affright. " What is the matter, my child ? " asked M. Hingant gently.

" He, it is he, the murderer ! " she gasped ; and at the same time she pointed to a man in a blouse who was passing along under the trees at some twenty paces from them, and who seemed bound for the gateway leading to the Rue d'Enfer.

" The murderer, what murderer? " asked M. Hingant, who was so surprised by this sudden exclamation that instead of looking in the direction indicated, he began gazing at the girl in alarm. He asked himself if her misfortunes had not unsettled her mind.

Rising up, however, with her arm stretched out towards the pedestrian,

who was walking swiftly along under the chestnut trees, she excitedly resumed : " It is the man whom you were looking for in my rooms; the
scoundrel who fired at my father from the window ! "
    This time Jean-Marie looked in the right direction, and perceived an in-
dividual, dressed like a working-man, and whose figure and bearing did
slightly remind him of the insurgent, of whom he had just caught a glimpse
between the half open shutters on the day of the conflict. The man was
already some distance off, however, and now only his back could be seen.
" You must be mistaken, my dear child," said M. Hingant to Marthe;
" you have been deceived by a chance resemblance."
    " No, no, I am sure that it is he.   When he crossed the path a moment
ago I recognised his bony face, stern eyes and swarthy complexion.   I saw
him only too near, in our rooms, to be able to forget him."
    " Then he must have changed his clothes," muttered M. Hingant, " for
he was dressed that day like a person of the middle classes.   After all, it
may be the same fellow, and in that case he ought not to be allowed to remain at liberty.   I shall hasten after him and summon a police agent to
take him to the station house.   If we are mistaken, as I fear, he can regain
his liberty by proving his identity and the manner in which he spent his
time on June 22nd."
    " You will never overtake him.   He has already disappeared under the
trees," said Marthe.
    " Oh, I'm no longer young, no doubt, but I still have good legs and I'll
catch him right enough.   I am mainly embarrassed as regards yourself,
my dear Marthe.   This man will certainly make a scene when he is
collared, and it wouldn't do for you to be mixed up in the matter.   On the
other hand I hardly like to leave you here."
    " But I can wait for you here without any risk of danger."
    " Hum ! there are several kinds of danger.   This garden is patronised by
students ; and then we shall miss our visit to Monsieur Gilbert.   But
now I think of it," exclaimed Jean-Marie feeling in his pocket, " take my
pass and go straight to the Val-de-Grâce.   It is only a few steps off, and you
can obtain admittance with this permit.   I will join you there as soon as I have
done with this scamp ; and you and Monsieur Paul can get along very well
without me for a quarter of an hour or so."
    " We shall be impatiently awaiting you," rejoined Marthe, expressing
her thanks in a glance.

                                VIII.

HAVING hastily handed the hospital pass to Mademoiselle Moulinier, the
old magistrate started in pursuit of the man in the blouse, who had now
had time enough to secure a long start.   M. Hingant caught sight of him,
however, as soon as he had passed the trees of the avenue leading to the
observatory.   The suspected individual was at this moment reaching the
gateway which led into the Rue d'Enfer, and he did not at all seem to imagine that he was being followed ; for, before leaving the garden, he
glanced on either side, like a saunterer undecided as to the best direction
for a stroll.   M. Hingant was not near enough to see the man's face, but
his doubts were revived by his careless manner, and he again feared that
he might make an egregious blunder by denouncing this quiet promenader
as a dastardly murderer.   What proofs could he supply to the police

authorities in support of so serious a charge? And in what an embarrassing position would he find himself, if the prisoner proved his innocence. This disagreeable prospect was worthy of consideration.

However, Hingant still hastened on, and drew nearer and nearer to the stranger, who was still standing near the gate. The old magistrate now regretted that he had not brought Marthe with him, for by sending her to the Val-de-Grâce he had deprived himself of the only witness who was in a position to recognise the murderer. Worthy Jean-Marie once more realised that he was prone to be over hasty. His heart always spoke before his mind, and he had at first only thought of pleasing his dear ward. Unfortunately, the mistake could not be repaired, for Marthe had already gone off in the direction of the hospital, and the stranger would certainly not await his pursuer's convenience. "The wine is drawn, and it must be drunk," said Hingant to himself. "Only I must be very cautious. I will take a closer look at this fellow, and if he really seems to be a scamp, I'll point him out to the first policeman I meet. Since that rising last week, the police are only too prone to arrest people, and when I give my name and address, and mention my former calling, they won't refuse to institute an inquiry. In that way I shall have my mind at ease, and I shall be able to reach the hospital almost as soon as Mademoiselle Moulinier. I ought to do so; for, young and pretty as she is, it is hardly proper, in fact it is almost imprudent, for her to present herself alone before all the soldiers guarding the entrance! There's another blunder of mine, and I begin to think that I am going into second childhood."

Hingant gained ground while thus reflecting. The stranger was still motionless, but, with annoying obstinacy, he refrained from looking round. Jean-Marie had barely a dozen strides to take to come up with him, when the fellow, suddenly making up his mind, began to cross the Rue d'Enfer, still without glancing back. One might have fancied that he feared some misfortune, similar to that which befell Lot's wife, or Orpheus, who is said to have lost his Eurydice for having looked behind him at an inauspicious moment. These comparisons did not occur, however, to the old magistrate, but he quickened his pace so as not to be distanced, and reached the gateway just as the stranger sprang into the first of a long line of cabs, standing on the other side of the street. Hingant hoped that the fellow would at least show his face, but he was doomed to disappointment. The driver, who had, no doubt, already received his orders, climbed heavily on to the box, while the stranger remained carefully ensconced in one corner of the vehicle. All that could be seen of him was his hand raising the side window.

Marthe's protector felt greatly embarrassed. He had not foreseen this flight in a cab, which upset all his calculations. He was now half inclined to relinquish the chase, but after a little hesitation, curiosity gained the upper hand, and he muttered, "I must satisfy my mind on the matter. That scamp is hiding, clearly enough. If he were a real workman he wouldn't amuse himself by driving about in a cab. However, cabs are to be hired by anyone, and by giving a handsome gratuity to another driver, I can follow the rascal, see where he alights, and note the number of the house he enters. Then I will drive back to the hospital, and this evening I will make a statement on the subject to the police."

To hasten to the cabstand, spring into the nearest vehicle, and give his orders to the driver, was only the work of a minute for the alert old magistrate. The two cabs got off almost at the same time, and the first one proceeded straight towards the Odéon, by a route which could not be followed, now that broad boulevards intersect the students' quarter of Paris in all directions. Hingant, who had no reasons for hiding himself, leant out of the window, and kept his eyes on the vehicle in front. Both cabmen drove rapidly down the Rue de Tournon, and then turned in the direction of the church of St. Sulpice. "I hope he won't take me like this to the other end of Paris!" sighed Jean-Marie. "There are only a couple of hours for visiting the hospital, and Marthe would be obliged to return home alone."

However, his apprehensions were promptly dispelled. After crossing the Place St. Sulpice the first cab turned into a narrow street, and drew up in front of one of the last houses on the left-hand side. M. Hingant saw the man in the blouse spring lightly to the ground, and then disappear up a passage. The driver, who had no doubt been paid in advance, at once proceeded on his way. The old magistrate now ordered his own Jehu to stop, and having alighted he walked down the street to examine the house in which the stranger had taken refuge. "It's singular," he said, "I believe I can recognise that house, and yes, this is the very street to which I was sent on my arrival in Paris, and which I have visited three times already without finding the man I want to see. Yes, indeed, unless I am greatly mistaken, he must live in that old house with a little door, next to the second-hand clothes shop." To satisfy himself on the point, the old magistrate proceeded to the end of the street, and looked up at the corner house, which bore an inscription. "The Rue des Canettes!" he exclaimed. "I wasn't mistaken, and the coincidence is a singular one. This insurgent, for I feel certain that he is one of the Red Republicans in hiding, has taken refuge in the very house where the private inquiry agent, who was recommended to me, resides? Who knows but what he is going to call on him? This would be a capital opportunity to kill two birds with one stone."

Thus reasoning, Jean-Marie approached the passage which the stranger had entered. When in front of the shabby shop, flanking the dingy entrance, he retreated to the middle of the street, and looked up at the house. Its front was high and grimy, and there was but one window on each of the six floors. The long dark passage giving access to the abode had a wicket gate, and as M. Hingant knew by experience, a bell rang loudly whenever this portal was pushed open. As for the shop beside the passage it all but disappeared from view behind the toggery and odds and ends, which hung in front of the windows outside. There were here, embroidered uniforms, workmen's blouses, hunting horns, guitars, top boots, frameless pictures, all tarnished, ragged, battered, cobbled and smoky; and amid them, the conspicuous scarlet tunic of an English officer at once arrested attention. M. Hingant had already had occasion to contemplate this striking display, but he had not previously paid much attention to it. That day however, he felt, despite himself, inclined to examine the house and its characteristics with no little care, and the more he did so, the more suspicious its appearance seemed. However, it was necessary for him to decide upon his course. "Twenty minutes past twelve," he muttered, looking at his watch. "I think that I shall have time to call on this inquiry-agent. He can't always be out, dash it all! If I now find him at home I will make an appointment to talk over the search which I wish to intrust him with, and, at the same time, I will say a couple of words to him about the rascal who has just entered the house, and ask him to make inquiries.

He won't refuse to do that, as inquiries are his speciality. I can trust him too, as he was recommended to me by Galmard, now of the Paris bar, and formerly my chum at the Rennes law-school. It will only be a matter of ten minutes; and I shall be able to reach the Val-de-Grâce by one o'clock, or a quarter past."

Such was worthy Jean-Marie's ardour, that he quite forgot that he had parted from Marthe with the intention of reaching the hospital almost as soon as she did. He was caught, however, in a network of complications, which might lead him very far indeed. Resolutely opening the wicket, he entered the passage amid the loud ringing of the bell, and climbed straight to the third floor as he had done on previous occasions. He here found himself in front of a door distinguished by a carefully polished brass knob, and a bell rope with a silken tassel. This door opened at his first ring, and a middle-aged woman, of plain but clean appearance, appeared on the threshold of a little ante-room. "I should like to speak to Monsieur Billebaude," said M. Hingant.

"I will see if he is at home," replied the woman.

"Pray tell him that I have come on urgent business, and shall not detain him long. Moreover, I was sent here by Monsieur Galmard."

"Oh! in that case, pray come in. I will take you to my master's private room at once."

The old magistrate followed the servant, who led him through a dining-room and a parlour, the modest aspect of which was well calcuated to inspire confidence. One would have fancied oneself in the abode of some provincial of the middle classes. The arm-chairs upholstered in yellow Utrecht velvet, the lamps shaped like fluted columns, the gilt bronze timepiece, and the two engravings representing "The Dog of the Regiment," and "The Trumpeter's Charger," could only belong to an honest, domesticated man. "I really think I have found the person I want," Hingant said to himself, while the servant, who had gone alone into the private room, was informing her master that someone wished to see him.

But a moment elapsed, and then M. Billebaude appeared on the threshold, with smiling face and gracious bearing: "Pray walk in, sir," he said, stepping aside to allow his client to pass him. "You are sent to me, I hear, by my old friend Galmard, and, in that case, I am completely at your service."

"Thank you, sir. I shall certainly have occasion to call on you again very shortly," said Jean-Marie, hastily, "but I will not trespass on your time to-day, for—"

"But there is certainly no reason why you should not sit down," interrupted M. Billebaude, bringing forward a chair.

Marthe's protector would willingly have dispensed with ceremony, for he wished to curtail the interview; however, he seated himself as requested near a mahogany writing-table. The servant having retired by another door, the two men found themselves alone. M. Billebaude was certainly over fifty, but he still had a pleasing appearance in his handsome cashmere dressing-gown, and embroidered smoking-cap. A Parisian would no doubt have taken him for a dentist, but worthy Jean-Marie considered that he looked majestic. There was certainly nothing repulsive about the agent's physiognomy. He had bright little eyes, a full placid face, a rather large mouth, which readily smiled, and carefully trimmed white whiskers, which served as a kind of framework to his countenance. M. Hingant did not hold inquiry agents in very high opinion, as a rule, but the sight of this genial-looking, elderly gentleman quite sufficed to dispel any prejudices that he may have entertained.

"Well, sir," he began with his usual frankness, "I have warned you that I should make you lose your time on this occasion, although I have but few moments at my disposal. I previously called here to speak to you about an important search which I wish to confide to you; but unfortunately, you were not at home."

"I greatly regret it, but you will understand that my profession often takes me from home. In future, if you will kindly write to me on the day before—"

"I certainly will, and as soon as possible, for the matter in question greatly interests me and might yield you a handsome honorarium. However for the time being, I merely wish to ask you for a little information."

"I am quite at your disposal."

"This is the case. A few m'nutes ago, just as I reached your house, a man who was walking in advance of me, entered it. He wore a blouse and trousers of blue linen stuff and had a cap on his head—in fact he was dressed like a workman. He was not very tall but extremely broad shouldered. I was, unfortunately, not able to see his face."

"The description is rather vague," said M. Billebaude, knitting his grey eyebrows, "but may I ask what is your object in supplying it?"

"I wish to know if it corresponds with that of a tenant of this house?"

"Dear me, no. It is true that I very seldom meet the other people living here, and that I never associate with them. However, I don't see that there is anything to show that this man does live in the house."

"At all events, I have reason to believe that he is now on the premises, and as there are important reasons for having him arrested, I should like—"

"To denounce him to the police, eh?" asked M. Billebaude, who seemed highly astonished and also a trifle embarrassed. "Pray, what has he done?"

"What has he done, sir? You ask me what he has done?" retorted M. Hingant, somewhat put out by Billebaude's supercilious manner. "In the first place he is an insurgent."

"Oh! I don't meddle in politics," interrupted the agent, "and if it's only a question of that—"

"If it were only that, I shouldn't think of denouncing him," replied the ex-magistrate firmly, "but I strongly suspect him of being the scoundrel who, on June 22nd, in cold blood and under my very eyes, deliberately shot a gentleman of position in whom I was interested. You will agree with me that this was a downright murder, which all the excitement attendant upon the insurrection cannot excuse; and every honest man ought to feel it his duty to hand the culprit over to the authorities."

"Very good; but if he is not in a position to do so?"

"But it was to ask you to help me in capturing him that I called here to-day. I should not have come in, otherwise, for I am expected elsewhere," exclaimed Jean-Marie, glancing at the mantelpiece on which stood a black marble clock, surmounted by a statuette of Belisarius holding out his helmet for the alms of charitable passers by.

"I am desirous of serving you, sir, out of regard for our friend Galmard; but I must warn you that criminal cases are not in my line."

"But this isn't a question of business; it is one of rendering a service to society by having a scoundrel arrested—"

"I certainly should not refuse to arrest him if I had him under my thumb; but it is not my business to search for him, for pray recollect that I am in no way connected with the police."

"Very well. I see I made a mistake," said M. Hingant, ill-humouredly. "I regret having disturbed you, and will wish you good day."

"Come, sir, be reasonable," rejoined the agent coaxingly. "You saw a man, whom you seem to suspect, but whom I have no knowledge of, entering this house. And you are convinced that he is still here, which seems to me very doubtful, for since you entered this room he has had plenty of time to get away. But in any case, how can I rush after him from floor to floor without causing a scandal which would only serve to compromise us both?"

Jean-Marie made no reply, for he was beginning to think that M. Billebaude was not altogether wrong. "Take my advice," gently resumed the agent, who already realised the success of his eloquence, "and don't pay any farther attention to this scamp. I will wager that he is already a long way off, and besides, in such times as these, a man cannot be too prudent. It is better to let the police act. The authorities have no doubt been informed of this murder?"

"Yes, certainly they have; for it was committed near the Porte St. Denis, in presence of more than sixty national guards who knew and esteemed the murdered man, poor Monsieur Moulinier, their captain."

A nervous contraction flashed like lightning over M. Billebaude's placid face. "It seems to me that I read something about the matter in the newspapers," he said, without displaying any further emotion. "May I venture to ask if you were a friend of the deceased?"

"No sir, no. I had had but a very slight connection with him," replied Jean-Marie, somewhat embarrassed.

"I am glad to hear it. I should have been extremely sorry if the misfortune had affected you personally. Then the matter which you thought of confiding to me, on Galmard's recommendation, does not concern Monsieur —Monsieur—Moulinier, I think you said."

"No, not at all; but I have not the time to explain it to you now."

"May I at least hope, however, that you will not retain an unpleasant recollection of our interview, and that at your next visit—"

"I—don't know, I will see," stammered Jean-Marie, who was not particularly well satisfied with his first dealings with M. Billebaude. "For the present, however, I must take leave of you." He was already on his feet, and seemed disposed to make for the door.

"What, sir, are you still annoyed with me?" the agent asked, barring the way under pretext of politely escorting him out. "Really now, you are very wrong, for I feel disposed to accomplish miracles to serve you, if only for the sake of effacing the unpleasant impression which you are perhaps taking away with you. I trust you will find that our mutual friend sent you to the right person. Litigation is my forte. I fancy I know something about it. Claims upon government, suits of every imaginable kind before any known tribunal, the settlement of accounts, the recovery of bad debts, the drawing up of genealogies—"

"It is not anything of that kind," M. Hingant hastily exclaimed, in view of putting an end to what threatened to be an interminable enumeration of the agent's 'specialties.' "I simply wish to find out what has become of a person—"

"Who is missing, disappeared, eh? And it perhaps occurred long ago. Upon my word, my dear sir, you could not have applied better. I am most successful in searches of that kind, for, without boasting, I have special gifts for following a scent and searching archives and registers. My instinct never deceives me, and I have accomplished incredible feats in that line. With the slightest indication, the barest particulars, I can discover a missing person if he be alive, or procure a certificate of his death, should he have died, just as Cuvier, the great Cuvier, with one fragment of bone reconstructed an animal of an extinct species."

The ex-magistrate opened his eyes in wonder and congratulated himself on having found such a skilful man. "Well, sir," he said, smiling, "in a few days from now, I will offer you an excellent opportunity to prove your skill, for by way of information I shall only be able to supply you with a name and a date."

"That isn't much, but it will suffice," replied Billebaude, with superb assurance.

"What, without any further enlightenment you would undertake to discover—"

"Well, just try me. Tell me the matter briefly now; and when you call again, I shall perhaps have some news for you."

Hingant was greatly impressed by the agent's imperturbable assurance, but there was another point to be settled. "Before trusting you with an affair which would cost you a deal of time and trouble," said he, "it would be as well to come to an understanding—"

"As to my honorarium! That's useless, my dear sir, quite useless. We will settle that later on, when we have succeeded. That is my invariable rule. There is no buying a pig in a poke here. Simply give me the few particulars you have and I will set to work this very evening."

"I would do so willingly, only I haven't time to add certain necessary explanations, for—" At this moment the clock bearing the statuette of Belisarius struck one o'clock. "Ah! good Heavens, I shall never get there!" added M. Hingant, and he darted to the door without finishing his previous sentence.

This time the agent was obliged to let his visitor pass by; only he followed him, bowing profusely and repeating formulas of politeness. "I am really grieved to have detained you, my dear sir. I trust I shall see you again speedily. It is unfortunate that I cannot begin my search in the meanwhile, for want of the person's name; I should feel very flattered, however, if you would kindly leave me yours."

"Here is my card, sir," said Hingant hurrying across the parlour. "I shall certainly call again before the end of the week. And as for the matter which I shall then explain to you, I can tell you that it concerns a Mademoiselle Marie Bréhal, who must have resided in Paris in July, 1815."

"And you wish to know what has become of her? Very well. I shall charge myself with the matter and am confident I shall succeed. If I didn't I ought to give up business, for searches of this kind are but the very rudiments of the art."

"I trust that you are right, sir, and I wish you a very good morning," exclaimed Jean-Marie as soon as he managed to reach the landing. And thereupon he began descending the stairs four at a time, at the risk of breaking his neck; while M. Billebaude, after closing his door, carefully entered the name of Marie Bréhal with the date, July 1815, in his note-book, examined the ex-magistrate's card, slipped it into a leather case which never left his person, and returned to his private room, rubbing his hands complacently.

Hingant did not seem to be equally pleased, and to tell the truth he could

barely congratulate himself on the result of the enterprise which he had
somewhat thoughtlessly undertaken. The murderer had escaped him, by
his own fault, for if he had contented himself with pursuing him up the
stairs instead of applying to M. Billebaude for help, he would perhaps have
succeeded in arresting him. Moreover, he now had no time left to search for
the fellow, for Mademoiselle Moulinier must be growing impatient, and he
had just lost a full hour, thanks to the agent's loquacity. However, he did
not regret having made the acquaintance of the skilful man who declared
that he would be able to find Marie Bréhal ; and the prospect thus offered
somewhat consoled Jean-Marie for his other misadventures. "To the
Val-de-Grâce and drive fast. I will pay you well," he cried out to the
driver of his cab, which was still waiting for him at a short distance down
the street.

IX.

WHEN Mademoiselle Moulinier cried out: "There is the murderer !" she
had given way to very natural fright. It was also quite natural that M.
Hingant should start in pursuit of the scoundrel thus providentially brought
within his reach ; and more natural still that Marthe should wish to ensure
the arrest of her father's murderer. And yet the result of this logical
sequence of feelings and actions was to place the girl in an extremely false
position. Scarcely had her old friend disappeared under the trees, than
she began to regret having allowed him to leave her. It was the first time
in her life that she found herself alone out of doors in Paris, and without
precisely knowing what she was afraid of, she began to feel a vague uneasiness. Everything contributed to disturb her, the large garden which she
had only visited once or twice with her schoolfellows when she was very
young, the soldiers camping beyond the shrubbery, and the long-haired,
carelessly-dressed students who ogled her as they passed by. It seemed to
her as if she found herself lost in an unknown country, inhabited by strange
people, and she was anxious to leave the spot as soon as possible. After M.
Hingant's departure she had remained standing, holding the permit in her
hand, without thinking of reading it, and not daring either to go off or to
sit down again. However, when her first emotion subsided she remembered
that her protector had given her an appointment at the military hospital,
and it was necessary for her to go there to join him ; besides she did not
wish to miss this opportunity of seeing Paul Gilbert.
    She now, however, had an inkling of difficulties which she had not pre-
viously foreseen. The idea of presenting herself alone and unprotected at
the gate of the Val-de-Grâce alarmed her in advance, and she said to herself that it was hardly proper for a young girl to enter all alone a ward full
of wounded officers. Jean-Marie's programme was simple but not prudent,
and, indeed, such a combination could only have occurred to some one
having but little Parisian experience. However, it was too late to retreat.
From the spot where Marthe stood she could perceive the dome of the hospital, and with this to guide her she ran but little risk of losing her way,
however unfamiliar she was with the neighbourhood. Accordingly, she
boldly walked up the Avenue de l'Observatoire, pulling her veil down over
her face and carefully avoiding all the people whose appearance inspired
her with distrust. She did not walk rapidly, however, for she indulged in the
hope that M. Hingant would soon have finished pursuing the strange man

he had gone after, and that he and she would reach the appointed spot at the same time.

No unpleasant incident occurred while she was crossing the garden; but just as she passed through the gate she caught sight of a young man who seemed to be following her. She quickened her pace without looking back, rapidly crossed the esplanade on which the statue of Marshal Ney now stands, and turned down a narrow street which seemed likely to lead her to her destination. It was rather deserted, having the high walls of various convents on either side, but it was also short and led straight to the Faubourg St. Jacques where there was no dearth of passers-by. Accordingly Marthe could hardly have anything disagreeable to fear, but she heard behind her a masculine footfall, which seemed to come rapidly nearer and nearer. Although ignorant of the system followed by the Lovelaces who stalk the streets of Paris in quest of adventures, her womanly instinct warned her that she was perhaps threatened with some peril. The nervousness which a repeated sound, due to a hidden cause, always produces made her lose her head, and she was scarcely half way down the street when she began to run as fast as she could.

Did the man behind her do the same? She knew nothing about it, for on reaching the corner of the Faubourg St. Jacques she gave a rapid glance to right and left and darted in the direction of an open gateway guarded by some soldiers. Chance had favoured her, for she saw the courtyard of the hospital extending in front. There was a crowd round about the entrance, visitors arriving and leaving in far greater numbers than usual. Young army surgeons passed by with a busy air, white-aproned nurses of the male sex darted between groups of lounging privates, and every now and then some officer, leaning on crutches or a cane, could be seen on the threshold bidding good-bye to some friends who had called to see him. On the other hand there was no dearth of spectators. The street was full of sight-seers who stood there killing time by watching the scene, much as they would have gathered in front of a booth at a fair. The policeman often had to tell the loungers to "move on," and the sentinels had a deal of trouble in keeping the gateway clear. A stalwart porter stood there, clad in a loose cloak and forage cap, and barring fully half of the way with his bulky form. He examined the permits, admitted the people who were duly authorized, and pitilessly dismissed the others, behaving, indeed, like a man fully convinced of the high importance of his functions. The fact is, order was very necessary, for the June rising had filled the hospital with wounded, and but few patients were not asked for by one or another visitor.

Marthe, surprised and intimidated by the crush, looked round her on all sides in the hope of espying M. Hingant, but the old magistrate was not to be seen. She then thought of waiting for him, and glided timidly along the side-walk bordering the railing of the courtyard. It was necessary to elbow one's way through the throng, and the spot was not at all suited to a girl whose toilet, simple as it was, strongly contrasted with the careless attire of the people round about. Marthe soon fancied that some of the loungers were eyeing her with mocking attention, and that her persistence in waiting provoked whispers and smiles. The women seemed to take her measure with a sneering air; it is true, however, that the weaker sex was mainly represented by some old, sordid looking harpies.

Martha was speedily disconcerted by all this; and reflecting that it would be best for her to enter the hospital, she drew together her courage, and with some difficulty succeeded in approaching the porter to whom she handed the permit with a trembling hand. The imposing functionary took it, read it and returned it to her, saying : "I'm very sorry, my little lady, but you can't go in with a pass made out in a gentleman's name, especially when one's as pretty as you are."

Marthe lacked the strength to answer a single word ; but she turned so pale that, despite her veil, the porter remarked her emotion. "You mustn't worry," said he with jeering complacency, "I know that it's hard to have to go home again without seeing one's lover, but it can't be helped. My orders are very strict to-day. Come back next week ; perhaps I shall then be able to let you in."

Mademoiselle Moulinier was no longer listening. She turned away from the gate, staggering and trying to pass through the crowd ; but her failure had had many witnesses, and it sufficed to rouse that cruel instinct which impels ill-bred people to jeer at the weak.

"Hallo !" said one old harpy, "so that pert looking thing wanted to get in without a pass."

"She needn't have rigged herself out so fine," said another.

"She's got plenty of bounce to run after her sweetheart at the hospital !" declared a third.

These coarse jibes resounded in Marthe's ears and she felt like fainting. Without quite understanding what was said, she realized that the bystanders were throwing mud at her. The jeers increased, moreover, and very soon people began to surround her. Fortunately, as it seemed, at this critical moment a voice whispered in her ear: "Take my arm, madame, and don't be afraid."

Marthe complied, scarcely knowing what she was about, and without even daring to look at the generous man who thus came to her assistance. His help seemed very appropriate, but at first it excited the crowd all the more. The clamour became almost threatening, and injurious epithets were showered like hail upon the girl and her protector.

"It seems she has two sweethearts, one inside and the other here," said one of the harpies who had spoken before.

"A soldier and a civilian !" echoed another.

"The trooper's jilted !" was the retort, and then came a burst of merriment.

Indeed, hoarse laughter followed each coarse jest, and in the whole crowd not one voice was raised in defence of poor Marthe. The stranger, who alone had taken her side, had the good sense not to try and answer the jibes, but to move on as fast as was practicable. The poor girl, leaning on his arm, scarcely had the strength to walk, her legs seemed to give way beneath her. "Fear nothing," whispered her protector, who was perhaps more uneasy than he seemed, "keep up for five minutes and we shall have escaped them."

Marthe barely listened, but mechanically tried to fly from this danger which she no longer exactly realised as she had pretty well lost her head. But one thought was clearly present in her mind. She hoped she would see M. Hingant appear. But the old magistrate was not to be seen, and the brawlers were still howling behind Marthe and her defender. The police were not numerous enough to assert their authority, and the tumult already threatened to become a chase, when a fresh incident fortunately occurred. An omnibus was coming at full trot down the Faubourg St. Jacques, which was then extremely narrow, and the throng had to disperse on either side, to avoid being crushed. The brawlers vented their spite on the driver, but the huge vehicle followed its course, splashing the mob by way of revenge with the muddy water in the gutters.

Marthe and her defender, who were slightly in advance of the crowd, had managed to glide between the houses and the omnibus wheels, while the shouting mass was still revolving in confusion in front of the horses. The stranger turned this momentary respite to good account with singular skill and speed. " Try and run," he said to the girl, " another twenty paces and we shall be free from danger." And at the same time, holding her firmly by the arm, he succeeded in dragging her along, so that before the thoroughfare had become clear behind them they had reached the corner of the Rue des Feuillantines.

"This way and we are saved," said the stranger whose assurance restored Marthe's strength; and she hastened on without even asking where she was being taken. If she had been calmer and more possessed, she would have hesitated before blindly darting under a broad archway the door of which stood open. There again, had she been able to recover herself, she would certainly have declined to proceed any further. But the tumult of the street was still ringing in her ears, and she imagined that she could ever distinguish the noise of the mob still hastening in pursuit of her; so that her only thought was to escape its persecution.

"Come in, quick," said the man in whom she fancied she could trust. She did not even take the time to look where he was leading her, and before she realised what had happened she found herself in a large room, lighted by two high windows. It was the main apartment of a suite situated on the ground floor of the house in which she had found a refuge. Her obliging guide had merely had to slip a key into the lock of a door on one side of the vaulted passage.

He was plainly at home; and indeed he soon shewed, in an unmistakable manner, that such was the case. He began by slipping a bolt, no doubt as a precautionary measure in case the crowd should think of invading his abode; then he laid his hat on a table, carelessly passed one hand through his hair, and giving himself a glance in a mirror, rolled an arm chair forward. Marthe who was breathless and half dying of fright, sank on to the proferred seat, and for the first time she raised her eyes in view of looking at her generous protector. He was a fair-haired young man, elegantly, or one might have said, sumptuously dressed, for a treble gold chain dangled across his white waistcoat, and there was a diamond pin in his blue silk cravat. Moreover, he wore a coat with metal buttons, pearl-grey kid gloves, and patent leather boots so shiny that one could see one's face in them. However, his features though regular were wanting in expression, and his bearing was anything but *distingué*, albeit he affected an easy air. He remained standing in front of the young girl, and looked at her with a smile. " How fortunate that I passed by ! " he exclaimed, without any preamble. " Had it not been for me, little one, you would have spent a very uncomfortable quarter of an hour. The Parisians are not easy to deal with."

Marthe started and a flush overspread her cheeks. She had never been spoken to in such a tone before, and she regretted that she had been so confiding. " I cannot do otherwise than thank you, sir, for the service you have rendered me," she said, "but—"

"Oh ! never mind the thanks, I am only too glad to have an opportunity of speaking to you—for I followed you from the Luxembourg without being able to overtake you. Do you know, you can trot along fast enough with those pretty little feet of yours?" exclaimed the young man, making a movement as if to draw nearer.

Mademoiselle Moulinier sprang up abruptly, indignation had restored her strength. "You are mistaken concerning me, sir," she said, with a cold dignity which momentarily calmed her host's transports.

"No, upon my word, I'm not mistaken," he resumed, sneering. "I see well enough how pretty you are, and as a fellow need not be very shrewd to guess that you were going to the Val-de-Grâce to see your lover, I don't hesitate to offer you a champagne dinner. That will certainly be preferable to tasting hospital *tisane!*"

"This is infamous," murmured the girl, who could barely repress her tears.

"Bah! and why, pray? Ah, I see, you take me for a humbug, because I reside in the students' quarter. But have no fear, I'm not a sawbones, and if I reside here, it is because I have friends in the neighbourhood, but when I want to make merry I cross the Seine. My means allow it. I am a landowner, my dear, and to prove it, I will show you this." As he spoke, he drew from his waistcoat pocket a glazed card, on which one read : CHARLES DU GENÊT, Land Owner. There was at least a half inch of space between the preposition and the name that followed it.

"I wish to leave this house, sir," said Marthe in a firm voice, "and I beg that you will allow me to pass."

"You are mad, my duck. Have you thought of the blackguards who are waiting for you in the street?"

"I would rather expose myself to their insults than submit to yours."

"I insult you? Not at all. It's you who misunderstand my compliments. Come, don't be pert, but sit down and let us have a chat."

"Will you open the door for me?" inquired Marthe taking a step towards the portal.

"May I ask where you mean to go, my pretty one?"

"To the house of a man in whose presence you would not dare to act as you are doing now."

"Your soldier? Come, come, you know very well that you won't be allowed to enter."

"I am going to my father's, sir, and I shall tell him some one has tried to take advantage of a young girl's inexperience and fright."

Marthe had thought of M. Hingant, and she hoped that by giving him the name of father before her odious persecutor, she would escape all further danger. But the handsome Charles began to laugh and twirled his moustaches.

"Pooh!" said he, "you have plenty of time, and I will see you home myself—when we have dined. In the meantime, little one—"

At this moment a violent ring at the bell interrupted him. "Who the devil can have come to bother me?" the young fellow muttered. "It can't be any of my neighbours, as it isn't yet the hour for absinthe. Can it be that some of the scamps who pursued us have thought of besieging my rooms? I shouldn't care for a joke of that kind."

Marthe said nothing, but she gently moved nearer to the door, for she had determined to call for help, and wished to be heard outside. There soon came a second ring at the bell, even more violent than the first one, then as a third resounded, one heard a voice, which made a great impression on the girl, calling : "Charles! Charles! Make haste and open the door. I know you are there, and I want to speak with you."

Charles no doubt recognised the voice, for he made a gesture of surprise and impatience. "That's all that was wanting," he growled sulkily, "What can have brought the old fellow here? Bah! I sha'n't let him in," he added, snapping his fingers.

"You will open the door at once, sir," now said Marthe.

"We will see about that."

"If you don't I shall call to the person who is outside."

Dugenêt, the most elegant of the old privateersman's three nephews, cut a sorry figure at that moment, and, not knowing exactly what decision to come to, cast furious glances at his piisoner. "Come, Charles, don't keep me waiting," resumed the visitor. "I'm in a hurry; and besides, I will not detain you long."

"The old fool! May lightning confound him!" muttered Charles.

And turning to the girl, he added: "Just be careful not to make a scandal. In the first place, I warn you that it will do no good, for I shall not let you escape." Convinced that this threat would suffice to intimidate Marthe, he resolved to draw the bolt, and set the door ajar with the intention of slipping outside, and talking to his importunate visitor in the corridor. But he had scarcely drawn the bolt, when the door, violently pushed, flew wide open, and a man burst in like a whirlwind.

"Ah, my friend," he exclaimed, quite out of breath, "if you only knew what has happened! A misfortune, a great misfortune, and it's all my own fault! I have come to you for help for you know the neighbourhood, and can help me to find her. I was told that she came this way."

"Find whom? What misfortune are you speaking of?" inquired Charles, trying to place himself in front of the intruder, so as to prevent him from seeing Marthe.

But this manœuvre did not succeed. A cry of joy resounded behind him, and before he had time to prevent it the girl, gliding along close to the wall, flung herself into the arms of the friend that Heaven had sent her, indeed into the arms of M. Hingant as the reader will have already guessed. "You—is it you? Ah, I am saved!" she faltered, clinging tightly to the old man's breast.

"And I have found you at last, my child," said worthy Jean-Marie, with tears in his eyes. "Ah, I have cursed my folly in leaving you unprotected. But if you only knew how one thing led to another, it was perfect fatality."

Léridan's nephew gazed at the embraces, listened to what was said in profound astonishment, racking his brain in vain to discover what possible bond could exist between the ex-justice of the peace and the pretty girl whom he had taken for a *grisette;* he even began to doubt Hingant's strict morality. At all events the adventure did not amuse Charles, who was extremely anxious to remain on good terms with his uncle's friend. Not that he in the least suspected that the magistrate held a will which might send him, the handsome irresistible Dugenêt, back to the broker's shop at Saint Malo; but he realised the necessity of relying upon the friendship of a justly respected man, and he was not a little proud of the interest which the old magistiate had continued to shew in his welfare since his arrival in Paris. So he tried to invent some clever falsehood to explain Marthe's presence in his rooms, but his imagination, by no means a fertile one, failed to devise one. Fortunately for him, Jean-Marie personally came to his aid. "Ah," exclaimed the old man, when his emotion had somewhat subsided, "this must certainly be an interposition of Providence—the selection of the nephew of my best friend to act as the defender, the protector of my adopted daughter."

"His adopted daughter!" said Charles to himself, in utter confusion.

"The nephew of his best friend!" muttered Marthe overcome with astonishment. Her heart revolted at the thought that this young man's infamous conduct was not even suspected by her protector, and she resolved to disclose the truth. "Tell me nothing, mademoiselle; I can guess all," said Hingant, with a cordial smile. And after making a friendly gesture which silenced her he shewed her that his heart was overflowing with benevolence by resuming: "I heard all about the affair outside the hospital. It was my fault if they refused to admit you with that accursed permit, my dear Marthe. I had not reflected that it was in my name. When I explained the matter to the porter he apologized. Then I spoke to a policeman, who described the abominable conduct of those loiterers, but he could not tell me what had become of you. He had seen a young man offer you his arm, and he thought you had made your escape by way of the Rue des Feuillantines. I felt disposed to tear my hair—that is, the little that remains of it. Where should I look for you? To whom should I apply for help? I couldn't question the wretched set crowding the street. I think I should have gone mad if an inspiration had not occurred to me. I recollected that Charles lived here, and thought of coming to ask him if he had seen or heard anything of the affair. Ah, I did not anticipate I should be so extremely fortunate." And suddenly taking hold of both the young man's hands, and pressing them affectionately, he added effusively: "What you have done, Charles, is worthy of the highest praise. I recognize the blood of Mériadec Léridan in you. If he were still alive, he would thank you, as I do with all my heart; but as we have lost him, recollect that you have in me, a friend, a father—"

Hingant paused, half stifled by emotion. It may be, such was his enthusiasm, that he had secretly vowed never to find the privateersman's legatee—the Marie Bréhal, whose discovery might utterly ruin this generous heir-at-law. Marthe lowered her eyes and asked herself whether she ought to undeceive the old magistrate to whom she owed so much. Charles's conduct had been infamous, but to reveal the truth she must deeply wound M. Hingant's kind heart. The rascally coxcomb stood there before her, eyeing her furtively, as if entreating her not to ruin him. She fancied she could read a feeling of repentance on his face, and so she remained silent.

"Come, my children, joy makes me garrulous," resumed the ex-magistrate, gaily, "and I have even forgotten to introduce you to each other. I really believe I am falling into second childhood. My dear Marthe, you are indebted for this service to my young friend and fellow-townsman, Monsieur Charles Dugenêt. My dear Charles, you have saved Mademoiselle Moulinier, the daughter of Monsieur Moulinier, a rich and honourable merchant of Paris, for whom she is in mourning. He was killed during the late unfortunate riots at the head of a company of the National Guard, to which I belong; and I have considered myself fortunate in being able to watch over his daughter until the business affairs which always follow such a sad event are settled."

"The daughter of a rich merchant!" Dugenêt said, to himself. "The deuce! and I took her for something disreputable."

"And now, my friend," resumed Jean-Marie, "you must understand that mademoiselle requires rest after such trying emotion. We will leave you now. My cab is waiting for me at the corner of the Rue Saint-Jacques.

C

Come, my dear Marthe ; and you, Charles, you must not defer calling on us. You will be received with open arms." And M. Hingant, after again pressing Charles's hand, went off with Mademoiselle Moulinier, who was only too glad to put an end to the unpleasant society of her persecutor.

Charles, left to himself, stroked his chin and muttered : "The girl is pretty, and must be a good match. Dear me, why shouldn't I marry her?"

X.

GREAT as had been M. Hingant s and Marthe's emotion on this eventful day, they did not devote the morrow to rest, much as they stood in need of it. It was time for the young girl to return to the rooms on the Boulevard Bonne-Nouvelle, if only to ascertain correctly in what situation her father's death had placed her. The ex-magistrate had decided to accompany her to her old home, and he felt somewhat uneasy concerning the investigation he was about to undertake, for Marthe's replies to his questions about M. Moulinier had been anything but reassuring. He divined that there was some mystery connected with the death of the deceased, with whose private affairs not even his own daughter was acquainted; the story of his life with his wife was fraught with ominous particulars, and Hingant suspected that an unhappy past had preceded a compulsory union of two uncongenial persons. However, the causes of M. Moulinier's marriage interested him less than the consequences of his decease. The first point was to watch over the orphan's interests and ascertain whether she was rich or poor. To tell the truth, M. Hingant felt almost confident that she would inherit at least a modest competence, for a fortune invested in business does not disappear with its possessor ; and, even admitting that the father had experienced reverses, the daughter ought still to inherit sufficient to be placed beyond the reach of want. In Paris the figure of one's rental usually serves as an estimate for one's income, and M. Moulinier's suite of rooms on the Boulevard Bonne-Nouvelle, must certainly have been expensive. However, the deceased had only kept one servant, who had thought proper to abandon Marthe as soon as the insurgents began throwing up their barricade. Still the fact that this woman had been the sole retainer of the household might have no importance after all. It might only be the result of habits formed earlier in life. Having taken all these considerations into account, Jean-Marie concluded that there would still be a satisfactory settlement of the deceased's affairs. So with a light step he escorted Marthe to her former abode.

The distance is short from the Rue Bergère to the Porte St. Denis and they speedily reached the house, the front of which was riddled with bullets. The girl was greatly moved on seeing the window where the murderer had stationed himself, and M. Hingant, to curtail her emotion, quickly led her under the entrance archway. They there met the doorkeeper, who was walking up and down with his pipe in his mouth and his hands in his apron pockets. This fellow, like M. Moulinier's servant, had deemed it prudent to decamp on the day of the conflict, and had only returned when quiet was re-established. M. Hingant was aware of this, having previously made some inquiries, so he held the fellow in but little esteem ; still he relied upon obtaining some information from him.

On perceiving Mademoiselle Moulinier, the doorkeeper opened his eyes wide, but condescended to lift his cap. "What! is it you, ma'm'selle?'

he exclaimed, sneeringly. "I really didn't expect to see you back so soon."

"Mademoiselle took refuge at my house," said Jean-Marie, drily, greatly displeased by the man's tone.

"Dear me !" exclaimed the scoundrel.

"And now she wishes to return to her own home," continued the old man, beginning to lose patience. "Give her the key to the apartments."

"Oh ! no key's necessary. The National Guards burst the door open, and anybody can go in who chooses."

"What ! you have left a tenant's furniture at the disposal of any chance comer, instead of having two or three broken boards and a lock replaced ? "

"Dear me, p'r'aps I ought to have met such expenses out of my own pocket. The landlord's in the country. So who would have repaid me ? You would, eh ? "

"I, or mademoiselle might. It matters little which. You might have been sure that you would lose nothing, and such negligence is certainly very culpable. You compel me to tell you so."

"That's all the same to me, as I don't know you, and, as for ma'm'selle, I have my reasons for not feeling confident. Her father already owed two quarters' rent, to say nothing of the one now running, and the 15th of July isn't far off."

M. Hingant turned pale, not so much from anger as from the consternation caused him by this revelation. He realized, however, the necessity of at once sparing Marthe any unpleasant humiliation, and he said, as coldly as he could : "I did not request any of these details. You shall be paid to-morrow. You need only send the receipts to me. Here is my address. Go up, mademoiselle," he added, turning to Marthe. "You, doorkeeper, fetch me a carpenter and a locksmith at once. Here are five francs for your trouble. I am going to inspect the rooms, and I shall not leave the house until the door is replaced."

The sight of a five-franc piece had a magic effect on the doorkeeper, and the perusal of the card which M. Hingant likewise handed him, came as an effectual damper upon his insolence. The words " ex-justice of the peace " inscribed below our old friend's name usually produced a salutary effect on impudent fellows. "If monsieur answers for the rent, that alters the case entirely," muttered the Cerberus. "Monsieur may rest assured that the workmen will be here in a quarter of an hour, and if monsieur needs me—"

"All I want you to do is to go for the men at once," Jean-Marie interrupted, dismissing the scamp with a peremptory gesture, and then he followed Marthe up the stairs.

Matters looked bad, the arrogance of doorkeepers always being in an inverse ratio to the good credit of tenants. It was evident that this fellow believed in the complete ruin of the deceased Moulinier. Perhaps he had proofs of it, and M. Hingant resolved to question him in private later on. For the time being he was solely occupied with Marthe, whom he watched furtively. Her manner was resigned, rather than irritated, and one was almost tempted to believe that she had expected this disagreeable scene.

The doorkeeper had told the truth about the door. The damage wrought by the captain's avengers had not been repaired—not even on the floor below, where the door of the flat had been so completely shattered that M. Hingant glanced inside and noticed that there was no furniture in the rooms—a proof that they had been unoccupied when the murderer secreted himself there. The ex-magistrate had investigated various criminal cases during his time, and it occurred to him that the doorkeeper had perhaps given the key of the apartments to the murderer before leaving the house on the morning of June 22nd. This was another matter for future inquiry. But a few fragments of the door leading into M. Moulinier's apartments remained. There was nothing to prevent entrance, so Hingant and Marthe stepped inside and went, though not without keen emotion, through the various rooms. The different articles of furniture were all in their accustomed places, and with the exception of some hangings, which had been pierced by bayonet thrusts, there was nothing that showed any signs of the invasion. The secret door had been left open, it had not been seriously injured, and the portrait of Marthe's mother was quite undamaged. "My dear child," said Jean-Marie, to divert her mind from the sorrowful feelings she plainly experiences, "it seems to me necessary that we should take away your family papers this very day, for I have no confidence in your doorkeeper. The papers will be much safer at my house, and we can examine them there more at our leisure. You must of course know where your father kept them."

"Well I don't," replied Marthe, "I even believe he kept nothing of the kind here. Still my mother and myself scarcely ever entered his study, and perhaps we may find something in the drawers of his writing-table."

"We will make sure of that at once," replied M. Hingant, whose face grew more and more gloomy. They again crossed the suite of rooms, and the old man now perceived for the first time that the luxury was only apparent. The furniture might have passed for sumptuous, had it been fresher; but on examining it closely, one easily perceived that the silk upholstery of the arm-chairs was badly worn, the hangings faded, and the mahogany warped. Threadbare carpets were still upon the floor, though it was the height of summer, a significant symptom of poverty to any one more familiar than Jean-Marie with the secret miseries of Parisian life. The owner had possessed the money to buy them in former years, but he had none left to pay men to remove them.

M. Moulinier's private sanctum was even less well furnished. Some faded green serge curtains at the windows, four straw-seated chairs, the familiar round-back leather-covered writing-chair, the usual walnut table on which stood an inkstand, in which the ink had long since dried up and a bundle of quill pens which had never been used; these were the only objects visible, and their appearance indicated not merely poverty, but also neglect and abandonment. It was evident that M. Moulinier had not worked in this room for a long time past, and that an inspection of his drawers would lead to no good result. Nevertheless M. Hingant opened them and examined them carefully, one after the other. They were all empty. "How strange," muttered the old magistrate, disconcerted. "Monsieur Moulinier must have kept some papers here. There must be some hiding-place, and if necessary I will have the walls sounded, the furniture taken to pieces, and—'

"Here are the locksmith and the carpenter, sir," at this moment said the obsequious voice of the doorkeeper, who suddenly appeared, cap in hand.

"Very well, I'll speak to them," said M. Hingant, and turning to Marthe, he added: "you will allow me to go and give the proper orders to these men, my dear?"

"I will wait for you in my mother's room," the girl promptly replied. Jean-Marie realised that she wished to pray beside Madame Moulinier's death bed, and with a pressure of the hand he indicated how much he approved of her filial piety. She went off thanking him with a glance; and Hingant entered the drawing-room where the men were waiting. They both had open, frank faces, and a mere look sufficed to show one that they did not belong to the class of pretended artisans who work three days a week and spend the other four in drinking. "I have brought you the carpenter and locksmith that the deceased used to employ," now remarked the doorkeeper.

"We worked for Monsieur Moulinier, during three years," exclaimed both men, at the same time.

"So much the better, my friends," replied Hingant. "That is an excellent recommendation to me, and I am really glad to be able to employ you. I wish you to repair the outer door as soon as possible, as well as a secret lock which has been forced."

"That of the little door leading to the servants' staircase?" asked the locksmith.

"You are acquainted with it, then?" said the ex-magistrate rather surprised.

"I should think so. It was I who placed it there."

"That's capital, you can set to work at once."

"And I," said the carpenter, "more than once repaired the furniture here. As I do a bit in that line, Monsieur Moulinier always sent for me. He wouldn't employ any one else."

"Indeed," remarked Hingant, and a new idea occurring to him he turned to the locksmith and said, "pray repair the spring concealed in the wood-work at once. However, Mademoiselle Moulinier desires to take the portrait away with her, and at present the spring is concealed in the frame."

"Oh, it will be easy enough—a screw to move and a hole to hide that's all. I'll go and see to it at once."

"And I will join you in a minute or two," replied M. Hingant.

"Has monsieur any need of me?" now inquired the doorkeeper, becoming more and more polite. "My duties call me below, and if monsieur will permit—"

"Certainly, certainly. You can go down, but come to my house to-morrow with your receipts ready—"

"Monsieur may rest assured that I will not forget to do so. I am known for my punctuality."

"Then it's settled," M. Hingant interrupted, impatiently. The doorkeeper finally decided to return to his post, and backed out of the room with a profusion of bows, with which Marthe's protector would have gladly dispensed. "Now, my good fellow," said Jean-Marie, on finding himself alone with the carpenter, "as I just told you I rely on you to repair the door, and I know the work will be done properly, for I saw at the first glance that you were an honest man. In fact you have inspired me with such complete confidence that I want to speak to you on another subject."

"Whatever you please, sir," was the reply.

"Well, you may be able to render me a great service.'

"Indeed!" exclaimed the man, greatly surprised.

"Yes. You just told me, that you knew Monsieur Moulinier very well, that he had often employed you?"

"Oh, yes; I knew the poor dear man very well indeed, and it grieved me to see that his affairs were not prosperous."

"It is true, then, that he was in bad circumstances?"

"Oh! quite so. Such a change had come over him that if a rascal hadn't

put a bullet through his brain, I have an idea he would either have killed
himself or died of grief, for, you see, gentlemen are not like working folks.
We have our hard times of course, but better ones come by-and-bye.
When a man's out of work he lives on his little savings or tightens his belt
till he gets employment. Among us fellows there's no shame in being hard
up, but with a person in trade it is very different. He must pay up on
settling days, even when his safe's empty—or else beware of bankruptcy ! "
   " Alas ! you are quite right, my friend; and I fear like you that Monsieur Monlinier was badly situated."
   "He couldn't console himself for having engaged in some bad speculation ; I guessed that, for he had been rich—very rich—and when he came
here to live he was still very well off. I knew the upholsterer who furnished these apartments, and what he supplied was good and handsome
and Monsieur Moulinier didn't count the cost. But from the day he took
these rooms he began to go down hill. He began with three servants, and
ended by merely keeping a cook. And meanwhile, with the tear and wear
of the furniture, I was often sent for, and though my bills were small enough
I often had a deal of trouble in getting them settled. If I had been better
off I shouldn't have bothered, for I often said to myself, ' Here's a chap
who's still more up a tree than you are, Courtin.' Courtin, that's my name."
   "I won't forget it, my friend," replied M. Hingant ; "but come, can you
tell me in what kind of business Monsieur Moulinier was engaged ? "
   "Oh ! I know nothing on that point, sir. I only heard that he was in
business, which means, of course, that a man has money, and works with it.
The butcher and baker ask nothing more, provided their bills are paid.
I always had an idea, however, that he speculated on the Bourse, and that
he had lost a deal of money, just about the time of the Revolution in
February, for lately he was in hard straits indeed, and when his poor wife
died, I'm sure he bled himself to the last penny to give her a decent
funeral."
   " Did you know her ? " asked Jean-Marie eagerly.
   "Not much, for she was always ill, and one very seldom saw her ; but
she seemed so kind and gentle that one would rather have gone hungry
than cause her any worry. I always took good care not to show any bills
to her. And the daughter, too, never put on any airs with us poor people.
The doorkeeper told me that you had taken her under your protection, and
I don't think you were wrong."
   M. Hingant, touched by this frank sympathy so artlessly expressed, felt
that he could speak without reserve. "I thank you," he said, "and since
you feel an interest in Mademoiselle Monlinier, it is in her name that I am
going to speak to you."
   "I will do anything I can to serve her, and you too, sir, for that matter ;
for if all the middle-class people were like you, we would do no matter
what to oblige them."
   "Then listen, my friend. As I told you just now, I fear that Monsieur
Moulinier died a ruined man. I have resolved not to abandon his daughter,
and I must first of all watch over her interests. But I find myself in a
most embarrassing position, for I possess no information whatever in regard
to any fortune she may be entitled to. It is not possible that Monsieur
Mouliuier's fortune can have entirely disappeared, and I hoped to find
some trace of it or at least some information in his papers. But I find none.
I have just explored the whole apartment in vain. Hearing you say that
you had often been employed here by Monsieur Moulinier, it occurred to

me that he had perhaps employed you to devise some hiding-place in which he could conceal his papers. He seemed to be fond of mysteries, judging from that secret door."

"Yes, and on account of his reserve, people said he belonged to the police. How stupid ! To my mind he merely had the secret door placed there so as to be able to go in and out without his wife knowing it. No man's perfect, you know. Now I don't recollect any hiding-place—though, wait a moment. Ah ! yes. I did fit a false bottom to the lower drawer of the writing-table in his study."

"You are sure of it; you could find it again ? " asked M. Hingant excitedly.

"Quite so, sir," was the reply.

"Then we are saved ! " exclaimed M. Hingant. "Come, my friend, come ; " and he dragged the worthy Courtin into the study.

"It is the same old bit of walnut," said Courtin pointing to the worm-eaten table, "and I remember that I told Monsieur Moulinier that it was a sin to spend money in changing the inside of such a tumble down affair."

"Well, don't let us lose a minute," urged the old magistrate.

"Oh ! it won't take long, you'll see," said Courtin kneeling down. Hingant watched him with mingled hope and nervousness while he began to withdraw the drawers, the last of which concealed a thin little board on one corner of which he pressed with his chisel. The board swayed and suddenly disclosed a hollow space. "Well, really now, there is a paper after all," cried the workman.

M. Hingant gave a cry of joy, and exclaimed : "Hand it to me, my friend, hand it to me ! "

The workman felt to ascertain if this paper was the only one in the niche and finding such to be the case, he gave it to Hingant who snatched hold of it as eagerly as if he had set his hand on a treasure. It was a simple leaf folded in four and bore no handwriting on either of its outer sides. Would it ensure Marthe's fortune or ruin ? That was the question. It must at least be of importance, for otherwise the deceased Moulinier would not have had a safe place of concealment devised for it. Hingant, after no little hesitation, at length decided to unfold the paper and peruse it. But, to his intense astonishment, he found that it was merely covered with figures separated by full stops, and occasionally with a letter or two intervening. There were at least twenty straight and closely written lines, traced in a firm hand by a man evidently accustomed to using this means of disguising what he wrote. Hingant turned the paper over and over but was quite unable to divine the meaning of these strange cyphers. "'This is all that was wanting," he muttered, with an air of consternation.

"Have you made an unlucky discovery, sir ? " inquired the worthy Courtin timidly.

"No, my friend, no, thank Heaven. This paper tells me nothing new. Only I hoped to gain some information from it. Still, perhaps, I shall be able to learn something by it later on, and I am no less grateful to you for having told me of this secret drawer. Do you think there is any other hiding-place elsewhere ? "

The workman expressed his conviction that there was not, but offered to examine the other articles of furniture to which proposal M. Hingant agreed.

However, he told Courtin to set about the search alone, and the carpenter passed into the drawing-room where he could soon be heard opening the cabinets and moving the arm chairs. M. Hingant took no part in this ex-

amination for the simple reason that he was quite upset by the discovery
of this enigmatical paper. He had been prepared for anything but such an
adventure as this. He tried to console himself by saying that this scraw-
was probably merely connected with one of the late Moulinier's speculal
tions, but his common-sense told him that a business man would not have
taken so much trouble to conceal the result of an ordinary transaction, and
his instinct warned him that the solution of all the mystery in which
Marthe's father had enveloped his life was to be found in this strange paper—a
solution which could no longer be deciphered by any one as M. Moulinier
was dead. Still after duly reflecting, M. Hingant came to the conclusion
that this paper must have been deposited in that drawer for somebody's
use. So, the cypher had a key, and this key was in the hands of a person
whom Moulinier alone knew, but who must now be discovered.

All this was very logical, but poor Jean-Marie was no farther advanced
by his deductions when Marthe, leaving her mother's room to allow the carpenter to continue the search, came and roused him from his barely pleasant
reflections. "What is the matter?" she asked on perceiving how disturbed
her protector looked.

"Alas! my dear child," sighed M. Hingant, "I have just experienced a
cruel disappointment. The carpenter shewed me a secret drawer in the
writing-table and found a paper there. I felt sure that I had come across
some valuable information, but see!—"

Mademoiselle Moulinier took the proffered paper, glanced at it, and
returned it to M. Hingant saying : " I expected something of the kind."

"What! did you know—"

"I knew that my father took every sort of precaution, even as regards
the slightest details of his daily life. He, who always seemed to me so
kind and just, acted as if he were continually surrounded by foes.
Hundreds of times I have seen him write notes in cipher, and burn the
letters he received ; and if I ventured a childish jest upon this excessive
prudence, he frowned, and drily told me that business matters did not
concern young girls."

"Yes, you previously alluded to this peculiar turn of his mind. But do
you recollect nothing whatever that could enlighten us as to this paper?"

"Nothing—absolutely nothing. I was not even aware that this
hiding-place existed, and I am sure that my mother knew nothing about it
either."

"Ah!" said M. Hingant greatly discouraged, "then we must renounce
all hopes, unless some lucky chance should, by-and-bye, explain to us—"

"I have no hope of that, and I am quite resigned to the fate which
Providence has in store for me."

"But, my poor child, you know nothing about social necessities, and
don't suspect that your fate would be—"

"Poverty. I do know it, and I shall try to earn my living."

"I entreat you not to think of such a thing," exclaimed M. Hingant,
with an emotion which he did not try to repress. "We will talk about
all this later on. I have a plan which I will submit to you, and which
you will approve of I trust. But see, here are our workmen back
again."

Courtin advanced the first, and Jean-Marie could read on his face that
he had been unsuccessful. "I have sounded everything," said the worthy
carpenter, "but I can find no hiding-place. I greatly regret it for the
young lady's sake.

"Well," interrupted M. Hingant. "There is nothing more to be done now. Bring me your bill to-morrow, and rely on my employing you whenever I have any work to be done."

The locksmith now stepped forward and said : "Half my work is completed, sir. I have removed the spring, and will place a new one in a day or two. Meanwhile, here is the portrait."

Marthe received her mother's precious likeness, and her eyes filled with tears. Hingant realised that it was time to go off. He was not merely anxious to leave a house which awakened such sad memories; but a new idea had occurred to him. He reflected that Paul Gilbert might perhaps be able to acquaint him with Mademoiselle Moulinier's real position; and he thought of going to the hospital alone, and having a long and serious conversation with the young officer. Moreover, he was anxious to make his acquaintance, and satisfy himself as to whether Marthe's intended marriage would really ensure her happiness; so he dismissed the two workmen, repeated his instructions to the doorkeeper as he passed out, and took the young girl back to the Rue Bergère. He had previously placed the mysterious document in his pocket; and, as he walked along the boulevard he said thoughtfully to himself : "Who knows but what my man in the Rue des Canettes may be able to decipher these hieroglyphics ?"

XI.

MAÎTRE * GALMARD, Jean-Marie Hingant's old chum at the Rennes law-school, did not often show himself at the Palais de Justice, although he had been called to the Paris bar more than twenty years previously. Now and then he pleaded in some complicated and scandalous case of judicial separation, or defended some dishonourable speculator, who was compromised in a nasty affair. His name then figured in certain newspapers, and acquired a passing notoriety in certain circles. One would have thought that the clients he preferred were guilty wives and swindling jobbers. However, Fame never occupied herself with him for long, and Maître Galmard's glory suffered periodical eclipses after shining for the transient period of two or three sittings of the court. It is true that his eloquence did not seem convincing either to judge or jury, for he lost all his causes with disheartening regularity. Being, however, prepaid by the unfortunate people, whom he deigned to plead for, his private interests did not suffer by his repeated failures. Moreover, pleading was but an accessory matter with him, his more important profits being derived from the legal consultations which he gave. His office, installed in the business quarter of Paris—Rue de Cléry, on the third floor, overlooking the court-yard—was known to all the shady characters of the city. The petty shopkeeper, who was meditating a skilful and lucrative stroke of bankruptcy, was certain of obtaining there, in exchange for a handsome honorarium, some excellent advice, as to the best manner of saving part of his assets from the wreck, without stranding on the reefs of the commercial code. Money-lenders at thirty per cent, also came in search of ingenious devices which would enable them to avoid the laws on usury; and more

* *Maître*, meaning "master," is a title of address bestowed by courtesy, and in lieu of the term *Monsieur* on all French notaries, attorneys (*avoués*) and barristers (*avocats*).— TRANS.

than one acting manager of a financial company glided stealthily up the stairs leading to Maître Galmard's office to obtain information as to some legal dodge which would close the mouths of over inquisitive shareholders.

The laborious advocate did not even disdain to interest himself in wives who wished to get up cases against troublesome husbands, and in widows claiming the liquidation of a pension, or desirous of prosecuting a recalcitrant debtor. Only he took good care to make inquiries as to the husband's fortune and the widows' solvability. The fact is, Maître Galmard did not care to work gratuitously ; but he was in the habit of saying that little streams make big rivers, and that a man ought to do everything in any way connected with his calling. In all these various branches of his quibbling profession there was certainly enough to occupy and enrich him, and yet his main hopes of wealth were not based on his establishment in the Rue de Cléry. He had a partner and a branch office. Indeed M. Billebaude, and the private inquiry agency in the Rue des Canettes, completed the organisation devised by Galmard's inventive brain. The affairs which he attended to at his own residence were not such as honourable members of the bar care to deal with, still, on the surface, they did not seem to be disreputable ones. A consulting barrister is at the disposal of the public, and Galmard might have claimed that it was not his fault if his clients seemed to concert together to bring nasty dodges under his notice, and to trust him with bad cases. The affairs that Billebaude attended to, did not belong to any particular branch of the legal calling, and Billebaude himself did not, in any wise, belong to the quibbling profession. When very young, he had begun life as a commercial traveller ; he had afterwards been employed in one of the Paris municipal offices, and, on reaching the prime of life, he had become a banker. None of these avocations have anything in common with the law, and people might have wondered how it happened that Billebaude had gained the experience and skill necessary in the exercise of his new calling. This was a secret between himself and his friend Galmard; and, at all events, he dexterously fulfilled the various delicate missions which the advocate confided to him. In appearance, they consisted of hunting for lost title deeds, or missing persons, and of supplying information as to an individual's solvability or habits. This somewhat resembled underhand detective business, but it could also be called "private diplomacy," a term which Billebaude himself had invented.

In point of fact, however, the great object of the two partners was to profit by the secrets which came to their knowledge ; in short, they practised black-mail. Maître Galmard was too cunning to operate in person ; he did not wish to compromise himself, for he knew that he was not popular among his fellow-barristers, and he feared that at the slightest scandal his name might be struck off the roll. Accordingly, whenever a promising affair presented itself, he contented himself with pointing it out to Billebaude, who examined the matter, made inquiries, estimated the probable result, and finally took the case in hand, providing it seemed likely to be a lucrative one. Galmard was kept informed of what was done, and whenever any difficulty arose, it was submitted to his appreciation. He almost invariably devised some means of overcoming it, gave judicious advice as to how the law might be eluded in any dangerous cases, and, as a matter of course, he pocketed his share of the ultimate profits.

He was always on the look-out for promising affairs, and did not neglect the slightest likely indication, whether it was furnished during one of his consultations or in the course of private conversation. Thus it happened that when M. Hingant came to see Galmard on his arrival in Paris, freshly come from Cancale, the advocate at first received him coldly, for he did not like to lose his time, and he took the old gentleman for an impecunious, petty magistrate, who, having lost his place, had come to try and win it back from the new Minister of Justice. Jean-Marie, who possessed all the fervour of a provincial, faithful to his youthful friendships, had considered this visit to be a duty, and without making any inquiries as to Galmard's standing, he had at once hastened to the address given in the Directory. After embracing the advocate as warmly as he had done on the day when they passed their examination together, he had begun in all simplicity to relate the story of his life since they had lost sight of each other. When he mentioned the income of ten thousand francs a year which his landed property yielded him, Galmard suddenly assumed a pleasant look, and the finish of the interview was very cordial.

What particularly delighted the advocate was to learn that Hingant had come to Paris to make a search respecting an inheritance. The old magistrate did not fully explain the matter, but he said quite enough for Galmard to prick his ears, like a charger at the sound of a trumpet. Then came the usual recommendation : " Go and see Billebaude. He is the most skilful inquiry agent that I know of, and the most honest into the bargain."

After that the two old chums separated, promising that they would speedily meet again ; but they were prevented from doing so by a chain of events—some of them of a political character and others privately concerning Jean-Marie. In those happy times the drum sounded almost every day, and even the least bellicose citizens had to leave home to do duty as National Guards. Moreover, Hingant was occupied with his friends, the privateersman's nephews, whom he saw very frequently. Thus it happened that when the advocate called on him to return his visit, he was away from home. Moreover, he had already been three times to see M. Billebaude, who was always absent, and having made the acquaintance of Mademoiselle Moulinier, he had gradually come to neglect the matter of Léridan's will. Such had been the position of affairs on the day when, by a strange chance, he had an interview with the private inquiry agent.

Galmard on his side forgot nothing, but duly apprised his partner of the approaching visit of a wealthy and simple-minded country fellow who was occupied with an affair which probably concealed a highly lucrative secret. Billebaude, greatly delighted, waited for the promised visit, but, like sister Ann in the story of Bluebeard, he saw nobody coming. The advocate was afraid to press Hingant on the matter, as he did not care to excite his misgivings, but he still kept the matter well in mind, and he started with delight on the day when the post brought him the following note from the Rue des Canettes : " I've seen our man, and am of opinion that a deal of cash could be got out of him ; but he did not unbutton himself on this first occasion. I am in need of some information. He will return, but I can't say when. Pray see to the matter."

Maître Galmard always did everything with proper expedition. Receiving this note in the course of the morning, he hurried through his consultations as fast as possible, instructed his servant to tell all visitors to call again the next day, and modestly climbed on to the omnibus going to the Place St. Sulpice. He was an economical man both by disposition and principle. Half an hour later he alighted at the end of the Rue des Canettes, and walked slowly towards the house which M. Hingant had visited on the day before. While proceeding along the street, with the

peaceful air of a gentleman taking a stroll, he gazed with marked attention
at the old clothes' shop, on the ground floor of Billebaude's residence.
"The deuce!" he muttered between his teeth. "The English officer's
uniform isn't there. Billebaude must have gone out. Still he ought to
have foreseen that I should call about this time of day." However, the
advocate walked on, and he had scarcely taken another dozen steps when
his face became serene again. "Ah! ah!" he muttered; "it seems I
have arrived just at the right time. There's old Mardochée leaving his
hovel to hang up the signal."

And indeed a greybearded old man had just shown himself on the pavement carrying a scarlet tunic at the end of a long pole. This bright tunic
had previously attracted M. Hingant's attention, and when it hung in front
of the old clothes' shop, it could be seen from the end of the street. On
perceiving it, Maître Galmard gave a little whistle, which was his usual
sign of satisfaction, and leaving the roadway he began to glide along the
foot-pavement, keeping close to the houses. The greybearded old man
espied him from afar, but did not give any signs of recognition. Two or
three loungers, rather shabbily dressed, were at this moment fingering some
of the second-hand clothes displayed for sale, or looking at the old
engravings in the shop window, and the advocate did not care that these
people should know that he was on intimate terms with the dealer. "How
much is this guitar?" he asked, pointing to a kind of stringless mandoline
which in days long past must have figured in many a serenade. To tell the
truth, he might have devised a better pretext for entering into conversation,
for with his white tie and solemn black clothes, he did not at all look like
a warbler of sentimental songs. However, the idlers of the Rue des
Canettes were not in the habit of looking into matters so closely, and they
did not display the slightest astonishment on hearing him ask the price of a
battered musical instrument.

"That's not for sale, sir," promptly replied the dealer; "it found a purchaser this morning, and I was just going to remove it to have it delivered.
But if you are an amateur of that kind of thing, sir, pray step inside—I
can show you some curious instruments, among them a three-stringed
lute which I received from Constantinople only the day before yesterday, a
spinet—"

"Indeed! Pray let me see."

The dealer at once ushered the collector of old instruments into his shop,
followed him inside, and carefully closed the door. "Well, Mardochée,"
said Galmard, as soon as he could speak without fear of being heard by the
idlers in the street, "it seems that I did right not to come earlier as I
shouldn't have found our friend Billebaude at home."

"He just come in, sir, at this very moment, and I was hanging up
the signal when I noticed you."

"Oh! I know that you discharge your duties properly."

"I do what I can, sir," said Mardochée, modestly.

"And how is business?"

"Mine is very quiet, sir; still, I earn a living. As for what goes on
upstairs, I don't meddle with it, as you know, and I wouldn't venture to
express an opinion."

"Why not?" asked the advocate promptly. "I gave you an interest in
our enterprise, so you at least have a right to hold an opinion on the manner
in which it is conducted. Besides, I have a high opinion of your judicious-
ness, and always take proper note of your remarks."

"Thank you, sir; but I'm only a poor beggar, and I shall never be worth much outside of my little trade."

"Why not? Don't affect modesty, but speak frankly. Have you any reason to complain of Billebaude?"

"I complain of my superior! I didn't say that, sir; I didn't say that."

"You didn't say it, but you think it. Do you fancy I don't know you well enough to read your thoughts on your face?" The old Jew made a grimace which might have been interpreted in a variety of ways. The fact is that one needed to be gifted with singular powers of penetration to divine the thoughts concealed by his hirsute face. "Come, confess it," resumed the advocate; "you have something on your mind."

"Nothing, sir, absolutely nothing, I swear to you. Everything goes on here as usual. I never leave my shop. Whenever Monsieur Billebaude comes home, I hang up the red tunic as a signal that you can go upstairs. When a ring of the bell warns me that anyone has entered the passage, I look at the person through the little window at the foot of the stairs, and if I don't know his face I touch the electric bell which communicates with Monsieur Billebaude's office. The rest doesn't concern me."

"Listen to me, Mardochée," said Galmard, assuming his most serious air, such as he held in reserve for important occasions, as when he had to influence a hesitating client. "I have a liking for you and I wish you well; but I don't mean you to try on your cunning with a man to whom you owe everything."

"Oh!" began Mardochée, "can you think, sir—"

"Let me finish. You shall talk afterwards. I presume that you haven't forgotten the day when you came to ask me for advice, when you were a jeweller in the Rue du Temple. Your position wasn't a pleasant one—hidden assets, the purchase of stolen diamonds, without speaking of false entries in your books. It smelt of fraudulent bankruptcy, or even worse. You were on the high road to Toulon, my good fellow." The Jew lowered his nose and plucked a few hairs here and there out of his beard, but he answered never a word. "Well," resumed Galmard, "I spared you the journey. Thanks to my advice, you escaped with a nice little bankruptcy, and your creditors took your failure in good part." Mardochée here raised his arms to the ceiling, as if to call heaven to witness his gratitude. "You admit all that," continued the advocate; "very well, but that isn't all. I guessed that you were an intelligent man, and I offered to set you up in business again, on certain conditions, which you accepted, though now you seem rather to have forgotten them—"

"Never, never, sir—not for one moment."

"Well, we will see. It was agreed that you should act as a sentinel to this house, and that in our joint interests."

"And I have never missed doing so for one minute."

"No doubt; but it was also agreed that you should remain my private agent and report to me, alone, whatever happened here; that you should warn me whenever Billebaude's conduct seemed suspicious; and mind he wouldn't hesitate about denouncing you if he learnt that you were dabbling in matters outside of the partnership. So now speak out and don't prevaricate. That may go down with fools, but it doesn't do with me."

The Jew drew himself up like a man who has come to a decision. "Well, sir," he said, "I know that I shall perhaps make an enemy of Monsieur Billebaude; but I prefer that to being thought ungrateful towards the man who saved me. I'm a rascal as much as you like, but not ungrateful, no, indeed ; I should think myself dishonoured."

"Then our friend upstairs isn't following the straight road ? " asked the advocate.

"There are goings on which I don't like."

"And you have waited till now to warn me ? "

"Oh ! the affair's a recent one, and yet it has been preying on my mind for a week or so."

"Well, what is the matter? Don't beat about the bush like that, but come to the point."

"The matter is that Monsieur Billebaude is mixing himself up in politics."

"You are crazy. Billebaude cares no more about politics than I do."

"So I thought, sir, only last week ; but my opinion has changed now."

"Dash it all ! Will you speak out? You would make even an investigating magistrate lose all patience."

"Well, sir, you know as well as I do that you have rented the whole house from top to bottom, and that we are all interested in having no strange tenants."

"And we pay quite enough to have the place to ourselves. Well, what besides ? "

"Well, since the June riots there has been a lodger on the fourth floor."

"And Billebaude has allowed it ?"

"He himself brought the lodger here."

"Ah, ah ! this is indeed something new," said Galmard, coldly. "Continue."

"When I say he brought this lodger, I make a mistake. It was a friend of Billebaude's who brought the fellow, a friend I'm not acquainted with, but who has frequently called to see him during the last two months, and who one evening at twilight came here with the lodger in question. Billebaude was waiting for them. He escorted the stranger to the apartment above his own, having already had a mattress placed there ; and the man still sleeps there."

"What kind of a fellow is he ? "

"Oh ! 'tisn't hard to guess. He's an insurgent in hiding, only he hides himself very clumsily, for he goes out nearly every day ; and sometimes when he comes home he can't as much as stand on his legs."

"Because he's drunk, eh ? "

"Yes, like a Pole ! And what's more, I believe that he was followed by a detective yesterday, for a fellow who looked as if he belonged to the Prefecture came up, close on his heels."

"Better and better. And now tell me something about this friend of Billebaude's—the man who brings him such nice associates."

"Oh ! I can't say anything in particular about that one ; he's well dressed and looks like a clerk, while the insurgent wears a blouse, and has the face of a rascal."

"And you don't think that the friend is simply one of our clients ? "

"No ; Billebaude receives him at all hours, and besides, if he were merely a client, he would have mentioned him to you."

"And he hasn't done so—unless—but no, that isn't possible," said Maître Galmard. For the advocate to talk to himself in another person's presence he needed to be greatly preoccupied. However, Mardochée did not attempt to disturb his superior's reflections, but assumed the satisfied attitude of a man who has just eased his mind. "Is that all you had to tell me?" asked Galmard, coldly.

"Yes, that's everything, sir, but it's quite enough to my mind ; for heaven only knows what trouble Monsieur Billebaude's imprudence may bring on us—"

"Be easy. I'll soon set matters to rights. Don't stir from here ; and don't sound the electric bell to warn the people upstairs. I'm going up, and I'll say a couple of words to you before I leave." Thereupon Maître Galmard disappeared into a room at the rear of the shop, where there was a door communicating with the staircase. "We must have a few words together, Monsieur Billebaude," he muttered between his teeth, while he climbed the stairs as swiftly as if he had been a young man, although, in point of fact, he was nearly sixty. It is true that he was not troubled with much fat, and that he possessed remarkably long legs. At the Palais de Justice his meagre figure, crooked carriage, and viper-like head had won him the nickname of the "asp of the Rue de Cléry;" and, for the time being, his anger by no means improved his looks. His naturally yellowish complexion had turned green ; his little grey eyes sparkled hatefully, and his thin lips were compressed as if preparing to discharge venom. The calm and majestic Billebaude would have felt positively frightened could he have seen the advocate gliding up the stairs to his office, much like a serpent winds round a tree to reach a bird's nest.

However, the shrewd advocate possessed the faculty of changing his expression of face in accordance with requirements, and he had scarcely touched the bell rope than his features looked as serene and phlegmatic as usual. He had become a diplomatist once more, whilst climbing the last flight of stairs. It must be admitted that he had never had greater need of all his calmness and cunning, for he was about to play a serious game. Billebaude, his confidential agent, and the executor of his vile schemes, was necessarily acquainted with his most precious secrets, and the slightest velleity of treason on such a man's part, constituted a danger which must at once be coped with. A front attack would have been a great mistake, however, for open warfare between two rascals always has disastrous results for both sides. It was preferable to try cunning, and endeavour by skilful strategy to wring from Billebaude a confession of his misdeeds, to pretend to condone them, and then to wreak vengeance at the first favourable opportunity.

"What, is it you?" cried the inquiry agent, who had so far departed from his usual habits as to open the door in person. "You come like March in Lent, for I have been longing to see you ever since yesterday."

"And I have been anxious to chat with you ever since receiving your note. I dealt with my clients as hastily as possible in my eagerness to come here; but it seems that I need not have hurried so much, as you have only just come in."

"Ah ! Mardochée has told you—"

"Nothing. There were some people in front of his shop, and I didn't enter it. But just as I reached the street I saw the old fellow hanging out the red tunic in front of his shop—"

"Ah, yes ! the signal—it does credit to the old Jew's inventive powers. But come into my private room. I want to confer with you on the point at issue. I can espy a lovely prospect, but I need a solid basis on which to raise my plans."

"Well thought, and well said !" rejoined the advocate. "We'll find a basis sure enough. I have come expressly for that purpose, so show me into the sanctum."

The sanctum was opened, and the two partners sat down in front of the statuette of Belisarius, who was as firmly fixed on his pedestal as the love of money was in M. Galmard's heart. "Have you done anything since you saw our Breton friend yesterday?" carelessly asked the advocate.

"Of course I have. I have just been the round of all the municipal offices in Paris. Four hours cabbing to go down to general expenses. It was even this excursion that delayed me."

"All the municipal offices, you say; pray, why did you go there?"

"To request the friends I have among the clerks and officials, to search the registers since 1815, in view of ascertaining whether they contain mention of a certain Mademoiselle Marie Bréhal's marriage or death. As the search extends over such a number of years, it will cost us dear, but I fancy our money will be well invested."

"Capital! I understand now. Marie Bréhal is the name of the person whom our old fossil Hingant wants to find. You have plenty of scent, Billebaude. Hingant told you however, I suppose, that it was a question of an inheritance, which this woman would be entitled to; and all affairs of that kind yield large profits, you know."

"He told me nothing excepting the woman's name, for he seemed in a terrible hurry. What kind of a man is he? Can he be relied on, and is he really an ex-magistrate as he asserts on his cards?"

"Quite so. He was a justice of the peace in Brittany, and what is more, he possesses some fat acres in the broad sunlight, so that if we don't succeed in working the inheritance we can always obtain a very handsome honorarium. If I didn't tell you all this before, it was simply because I don't care to waste my words. Words are like money, they must be made to yield interest. I was waiting for the fish to swim round the net, it's now only a question of getting him in the meshes, and I've a bait all ready to ensnare him."

"Let us see the bait then. I have full confidence in your experience as a fisherman," said Billebaude politely.

"Well, this is the point. Hingant honours me with his confidence. He was formely my schoolfellow and barely knows any one but myself in Paris. The question is to keep him isolated, under my thumb as it were."

"But are you quite sure he has not made some friends since his arrival here? Remember that he did not shew any great haste in renewing his visit to you or in calling on me. And, besides, yesterday he repeated three or four times over that some one was waiting for him. So he must have some connections here."

"Oh! I don't pretend that he hasn't spoken to any one during the last two or three months. I mean that he has no *friends* in Paris, and we must prevent him from finding any apart from Messrs. Galmard and Billebaude."

"Very well; but how do you propose to accomplish your object?"

"In a very simple manner—by offering him hospitality—lodging him gratis, so to say. He will be very grateful for the attention."

"Lodging him—at your place?" asked the inquiring agent somewhat surprised by his partner's generosity.

"No; not at my place, there is no room," said Maître Galmard coldly, "we will lodge him here."

"Here? But I'm too much pressed for space as it is!" cried Billebaude.

"Oh! don't be worried, my dear fellow. I don't mean to inconvenience you ; but the house is at our disposal from cellar to garret, and we have plenty of room to give our friend a lodging. I have decided to give him the pretty little suite on the fourth floor, just overhead."

Billebaude moved uneasily on his chair, and with a slight tremor in his voice replied, "There's one annoyance, the suite isn't furnished."

"Oh, everything can be quite ready by the day after to-morrow if I choose. I need merely send Mardochée to the auction rooms."

"But have you reflected how inconvenient it will be for me to have this man so close by—close enough to see the people who visit me and hear what they say?"

"Oh! old Hingant wouldn't think of prying into our affairs, while we shall be able to study him thoroughly. I shall make the proposal to him this very evening, and I am certain that I shall prevail upon him to accept it."

"Well, I doubt that ; and I don't quite see the use of so much politeness ; still if you are determined on it—"

"I am ; and if I came to day it was in a measure to visit the rooms. Let us go up to them, my dear fellow ; I'll take some necessary measurements and you shall make out a list of the articles of furniture which will be required. Oh! I'm not going to be prodigal ; Jean-Marie is a man of simple tastes and he will be quite satisfied with a suite in walnut."

If M. Billebaude's chair had been stuffed with thorns he could not have wriggled more atrociously ; however, he made no answer. He had for a moment fancied that he would be able to extricate himself from a nasty predicament. With a couple of days' respite he could have cleared the apartment upstairs ; but his partner's last proposal drove him to the wall—the more so as it was as imperative as an order, "Well, are you coming, my dear fellow?" asked Galmard preparing to rise.

"The fact is, I haven't got the key" stammered Billebaude.

"What does that matter? you know very well that we can go up by the inner staircase—there, behind the partition. We'll nail the door up when Jean-Marie is in his new quarters, but it can still be used, I presume."

"Of course—only—"

"Only what? are you afraid of the rats and mice upstairs? They are the only tenants at present, I presume, unless—but now I think of it, where was that man in a blouse going, who climbed the stairs ahead of me and seemed to stop on the upper landing?"

"A man in a blouse?" repeated Billebaude, overwhelmed.

"Yes, and he looked queer—just like a man who has been up to some nasty tricks. One can't be too careful in such times as these, my dear fellow. We should have a deal of trouble if the police had a pretext for entering the house. You know that the insurgents are being tracked right and left just now. How can that fool of a Mardochée let such suspicious characters enter the house without sounding the alarm? I shall give him a good blowing up when I go out."

"It's useless. I will attend to it," stammered Billebaude who was beginning to lose countenance. "Besides that man, even if he did go up to the fourth floor, will have found there was no one there—and have gone off as he came."

"Do you think so? well, it's quite possible," said the advocate assuming the look of a simpleton. "We'll let him go and get hanged elsewhere ; as for ourselves, as we are not stupid enough to dabble in politics, let us go and inspect the rooms. I particularly wish that Hingant should have proper accommodation, and we have barely the time to prepare everything for his reception. So let us go up at once." Thus speaking, Maître Galmard rose and approached the chintz hanging which concealed the door conducting to the secret staircase.

Billebaude was livid and his partner pretended not to notice it. The time for a decision had arrived, however, and the inquiry agent found it necessary to confess everything. Frankness was not his *forte* but he knew how to resort to it on great occasions, and it may be said that he held it in reserve as a last resource, like Napoleon kept the Old Guard on days of decisive battle. Accordingly, with a great effort, Galmard's partner articulated : " Don't go up—the man's there ! "

" What ? the man ? " asked the advocate with cleverly feigned surprise. " The man I saw ahead of me ? Come, you are dreaming, my good fellow. Who could have opened the door for him ? "

" He has a key, and has been sleeping up there for the last week or so."

" With your authorization then ? "

" Well—yes."

" And you said nothing about it to me, Billebaude ? That was wrong, very wrong ! To hide things from me—when I have confided my most secret thoughts to you—"

" When you have listened to me you will admit, I think, that there are extenuating cricumstances in the case."

" Well, the court is ready. Begin," said Galmard sitting down again.

" First of all, pray believe that I don't share the socialistic folly which has led to such strife this year. If my tenant were merely an insurgent—"

" So he is one then ? "

" To some extent, but if he were only that, I should have turned him out on the day he first came to me. But he is something else besides. You know that I was a banker in happier days—"

" Happier days ? not for the people who deposited their money with you," interrupted the asp of the Rue de Cléry.

" Alas ! one can't always succeed ! " said Billebaude without displaying the least resentment for this venomous thrust. " However, you are also aware that, thanks to your intervention, all my creditors consented to allow me to go into liquidation, that is excepting one—"

" Excepting your principal backer, whom you all but ruined."

" That was so; you cannot have forgotten either that this person threatened me with the assize court and that, by your excellent advice, I promised him a share in the profits of the new calling which I was about to embrace."

" And you had to keep your promise ; and I know that it has already cost you a pretty penny. That is what comes of leaving written proofs behind one, when one dabbles in matters which the law may interfere with. If that fellow had not held everything necessary to have you condemned, you could afford to laugh in his face, whilst now, you are sentenced to pay him a pension for life."

" I shall not pay him one any longer, for he has just died."

" Really ? "

" Yes. He was killed on the 22nd June at the head of his company, for he was a captain in the National Guard."

" Hum ! hum ! It seems that politics sometimes lead to something good, and I must own that you are lucky, Billebaude. But this pleasant affair has made you lose sight of the man in the blouse."

" Less than you think, for he fired the shot to which I am indebted for my release from liability."

"Oh! oh! that is another matter," said Maître Galmard, frowning. "Did you by any chance commission him to undertake this nasty job?" "I? Whom do you take me for? No, no, I don't work in that line. Chance did everything."

"Then pray explain this chance."

"I must tell you, then, that of an evening I often spend a few hours at a café near—"

"No matter where, come to the point!" said Galmard, in the tone of a judge reproving a loquacious barrister.

"Well, the fact is, I there became acquainted with a country bumpkin who had just arrived in Paris with the view of going into business. What business? He himself hardly knew, but he was very eager about turning his capital to account and did not seem at all scrupulous as to the means employed. I scented a mine to be worked in this provincial intriguer, for I had made inquiries and had learnt that he possessed a snug little fortune."

"Ah! ah! that's not bad," said Maître Galmard licking his lips.

"Well, I suggested he should come and see me, and he made a point of doing so. I need not tell you how I convinced him that my agency here brought me twenty-five per cent clear profit."

"I hope, however, that you didn't let him into the secret of our real transactions."

"No fear. I wasn't so foolish. He believes that I merely occupy myself with searches and inquiries about persons and property, disputed accounts and Bourse speculations So he took a good bite at the hook and shewed himself disposed to trust a hundred thousand francs to me to begin with."

"And you have received them?" asked the advocate with a keen glance at his partner.

"No. I hope to do so; but we haven't got so far as yet. These village financiers are extremely mistrustful, and slip between your fingers just as you fancy you hold them. This fellow is smelling round the safe, but he doesn't deposit anything in it, and I fancy that to bring him to a determination we shall have to employ him in some affair (which we need only partly explain to him), and then hand him something handsome, on the pretence that it has succeeded. This would be sowing to reap, for these peasants only make a venture when they have seen and felt hard cash."

"Perhaps so. We will see to it. But how about the man in the blouse?"

"I'm coming to him. I was warming my provincial friend as well as I could, when one evening last week he came to the café, looking quite upset, begged me to step outside, and there set me face to face with the man you speak of. He told me that this fellow was a near relation who had been foolish enough to take part in the insurrection, and that the police were looking for him to shoot him. Finally, he asked me if I could find a place of refuge for the fellow, saying that he himself could not shelter him as he was staying at a hotel. You can picture my embarrassment. The brute gives me to understand that if I oblige him in the matter he will bring me the hundred thousand. I raise objections, and to gain time I question the insurgent, who tells me his story right away; what do I learn?—that he is "wanted" for having shot a captain from a window in a house near the Porte St. Denis. I had read about the affair in the newspapers which gave the name of the deceased—none other than that of the scamp who furnished me with the means of setting up in banking business. Well, the knave in the blouse had, without knowing it, rid me of a vampire who for some time had been sucking up most of my profits—"

"I can understand that you felt grateful," said Galmard with an ironical smile. "And so now the man is installed upstairs."

"Oh ! he merely has a straw mattress there, but that's quite good enough for a scoundrel who will go out in spite of my prohibition and persists in coming home drunk."

"And who will end by seriously compromising us," retorted Galmard. "On the other hand, you haven't received a copper from his estimable relative."

"No, but—"

"Billebaude, my friend, the imprudence you have been guilty of smacks of treason."

"Treason ? you accuse me of treason towards you ? "

"I do. Pray explain to me why you never spoke to me about this pretty combination, before."

"Because I wished to get rid of the insurgent before telling you about the pigeon that there is to be plucked. I realised that I had acted very foolishly in housing this scamp, and I was only thinking of how I could get rid of him."

"The excuse must be taken at its value ; only I warn you, my dear fellow, that henceforth you will have to shew me your hand. In the first place I need some security. I must see this so called country bumpkin and have a chat with him."

"That can be easily managed," said Billebaude, who seemed disposed to make every imaginable concession. "He will probably come here to-day, and I will introduce you to him. In the meantime, if you care to speak to the man upstairs—"

"Oh ! I have no desire to have anything to do with the brute. It is the other fellow that I want."

"And you will have him if I am not mistaken. There is a ring at the bell at this moment, and in all probability it's he."

"If that should be the case," said the advocate, promptly, "you must receive him at once, and let me manage the conversation. By-the-way, is he aware that you have a partner ? "

"I—have not yet spoken to him about you," replied Billebaude with evidant embarrassment.

"Ah ! I expected as much. Well, you must begin now by introducing me—or no—I will rather introduce myself."

The agent's servant at this moment discreetly entered the room, and approaching her master, whispered a few words in his ear. "Let him come in," was Billebaude's clearly articulated response. The agent had resigned himself to Galmard's exigencies, reflecting that he would at least extricate himself from a difficult position, a prospect which slightly consoled him for the fact that he would not be able to keep the whole of the country bumpkin's hundred thousand francs to himself.

Maître Galmard, in the meantime, was wriggling on his chair and rubbing his hands with a very satisfied air. The door soon opened and the client appeared on the threshold. He was a man still young in years, who looked somewhat old on account of his spectacles and pale complexion. His embarrassed manner and ill-fitting clothes shewed clearly enough that he had only lately arrived from the provinces, and, at first sight, one might easily have taken him for a perfect fool. Such, indeed, was M. Billebaude's opinion, but the advocate, who was in the habit of judging men at a glance, could read certain unmistakable signs of acumen on the stranger's pale face. His nose was slight and bony, his lips thin, his gaze oblique—all so many tokens of remarkable cunning, and Galmard at sight of them decided to play a close game.

"Excuse me, Monsieur Billebaude," said the visitor in an obsequious tone, "I see that you are engaged, and I won't disturb you—I will call again at some other time—"

"Not at all, not at all!" exclaimed the agent, darting forward to usher the stranger into the room. "We were expecting you, and my partner will be delighted to make your acquaintance."

"Ah! this gentleman is—"

"Maître Galmard of the Paris bar," said the advocate, keeping the promise he had made to introduce himself,

"Your very humble servant, sir," rejoined the stranger. "Pray accept my apologies; I was not aware—"

"That our dear friend Billebaude had a partner? He was telling me that, only a short time ago, and I reproached him for his neglect in not apprising you of the circumstance; for on the other hand he had often mentioned you to me, and, as I need not add, in the most favourable manner."

Whilst Galmard was delivering this gracious speech his partner brought a chair forward. The stranger timidly sat down, placed his hat on his knees, drew a coloured handkerchief from his pocket, and blew his nose with a formidable noise. "The scamp is really cunning," thought the asp of the Rue de Cléry. "He has no more of a cold than I have; only he wants to study us through his glasses." The advocate then resumed aloud: "I am aware, sir, that you are an intelligent man, that you understand the spirit of the times, and that you wish to take part in the great financial movement which now-a-days absorbs the energies of our most enlightened contemporaries. Ah! the provinces are slandered when people pretend that country folks content themselves with hoarding their savings in old stockings, or investing them in land which only yields two per cent."

"Land has its merits," said the rural capitalist, softly.

"No doubt; but speculation alone can give large and speedy profits. My land is my practice, which I in no wise neglect. Thank Heaven, it is fairly lucrative, but, apart from the revenue derived from work, there are splendid profits which a judicious person can easily reap from some skilfully conducted financial operation, and I confess it, I don't allow such opportunities to escape me."

"That is quite natural. Monsieur Billebaude mentioned to me various matters which yielded large profits, and I should like to deal with them, providing they were not above my ability; only I am not a Parisian, and my intelligence has never been remarkably acute, so that as yet I do not quite understand—"

"What are the matters in question? Well, sir, we have no secrets for people like you. In the first place, good strokes are to be made on the Bourse. When you know how the land lies, you can speedily double your capital without running any great risk."

"Unless a revolution takes place," muttered the visitor.

"Oh, in that case there is no settlement of differences. After the Revolution last February, no liquidation took place at all on 'Change. However, another remunerative channel may be found in private diplomacy—"

" Excuse me, sir, hut I don't quite understand—"

" I will explain myself. Suppose, for instance, that a title-deed has heen mislaid, or that some fortune remains unclaimed on the death of its possessor. You will understand that the person to whom the title-deed is restored, or the heir who learns that he is entitled to a fortune, does not refuse to give a handsome sum to the person who enriches him."

" Yes, yes, I understand—yon say to him, we must share with yon."

" Quite so, my dear sir."

" However, I don't quite see how I could be of any assistance to you in these delicate matters—"

" Oh, if you really intended to interest yourself in our operations, I would speedily prove to you that you are in a position to be very nsefnl indeed ; only you must not consider yourself hound to follow up the views which Billehaude mentioned to me. We two suffice for our requirements, and if we took a fresh partner it wonld only be to extend our husiness, which is remarkahly prosperous as it is."

" May I venture to ask you what my duties would consist of ? " asked the visitor, who plainly enough was greatly impressed by Galmard's skilful retreat. Men only willingly give that which is not asked of them, and the best means of obtaining anything is to pretend that you don't care for it.

" It is a very simple matter," replied the advocate. " We have all we need in Paris, but our organization is not so complete in the provinces, and a partner acquainted with the departments, merely with those of one part of France, would be of great assistance to us in making inquiries, searches, &c."

" I myself come from Brittany ; only—"

" Really ? From Brittany ! Why, we have an important affair in that direction, and we are precisely in need of information."

Billehaude was looking anxiously at the advocate, but the latter gave him a glance which clearly implied : " Let me continue, I know what I'm ahout."

" I will add," resumed Galmard, " that I don't propose to you to hecome one of us for good, but it often happens that in some special case we apply to a third person for help. In the event of success, the profits are divided equally, and the ally we have momentarily secured is not involved in any subsequent transactions."

" Oh, under those conditions, I should be quite disposed—"

" To make a trial, eh? Well, that would suit us, and by-and-bye I will tell you what the matter is ; but first of all there is another question to be settled—I allnde to the position of the friend whom Billehaude is sheltering at your request—"

" Ah, you are aware then—"

" Quite so ; and I am delighted to know that my partner was ahle to be of assistance to yon in the matter. Besides, I have no prejudices in politics, and I invariaby sympathize with the defeated. Your friend did duty in the insurgent ranks ; it is his own concern, and I sha'n't try to harm him. Only, in his own interest, he must not remain here."

" I am certainly afraid of his being discovered ; hut—"

" He will he so if he stops here ; he is so imprudent. Would you like me to find him a safer place of refuge ? "

" Ah ! if you did that, sir, I shonld he eternally grateful to yon, for I tremble at the thonght that this unfortunate fellow may compromise me—compromise himself, I mean—"

"Good ; it is understood. He shall be installed elsewhere to-morrow in perfect safety. Now, to return to our affair, will you take upon yourself to follow up a search which has been confided to me by an ex-magistrate residing near Saint Malo ? "

" Saint Malo ? That is just my part of the country."

" Well, it is a question of ascertaining what has become of a certain Mademoiselle Marie Bréhal, who is entitled to a very large fortune."

" I'm not acquainted with that name, but if you gave me that of the ex-magistrate, it might perhaps set me on the track."

" He is called Hingant, and was formerly justice of the peace at Cancale. He is a particular friend of mine."

" Hingant ! " exclaimed the visitor, half-starting from his chair. " Hingant, you say ? "

" Yes, Hingant, Jean-Marie. He was my chum at the Rennes law-school. He subsequently became a solicitor and afterwards a magistrate. Do you happen to know him by any chance? That would really be providential."

" No, no, I don't know him," stammered the visitor, " but I have often heard him mentioned."

" It is not at all necessary, you know, for you to be brought into contact with him."

" Ah ! " muttered the client, whom this assurance seemed to relieve.

" Hingant only knows us, and ought not to have dealings with anyone else. It will suffice for you to occupy yourself about this Marie Bréhal, and if you find her you can rely on a very handsome honorarium. We always act liberally in business, and the least information that would set us on this woman's track would be paid for at once."

" I am greatly obliged to you, sir, and I will do my best ; but if you will give me some information as to this woman's antecedents, my task will be made much easier. A mere name is very vague."

"No doubt, and if you will take the trouble to call on me to-morrow, at my office, 135 Rue de Cléry, between two and three o'clock, I will communicate all the documents I possess to you." The advocate had good reasons for replying in this manner, for he knew no more of the affair than the visitor did ; only he hoped to see M. Hingant in the course of the evening, and ask him for full information respecting this Marie Bréhal.

" However," said the stranger with some embarrassment, " it is certain, I suppose, that an inheritance is in question ? "

" Oh, quite certain."

" Is the inheritance a large one ? "

" Yes, very large indeed."

" And what does it consist of, land or cash ? You are no doubt also acquainted with the name of the person who has left so much unclaimed wealth."

" I will tell you everything to-morrow, my dear sir ; I must look at the papers again ; I have had other and more pressing matters in mind. For the time being I will occupy myself about the removal of your friend, who must feel very bored upstairs. Shall we go up together to see how he is getting on ? "

" It's useless," replied the visitor, " I rely on you, and I won't hide the fact that if you could get this unfortunate fellow out of Paris you would render me a great service."

" I'll try, my dear sir, I'll try. However. to-morrow I will give you an answer for certain."

"Then I will thank you and retire. Your servant, sir, and yours also Monsieur Billebaude. I hope you will have the leisure to spend an hour or two at our little café this evening."

"Certainly, and we will have a fine game of dominoes."

The visitor had risen to his feet and was about to leave the room, when the servant appeared and approached Billebaude, to whom she whispered a few words. "Let him wait a moment in the parlour," said the agent, "and shew this gentleman out by way of my bed-room. You will excuse me, I hope," he added, turning to the countrified-looking client, "every-thing here is conducted with due secrecy, and we don't let the people who visit us meet in the same waiting room. It might be unpleasant at times."

"You are quite right, sir," said the man with the spectacles, and after shaking hands with the two partners, he followed the servant into the bed-chamber.

"Who is it?" Galmard asked Billebaude at the same time pointing to the parlour door.

"Why; Monsieur Hingant in person."

"That's capital. I sha'n't have to run after him!"

"And it's fortunate that he didn't meet that other fellow on the stairs. I fancy that they know each other, and, between ourselves, in my opinion it was rather imprudent of you to talk about the Marie Bréhal affair."

"Oh, let me be, Billebaude, you worry me with your apprehensions. I floored your visitor, and I shall have him bound hand and foot when I've rid him and you of that insurgent, and given him three or four thousand francs for his help in the Bréhal matter. He'll then come and beg us to take his hundred thousand."

"Well after all, it's quite possible, but what are you going to do with the man on the fourth floor?"

"Oh! I know where to lodge him. He shall go off to-night with Mardochée as an escort. And now let us deal with Hingant. I want to find out what he has in his bag, and besides an ex-magistrate ought not to be kept waiting."

"I will go and fetch him," said Billebaude, opening the parlour door; and a moment later he reappeared in the wake of Marthe's protector, whom he ushered into the office with a cordial gesture.

"Ah! how are you, old fellow?" said the advocate hastily approaching Jean-Marie. "How have you been getting on since your first and last visit? It dates some time back, and I ought to reproach you, but I am so glad to see you now, that you may consider yourself excused."

"What would you have, my friend?" said M. Hingant. "I have had a lot of things to attend to since my arrival in Paris; and then there was that fatal insurrection last month. However I have been here several times already—"

"And you only succeeded in seeing Billebaude yesterday. I know that; and I am very glad that you have returned to-day."

"And I am glad to find you here for more than one reason."

"Ah!" said Galmard in a tone of restrained emotion. "You haven't changed a bit, my old friend. I should have recognised you thirty paces off—"

"But my hair has grown white and I have lost the legs I had," said the ex-magistrate sitting down.

"Oh! you'll find them again so as to come one day with me into the country. We'll have a nice long walk together, as we used to have in the old days. Do you remember how we used to go and milk the cows at the farm of La Prévalais—"

"Ah! my poor Galmard, my thoughts are far from those pleasant times—I don't feel merry by any means and I have come—"

"The fact is that you do look out of sorts," rejoined the advocate. "Come, tell me your troubles. Billebaude won't be in the way as he's a friend. But, by-the-bye, is it that inheritance affair which is worrying you?"

"No, there is nothing new in that direction except that Monsieur Billebaude promised me yesterday—"

"And I have begun to put my promises into execution," interrupted the agent. "All my people are at work and we shall soon have some good news, at least I have every reason to presume so. Only we need a little enlightenment—"

"I will tell you everything I can, and as completely as possible; but to-day I have come to speak to you about another matter, as singular as the first one and quite as interesting to me,"

"Really?" said the advocate laughing, "you are like a surprise-box, Jean-Marie. While Billebaude is finding the solution to one enigma, behold you present him with another one."

"Alas! I hardly hope that he will find the solution of it."

"Let us see what it is, at all events."

"Well, it is a question of deciphering what is inscribed on this paper," said Hingant exhibiting the mysterious document found in the secret drawer.

Maître Galmard took hold of it and began to examine it attentively while Billebaude looked over his shoulder. "This comes quite within the scope of our calling," said the advocate after a prolonged scrutiny. "We have accomplished miracles in this line, and if it were only a question of conventional signs corresponding with letters of the alphabet I would engage to decipher the document in twenty-four hours."

"There is an infallible method with those kind of systems," said Billebaude. "You take note of the figure which most frequently occurs, and you may be sure that it represents the letter which is most used in the language. In French the letter ' E ' is the one which figures more often than any others. That point established you pass to the other figures, and by dint of deductions—"

"That will do, my good fellow," interrupted the advocate, "we know that you are very clever; but unfortunately your attainments cannot accomplish more than mine in the present case. It is sufficient to study these figures a little to perceive that they are connected with some book which is only known to the person who wrote them and the person for whom they were intended."

"What, a book!" exclaimed Hingant.

"Yes, it is simple enough. Pray note, that on this paper a large number is always or nearly always followed by a smaller one and then by one still smaller. Take the three first for instance, 636—22—9. This implies that one must look in a certain book for the ninth word on the twenty-second line of page 636."

"Yes, that seems probable."

"It is certain. The letters which you can see here and there refer perhaps to some word which is not contained in the book in question, and for them another key would have to be found. However, the exception confirms the rule. See how regularly the order of the numerals, which I just pointed out to you, is followed—"

"In that case it would be very easy to decipher these figures."

"No, on the contrary it will be very difficult for we need the book which was used. Now what book was it? This system of cipher writing is the only one that ensures secrecy, as it is based on something one is ignorant of."

"So there is nothing to be done," said Hingant sadly.

"I can't say. To give an opinion I need to know who wrote the paper, and where it was found."

"I found it in a secret drawer, and everything leads me to believe that it contains information which I greatly need to prevent the ruin of an unfortunate orphan to whom I am greatly attached—Mademoiselle Marthe Moulinier."

It was no doubt written that this name of Moulinier should, at regular intervals, unexpectedly fall upon Billebaude's ears, and each time it was pronounced it had the same effect on his nervous system. He had changed countenance when M. Hingant had alluded to the captain's tragical demise on the occasion of his first visit, and he became ghastly pale now that he learnt that the ex-magistrate had taken Marthe's interests in hand. Maître Galmard had not the same reasons as his partner for shewing emotion, but he had previously learnt sufficient to understand the situation. The Moulinier in question was evidently the person who had supplied Billebaude with money to set up in business as a banker many years previously, and over whose death the agent had so much rejoiced. The advocate took mental note of all this, and then resumed his instructive conversation with M. Hingant : "Come, my dear fellow," he said gently. "Try and be precise, for I don't know what motives lead you to attach so much importance to this paper. You talk to me about a secret drawer and information and an orphan. This is rather vague. Be precise, Jean-Marie, be precise."

"Well, my dear Galmard, I must tell you that on the 22nd of June, having witnessed the death of the captain, who was killed or rather murdered close to me—"

"What! you have been under fire at your age! That's heroism, if I know anything about it."

"I did my duty—that was all. I was saying, however, that having witnessed this catastrophe and the search of the house whence the shot was fired, I was led by a succession of events, which it would require too long to relate to you, to take the only daughter of this unfortunate Monsieur Moulinier under my protection."

"Ah ! ah, my fine fellow. She's young and pretty, eh ? "

"Pray don't joke—this is no laughing matter," replied the old magistrate. "I feel a fatherly affection for this poor orphan, and I hope to see her soon married to a young man whom she loves and who reciprocates her attachment. It is this matter of her marriage that worries me ; for money is required to begin housekeeping, and I fear that Mademoiselle Moulinier will never recover whatever her father left behind him."

"What was her father's avocation ? "

"I hardly know, for he seems to have kept his daughter in complete ignorance respecting money matters : however he had evidently been in business and had met with reverses of recent times. Still he lived in comfortable style, after all ; and however moderate his income may have been it must certainly have been derived from something. It is there that the mystery begins. No one knows the source of his income. He recently lost his wife, and his daughter has not been able to give me the name of any relative or friend to whom I could apply for information. I thought I might solve the question by examining the deceased's papers, but no writing has been found save this puzzling scrawl in cipher. Do you realise now why I am so anxious to discover its meaning?"

"Oh! I understand you perfectly well, and I am of your opinion that the deceased has here given all needful information as to his belongings, supposing that any remained to him. If he possessed any stocks or shares, the name of the person with whom they are deposited must be inserted here. If he simply had an interest in any commercial business we shall here find the name of his partner—and also the name of his debtors, supposing anyone owed him money." As Maître Galmard concluded he gave his friend Billebaude an expressive glance as much as to say, "I know very well whose name is set down on this scrap of paper, and you know as well as I do."

"Yes, all that is only too probable," sighed M. Hingant, "but we are no further advanced, for you admit that this fatal paper will never yield its secret."

"Excuse me, my dear fellow, I did not precisely say that. I merely asserted that the key of this sample of cyptography—that is the technical term—could only be found in a book. What book? That is the question, and may be it can be answered. I already know that it must be a large book."

"How do you know that?"

"Why because certain numbers are very high. Look," added Galmard, again examining the mysterious scrawl. "We have 636 to begin with; then 682, 647 and 674 further on, and several similar numbers besides. They plainly refer to pages, as I pointed out before; so the book in question must have nearly 700 pages and be a bulky affair."

"It's a dictionary, perhaps."

"I don't think so, and will tell you why. The third numbers of each lines—those indicating the position of the words on certain lines—are rather high. I find 17, 15 and 19 for instance. Now dictionaries have two or three columns per page, and no line of one column contains as many as nineteen words."

"That's true," muttered Jean-Marie.

"Well, to judge of the book's size, we need only refer to the second numbers of each series. They will tell us pretty nearly the number of lines on a page. I find 33, 36, 38, nothing above that. So the book hardly has more than forty lines to a page; and to sum up I believe that the work in question must be a bulky octavo volume, printed in rather large type, with margins of the usual width."

"That seems certain, and your deductions are extremely clever."

"I told you that the matter came within my province. This is only child's work, however, and you will see some much stranger things before we have finished with the matter. For the time being, we know that the book is neither a dictionary nor a circulating library novel, which contains more white paper than letter-press. Nor can it be a pocket volume. Despite these negative certainties, however, we are still at sea, and it is time to turn to another side of the question. Have you any suspicions concerning any person to whom this Monsieur Moulinier might have confided the volume which contains the key of the cipher?"

"No; it can't be his daughter, for I shewed her this writing and she had no idea as to its purport. If her father had left the paper for her benefit, he would not have failed to inform her of his strange combinations."

"That's quite true, but another supposition presents itself. You told me that he had only recently been left a widower."

"His wife died three or four months ago."

"Well, then, he may very well have confided his secret to his wife, and she, for some reason or another, may have neglected to reveal it to her daughter before dying."

"Yes—that is possible; and yet— However, I will ask Mademoiselle Moulinier to try and remember if her mother ever said or hinted anything on such a subject."

"Now, did the deceased possess a library? If he did, each volume it comprised ought to be carefully examined."

"I did not notice a single book in the place, still, there may be some. I cannot speak with certainty, as all this was far from my mind at the time. However on my next visit—"

"I can go to the place with you if you like—"

"Thanks, my dear fellow; your help would certainly be very valuable, but I must first of all talk the matter over with Marthe."

"As you please. Will you leave me this scrawl? I will go through it attentively at my leisure, and may be I shall make some unexpected dis· covery."

"I ask nothing better; only I don't think I have a right to dispose of the paper without Mademoiselle Moulinier's authorisation."

"That's quite true; so keep it. However, there is a means of con· ciliating everything. Let my friend Billebaude take a copy of the figures, here at once. In this manner I shall be able to investigate the matter on my side, while you are tackling all the books you may happen to come across."

"I don't think there is any reason why that shouldn't be done."

"Very well then. Come, Billebaude, to work," cried Maître Galmard flinging the paper on the writing table.

The agent did not need any pressing to do as he was bid. For a long time past he had been waxing frantic as he heard the advocate giving precious advice to M. Hingant at the risk of setting him on the right track. The deciphering of the scrawl might be attended by the most disastrous consequences, at least so he, Billebaude, imagined; for to his mind, these incomprehensible numbers concealed a statement of his connection with the deceased Moulinier. If M. Hingant had been willing to part with the paper, Billebaude would have liked to have thrown it into the fire; but failing this desired annihilation of the mysterious document, he was glad to be able to take a copy of it; no one knew what might happen. Whilst the agent was engaged in carefully copying the strange medley of numerals, Maître Galmard endeavoured to enliven his old chum, Hingant; but he failed to do so, for the ex-magistrate did not see any means of improving his ward's position as regards the paternal inheritance, and besides, with his natural straightforwardness, he felt ill at ease amid this entanglement of mystery. He who for thirty years had lived in a glass house, without concealing either thought or action, seemed to have landed on an unknown shore, and to a man of his frankness and loyalty, all this concealment, all these tortuous dodges, were highly displeasing. The advocate now tried to bring the Marie Bréhal matter forward, for he was greatly interested in this affair—far more indeed than in the Moulinier inheritance, on which he had a very decided opinion; but he soon realized by Jean-Marie's manner that the moment was ill-timed for referring to business, and as he was by no means a fool he refrained from insisting. "When shall I see you again ?" he asked as Hingant rose to his feet and stowed the mysterious paper, which Billebaude had just copied, away in his pocket.

"In a few days' time," replied the old magistrate, "that is if I am likely to find you at your place in the Rue de Cléry. But as for coming to the Rue des Canettes that is another matter; it is a long way off, and for a short time I shall be fully occupied."

"With your orphan's wedding, eh ? Your mind is set on it. Well, no matter. I shall be at home every afternoon at four, and I hope that you will look in some day or other."

M. Hingant parted with the two partners on the best of terms; but as soon as the latter were alone again Billebaude somewhat peevishly asked : "Why to the deuce did you tell him so much about the way to decipher this cursed paper which may ruin me ?"

"So as to have you under my thumb," answered Maître Galmard coldly.

XII.

AT noon on the morrow of this busy day M. Hingant was lunching with Mademoiselle Moulinier. The repast was more silent than usual. Marthe seemed absorbed in sad thoughts, and the ex-magistrate was scarcely in better spirits than the young girl. His conversation with Galmard had left him but little hope; he felt that it was time he should have a serious explanation with Marthe, but he did not know how to begin. "My dear child," he said at last, "my inquiries yesterday proved unsuccessful, and, despite the cleverness and experience of the man I consulted, he could only give me a very vague explanation of the probable meaning of the cipher writing."

"I am not surprised," sighed the orphan. "What is the use of your taking so much trouble ? my poor father's ruin is only too certain, and the deciphering of this document would hardly alter my position."

"Perhaps not; but, in any case, you ought to know its contents, and my friend Galmard's advice should not be neglected. He proved to me that these figures must designate the pages, lines, and words of a book, which must be in the hands of some person to whom your father had confided his secret. Have you no recollection of his having given your mother any bulky volume, of octavo size ?"

"No. My mother read very little, especially of late times, for her eyesight had grown very weak; besides, if such a book had been in her possession, she would have attached importance to it, and have shown it to me, or at least have spoken of it."

"Still, I think it would be as well to carefully examine such books as may have remained in the apartment."

"There are only the books I used at school. My father was never fond of reading, and, of late times, business cares fully occupied him."

"Then I must look for the volume elsewhere," said M. Hingant, sadly. "But, before clearing up all this mystery, don't you think, my dear child, that we ought to occupy ourselves about someone whom we have rather neglected? I refer to Monsieur Gilbert, of course. You announced our visit to him, and he must be growing very uneasy. It seems to me we should do well to relieve his anxiety."

Mademoiselle Moulinier hung her head, and made no reply.

"I, for one, particularly wish to see him," continued Jean-Marie. "I will not conceal from you that the dearest hopes of my declining years are connected with him and yourself, my dear Marthe." The orphan gazed at her protector with a look of deep emotion. "Yes," resumed M. Hingant, "I am old, and I am alone in the world. What can I hope for now, but to see you two united and happy, and to end my days near you?"

"Ah! sir," said Marthe, in a voice that trembled, despite all her efforts to appear calm, "you have been a father, more than a father to me, and I would gladly devote my life to testifying my gratitude to you, but I shall never marry."

"What are you thinking of, my child? Why, this is folly. You love this young man; he is worthy of you, I'm sure, and yet you won't—"

"Yes, I love Paul, and it is because I love him that I will not allow him to share the sad lot that awaits me."

"What, because you have no fortune? But there is nothing to prove that; and besides, you forget that you still have a friend—that I have come to regard you as a daughter."

"You are altogether too kind, sir; pray listen to me," interrupted Mademoiselle Moulinier, with a firmness of tone which indicated great decision of purpose. "I have reflected during the past few days, and I perceive but one honourable issue to my situation—work! Paul has only his pay to depend upon; by marrying me he would ruin his career, and I will not consent to such a sacrifice."

"Ruin his career? But am I not there to—"

"I know what you wish to say, and certainly there is no reason for me to blush at the thought of accepting your bounty; but I do refuse it, and I hope you will forgive me for doing so, for I rely upon you to help me in carrying out the plan I have formed."

"A plan? Alas, my poor child, you know nothing of life; you do not know that at your age—a young girl, brought up as you have been."

"I can teach English, and the piano, and I can embroider very well I know. Even if I have to work day and night, I will succeed in earning my living, and I ask you to find some pupils for me. You see I don't refuse your protection."

She spoke these last words in a tone of affection that completely disarmed M. Hingant, and brought tears to his eyes. "Ah," he exclaimed, "this is not what I dreamed of for you and me; but you know that I shall always be only too glad to serve you, and if it only depends on me—"

"Beg pardon, sir," said the old servant-woman, opening the door, at this moment. "But there is an officer here who wishes to see you."

"An officer!" exclaimed Hingant, greatly delighted; "it must be Monsieur Gilbert, and I will—"

"Monsieur Hingant," said Marthe pleadingly, "pray excuse me from being present at this interview."

"What! you decline to see him?"

"I should not have the courage to inform Paul of the decision I have arrived at, and I rely upon you to apprise him of it." And, without waiting for any reply from her old friend, the girl rose up, and took refuge in an adjoining room.

The old magistrate was overwhelmed with consternation, and it became necessary for the servant to remind him that the visitor was waiting. However, he did not have to give orders for his admission, for the door now opened, and a young man, wearing the undress uniform of a lieutenant of chasseurs, hastily entered the dining-room. He carried his arm in a sling, and wore the red ribbon and cross of the Legion of Honour on his breast. This was quite enough for good Jean-Marie to know whom he had to deal with, and yet he surveyed Marthe's chosen lover with kindly curiosity. Paul Gilbert was of medium height, well built, rather dark complexioned, and with very black eyes and hair. His regular features had an expression of unusual firmness, and in his clear, straightforward gaze one could read frankness, honesty, and decision. At first sight he intimidated rather than pleased one, and the ex-magistrate felt a trifle disconcerted. He had pictured to himself a hero of romance, but beheld a proud-looking soldier, who was very reserved in manner.

"Is it to Monsieur Hingant that I have the honour of speaking?" asked the lieutenant, rather curtly.

"That is my name, and I am glad to see you, for I have long been desirous of making the acquaintance of Mademoiselle Moulinier's betrothed. On the day before yesterday, an accident deprived me of that pleasure. We went to the Val-de-Grâce."

"Oh! I know what occurred there," interrupted Paul Gilbert, "and I also know that Mademoiselle Moulinier has been residing with you since the death of her father, so you will not be surprised if I have come here to ask you for an explanation of this singular circumstance."

"I am entirely ready to furnish it, and it is very simple. Chance led me to the house in which Mademoiselle Moulinier had been left alone, exposed to all the dangers which threatened a young girl during that frightful insurrection. Her father had just been killed by my side, for I was a sergeant in the company of National Guards which he commanded. I only thought of the safety of a poor, desolate girl, and she merely saw in me an old man glad to protect and shelter her."

This was said with such perfect simplicity that the lieutenant departed somewhat from his stiffness of manner. "Excuse me, sir," he said politely, "and allow me to inquire if Mademoiselle Moulinier is here. You will readily understand that I am anxious to see her."

"Certainly; and it is no fault of mine if she did not remain in this room where she was sitting only a moment ago. It was her wish to retire, however, and it is at her request that I receive you alone."

"She had some motive, of course, in acting thus. May I inquire what it is?" asked Paul Gilbert, becoming cold and stern again.

"Ah! I wish I could be spared the necessity of telling you!" exclaimed Monsieur Hingant, with emotion. "She has formed a resolution which I disapprove of, and which I have opposed with all my power, and she has imposed upon me the sad task of acquainting you with it."

"And what may it be?" inquired the lieutenant, who was evidently forcing himself to remain calm.

"Mademoiselle Moulinier has ascertained that her father died insolvent. She is poor; she loves you; and she voluntary renounces her most cherished hopes. She refuses to marry you because she is unwilling to prove an obstacle to your success in life, and yet if she would listen to me—" Jean-Marie's voice failed him, and big tears rolled down his cheeks.

Paul Gilbert gazed at him with a strange expression. "I knew a long time ago that Monsieur Moulinier had lost his fortune," he said slowly.

"And you loved his daughter none the less, I am sure of it," exclaimed M. Hingant, "and I feel certain that you will join me in overcoming Marthe's scruples."

"Oh, Mademoiselle Moulinier is right, sir. Our marriage at the present time would be impossible, for an officer can only marry a woman possessing an income of twelve hundred francs. Upon this point the army rules are inflexible."

The old man turned pale and his head drooped. This cold response had wounded him to the heart. "Ah, sir!" said Paul Gilbert, taking a seat, to Jean-Marie's great astonishment, "I can read your thoughts on your face; I can guess what you think of me; but pray, listen to me a moment."

M. Hingant on his side seated himself again without saying a word. He scarcely knew what to think of this strange lover who reasoned like an old man. "Naturally enough I was greatly irritated when I came here," resumed the officer. "I did not know you, and appearances were against you. I could not imagine any circumstances which had made it necessary for you to take Mademoiselle Moulinier under your protection. My confidence in her was unshaken; but I distrusted your motives, and I feared she was deceived when she wrote that you treated her with fatherly affection."

The ex-magistrate here made a gesture indicative of sorrowful surprise. "The painful scene which occurred at the gate of the hospital," resumed the lieutenant, "was related to me, with comments which I need not repeat to you; and moreover, the doorkeeper of the house in which Monsieur Moulinier resided informed me this morning that you had paid the arrears of rent."

"Was not that natural under the circumstances? Ought I to have left an orphan girl exposed to the impertinence of such a rascal?"

"Well, it was something that a stranger had no right to do, and I then looked upon you as a stranger; but it has sufficed for me to see and hear you, to become convinced that I was mistaken, and that I have a kind-hearted honourable man before me. It is now my duty to justify myself, and to explain the words that wounded you so keenly just now."

"Justify yourself? That is unnecessary. I did not blame you."

"Well, you attributed to me certain sentiments of cold calculation which I shall never have, but which my reply seemed unmistakably to indicate; and I esteem you the more for your signs of displeasure. If I were capable for a moment of hesitating between my love for Mademoiselle Marthe and pecuniary interest, I should deserve your scorn; and it is time for me to tell you why I spoke as I did."

Hingant, greatly touched, took Lieutenant Gilbert's hand, and pressed it cordially. "Has Mademoiselle Moulinier ever told you how we became acquainted?" inquired the lieutenant, after returning the pressure.

"Yes, she said it was at the boarding-school, where she was educated," stammered Jean-Marie.

"Well, excuse me if I relate to you the story of my life. It is very simple and very short. I never knew the name of my parents, and that by which I am called is certainly not theirs. I figure upon the register as the child of parents whose name was unknown, and the one I bear was given me by the midwife who carried me to the mayor's office; still I had a sister seven years younger than myself, registered, like myself, under the surname of Gilbert, and the Christian name of Paule, as if to indicate that we were of the same blood. It was unnecessary, for the resemblance between us was striking."

"But," interposed the ex-magistrate, "how did you learn—"

"That Paule was my sister? I was fourteen when I learnt it. I was still at the school where I had been placed when a mere child, where no one ever came to see me, and where I remained even at holiday time. One day, however, the master sent for me, and said : 'My boy, it is time for me to tell you that you have no one to depend upon excepting yourself. Your schooling here for three years more has been paid in advance ; but when this period expires, you will be obliged to earn your own living. I must also tell you that you have a sister, and that she will need your help some day. Next Sunday I will take you to the school where she is beginning her education, and where she will complete it. In ten years—she will then be seventeen—I hope you will have gained a position which will enable you to support her.' "

" Poor children," murmured M. Hingant.

" My schoolmaster kept his promise. He took me to a girls' boarding-school in the district of the Marais, and I met Paule for the first time under the old trees of the playground. Strange as it may appear, it seemed to me as if I had always known her, and she experienced a similar impression. We had loved each other without ever having seen each other."

" And Marthe ? " interrupted M. Hingant.

" I did not meet Mademoiselle Moulinier until some years later. On the day when I learned that I was no longer alone in the world, my character underwent a change. I had been a gay and thoughtless youth. I became taciturn and industrious. I fully realized that some one—my sister—was dependent upon me. Every Sunday I hastened to the school where the dear little girl was impatiently awaiting me. Of the childish conversation which took place under the lindens of the walk, I retain only an indistinct recollection ; but I remember that we solemnly vowed never to part from each other when we had gained our freedom. We seldom or never alluded to the past. Paule had been sent to school when very young, like myself, and her earlier recollections were most confused."

" What a strange story," murmured M. Hingant.

" Yes," replied the young officer, sadly, " and if I were superstitious, I should almost be tempted to believe that a sort of fatality follows me and those I love. But in the old times I was hopeful concerning the future. I said to myself that my sister would not need my help until her education was completed, and that, consequently, I had ten years before me, which I intended to devote to the acquisition of a small sum that would suffice for Paule's support, and serve her as a modest dowry. At an age when other boys dream of liberty and amusement, I only thought of preparing myself to achieve success in life. With the kind of education I received, and my natural taste for the exact sciences, I could have easily obtained admission into the Government schools; but I knew it would be impossible for me to pay even for my outfit, and I had no claim to a scholarship, so that was not to be thought of. If I turned to business pursuits, or reconciled myself to teaching children, the conscription would abruptly prevent me from continuing my work, as I had not the money to pay for a substitute. If I were drafted into the army at the age of twenty, my term of military service would not expire by the time that my sister would need assistance. Thus after serious reflection, I concluded that the best course for me to pursue was to enlist on leaving school. I should thus gain three years, and my term of service would expire the same year that Paule left school. It went hard with me to enlist, I assure you ; however, I did so. At the age of seventeen, I joined a regiment of Zouaves, and started for Algeria. I was robust and vigorous, and had no parents' consent to obtain. Six months afterwards, I was a corporal. At the end of a year, I received my first

D

wound and a sergeant's shoulder-straps. At the close of my fifth campaign, I was promoted to a sub-lieutenancy in a regiment of foot-chasseurs, and I returned to France."

"That was splendid! noble!" muttered Jean-Marie, whose enthusiasm was aroused by this narrative of a courageous life.

"My success had surpassed my hopes, and by enlisting in order to be free the sooner, I had unwittingly opened for myself an honourable career, which I no longer thought of abandoning. My regiment was soon ordered to Paris for garrison duty, and I had the unspeakable happiness of seeing my sister again. She was now almost a young girl, and I felt proud of being her brother, proud and happy, for I was no longer troubled by anxiety as to the future. My pay was not large, but we receive, you know, a more liberal allowance when we are abroad, and I had practised the most rigid economy, saving a sum for my sister's future use. She still had two more years to spend at school, and I was almost sure of not being ordered away from Paris, so we resumed our pleasant chats and dreams; only now there were three of us, for Paule had a friend—"

"Marthe!" exclaimed M. Hingant. "Ah, the dear child has often spoken of the happiness of those fleeting days, and of the bitter anguish of the final parting."

"Then I need not allude to them," resumed Paul, in a husky voice. "Just as my sister's most intimate friend was returning to her parents, poor Paule fell ill and died about a month afterwards. Before her death she made me solemnly promise that I would never marry if Mademoiselle Moulinier could not become my wife."

"And that oath you will keep! And the husband will lavish upon the poor orphan the tenderness and devotion that the brother displayed towards his departed sister."

"I shall keep the oath whatever happens," said the officer, gravely.

"Whatever happens!" repeated Jean-Marie, in anguish. "Do you mean to say that this marriage has become impossible?"

"I hope, sir," replied Paul, "that you esteem me enough to believe me incapable of breaking a sacred promise or of feigning sentiments I do not feel." M. Hingant protested with a gesture. "Well," resumed the young officer, warmly, "I love Mademoiselle Moulinier with all the strength of my being. I would willingly sacrifice my life for her, as I would have given it for the poor child who is no more; but I have no right to bring misery upon a young girl—"

"Misery!" cried M. Hingant. "But that is the same language that Marthe used to me. She also fears to impose a sacrifice upon you. You see that this is an exaggerated sentiment of delicacy, and that her love, like yours, is superior to all the trials of life."

"I know it," replied Paul quietly, "but when you have heard me to the end you will perhaps come to the conclusion that it is my duty to act as I propose. When we first began to love each other, we both felt that it was our duty to inform Marthe's parents of our hopes. My scruples then were of an entirely different nature. I, friendless, nameless, and penniless, felt that I had no right to aspire to the hand of Mademoiselle Moulinier, who seemed likely to be rich, and I did not want my motives to be misconstrued. To my great surprise, however, Marthe told me that my pretensions to her hand had been favourably received. Her mother had been aware of her growing affection for some time, and greatly desired our marriage. Her father appeared less enthusiastic, but did not refuse his consent. Indeed, he readily allowed me to visit the family. I had resolved not to accept from Monsieur Moulinier any dowry above the sum which the regulations of the War Department rigorously exact for the wife of an officer. Marthe was acquainted with my ideas on this subject and approved them. The humble character of our future life did not frighten her ; she asked nothing better than to share the privations of a poor lieutenant, feeling sure that the day would come when her devotion would be rewarded."

" I assure you that her feelings have not changed. Misfortunes have not impaired her courage."

" I believe you, sir ; but what was then possible, is now impossible ! "

" What ! " said M. Hingant, bitterly, " your love bows to a regulation ? You would renounce Marthe for want of a paltry sum of money which a friend would be only too happy to give—to lend you."

" Mademoiselle Moulinier shall be the judge. My honour is hers, and I am sure she will advise me to refuse charity under whatever disguise it may be offered, even from a man whom she respects, and whom I esteem above all others." Kind-hearted Jean-Marie groaned aloud. " Consequently," continued Lieutenant Gilbert, " I can only marry Mademoiselle Moulinier by sending in my resignation."

This plain conclusion, delivered without any preamble, fell upon the ex-magistrate like a thunderbolt. " He has resolved to break the engagement," said Jean-Marie to himself, and the thought filled him with consternation.

" I shall soon be twenty-six," continued the lieutenant, " and I know barely anything, save commanding soldiers and leading them to battle, for I have had time to forget all I learned at school. Still, I think I might yet find some position in civil life; and my military record, and the decoration I have just received, would be excellent recommendations. Perhaps I should not succeed in finding employment at once, but I think I should do so eventually, though I should be obliged to content myself with the petty salary accorded to beginners. Marthe would, I am sure, know how to endure this ordeal of poverty, unlightened by the hope of rapid advance-ment, but I cannot assume the responsibility of condemning her to such an existence—"

" You are quite right, sir," said M. Hingant, wounded to the heart. " A glorious future opens before you, and it would be wrong to renounce such prospects. Mademoiselle Moulinier would not allow you to resign, and I should never cease reproaching myself for having advised you to do so."

" You have misunderstood me," replied Paul Gilbert, reproachfully. " Here is my resignation." And he handed Marthe's protector a large envelope bearing this superscription : " To Monsieur, the Minister of War."

" Indeed ! " exclaimed M. Hingant, deeply moved, " you tender your resignation ! You would abandon a military career without regret—"

" Without regret, is saying a good deal," muttered Lieutenant Gilbert, " but certainly without hesitation. I don't wish Mademoiselle Moulinier to accuse me of possessing a calculating spirit, and even if I were certain of becoming a Marshal of France, I should infinitely prefer the happiness of being Marthe's husband to such an honour. But I do not desire to influence her in her decision, and for that reason, I congratulate myself upon having had an opportunity of conversing with you alone. Take this letter, pray, hand it to Mademoiselle Marthe, and repeat our conversation to her. I make her absolute mistress of our joint destinies. If she thinks she will never regret her resolution, she has only to forward this letter to its address. As soon as the Minister receives it, I shall be free, and I swear to you that this is my fondest desire."

"Is this really true?" asked Jean-Marie, with a joyful heart.

"Can you doubt it for an instant? Ah, you do me great injustice if you deem me ambitious, if you think there is room in my heart for any other feeling than love for Marthe—Ambitious!" Paul repeated, sadly. "Ah, it is for her, and for her alone, that I might have been so. Yes, I should have been glad to see her in the foremost rank, so that she might be proud of the humble lieutenant, who, at the price of his blood, had won a colonel's epaulets, perhaps even a general's stars. But neither rank nor glory is, in my eyes, worth a single day of the life that would await me if she consented to link her destiny with mine."

"Will you authorize me to repeat to her the words you have just spoken?" inquired the old man, eagerly.

"Certainly, for they are perfectly sincere. Still, if you were to use them to influence her decision, I shall regret having given utterance to them. Mademoiselle Moulinier must be free, absolutely free to decide; and if I have a favour to ask of you, it is rather to point out to her how cheerless would be the life to which she would condemn herself by marrying me."

"That is unnecessary; my mind is already made up," said Marthe, suddenly making her appearance, pale but with a firm expression of countenance, and unflinching gaze. M. Hingant hastened towards her, and the young officer, in his excitement, rose so hurriedly that he tottered and almost fell.

"Ah, my dear child, this is very wrong. You have been listening," gaily said Jean-Marie, confident that everything would finally be arranged to his liking. "I am not angry with you, however," he continued, "for as you have heard Monsieur Gilbert, I feel sure that our cause is won. Come, I am going to take this letter to the War Department; but before I start we must fix the wedding day."

"No, my friend," said the young girl, with an effort, "I cannot be Paul's wife, and I beg of him to forgive me for refusing such happiness."

"Marthe," murmured the lieutenant, who was almost fainting.

"I, too, shall suffer, Paul," Mademoiselle Moulinier continued, "but I shall not lack courage; though I have not enough to accept the sacrifice you offer." Hingant sighed, and lifted his hands to the ceiling. The officer remained silent and motionless. "I might attempt to convince you that poverty frightens me, but I know you would not believe me," resumed the orphan with a proud gesture; "so, instead of that, I will merely say that by insisting you would only cause me fresh and increased grief."

"But this is folly," exclaimed Jean-Marie. "In Heaven's name what do you intend to do?"

"I have already told you, my friend. I shall support myself by my own work, and I depend upon you to enable me to do so. By the sale of my father's furniture, I trust that a sufficient amount will be realized to pay the arrears of rent which you so generously advanced to me, and to furnish a modest room."

"No doubt, no doubt," stammered the worthy man, secretly determined that these expenses should be defrayed out of his own purse.

"The lessons I shall give will suffice for my wants, for I am sure you will procure some pupils for me," added Marthe, forcing a smile.

"I must do so, and yet, if you chose—but have you no thought of Monsieur Gilbert and the sorrow you cause him?"

"Monsieur Gilbert, like myself, will have sufficient courage to resign himself—and to hope," said the girl gravely.

"Hope!" repeated the officer, bitterly, "what have I to hope for now?"

"Mademoiselle Moulinier's situation may change," replied M. Hingant, hastily. "There is positively nothing to prove that her father has not left a fortune; and, really, when we reflect a moment, we cannot admit that the capital from which he undoubtedly derived his income has altogether vanished into smoke." At this point Paul Gilbert made a gesture of indifference. "Oh! I know very well," resumed M. Hingant, "that your mind is not set upon wealth, but you would certainly be pleased if Marthe recovered sufficient to constitute the dowry which the army regulations require. And all is not lost; the paper I discovered may prove our salvation, for the clever man to whom I showed it says he is confident he shall soon succeed in deciphering it." Marthe tried to speak, but M. Hingant instantly resumed: "I know all the objections you are about to offer, my dear child. You are going to say that it is useless to take so much trouble, and that the deciphering of these mysterious figures will not benefit you in the least. Ah, well! I was desirous of keeping all this to myself, but you compel me to confess that I have serious reasons for thinking the contrary."

"Is it possible! but what reasons are they?"

"I cannot disclose them at present. It is my secret, a very pleasant secret, I assure you. I certainly have a right to reserve myself the pleasure of giving you a surprise."

The girl's face brightened, and the officer looked at her with beseeching eyes which seemed to say: "If it is an illusion let me share it." Worthy Jean-Marie on his side smiled and rubbed his hands complacently, for he had just devised a plan which seemed to him an admirable one. He said to himself that it was necessary at any cost to unite these two lovers who were too proud to accept favours, and so he had decided to resort to a pious falsehood. There was nothing, after all, to prevent him from announcing some fine day that his search had proved successful, and that the strange document which was Marthe's sole inheritance for the time being had indicated where her father's money was invested. He could, in this way, arrange a little comedy with Maître Galmard; prepare a plausible story, and bring the orphan the product of his pretended discovery, that is to say some thirty thousand francs, which he of course intended to draw from his own capital.

Everything seemed to be progressing as smoothly as he could desire, for neither Paul nor Marthe appeared inclined to reject the hope he held out to them! Now or never he must fully win their confidence by adroit concessions. "As you know my plans at present," he said, gaily, "I am quite ready to confess, my dear child, that I entirely approve of your resolution to try and secure an independent position. The sale of your furniture is an excellent idea, and I am sure it will yield a handsome amount." The good man had excellent reasons for this opinion, for he had determined to bid vigorously on his own account. "I will try to find some rooms which will suit you," he added, "and which must not be too far from mine. In less than a week you shall be installed in your new home. As for pupils, you will soon have some. My friend Galmard is well acquainted with the lawyers of the Palais de Justice, and with business men also; he will find us what we want. And, besides, now I think of it, I already have one pupil for you. The niece of my poor friend Léridan is iu Paris, and I know she wishes to learn a great many things, for her education was very neglected. I even hope that she will soon become your friend. What do you say to my plans?

"That we shall owe our happiness to you," replied Marthe, throwiug her arms round the old man's neck. Jean-Marie's offers had conquered her, and she no longer thought of resisting the impulses of her heart.

"And I shall owe you my life as well, for I had resolved to die," whispered Paul Gilbert.

"No, no; I am determined that my dear Marthe shall be a general's wife some day, and I utterly refuse to accept your resignation," joyfully exclaimed the old magistrate, and he thereupon tore up the letter addressed to the Minister of War.

XIII.

TIME passes swiftly in Paris, and despite M. Hingant's industry, a week elapsed without his being able to do more than carry out the first part of the programme which he had exposed to Marthe and Paul. At first, his time was fully taken up in searching for a suitable abode for the orphan girl; and he climbed many a staircase before he eventually found, on the fourth floor of a respectable house, in the Cité Bergère—close to his own residence—three cheerful rooms, the windows of which overlooked a large garden. He took the rooms in the name of Mademoiselle Moulinier, teacher, and, having paid a quarter's rent in advance, he occupied himself with furnishing them. Marthe wanted to wait until the sale of her father's furniture yielded a sufficient sum, to defray the expenses of fitting up her new home; but Hingant showed her that there were certain for-malities to be accomplished before sending the parental furniture to auction, and he prevailed upon her to install herself in the Cité Bergère without delay. She only assented, however, on conditions that her protector would reimburse himself for his advances, as soon as the Moulinier estate was wound up. Worthy Jean-Marie laughed in his sleeve at this, for he knew very well that but little money would be obtained from that scource; however, he took good care not to undeceive his ward, and he decided that he would profit by her ignorance of prices, to let her imagine that a few hundred crowns were still left to her, when everything was settled. Meanwhile, he made an agreement with an upholsterer, who only asked three days and a lump sum, to place the rooms in the Cité Bergère in habitable condition. The man had a little taste, and his arrangements were intelligent. Marthe was provided with a bed-room, hung with white muslin, like a schoolgirl's chamber; and a lesson-room, furnished with a handsome bookcase, an embroidery stand, and a very fair piano. There was nothing superfluous, and yet nothing deficient in this modest abode, which greatly pleased Marthe, and which was, indeed, as perfect as she desired, both as regards comfort and the proprieties. M. Hingant's old servant undertook to find a respectable woman to prepare the young girl's morning meal, and it was arranged that she should go every day to her foster-father's to dine.

The question of obtaining pupils remained, and, in this respect, the ex-magistrate had perhaps been over forward in promising such wonderful success. In point of fact, he was only sure of Mathilde Pelchat who, as an heiress, aspired to enter fashionable society. The art of playing the piano would seem to her a very desirable accomplishment, thought Hingant; and as her parents'—petty tavern-keepers—had not made a musician of her for that best of reasons, lack of money, it was as good as certain that she would be delighted to take lessons from Mademoiselle Moulinier. The old magistrate reflected that this would suffice as a beginning, and besides, as Marthe embroidered wonderfully well, he meant to procure her some very remunerative work of that description. It was only a question of coming to an understanding with some tradesman, who would pay her more than the embroidery was worth, on conditions that the surplus was refunded to him by M. Hingant. Thanks to these ingenious arrangements, Jean-Marie hoped to provide for the first requirements of the situation, pending the time when, without too much improbability, he could announce that the search respecting the inheritance had succeeded, and that Marthe was entitled to a little fortune. To his mind a couple of months would suffice to arrive at this result.

Everything was progressing favourably as regards Paul Gilbert, who felt so happy at being still allowed to hope, that he accepted M. Hingant's suggestions with closed eyes. His battalion was not likely to leave Paris before the end of the year; and as nothing prevented the lovers from seeing each other during the period of probation, now beginning, they agreed to meet at the residence of the worthy man, who had so generously undertaken to smooth away all the obstacles which misfortune had scattered across their paths. The lieutenant had been decorated for his gallantry, and Marthe was now rapidly recovering health and spirits. To finish with the past, their old friend now only had to send the late M. Moulinier's furniture to auction, and in mid-July he found himself able to do so. For the success of his plans, it was needful that Marthe should not meddle in this matter, for he did not wish her to know the real figure which her father's belongings fetched at the sale. He therefore prevailed upon her to give him a power of attorney, removed such things as Marthe wished to preserve, to her new lodgings, and sent the remainder to the public auction-rooms, which were then installed in a building called the Hôtel Bullion, situated on the Place de la Bourse.

On the day appointed for the sale, M. Hingant repaired there, and elbowed his way up the narrow staircase to the first floor, where, after a short search, he succeeded in finding the furniture in which he was interested. The auctioneer had not yet arrived, and the public strolled to and fro among the various articles which were to be offered for sale. Dealers in second-hand goods were plentiful, and M. Hingant especially remarked one old man, who had a hook nose, bright little eyes, and a long, ill-combed, grey beard. This man, who was plainly a Jew, was engaged in opening the drawers of all the buffets, chiffoniers, and so on, taking a good look to see if they were quite empty, and even rummaging inside with his fingers.

Jean-Marie had no right to prevent him from acting in this style, still he began to watch him, for this conduct displeased him, though he scarcely knew why. Nor was he the only person who noticed the Jew's singular manœuvres, for another dealer, who was strolling about, suddenly approached and exclaimed sneeringly: "I say, Mardochée, what you are up to there is scarcely fair. Come, come, put back the trinket you just found in there, and keep your hands off."

The old Jew bestowed a malevolent look on the speaker, replied by an

inarticulate growl, and quickly withdrew his arm, which he had introduced
as far as the elbow into one of the drawers. " Come !" resumed the other
dealer, "you need not take the trouble to glare at me. We all know
you, Mardochée, and this wouldn't be the first time you've taken possession
of an article without waiting for it to be knocked down to you by the
auctioneer."

"That's false !" growled the dealer of the Rue des Canettes. " I have
been looking for an ebony chiffonier for a month past. I find one here, and
I certainly have a right to examine it."

" Yes ; but not to take what's inside it."

"There is nothing inside it."

"We will see that by-and-bye, when it is put up. You can bid for it
then, and for the thing you were handling inside of it as well, if you like.
In the meantime, move on, Old Clo's, or I'll call the superintendent, who
will show you the door."

Mardochée, usually yellow, now became green with rage ; however, he
walked quietly away, and stationed himself in a corner, where he could
keep his eyes upon the article of furniture he coveted. To tell the truth,
he was accustomed to such insults, for he was not a favourite with the
other dealers, who often united in teasing him. After all, it was simply
trade jealousy, for none of the dealers were strictly honest men.

M. Hingant had witnessed the scene, and had not lost a single word of
the edifying conversation between the two dealers, for a vague instinct
made him anxious as to the slightest incident connected with this sale.
He did not know what this hook-nosed old man had discovered in a
drawer which he, Hingant, felt sure he had examined with the others ; but
it was certain that the Jew had found something, and whatever that something might be, he had endeavoured to appropriate it. This was enough
to furnish Hingant with abundant food for reflection, and to induce him
to keep sharp watch on the bearded dealer, who was a perfect stranger to
him, for he had not caught sight of him on the occasion of his visits to
Billebaude, and he did not for a moment suspect that Mardochée was ever
hidden behind his old clothes watching the comings and goings of the private
inquiry agent's clients. After taking a good look at the fellow Jean-Marie
came to the conclusion that he was not worthy of notice, being merely a
dealer in second-hand goods—nothing more or less. Still the ex-magistrate
felt a strong desire to go and ascertain what the chiffonier contained ; but
he was so ill at ease in the somewhat disreputable crowd which filled the
room, that he did not care to attract attention. After a little thought he
decided to watch the piece of furniture until it was offered for sale.

This chiffonier, as Mardochée styled it, was a product of Parisian industry, dating from the Empire or the Directory, and made in the detest-
able style which was in vogue in the early part of the present century.
It comprised a sort of massive table, supported by bronze feet, and surmounted by a ponderous structure in ebony, with folding-doors, deep
drawers, and shelves. It might have been used with equal convenience as
a lady's workstand, a cabinet for coins, or as a book-case. From afar it
still looked tolerably handsome, but close inspection showed that it was
falling to pieces. M. Hingant distinctly remembered having seen it in the
room formerly occupied by Marthe's mother, and he was almost certain that
he had examined it carefully and found nothing inside. It was scarcely
probable, therefore, that the old Jew had lighted on some object which had
escaped previous notice.

However this may have been, the old magistrate's reflections were interrupted by a commotion in the crowd. The auctioneer had entered the room, accompanied by his clerk and followed by his crier, while the men whose duty it was to bring the goods forward formed a sort of rear-guard. The crowd of people hastened to take up their positions—some seated on rush-bottomed chairs and some standing in front of a long table, forming a sort of line of intrenchment, which the public had no right to pass. The auctioneer, attired in black and wearing a white cravat, ascended the platform, on which his desk was perched, with the solemn tread of a judge, and bestowed a majestic glance on the throng, while the clerk put his papers in order, and the crier talked familiarly with an old-clothes' woman of his acquaintance.

M. Hingant did not care to sit down, but he drew near a group of intending bidders in order to be within hearing. As for old Mardochée, he remained hiding in his corner, with his eyes and ears on the alert, his back bent, his chin buried in his beard, and his hands in his pockets ; he looked exactly like an owl perched just outside his hole and awaiting the passage of the bird he wishes to devour.

The auctioneer, probably thinking that he had made due impression upon the feminine dealers below him, suddenly seized his hammer with an Olympian gesture, and struck three blows to announce the opening of the sale. The crier instantly raised his voice, reading with wonderful volubility a kind of prefatory " puff" which spoke of the sale of a quantity of rich and superb household furniture, almost as good as new. The old magistrate had never before witnessed the doings of a Parisian auction-room, and in his simplicity he believed that this glowing description was a favourable augury for the success of the sale. However, the illusion was short-lived. As usual, the bids began with the household utensils, and the absurdly low prices at which these things were knocked down enabled M. Hingant to conjecture how extremely small the sum total would be. The crier bawled aloud the sums offered by the dealers, who in the various intervals joked together and underrated the goods, and Hingant began to regret having advised Marthe to let the things be sold. Everything indeed was disposed of at absurdly low prices, and in the twinkling of an eye ; and one might almost have sworn that there was a tacit agreement between the dealers, to the effect that the spoils offered to their rapacity should be shared at the least possible expense.

To compete with these fellows, it was necessary to possess a thorough knowledge of auction-room customs, and the justice of the peace was a novice in such matters, being even ignorant of the signs which are so familiar to the frequenters of sales of this kind. Meanwhile the auctioneer pursued his task with a bored air and without waiting for bids, the blows of his hammer falling like hail. Like a general who judges at a glance the importance of the conflict in which he is about to engage, the auctioneer had promptly come to the opinion that the sale would be a tame one, and so he wished to have it over as soon as possible. There was not a rich connoisseur in the crowd ; the furniture was worn and old-fashioned, and there was very little profit to be obtained from such a day's work, especially so soon after a formidable insurrection. Before Hingant's eyes there passed, in rapid succession, various antiquated clocks, faded curtains, rickety arm-chairs, and even the writing-table containing the secret drawer. None of these articles were honoured by any competition among the dealers. Each article was placed upon the table. The crier announced the upset price. There were two or three bids, and in a moment the article was sold—the various belongings of the deceased Moulinier, caught up by brawny arms, being straightway consigned to the store-place behind the auction-room.

Hingant, now quite resigned, made no attempt to interfere, but he did not lose sight of Mardochée, who as yet had neither moved nor opened his mouth. Suddenly, however, the monotonous voice of the auctioneer was heard saying to the porters : "Put that pretty ebony chiffonier upon the table—yes —that one over there, behind the large wardrobe with the glass door. Come, come, make haste."

The old Jew evinced no excitement on hearing these words, but M. Hingant, who was still watching him, saw him leave his corner and draw near to the desk behind which the auctioneer was enthroned. It was not difficult to guess his object. He evidently intended to bid ; and nothing more was needed to arouse Hingant's flagging interest.

In the meantime the porters had fetched the chiffonier, and placed it upon the long table, to enable the people present to examine it more closely. "Gentlemen," began the auctioneer, probably glad of an opportunity to enliven the sale, "here at last we have a really artistic article—a chiffonier with compartments, a table with a folding leaf all of pure Empire style massive ebony, and in excellent condition. All that is wanting are two or three handles to the drawers."

A few women in the crowd responded with derisive laughs to this facetious description, but the majority of the spectators remained unmoved. "Come, gentlemen, how much for this artistic affair—an old chiffonier, almost new ? With a few repairs, it will be worth a thousand francs if it is worth a penny." This time there was a general outburst of merriment. "Make haste, make haste, gentlemen," urged the auctioneer. "Will you start at five hundred francs—four hundred ? I think I hear three hundred."

"Three hundred ha'pence," sneered a woman and this was the only response. Hingant was anxious to bid, but a sort of timidity prevented him from speaking first ; besides, he had no idea of the real value of the article, and feared he might do the Moulinier estate an injury by bidding too small an amount.

"Fifteen francs," at last growled old Mardochée, in a voice that seemed to come from his boots.

"Fifteen francs ?" exclaimed the auctioneer. "You must be jesting, gentlemen. Fifteen francs would scarcely pay for the ebony used in the manufacture of this little masterpiece."

"Then keep your masterpiece," muttered an Auvergnat dealer, who had just purchased, at an absurdly low figure, the shovels, tongs, irons, and saucepans of the late M. Moulinier.

"So it's decided, gentlemen ? Well, we will start the chiffonier at fifteen francs ; but make haste, if you please."

"Fifteen francs, gentlemen, fifteen francs; that is for nothing !" chimed in the crier.

There was a profound silence ; the assemblage evidently lacked enthusiasm, although the dealer who had so severely reproved the Jew before the sale began, whispered to his neighbour : "I have a half mind to bid a franc more, just to make the old fellow wild."

"Bah !" was the reply ; "let him alone. What use is it for us to spoil each other's game ?"

"We are losing time, gentlemen," resumed the auctioneer. "One more bid, and I will knock it down. There is no response. Then on the part of the owner I bid twenty francs. It sha'n't be said that at one of my sales only fifteen francs was given for a superb chiffonier of pure Empire style, with a table—"

"Twenty-one," whispered Mardochée.

"Twenty-one francs, eh; that's very little, but I promised to knock the lot down at the next bid."

"Thirty francs," murmured M. Hingant in a husky voice.

It was time he spoke for the auctioneer had already raised his hammer. "That's right, gentlemen," said he. "You are waking up a little. Thirty francs—thirty francs are offered."

"Thirty-one," resounded like an echo from the Jew's beard.

"Forty," responded Hingant.

"Look out!" whispered Mardochée's enemy to his neighbour, "an outsider is bidding; we must look alive."

"Let us pay him for interfering," replied his neighbour in the same tone. And he made a sign to the auctioneer, who announced : "Forty-five francs are bid, gentlemen, for the Empire style chiffonier, and that is very cheap."

"Six," rejoined the dealer of the Rue des Canettes.

"Forty-six are offered."

"This man certainly has hidden reasons for persisting," thought the old magistrate, and he cried in a resolute tone : "Sixty francs."

The dealers stared at each other, and one man said : "I should like to look at the chiffonier."

The porters pushed it across the table, and the speaker began to open the drawers and examine the panels. "See, gentlemen," began the crier, "how beautifully it is arranged and neatly put together. Look! examine it. That will cost you nothing."

"Hallo! there is a big book inside," said one woman who had profited by the permission to examine the interior.

"Ah! I suspected as much," muttered Marthe's friend. "That's why the old scoundrel is so anxious to purchase the article ; and yet, how can he possibly have suspected—" Hingant did not finish this soliloquy, but the following reflections flashed across his mind : "What strange chance has led that ragged great stranger to attach such great importance to the possession of a book left in a drawer? Does this book contain an explanation of the mysterious document written by M. Moulinier? And, above all, how can this volume have escaped the careful search I made on two different occasions?"

This last problem was soon solved. By peering over the heads of the people seated in front of him, M. Hingant could see in the side of the chiffonier, and it was plain that the principal compartment had originally been divided by a vertical partition, which had fallen amid the jar of removal and transport in a springless cart, so that the volume formerly concealed behind it had abruptly come to light. At the same time Jean-Marie caught a glimpse of the book itself, and saw that it was a thick octavo volume, corresponding perfectly with the description given by the prophetic Galmard. The woman who had discovered it was holding it in both hands, and seemed to be so embarrassed by her discovery that a loud laugh resounded down the whole line. "Hand it here, Jean," said the auctioneer to the crier. "This is out of my line, but as it is an odd volume, my colleague in the

108 A FIGHT FOR A FORTUNE.

book department will excuse me for not sending it to him in the Rue des Bons-Enfants. I will offer it for sale by-and-bye."

"Why not put it up with the chiffonier?" some of the dealers asked, sneeringly. "The two will make a pair."

"Well, with the chiffonier, if you like," replied the auctioneer. "That will expedite matters; Jean, put the book back into the drawer, that is, unless someone wishes to examine it."

"That isn't worth while. The paper will always do for a grocer to make up screws," cried a wag.

Hingant made no objections. He could not verify the truth of Galmard's predictions at that moment, and he trembled at the thought of missing an opportunity of becoming the owner of the precious volume. "We were saying then that we have here a beautiful piece of antique furniture, with a number of drawers, one of which contains an odd volume," resumed the auctioneer. "What was I offered, gentlemen?"

"Sixty francs," replied the crier.

"Sixty-one," sighed Mardochée, faithful to his modest increase of a franc per bid.

"Eighty," said Jean-Marie, boldly.

"Eighty francs," repeated the crier. "That's nothing for a massive ebony chiffonier, Empire style."

"They are mad," muttered the Auvergnat dealer, who only bought tongs and saucepans.

"Perhaps not," replied his neighbour. "The book is perhaps worth a deal of money."

"I know nothing about that; it isn't in my line," was the reply.

"Nor do I, but old Mardochée is a shrewd fox, and if he bids, he must have an order from some collector, and it certainly isn't for that old wooden rattle-trap."

"No, Mardochée is no fool; but, all the same, there's an old gentleman behind him who is going to make him pay dearly for his prize."

"I know that, and I am going to amuse myself by tormenting them a little," and the dealer shouted in thunder tones: "Eighty-two francs and a half."

These words were followed by a grimace addressed to the Jew, who ran his trembling fingers through his beard, which stood out like a hog's bristles, and then added half a franc to the bid first made. "Eighty-three francs," proclaimed the crier.

"Gentlemen, gentlemen!" exclaimed the auctioneer, "it is ridiculous to think of bidding fifty centimes in connection with a rare piece of furniture, which, probably, figured at Malmaison or the Tuileries, and very possibly belonged to the First Consul."

This hazardous supposition was evidently intended to make an impression upon M. Hingant, whom the auctioneer supposed to be a greenhorn. He indeed thought he had struck home when he heard that gentleman reply with the imposing amount of two hundred francs. Jean-Marie did not care in the least about the First Consul, but he wished to end the matter. He gave his adversary a stealthy glance, and saw that he turned pale, which seemed to him a good omen. An all but admiring murmur greeted this bid, and the auctioneer, astonished by his success, but scenting a lucrative competition, exclaimed triumphantly: "Two hundred francs, gentlemen, two hundred francs, and we shall not stop there."

While he waved his hammer, Mardochée kept his little grey eyes fixed on the darkest corner of the room. One would almost have sworn that he was looking for some one to ask advice. This entirely escaped the notice of Jean-Marie, who was anxiously waiting for the decisive word to fall from the lips of the auctioneer ; but instead of this desired conclusion, he heard the Jew say, "Two hundred and five." If he were bidding for some person concealed about the room this person must have made him a sign to go on, for he made the bid quite cheerfully.

"Two hundred and twenty," retorted M. Hingant, who was bent on winning the day. There were certainly excellent reasons for his being determined to obtain possession of the book at any price, but the excitement engendered by the feverish atmosphere of the auction-room also had its effect upon him. This is a malady well known to all those who have competed with a rival for a rare book or a long-coveted picture.

"Two hundred and twenty-five," now sighed Mardochée.

"Two hundred and fifty."

"Fifty-five."

"Three hundred," cried Jean-Marie.

This bid made the Jew pause and he again began fumbling his beard.

"It is becoming amusing," said the dealer who disliked him.

"Not so very amusing," growled his neighbour. "Perhaps we are missing a good bargain."

"There is still plenty of time for you to bid. Go ahead, old fellow." But the saucepan purchaser lacked courage, and, instead of bidding, he blew his nose. "Gentlemen," said the auctioneer solemnly, "it is a pleasure to conduct a sale in the presence of persons who know how to appreciate beautiful articles, but time presses, and I have the honour to inform you that I am about to knock the lot down. Going at three hundred francs ! three hundred francs ! I repeat it for the last time."

"Five," said the persevering Mardochée, softly.

"Three hundred and five !" repeated the auctioneer, with a persuasive look at Jean-Marie and at the same time raising his hammer.

Hingant saw that it was ready to fall, and he had only time to cry : "Four hundred francs ! "

"Five," said the invincible son of Israel.

"Once, twice," exclaimed the auctioneer. "No one bids in front of me. Going, going—"

"Four hundred and twenty."

The hammer paused but two inches from the table at the very instant when Jean-Marie opened his lips. The old magistrate had changed his tactics, hoping that by making a smaller advance each time, he would weary the patience of his adversary, but Mardochée, following his example, this time bid two francs instead of five, and Hingant, annoyed and resorting again to extreme measures, cried out : "Four hundred and fifty."

This time, the auctioneer, while flourishing his hammer, turned to the Jew, and if Hingant had been less excited, he would, perhaps, have perceived the exchange of certain winks between them.

"Six," exclaimed the Hebrew.

"Five hundred ! "

"Five hundred and ten ! "

"Five hundred and ten ! You hear, gentlemen ? Going at five hundred and ten. Come, the last bid—"

The old magistrate was on the point of making this last bid, when someone standing behind him struck him so violently on the shoulder that he turned round; if he had only turned and then faced about again, there would have been no great harm done, for the auctioneer, instead of striking the final blow, was engaged in making those little demonstrations with his hammer, which always precede the irrevocable decision. He lifted this hammer, lowered it to within three inches of the table, raised it again, and let it describe all sorts of capricious curves in mid-air. One would have thought him the conductor of an orchestra, leading a body of musicians with his bâton. It was evident that the love of his profession had won the day, and that he took great interest in this obstinate contest. Consequently he did not care to knock down the article in spite of the mute entreaties of Mardochée's tiny eyes. On the contrary he was waiting for the stranger to bid, and trying to tantalize him. Unfortunately, however, Hingant, on turning round, found himself face to face with the last person he expected to meet in such a place: Maître Galmard, in person, Joseph Népomucène Galmard, attired in black, freshly shaven, with bright eyes and smiling lips.

"A strange meeting, indeed," exclaimed the advocate; "I certainly had no idea of finding you here, but you are going in for curiosities now, I presume."

"No, I will explain everything to you in a moment," hastily replied Jean-Marie, at the same time trying to face about, and catch a glimpse of that terrible hammer.

But Galmard, holding him by the lapel of his coat with one hand, passed the other affectionately round his waist, saying, as he did so: "Ah! you may say what you like, my fine fellow, you are certainly going in for curiosities, unless you have come to purchase some furniture for a lady." And he laughed so boisterously, that the crier bawled, "Silence, gentlemen!"

"I assure you that you are mistaken," stammered Hingant, crimson with anger, and still struggling.

"Five hundred and ten are bid," cried the auctioneer, who was beginning to grow impatient. "Five hundred and ten. Do you hear, gentlemen?"

"In Heaven's name, release me," entreated poor Jean-Marie; but his persecutor pretended not to hear him, and clung so tightly to his coat-collar, that the unfortunate ex-magistrate could not even turn his head. The scene greatly amused the dealers, and the gentleman, who purchased saucepans, exclaimed: "Serve the old fellow right. He'll miss his bid, and that'll teach him not to poke his nose in our affairs again."

"I warn you, gentlemen," now cried the auctioneer, "that this is your last chance. For the third and last time—"

Hingant could not see the hammer, but he felt that it hung suspended over his head, and despair gave him strength to cry: "Five hundred—"

He intended to say five hundred and fifty, but the word fifty stuck in his throat, for a loud knock cut the sentence in twain. The auctioneer, tired of waiting, had just struck the decisive blow, uttering the word "sold," as he did so.

"Ah, good Heavens!" murmured Marthe's protector, who could not have felt greater consternation had he heard his death-warrant read.

"Why, what is the matter with you, Jean-Marie? Are you ill?" inquired the lawyer, hastily restoring his old friend to liberty, as soon as he was no longer in need of it.

"Let me alone," said the ex-magistrate, curtly.

"No, no, you are ill, I am sure of it, and I won't leave you. The air is stifling here. Take my arm and let us go outside. The fresh air will do you good."

"Let me alone, I tell you. You don't know, you cannot understand—"

"An ebony chiffonier, and an odd volume—five hundred and ten francs—to Monsieur Mardochée. What street?" inquired the clerk in a nasal voice.

"The buyer will pay and remove the articles himself," replied the auctioneer, to whom the old Jew had just whispered a few words.

"He is taking it away—all is lost!" sighed the unfortunate Hingant, striking his forehead despairingly with his clenched hand.

"You must be losing your senses," laughed Galmard. "'He is taking it away,' what do you mean by that?"

But Jean-Marie, instead of listening to his consoling friend, remained in a despairing attitude, with his arms hanging down, and watched the movements of Mardochée, who had just finished counting out his five hundred and ten francs, plus the expenses, on the auctioneer's desk. Having done this, the bearded Israelite engaged with the porters in a short colloquy, which Jean-Marie could not hear, though he beheld the result of it with the utmost grief. Mardochée consigned the chiffonier to the storeroom, placed the book under his arm; and then turned to leave the place, not in the least disturbed by the sneers and ridicule of his brother dealers. On his way out, he passed close to the two friends, but one would have sworn that he and Galmard had never seen each other before. Hingant, on the contrary, trembled on coming in contact with his fortunate opponent, who was quietly retiring with the coveted book; and an inspiration suddenly occurred to the old justice of the peace. "Sir," he said, catching the Jew by the sleeve, "will you sell me that book? I will give you a hundred francs above what you paid for it."

Mardochée paused; but instead of replying, he began to look at Hingant with an astonished air. The latter thought that the noise had prevented the man from hearing him, for the sale was proceeding, and the blows of the hammer resounding. "I will give you six hundred francs for the volume," repeated Jean-Marie in a louder tone.

The Jew did not reply even this time, but shook his head, and tapped his ears with his fingers, after which he gently disengaged himself, forced his way through the crowd, and speedily gained the door. "He is as deaf as a post," said Galmard, with an air of conviction.

"Deaf? Why, didn't you hear him bidding against me just now. He wanted to poke fun at me, but I won't be humbugged. I am going after him—"

"To repeat your senseless offer of six hundred francs for a shabby old book."

"Yes. Let me go. I can overtake him."

"I sha'n't allow you to commit such an act of folly, Jean-Marie. It is bad enough to offer extravagant prices for old furniture, but to ruin yourself for a book is absurd, and it sha'n't be done," said the lawyer, who was now holding Hingant by one of the buttons of his waistcoat.

"Do you mean to drive me mad?" cried Hingant. "Don't you understand that this furniture belongs to Mademoiselle Moulinier, the orphan in whom I am interested.

"The orphan!" repeated Galmard, in feigned surprise.

"And that this book probably contains the key to the cipher I showed you."

"Ah, yes, yes ; now I understand, the cipher—Mademoiselle Moulinier, eh? You are right, my friend. We must lay hands on that scoundrel."

"Come with me, then, instead of preventing me from starting off in pursuit of him," said Jean-Marie, sacrificing 'his waistcoat button in his struggle to free himself from his companion's determined grasp.

"I am coming. I am coming. Why didn't you speak sooner ?" growled the wily lawyer.

Had M. Hingant been more familiar with auction-rooms, he would have known that the dealers who frequent them are acquainted with each other, and that by questioning one of them, he might easily have learnt the name and address of the bearded Jew. But he didn't think of resorting to this simple method, and Galmard took good care not to suggest it. On the contrary, the asp of the Rue de Cléry hurried Jean-Marie towards the staircase, which was unfortunately very crowded, so that the two friends lost five minutes more. When they reached the Place de la Bourse together, they looked round them on all sides in vain ; they saw no sign of the old Jew. He and the book had both disappeared.

XIV.

HINGANT was strongly inclined to tear his hair, but such a frantic demonstration of despair not being allowable in the street, he confined himself to striking his forehead, while he exclaimed : "Fate is against me, that's certain. It seems to be ordained that I shall only commit acts of folly."

"Come, come, don't lament," said Galmard, in a much calmer tone. "You know very well that it will do no good."

"It is very easy for you to talk, but if you were in my place—"

"If I were in your place, instead of worrying and raising my fist to heaven, I should beg my old friend, Joseph Galmard, to take the matter in hand, and friend Joseph would take the necessary steps to discover this old scoundrel with the goatee."

"What ! you think that would be possible ?" exclaimed Jean-Marie, inclined to clutch at the slightest hope.

"Nothing is impossible with patience and money. Now, I am patient, and you are rich, so that—"

"I don't pretend to be rich, but I am willing to pay twenty times its value for this book if necessary."

"I don't doubt it. You have just offered six hundred francs, and it is certainly not worth five."

"But recollect, my friend, that Mademoiselle Moulinier's fortune depends upon our possession of this volume."

"And Mademoiselle Moulinier's is very dear to you ; very dear, for the searches you undertake will probably cost you a lot of money," said the advocate, laughing in a manner that was not altogether pleasing to Marthe's protector.

"That matters little provided you are successful," said Jean-Marie, drily ; "but I don't see how you will set to work—"

"What a child you are ! Do you suppose for a moment that a man like myself is embarrassed by such a trifle ?"

"I have great confidence in your ability, but I doubt whether you will really be able to find this man and prevail upon him to part with that book."

"Oh ! I'll find him, never fear ; as for his parting with the book, that depends upon the price you are willing to pay for it."

"I will give a thousand francs, if necessary," rejoined the ex-justice of the peace.

"With the expenses that'll make fifteen hundred, for I shall be obliged to set my agents on his track."

"Very well. But, now I think of it, if instead of buying the volume, you asked the Jew to let you examine it. I fancy that a few moments would suffice to explain the meaning of the document you copied the other day."

"Jean-Marie," cried the advocate, "you are growing stupid. Do you really imagine that this fellow paid five hundred and ten francs for an odd volume merely for the pleasure of increasing his library ? "

" Then you think—"

" I think that the Jew was employed by some one who had an interest in obtaining possession of the book," said Galmard, authoritatively.

" And this person can be only an enemy of Monsieur Moulinier, a man acquainted with the secret, and anxious to preserve it for his own benefit. You are right ; we shall obtain nothing from his agent."

" I didn't say that. I only said that the Jew must know that the book is of exceptional value, so that unless he is well paid he won't allow me a glimpse of it."

" Yes ; he will realise that he would be betraying his employer," said Jean-Marie.

" Certainly ; but treachery has its price like other goods, and by paying this fellow better than his employer we may succeed in our object. The question is to act promptly."

" Yes, but it may be too late already ; this old scoundrel may have joined his employer and delivered the book into his hands ? "

" That would be unfortunate, certainly, still everything would not be lost, for we could bribe the old Jew to give us his employer's address and name, which might perhaps remind Mademoiselle Moulinier of some circumstance likely to set us on the right track. The question is to act according to circumstances. Come, will you give me *carte blanche ?* "

" Certainly."

" Then don't detain me, for each moment is of importance."

" So you are going—"

" To hunt that Jew up ? Call on me to-morrow at three o'clock, and I will tell you how I have employed my time." As Galmard spoke, he bestowed a cordial hand-shake on his friend, and, to prevent any new objections, stopped a passing cab, sprang into it, and disappeared before M. Hingant had time to recall him.

The ex-magistrate remained standing outside of the auction-rooms very perplexed ; and, as is usual, when a man has done anything foolish, he reviewed with infinite regret the unfortunate incidents of the sale. At last an idea, which ought to have occurred to him much sooner for it was so very simple, flashed through his mind. It would have sufficed for his purpose if he had only learned the title of the book. He could then have procured another copy or have consulted one at a public library ; but unfortunately, in the excitement of the contest, he had overlooked that point. However, perhaps, it was not too late; the auctioneer had held the book in his hands, and, although he had not announced its title he might certainly have read it and still remember it. Impressed by this idea, Jean-Marie hastened back to the auction-room. But fate was decidedly against him that day. His conversation with his friend Galmard had occupied fully a quarter of an hour, and when he reached the auction-room again, the sale was over, the dealers were going off, the auctioneer had left the place, and only the porters remained. Hingant made some inquiries, but gained no further information than the address of the auctioneer. This was not much, but he resolved to make the most of it and took himself off in his turn.

While he was returning home, pondering over the difficulties of the situation, Maître Galmard was rolling along towards the Rue de Cléry, in a capital humour. He rubbed his hands, and constantly looked out of the cab window to see if he was approaching home. In point of fact, his destination was only a short distance from the Place de la Bourse, and he must have been greatly pressed for time to have indulged in the luxury of a cab. On approaching the house he lived in, he had the satisfaction of seeing Mardochée's grey beard ahead. The old man had sturdy legs, and he had hurried on so fast that he had arrived in advance of his worthy patron. Galmard stopped the driver a short distance from the house, paid him, and joined the Jew who was waiting for him in the hall. "I have it," said Mardochée, with a diabolical smile, at the same time showing a corner of the book, which was carefully concealed under his long overcoat.

"I know it, and I am well satisfied with you, Mardochée," replied the lawyer. "But you shouldn't have remained here. If my country friend had taken it into his head to accompany me home, we should have been caught." Mardochée rolled his eyes as if reproaching himself for his blunder, and mumbled a few words of excuse. "Come, come, I am not angry with you, old fellow," resumed Galmard. "All's well that ends well. But don't let us dawdle here. The place is dangerous, for my friend may turn up unexpectedly. I am going upstairs; follow me. I want to speak to you."

Mardochée did as he was bid, and followed close on the heels of the lawyer, who fairly flew up the staircase in his eagerness. Galmard lived on the third floor, and his modest apartments were entered by an ante-room hardly large enough to accommodate three persons; then came a parlour, which also served as a waiting-room for serious clients, and one next entered the famous consulting-room. Clients only saw these three apartments and were at liberty to suppose that the lawyer expended his money on those they did not see; the fact is, the offices were very meagrely furnished. There were no velvet arm-chairs or mahogany desks; not even a clock adorned with a historical figure, as at the private inquiry agent's office in the Rue des Canettes. The unfortunate beings who were obliged to seek the expensive advice of this lawyer sat upon straw-bottomed chairs, signed their engagements upon a painted wooden table, and learned the time from their own watches, if the latter were not already in a pawnbroker's keeping. This Lacedæmonian simplicity contrasted strikingly with the pretentious adornments of Billebaude's apartments. The valet eclipsed the master; and this was logical, for Billebaude had need to dazzle the clients who came to him only second-hand, while Galmard, for whose advice embarrassed persons came of their own accord, found it to his interest to play the part of an austere jurist. The petty tradespeople who formed the great majority of his clients would have taken him for a charlatan if he had indulged in a showy dressing-gown or handsome furniture;

but they accorded him implicit confidence when they beheld in him what may be called a threadbare advocate, for his soiled white cravat, his creased dress-coat, and old black trousers, shiny from long wear, seemed to them conclusive proofs of integrity—a man so poorly clad, and living in such a scantily furnished house, must necessarily be honest and skilful.

Mardochée knew what to believe on this point; but he approved of these austere surroundings as much as he despised the charlatanesque manners of Billebaude, and he always entered the scantily furnished sanctuary of his chief employer with pleasure and even awe. This child of Israel loved and practised humility through instinct as much as calculation.

As he passed, he bestowed a discreet smile on Galmard's servant, an old, toothless creature, with but little resemblance to Billebaude's trim waiting-maid, and harmonising admirably with the advocate's miserable surroundings. Galmard had undoubtedly chosen her on this account. He had no great merit in feigning poverty, for his one passion was avarice—a sordid and yet logical avarice—for though he could sleep upon straw, and make his dinner off a black radish, he also knew how to draw a large sum of money out of his cash-box, and risk it whenever he had any promising scheme on hand. "Has anyone been here?" Galmard curtly asked his servant.

"Yes, several people; but I told them to call again to-morrow," growled the female Cerberus. "Will they come or not? That remains to be seen. But certainly closing the shop is no way to attract customers."

"Never mind; never mind; I know what I'm about," said the lawyer, pushing Mardochée into the private office.

"Here is the book," sighed the venerable Jew, "and one may say that it has cost its weight in gold."

"That is your own fault. If you had been quicker, we could have had it for nothing."

"I assure you, sir, it wasn't an easy matter. Recollect what a crowd there was. Besides, I was obliged to examine all the articles of furniture; and very fortunate I think myself in having discovered the book at all, for I had previously searched everywhere and found nothing."

"Well, well, I don't complain. You did the best you could, and we have the book. Where is the change out of the thousand-franc note I gave you this morning?"

Mardochée drew a greasy portfolio from his pocket. "Five hundred and ten francs, and the auctioneer's expenses," he said, "amount to five hundred and thirty-seven francs fifty centimes, which is equivalent to twenty-six twenty-franc pieces, or at least twenty-five, allowing for the premium on gold."

"I did not bring you here to hear an essay on banking," the lawyer interrupted. "Let us settle our accounts and you go back to your shop."

"Isn't my day's work worth the sixty-two francs fifty centimes that remain in my pocket?" asked the Jew in a wheedling tone.

"Ah, you never forget yourself, you old Barabbas," replied Galmard, frowning. "Sixty-two francs for spending a couple of hours in an auction-room. You don't mince matters. How many dozen old coats would you have to sell to make up that amount?"

"Old books sometimes bring better prices than old clothes," retorted Mardochée, with a meaning smile.

"Well, well," said the advocate, "I don't haggle when I'm well served, so I will make you a present of what you ask. However, mind you per-

form your duties properly. Keep your mouth shut. Billebaude must
know nothing about what occurred to-day."

"There is no danger of that. I don't like him well enough to make him
my confidant."

"You are right to be discreet, for if any tattle comes to my knowledge,
I shall he very angry, and you'll spend a nasty moment. Is there anything
new in the Rue des Canettes?"

"Nothing."

"Has Billebaude's friend, the man with the gold spectacles, called
again?"

"Twice during the past week."

"And the insurgent he concealed in the garret, has he been there again?"

"No; I have an idea that he won't show himself again."

"What makes you think that?"

"Because the wearer of the spectacles and Billebaude are both too well
pleased to be rid of him. If he did return, he would meet with a bad reception."

"I think as you do, that he won't return," said Galmard, in a tone of
conviction. "But now one more question: Does the auctioneer who conducted the sale know you?"

"By sight, yes; but I don't fancy he knows my name."

"Then he hasn't got your address?"

"I wasn't fool enough to give it to him. You must have heard me tell
his clerk that I would pay cash and take the goods away myself."

"Yes, but your brother dealers know you, eh?"

"Only slightly. I have very little to do with them, and they do not
often see me at the sales. There are two or three who call me old Mardochée."

"Including the man who caught you while you were rummaging in the
drawer?"

"Yes, and I will pay him for his impudence some day. He keeps a
second-hand shop near the Pas-de-la-Mule in the Marais. He knew me
when I was a jeweller, and he has a grudge against me because I once got
the better of him in a bargain; however, he hasn't troubled himself about
me since I left his neighbourhood, and it is more than a year since I met
him."

"You, of course, understand why I ask you all these questions?"

"Oh, yes; it's plain enough. You want to know if there is any danger
of my competitor finding out my name at the Hôtel Bullon; but there's
nothing to fear on that score, and if he makes the attempt, he will have his
trouble for nothing."

"Unless you are in your shop when he goes to see Billebaude, for you
know that the old gentleman is one of our clients," said Galmard, after a
pause.

"Oh, yes, I saw him enter the house on the day he was pursuing the insurgent, and once afterwards also. But I'll take my precautions; I have good
eyes, and whenever I see him coming I shall creep into my den."

"That's right; but in case he should surprise and question you, how
will you get out of the dilemma?"

"I shall tell him I bought the book for a gentleman I don't know, but
who gave me the money in the auction-room, and went to wait for me
behind the Bourse."

"You are certainly shrewd, Mardochée. The story isn't a remarkable one, but I can think of no better one myself. Try to keep out of sight as much as possible. I have nothing more to say. You can go."

The bearded patriarch silently obeyed, withdrawing on tiptoe, with his hand pressed lovingly upon the sixty-two francs reposing in his waistcoat pocket.

"Now let me see what the book of the late Moulinier contains," said the lawyer, joyously, as soon as he found himself alone. The book was still on the corner of the table where Mardochée had laid it, and Maître Galmard only had to stretch out his hand for it. "Ah ! it is a volume of the Encyclopedia, Panckoucke's edition," he remarked, opening it at the title-page. "Who the devil would have guessed that ? My friend Hingant will search in vain. He will never imagine for a moment that the deceased Moulinier cultivated the philosophers of the eighteenth century, or that he concealed his secret in the ninth volume of their great work." And the lawyer, smiling at the thought that poor Jean-Marie was so far off the track, resumed : "After all, Moulinier had been a trader and belonged to the National Guard. Voltaire's opinions are in favour of that corps, so there is nothing so extraordinary about his having bought this book. But to work, to work !" With this conclusion Galmard opened a drawer of the table at which he was seated, and drew a bundle of papers from it. He soon found the leaf upon which Billebaude had faithfully copied the characters traced by Marthe's father ; and he laid this interesting document on the table beside the precious volume. It was not without great reluctance that the detective of the Rue des Canettes had relinquished it ; but the lawyer had demanded it with such threats that the unfortunate Billebaude had been obliged to hand it to him.

Before proceeding with his investigation, Galmard remained for a moment absorbed in contemplating the manuscript and the volume. He found himself somewhat in the situation of Ali Baba, examining the door of the cave in which the Forty Thieves had concealed their treasure, and hesitating to utter the "open sesame" which would make him possessor of the hidden wealth, for he firmly relied on discovering in this book, not merely full proofs of Billebaude's knavery, but also information in regard to the property left by the deceased Moulinier ; or, at least, the revelation of some curious family secret which would be of value to him. He had not risked six hundred francs for nothing. He had sown, he expected to reap ; and so it was not without emotion that he began his work. "Let us see," he muttered, looking at the sheet covered with figures ; "we have first, 636, 22, and 9. Seek, and ye shall find. I shall surely find, but what ? That is what I should like to know, for the first word will decide everything. If, for instance, it proves to be a conjunction, an adverb, or some technical term, my calculation will be erroneous."

As he spoke, he turned over the leaves in pursuit of page 636, which was near the end of the volume.

"Line 22nd," he muttered, on finding the desired page, and he began to count. "Now the ninth word," and he ran his forefinger along the line. "The ninth word is Marie," he exclaimed, after a moment, with a violent start. "The deuce ! I don't know what to make of that. Marie ! What does that mean ? That, certainly, is a singular way of beginning an important document, a sort of will." He counted the words over again with the same result, and then, with his elbows on the desk, his head on his hands, he began to reflect. He thought of his six hundred francs, and could not help admitting that he had been rather venturesome. Suddenly, however, his face brightened, and looking up, he exclaimed : "Well, I must be a fool, after all. The deceased is addressing a person of the female sex called Marie. There is nothing very strange about that. And this person can only be his wife or daughter. His daughter? No. Hingant told me her name was—Marthe ; yes, that was it. So it must have been his wife. And, really, it was quite natural for him to leave his last instructions to her ! However, his wife is dead, if I am not very much mistaken. Yes, for Hingant called that girl an orphan. Then, how is this? But, bah ! why do I rack my brain when I have only to continue my work to elucidate the whole matter. We will see—*videtimus infrà*, as we used to say at Rennes," murmured Galmard, again turning to his book.

After ten minutes of diligent investigation, he uttered a cry of triumph. He had just deciphered word by word the first line of the document with the following result : " Marie, you will here find directions to which I beg you will scrupulously conform." There was no longer any possible doubt. The paper contained the last wishes of M. Moulinier, and had evidently been intended for his wife.

Encouraged by this success, the advocate eagerly resumed his work, but he was obliged to take one word after another, and this was no slight task, for the figures, even in Billebaude's compact writing, covered nearly the entire sheet of paper. However, Galmard was not easily discouraged when he expected to reap a handsome remuneration for his work, and he would have laboured through the whole night rather than have left his task un-finished.

Besides, the operation was very like a voyage of discovery, and each new "find" encouraged him to persevere. At the end of an hour he had com-pleted nearly half of the work, noting down each word taken from the encyclopædia ; and he then stopped to rest and to read over what he had written. "You know that I am a ruined man," continued Moulinier, after the aforesaid introduction. "All I possess to-day is a small income—the principal of which is virtually irrecoverable. A certain Billebaude, formerly a banker, deprived me by fraudulent bankruptcy of two hundred thousand francs which I had deposited with him, and which was the only resource left to me. I might have dragged him before the courts, and had him condemned to the galleys, but I thought it better to compromise with him, and I agreed not to institute proceedings against him on condition that he would pay me or my heirs, the sum of six thousand francs annually. This man, who is a scoundrel capable of any crime, even of having me murdered, has hitherto kept his promise, but only from a fear of being denounced to the authorities. After my death, he will certainly try to shirk his obligations, and to make him carry them out, you must threaten to produce a paper which he has signed, and which contains a confession of his dishonesty. This paper, with other proofs of forgeries committed by him, has been intrusted by me to the keeping of Catherine Pirou, Marthe's nurse, who will give it to you whenever you ask for it. This Billebaude now calls himself a private inquiry agent, and resides at No. 59 in the Rue des Canettes ; you must let him understand that you are in a position to send him to the Assizes, in case he refuses to pay you. This is the only means of insuring a livelihood for yourself and your daughter whom you must acquaint with this secret. Having said this, I will now pass to a subject which affects you more particularly, and I am willing to point out to you the means of establishing your claim to the very large inheritance to which you may some day become entitled."

Here Maître Galmard's translation ended. He read the last sentence aloud, and exclaimed joyfully : "Now we have it !"

The interesting part of the document was close at hand, and this was the moment for pushing ahead. "Well," he exclaimed, tilting his chair with a complacent air, "I must say that I am lucky, and that Moulinier was a perfect fool. If instead of devising all these mysterious precautions, he had simply told everything to his wife, I should never have learnt anything, while I am now master of a secret for which Hingant will have to pay me dearly, if I consent to sell it to him. These retired merchants are strange creatures, upon my word ! Here's a fellow who makes a will in cipher, and who gives himself no end of trouble—all to what purpose ? To enrich me, to the detriment of his own family. Billebaude told me he was eccentric, and I agree with him. When I think of the time he must have spent searching out the words in this encyclopedia ! And what a deal of trouble with the proper names ! To coin Billebaude he had to look in the book for *bille* and *baudet*, and scratch out the 't' of the latter word. Ah ! it would have been an easier task to compose an epic poem, or a tragedy in five acts."

After indulging in this facetious remark, Galmard began to laugh heartily. But his gaiety was not of prolonged duration. He soon resumed a meditative attitude, and again began to study the paper before him. "A singular style for a husband to adopt in informing his better half of his last wishes," he muttered, after again attentively perusing the translation. "There isn't the slightest approach to familiarity in all this. It is written in the manner of a master givings his orders ; or, at least, of an offended husband who has not forgotten former wrongs. 'I am willing to point out to you the means of establishing your claim to the very large inheritance to which you may some day become entitled'—that is to say : 'I am under no obligations to a woman against whom I have grave cause of complaint ; still I consent, out of pure charity, to give her some good advice.' It is plain that Madame Moulinier had grievously offended him in some way or other, and that he had no affection for her. As for Mademoiselle Marthe, Hingant's ward, Moulinier doesn't appear to have had any very great fondness for her. In fact, his paternal love seems to be decidedly lukewarm, as witness this sentence : 'This is the only means of assuring a livelihood for yourself and your daughter'—*your* daughter ! Ah, ah, that is not very tender talk, and in my opinion Moulinier had very grave suspicions in regard to the parentage of that charming girl. It is as well to note all these points before proceeding further."

The information so far yielded by the document was not particularly novel, save as regards the fact that Marthe's nurse, who must be found, held proof of forgery committed by Billebaude. However there was the promise of a revelation respecting an enormous inheritance, and this made Galmard's mouth water. He resumed his work with intense eagerness. The pages of the encyclopedia fairly flew under his agile fingers, and his pen scratched noisily as he noted down upon the paper each word extracted from the book. He indeed had the appearance of an augur consulting one of the Sibylline volumes. At the end of a quarter of an hour of diligent labour he had translated the following paragraph : "In my last conversation with you, I explained to you where you would find this document after my death and how you might decipher it with the help of Volume IX. of the encyclopedia, but it was impossible, for reasons you can readily understand, that there should be any allusion to the inheritance in question. Although

I consent to give you on this point certain information by which, I persume, you will not fail to profit, I am most unwilling that it should fall into other hands than yours or your daughter's. I cannot take too many precautions to prevent this, so I have devised another plan."

"Upon my word, this is too bad!" exclaimed Galmard. "How could he have devised any better means than this cipher for preserving his secret? This man certainly missed his calling. He was certainly born to super-intend the cipher service at the Ministry of Foreign Affairs. How-ever let us see what his new combination is."

It was not without considerable anxiety that the indefatigable Galmard returned to his work, for this last sentence seemed to indicate unforeseen complications. His face lengthened, and he bestowed redoubled care upon his translation. He examined each word attentively, and even pronounced it aloud for fear of making a mistake. "For this reason," the late Moulinier went on to say, "you will have to look elsewhere for the words indicated by the following figures."

Maître Galmard turned ghastly pale at this announcement, and muttered between his teeth : "What! Elsewhere! What can this mean? Can he have had the infernal idea of changing the key to his cipher. No, a retired trader couldn't have been so cunning. Let us go on."

He did so, with the following result : "From the close of this sentence, the figures correspond with the words in a book with which you are familiar."

"But with which I'm not," exclaimed the advocate, in perfect agony. "If he doesn't designate it more plainly than that, all is lost! I will see, however," he added, again turning to the pages with a trembling hand. "It is the book I gave to your daughter on the day of her first communion."

"Ah, the rascal!" muttered Galmard, in consternation—"the scoundrel! People ought not to be trifled with in this manner. But it is impossible. There must be something more; and, by continuing my translation, to the end—"

Again he set to work, turning over the leaves and counting, but the re-sult now proved disastrous. The next figure corresponded with the word "metaphor," and the following one with the word "cocoanut." There was no longer any hope. The thread was lost, and the lawyer had no means of recovering it. "I have lost my six hundred francs!" he said, in a voice husky with emotion. "The fiend take Hingant and the simpleton he pro-tects." Then, angrily pushing aside the book, Maître Galmard rose and began to stride up and down his office. "Yes; go on, fool, go on!" he growled. "Go and run after that little jade, and ask her to lend you her catechism."

The insults he heaped upon himself were of some use, for they soon calmed him. "And why not?" he suddenly exclaimed, pausing in his furious pro-menade. "What prevents me from obtaining an introduction to her through that fool Jean-Marie? The game isn't lost, after all, perhaps."

Having arrived at this consoling conclusion, the advocate reseated him-self at his table, and fell into a profound reverie. The case did not seem so desperate. He had often triumphed over greater obstacles, and to save his six hundred francs he felt capable of doing almost anything. After prolonged reflection he rose up, locked the paper and the translation in a drawer, closed the book, placed it in a cupboard which served him as a book-case, and muttered with a sneer : "Moulinier has played me a shabby trick but his daughter shall pay for it."

XV.

M. HINGANT became greatly depressed in spirits after his unfortunate adventure at the auction-rooms. The visit he paid on the evening of the same day to the auctioneer yielded no information whatever in regard to the competitor who had become the fortunate possessor of the coveted volume. The purchaser was not known to the auctioneer, who was extremely courteous, however, and very anxious to help an ex-magistrate. He promised to make some inquiries of the frequenters of the Hôtel Bullon, declared that the old Jew would certainly return if only to claim the ebony chiffonier, and promised to give instructions to the porters, who would certainly discover who the Jew was, and, if necessary, follow him home. In short, he made so many promises that if he had fulfilled merely half of them, Mardochée would certainly have been captured.

But, unfortunately, matters turned out very differently ; the bearded Jew did not call for the piece of furniture he had purchased, and though the obliging auctioneer made some inquiries of various dealers in second-hand goods, they could not, or would not, give him any information on the subject.

The interview which M. Hingant had on the following day with his friend Galmard yielded no better result. The advocate declared with wonderful assurance that the mysterious purchaser did not reside in Paris, but must have come from the provinces to play them this trick, and have already returned home. Galmard had not given up all hope of discovering him later on, but time, considerable time, would be required. The lawyer had his reasons for speaking in this evasive manner. He wished, in the first place, to lay his hand on the book from which he could learn the rest of Moulinier's intentions ; but, being by no means sure of success, he intended to reserve as a last card the chance of selling Volume IX. of the encylopedia to Hingant for a very handsome sum, that is, when all other means of recovering his disbursements had failed.

However, the ex-magistrate had begun to lose faith in his friend's ability, and to think him a little too much inclined to boast of the skill and zeal of the agents he employed. Billebaude, too, had fallen considerably in his estimation, for despite his formal promise to find Marie Bréhal, he had not made the least progress in the matter. Hingant was indeed fast coming to the conclusion that the Parisians were all alike—prodigals so far as words are concerned, but accomplishing little or nothing. Instead of employing agents it was better perhaps to have recourse to legal measures, to which he, Hingant, was naturally inclined.

At the same time, another revulsion of feeling, as it were, had taken place in Jean-Marie's mind. For nearly a month he had been devoting himself exclusively to Marthe, and his devotion to her interests had almost caused him to forget the object of his visit to Paris. The privateersman's will was still in his pocket-book, and he often thought of it ; but since his departure from Cancale he had done little to insure its execution. Moreover, he had greatly neglected the moral side of the question, that is to say, the study he had intended to make of the characters and conduct of his deceased friend's heirs-at-law. It seemed to him that the time had now come to devote himself exclusively to the fulfilment of the mission he had assumed. Mademoiselle Moulinier had begun leading a new life, and seemed to be getting on very comfortably. She and Paul Gilbert met almost every day at the home of their mutual friend, and their marriage was only deferred until this friend had succeeded in rescuing from the remnants of M. Moulinier's fortune the sum necessary for the young girl's dowry. Hingant had taken good care not to tell them of the disappointment he had experienced at the auction-rooms; on the contrary, he tried to persuade them that everything was progressing favourably, that they were on the eve of an important discovery, and that he would soon have some good news to announce to them. Lovers are always confident, and Jean-Marie was delighted that they so readily indulged in these hopes. As he had fully decided to insure their happiness by an innocent subterfuge, there was no longer any necessity for anxiety in regard to their future. Still, as a methodical man, he wished to fix upon a date when he might consider his double mission ended. It was now July, and he gave himself until the end of October to come to a decision in regard to the privateersman's property. If, by that time, he had not succeeded in obtaining any information concerning Marie Bréhal, and if his old friend's nephews had behaved themselves creditably, he was determined to leave them to the peaceful enjoyment of their fortune, and return to Cancale. He also resolved that the marriage of the two young people who had become so dear to him should not be deferred beyond that time. When September arrived he intended to announce the miraculous recovery of some forty thousand francs, left by the late Moulinier, but which, it is needless to say, he proposed taking from his own fortune. A few weeks would suffice for the formalities insisted upon by the War Department, and the ex-justice of the peace would then be able to return to his old house, his garden, and his servant, Brigitte, taking with him the promise that the newly married pair would as often as possible share his quiet life.

This return home, after making two dear ones happy, and satisfying any lingering scruples of conscience, was a prospect which fully reconciled Hingant to his prolonged sojourn in Paris. When he had once adopted a plan he followed it out, and he began by utterly renouncing the chimeras which had already cost him so much time. The lost book, the bearded Jew, Billebaude and his gorgeous dressing-gown, Galmard and his ingenious conjectures—all these were soon almost forgotten. The advocate paid him several visits, made all sorts of glowing promises, expressed, in the warmest terms, his sympathy for Mademoiselle Moulinier, and requested an introduction to her; but Jean-Marie remained unmoved, and turned a deaf ear to all proposals. "If you find the key to the cipher," the ex-magistrate said to his friend, "you can rely upon the sum you asked for. If your agent discovers Marie Bréhal, I will reward him generously; but I confess that I rely very little upon success in either undertaking; besides, I am growing weary of Paris, and long to climb into the Saint Malo diligence— so pray make haste." This was all he would say, and his words decided Galmard not to change his plans, but his mode of attack.

Having settled matters on this side, Hingant went to the Palais de Justice, where he found a magistrate who greeted him very cordially, and promised to institute a search for a certain Marie Bréhal, of whom nothing had been heard since 1815. The old justice-of-the-peace then had an advertisement inserted in the newspapers, and depended on Providence to do the rest. After thus satisfying his conscience, he began to think of resuming his intercourse with the privateersman's nephews, whom he had rather neglected during his stay in Paris; for, though he had called upon them soon after his arrival there, he knew very little about the life they were now leading. Charles Dugenêt was the only one whom he had seen at all often since the adventure outside the Val-de-Grâce hospital. The privateersman's handsome nephew had lost no time in calling upon M. Hingant and his ward, whom he supposed to be rich, and of whom he had secretly resolved to make a conquest. But Marthe received him very coldly, although good Jean-Marie knew not why. Jacques Le Planchais nominally resided on the Ile Saint-Louis, a long distance from the Rue Bergère, and was never found at home. François Dolley, on his side, lived in the Rue Feydeau, but it was almost as difficult to find him indoors. As for the stylish niece, Mathilde Pelchat, she had rented and furnished a rather nice suite of apartments in the Rue d'Amsterdam, where Hingant had called but once, and then only when the idea of asking her to take some lessons of Mademoiselle Moulinier occurred to him. The ex-belle of the Café Militaire had no desire to miss such a fine opportunity to learn the accomplishments of society, and the arrangements were instantly concluded. Marthe was to spend two hours, three times a week, with her pupil, who was exceedingly anxious to become the friend of a young lady of good social standing. It was in this way that M. Hingant had spoken of his adopted daughter, and this was more than enough to make the ambitious Mathilde dream of initiating herself into the mysteries of good manners by imitating so perfect a model. She felt some disappointment when she saw that Marthe's manners were as simple as her toilet ; still all went well, and the old magistrate soon thought of utilising Mademoiselle Pelchat to renew his intercourse with her cousins.

He insinuated to her that it would be appropriate to assemble them occasionally in her drawing-room, a suggestion which was eagerly adopted, and one Saturday, the charming Mathilde invited Marthe Moulinier and her protector to honour with their presence a little family gathering which would take place that same evening. M. Hingant was careful not to miss such an excellent opportunity of having a chat with the various heirs of his friend Mériadec, so he eagerly accepted Mathilde's invitation. Mademoiselle Moulinier, however, displayed much less enthusiasm, and even made several timid objections so far as her own acceptance was concerned. She was in deep mourning, and it seemed scarcely proper for her to attend anything like a *soirée*. But her pupil declared that it was only a small family meeting which no strangers would attend, and that a refusal would cause her deep regret. Still, Marthe would probably have persisted in absenting herself, had she not seen that her adopted father was extremely anxious for her to accept. Her repugnance to attend the gathering was due in a great measure to the certainty of meeting that odious fop, cousin Charles, against whom she had such just cause of offence Unfortunately, it was too late to acquaint M. Hingant with the young fellow's unseemly conduct, and Marthe, reduced to silence respecting the scene in the Rue des Feuillantines, could think of no good pretext for excusing herself.

Jean-Marie, in his efforts to explain the real cause of his ward's reluc-tance, finally came to the conclusion that she regretted the loss of Paul Gilbert's daily visit, and he thought himself very clever in suggesting to Mademoiselle Pelchat that she should also invite the lieutenant. Nothing could have pleased Mathilde better. She delighted in the company of young officers ; besides, she was not sorry of a chance to see if Mademoiselle Moulinier had any good taste ; and Marthe then accepted, thinking that the presence of her betrothed would perhaps put an end to the unwelcome

attentions of the handsome Dugenêt. Eight o'clock was the appointed
hour, Mademoiselle Pelchat promising to have her three cousins at hand,
and M. Hingant pledging himself to bring Paul Gilbert.

It may seem strange that the old magistrate should not have hesitated
about encouraging an intimacy between the privateersman's niece, whose
position was ill-defined, and a well-born, well-bred young lady like Marthe.
Mathilde was of age and independent, as her respectable parents had long
since passed out of the world. So she had a right to live as she liked, and
she had early availed herself of the opportunity by consenting to preside at
the desk of the Café Militaire, in the midst of a cloud of tobacco smoke,
the jingle of glasses, and the click of billiard balls. It is only just to add
that the gossips of Saint Malo had never accused her of any greater sin
than coquetry, and that at the time she came into possession of her fortune,
she was about to marry a young non-commissioned officer who stood well in
his regiment, and who had saved some little money. Hingant had consequently come to the conclusion that the companionship of Mademoiselle
Pelchat was not dangerous for his ward. The fact that Saint Malo had
never spoken against Mathilde was a sufficient guarantee for the old justice
of the peace.

But Saint Malo is not Paris, and in Paris very little credence is placed in
the virtue of young women who lead isolated lives. Mathilde was not long
in finding this out after her arrival in the city of her dreams, for she had
met with a great deal of difficulty in finding suitable apartments. The
doorkeepers looked at her askance when she asked to rent an apartment,
and invariably replied that the landlord did not wish to have any single
lady in his house. This reception surprised the ex-queen of the Café Militaire, all the more, from the fact that she had provided herself with a respectable companion. The person who had gladly consented to serve as
her chaperon was the widow of a drum-major, and was named Madame
Tromblas. She had formed Mademoiselle Pelchat's acquaintance at the
Café Militaire, where her husband had sometimes taken her, and that brave
warrior's premature death had only strengthened the friendship between
the two women in spite of the disparity in their ages and bringing up. The
Widow Tromblas accompanied Mathilde in all her house-hunting expeditions,
although her presence did not seem to have any beneficial influence on the
greetings of the doorkeepers. It is true, however, that the widow was not
remarkable for the elegance of her attire or the distinction of her manners.
She had a loud voice, a brick-coloured complexion, a stalwart form, and
man-like tread; and in her chintz dress and cap decked with gay ribbons,
she looked very like a cuirassier disguised as a woman.

However, Mathilde had finally succeeded in finding a tolerably pleasant
suite of apartments on the fourth floor of a new house in the Rue d'Amsterdam. Madame Tromblas took all the duties of furnishing upon herself,
and conducted the business in such an expeditious manner that by the end
of a fortnight Mademoiselle Pelchat was prepared to receive the most
brilliant society. Indeed, the drum-major's widow solemnly assured her that
the wife of a general of division would be well content with so splendid an
abode. But this much is certain; the brilliant society did not come. Only
the cousins were now and then entertained in the coquettish drawing-room.
No ladies called, although Mathilde tried hard to ingratiate herself with her
neighbours residing on the lower floors of the house, and she was compelled
to acknowledge that Paris did not equal her expectations.

Her only diversions were driving through the Champs Elysées in a cab, and spending her evenings at a theatre. Madame Tromblas, on her side, consoled herself for this isolation by an excellent table, for she had assumed charge of the culinary department; still this did not prevent her from accompanying Mathilde whenever the latter went out. The piano lessons afforded some relief to the monotony of daily life, and the pupil seemed to be full of affection for her young teacher; but to Mathilde's great disappointment, she made even less progress in her intimacy with Marthe than in the art of music. Mademoiselle Moulinier was a teacher of exemplary patience, but she talked very little; and as soon as the lesson was over she took her leave, without even waiting to listen to the stories that the widow tried to relate to her.

Such being the state of affairs, M. Hingant's suggestion respecting a family gathering was eagerly adopted, and no time was lost in organizing the entertainment. The heiress once more began to dream of social successes, for she hoped this would not be the end by any means, but that the day would soon come when the circle of her guests would be enlarged. In the meantime, as one is obliged to be content with what one has in this world of ours, she dispatched a messenger to each of her three cousins; and as she did not lack shrewdness, she took good care to say in her notes that she wished to speak to them on business. She distrusted their willingness to gratify her partiality for society, and rather relied upon their well-known solicitude for their pecuniary interests.

An important question respecting the evening's entertainment remained to be decided, that of the requisite refreshments. Madame Tromblas voted for kirsh punch, but Mathilde assured her that this beverage was not in vogue in refined society. Finally, it was decided to serve tea and cakes, to which the widow insisted that warm *pâtés* should be added, declaring that at the house of the colonel, in whose regiment the late Tromblas had served for fifteen years, *pâtés* had invariably figured on the bill of fare at all similar entertainments.

On the evening of the memorable day everything was in readiness long before the appointed hour. Mathilde had chosen her prettiest dress, the *chef d'œuvre* of the best dressmaker in Saint Malo. The Widow Tromblas had donned a fiery red costume, cut audaciously low about the neck, and a cap trimmed with black and yellow ribbons, which strongly resembled a dragoon's helmet. The servant, a Burgundian girl whom the ladies had secured at an agency, was also gaily attired. Flowers had been placed upon the balcony, for there was a balcony to the apartment, in accordance with the fashions which prevail in the erection of new buildings. The water was singing merrily in the tea-urn, which stood in the middle of the table, surrounded with such a profusion of plates loaded with cakes, that one would almost have fancied one's self in a pastry-cook's establishment. And meanwhile Mathilde, quivering with anticipated delight, did not take her eyes off the clock, so eager was she for the arrival of her guests.

M. Hingant was as punctual as a soldier. The clock was striking eight when he entered the room with Mademoiselle Moulinier on his arm. It would be a difficult task to describe the enthusiastic transports and overwhelming courtesy that greeted them both. Mathilde caught hold of both of Marthe's hands and the drum-major's widow ventured to kiss her upon both cheeks. M. Hingant, touched by this reception, congratulated himself on the success of his scheme, and inquired after the cousins. "Oh, they are coming," said Mathilde. "There can be no doubt about it for they know that Mademoiselle Moulinier will be here. Charles will surely come," she added, glancing at Marthe, who did not even deign to smile. "But it seems to me—I hoped you would have brought—"

"Ah! Lieutenant Gilbert. He has promised to join us as soon as he is at liberty. He is on duty to-day, and you know that an officer—"

"I think I hear the bell now. Perhaps it is he," interrupted Mademoiselle Pelchat, blushing slightly. The throbbing of Mathilde's heart had quickened unnecessarily, however, for it was not the young officer whose approach was heralded by a cautious ring at the bell. The servant suddenly threw open the drawing-room door, and exclaimed: "Madame, here's your cousin!"

Mademoiselle Pelchat's cheeks turned from pink to scarlet, for this style of announcing people was not that which she had been trying to inculcate. But the Burgundian girl was thick-skulled, and in spite of several rehearsals she had not been able to remember her mistress' instructions respecting social usages. "You will never be anything but a simpleton," exclaimed Madame Tromblas, indignantly. "You were told to announce the gentlemen by name, but you burst in with a 'Here's your cousin!' Upon my word! in the Twenty-ninth the corporals wouldn't tolerate you as a waiter."

"I can't help it. I do not understand all your manœuvring," muttered the servant, before disappearing.

M. Hingant bit his lips to keep from laughing, and even Marthe could not repress a smile. As for the mistress of the house, she would have been glad to sink through the floor.

Fortunately for her, Charles Dugenêt's entrance afforded a welcome diversion. The handsome cousin advanced hat in hand, and smiling. He was freshly gloved, shaven, curled and pomaded, looking as trim as if he had just emerged from a band-box, and one could read on his face his perfect contentment with his person and attire. The fact is he had undergone a change since his arrival in Paris. At Saint Malo he had looked like a café loafer, whereas now he strongly resembled a hairdresser. This was certainly progress, and Mathilde envied him his perfection. "Mesdames! Mademoiselle! Monsieur!" he exclaimed, punctuating with a low bow each of these words, which were pronounced in the most deferential tone.

"Good evening, my dear Charles," said Hingant, with his accustomed cordiality.

"It is very kind of you, cousin, to have come early," remarked Mathilde, simperingly.

"Young man, punctuality is the chief requisite in a soldier, and in civil life one should never keep beauty waiting," said the Widow Tromblas, gravely.

Marthe's only reply to the fop's genuflexions was a cold bow. But he was not easily disconcerted, and he took a seat between the two young ladies without displaying the least embarrassment. "May I venture to ask for whom you destine this pretty work?" he asked, touching the embroidery which Marthe had just opened upon her lap to the profound astonishment of Mademoiselle Pelchat and the widow, for these good people had very vague notions about fashionable customs, and thought it very strange that at a soirée, as they styled their entertainment—Sam Weller would have said a "swarry"—one should do anything at all except gossip and eat cakes.

"This work is intended for the tradesman who ordered it," said Marthe, without deigning to raise her eyes.

"Oh, mademoiselle, you are jesting," cried the young fop.

"Not at all, sir. I embroider for a living, as well as give music lessons to Mademoiselle Pelchat, your cousin," responded the orphan, drily.

This straightforward but entirely unexpected declaration caused a sudden silence, but Mademoiselle Moulinier had not made it without a motive. She was too clever not to perceive that M. Dugenêt still believed her to be a rich heiress, and she wished to put an end to his intrigues, and thought she had now succeeded. There had been no conversation respecting her position when Charles had called upon M. Hingant. Joan-Marie, although surprised by his ward's manner, did not deem it advisable to add any explanation. Mathilde fidgetted on her chair, but did not know how to give a fresh start to the conversation. The widow coughed and blew her nose loudly. As for Dugenêt, he mentally resolved to find out the truth from M. Hingant, and to change his tactics if he learned that Marthe was really penniless. In that case he might make love to her without any idea of matrimony.

The silence was still unbroken when reinforcements arrived in the person of cousin Dolley. He entered the room almost unperceived, for the servant girl, fearing she might commit some fresh blunder, abstained from announcing him, and contented herself by pushing him into the room. The ex-schoolmaster had not made the same progress in foppishness as handsome Charles and pretentious Mathilde, he still wore the gold spectacles, brown coat, and stout laced shoes he had sported at Cancale; while his face had become thin, and his skin as yellow as a pumpkin's rind. In fact he looked careworn. He approached the group with the annoyed and hesitating step of a man who finds himself among persons he had not expected to see; but when his eyes fell upon M. Hingant his expression changed. He went straight up to him without even waiting to bow to the ladies, and seized hold of his hands with an eager cordiality that his anxious face belied. It was very evident that he was wondering what the worthy old man was doing there, and why Mathilde Pelchat had planned this surprise. "You were not expecting to see me here, were you, my dear François?" inquired M. Hingant, with his genial smile.

"I must admit that—that my cousin neglected to warn me—"

"It was I who begged her to invite you, for, really, for some time past I have been reproaching myself every day for neglecting my poor friend Léridan's nephews. Since my arrival here I have scarcely had a day to myself. And then, Paris is so large. But now I have got hold of you, and I earnestly hope we shall frequently have a sort of family gathering, for I make so bold as to regard myself rather in the light of a relative. Our party will be complete to-night. Here are Mathilde and Charles, and although Jacques has not yet arrived, he will be here before long."

"Jacques! what! is Jacques Le Planchais coming?" exclaimed Dolley, with ill-disguised emotion.

"Certainly. I was anxious to see you all, and your cousin very kindly engaged to assemble you all at her house. But it is time I made you acquainted with Mademoiselle Moulinier, the daughter of one of my friends.' This assertion was not altogether accurate; but the old magistrate rightly judged that this was not a proper time to enter into an explanation of his ward's real position.

François bowed awkwardly, and Marthe bent her head without laying aside her embroidery. This third heir to the privateersman's property impressed her no more favourably than the others. She had bestowed only a glance on him, but it was enough for his pale face to excite her antipathy, and her instinct warned her that none of these persons were worthy of M. Hingant's friendship. "It seems to me it is time to pay our respects to the jam tarts," exclaimed Madame Tromblas.

The respectable widow was beginning to find the evening tiresome, and thought it time to pass to more solid enjoyment. "Not till the tea is ready," muttered Mathilde. "People don't do that!"

"Oh, they did it in the Twenty-ninth," retorted the widow, aloud. "Come, we will attack the cakes while you pour the hot water on the tea. This young lady and your cousin will keep me company, and the older people can talk politics if they like. You, my dear, will take charge of the tea, and be sure not to forget to add a drop of rum."

Hingant and cousin Dolley had no thought of talking about affairs of state, but they had several things to say to each other. "We are the old persons, my dear François," said the ex-magistrate, gaily. "If it suits you, we will leave Mathilde to do the honours of her drawing-room to the young folks, and go out on the balcony for a little fresh air."

François asked no better; so they went and seated themselves side by side among the flower-pots with which Mademoiselle Pelchat had adorned her balcony. "This was an excellent idea of yours, Monsieur Jean-Marie," said Dolley. "I have some information to ask of you."

"Upon what subject, my friend?"

"Respecting a certain private inquiry agent, who lives at No. 59 Rue des Canettes."

M. Hingant was certainly not expecting to hear François Dolley ask him for information concerning the detective of the Rue des Canettes. He had never spoken of his visits there to any one, nor of his acquaintance with Galmard; and the ex-schoolmaster was certainly the last individual whom he would have suspected of being aware of these matters. Consequently the question disturbed him a little, and he would have been glad to evade it, but deception was not his habit. "You mean, I suppose, a man named Billebaude, who resides at the place you mention."

"Precisely."

"Well, I have had some dealings with him, but—well, but how could you have heard of that?"

"I can readily understand your astonishment, Monsieur Jean-Marie; still the matter is very simple, and if you will allow me, I will explain myself."

"If I will allow it! Why, my friend, that is the very thing I beg of you to do, for I am truly curious to learn why you have spoken of this person."

"Then I will proceed to explain. You are probably aware that I came to Paris with the intention of investing my capital to advantage."

"Your capital! I thought that your uncle only left you landed property."

"That is true; but one can easily raise money on landed property, especially in our province."

"Humph! in revolutionary times like these, it is not an easy matter, even in our part of France."

"Oh, yes, Monsieur Jean-Marie, it is. I have borrowed one hundred thousand francs upon a first mortgage, from a Saint Servan notary, who would not have lent me fifty crowns when I was merely a teacher."

"A very unwise thing, my friend; and if you had consulted me—"

"Not so very unwise; for the three farms that fell to my share don't yield me three per cent on their value; and here, in Paris, in six months time, I shall perhaps double my hundred thousand francs."

"I doubt it, my dear François. Speculations are always risky, and at this particular time they seem to me terribly dangerous. But was it that man Billebaude who advised you to do this?"

"He did more than advise me. He called my attention to a particular branch of business, from which a person is sure to derive large profits. I have had proofs of it. In less than a fortnight he has enabled me to clear a thousand francs. You see that with a dozen such operations in the course of a year, I shall do very well."

"Then you have trusted this man with a sum which represents nearly half of your entire fortune?"

"Yes, Monsieur Jean-Marie, and I don't regret it, I assure you."

"But, my dear fellow, this is a grave imprudence. How can you, at your age and with your experience, believe for a moment that money will yield such an exorbitant rate of interest without your incurring great risk of losing it? If it was at the Bourse that you achieved this miraculous result—"

"It was not at the Bourse."

"Where, then?"

"In private diplomacy," replied Dolley, with superb assurance.

For a moment, M. Hingant thought that the ex-schoolmaster had lost his senses, and with mingled gentleness and compassion, he said to him: "Explain yourself more clearly, my friend, for I confess that I don't understand what you mean by 'private diplomacy.'"

"It is the art of discovering certain secrets of interest to certain parties, and of selling the said secrets to them," said the ex-schoolmaster, repeating almost word for word the definition given him by Galmard.

"What secrets?"

"Oh, they are of more than one kind. In the first place, there are estates for which there are no claimants—"

On hearing this response, Hingant pricked up his ears, and began to think that cousin François was not so mad as he appeared. "Can it be," he secretly wondered, "that Billebaude has spoken to him about the inquiries I charged him with?" And he resumed aloud: "All this, my dear fellow, is Hebrew to me; but we are wandering from our subject. You promised to tell me how you learned that I was acquainted with the private inquiry agent in the Rue des Canettes."

"I am coming to that, Monsieur Jean-Marie—I am coming to it. Monsieur Billebaude, in giving me an interest in his business, seemed to care less for the money I could advance, than for the personal help I might give him. It was agreed that I should utilize my capacities by taking charge of a part of the business. Judge, then, of my surprise, when I learned that the very first case confided to me concerned the best friend of my lamented uncle—a friend whom I love and revere."

"If it is to me you allude, be brief, my friend, I entreat you. To what work do you refer?"

"That of finding a certain Marie Bréhal, the heiress to a large fortune, and whose whereabouts should be communicated to Monsieur Hingant, formerly justice of the peace at Cancale."

The blow struck home. Hingant could not help blushing, and half a minute elapsed before he felt able to reply. It must be admitted that Dolley's manœuvre was both bold and clever. The country bumpkin whom Billebaude had imposed upon, was none other than François, who, since the day when Galmard had initiated him into the Bréhal affair, had passed

E

through many tribulations. The first idea that had occurred to him was that the woman whom M. Jean-Marie wished to find was a person in whose favour a will had been made by his deceased uncle, and as he had no desire of losing his inheritance, he had determined not to find her, although he might pretend to be trying to do so. All this had considerably influenced him in deciding to enter the firm of Billebaude & Co., for he wished to keep himself informed of all that was learnt in regard to the mysterious heiress. However, to his great disappointment, his fellow-partners had given him no further information about Marie Bréhal, and this for the excellent reason that they themselves knew next to nothing; so they pretended that their attention was engrossed by other and more urgent matters. Galmard had certainly given him a thousand francs to compensate him for his first efforts, which solely consisted in writing to several notaries in the neighbourhood of Saint Malo, in order to ascertain if they had any knowledge of Mademoiselle Bréhal's existence. This was liberal pay, as the replies had all been negative ones. So Dolley could not complain; and after being foolish enough to exchange his hundred thousand francs for a receipt from Billebaude, he had contented himself with watching and waiting.

Still he was a prey to the most intense anxiety, and he had more than once thought of going to M. Hingant and stating the case to him. He had such implicit confidence in the old magistrate's honesty that he had no doubt of being able to obtain a truthful reply. However, the situation was so delicate, that he had not yet dared to risk a visit to M. Hingant, but when chance brought them together in Mademoiselle Pelchat's drawing-room, he suddenly resolved to put the difficult question. Jean-Marie was quite unprepared for this onslaught, and if he disliked deception, on the other hand, how could he tell this poor devil of a schoolmaster, enriched by an unexpected windfall, that he, Hingant, his uncle's friend, had no other aim but that of despoiling him for a stranger's benefit. He would also have to confess that the will was in his possession, excuse himself for not having burnt it, and expose himself to countless reproaches. From this prospect the old magistrate naturally recoiled: and fortunately a new idea occurred to him. "My dear fellow," he said, carefully choosing his words, "I take no interest in anyone but Mademoiselle Moulinier, the young girl sitting there beside your cousin, and I have no reason for concealing from you that I did ask my former schoolmate, Galmard, and his partner, Billebaude, to interest themselves in her behalf."

"What! Was it merely to establish her right to the property of—of whom?" asked Dolley, divided between fear and hope.

"It was a question of discovering where her father's money was invested, and these gentlemen are now engaged in the task. I was not aware that you were their auxiliary, my dear François, but I can only congratulate myself that such is the case, for I feel sure you will do all in your power to insure our success."

"Don't doubt it, Monsieur Jean-Marie, for I am yours body and soul. Shall I undertake the case alone, or shall I merely stimulate the zeal of my partners? You have only to speak." A heavy weight was raised from his heart, since he had learned that Mademoiselle Moulinier did not lay claim to his uncle's estate.

"I scarcely know what to answer," replied M. Hingant. "Galmard gave me hopes that have not been realised. Once I thought I held a clue. I almost had my hand upon a book which can give us the information which is needed to put us on the track."

" A book ! "

" Yes. Connected with the matter, there is a story—altogether too long to be related here. But I will give you all the particulars if you will call on me, as I sincerely hope you will. "

" I will come to-morrow afternoon, and I will make every effort to secure the volume you are looking for. What kind of a book is it ? "

" A large octavo book, in an old-fashioned binding, and the leaves are red edged. If I only knew the title all would be well ; but, unfortunately, it was purchased at an auction sale by an old grey-bearded Jew, whom Galmard has not been able to find. "

" An old Jew ? Do you know his name ? "

" We heard him called Mardochée, but we are not much the wiser for the information. However, here is my young friend, Lieutenant Gilbert, entering the drawing-room. Come and let me introduce you to him. "

François promptly rose, and followed M. Hingant into the drawing-room, saying to himself as he did so : " Mardochée—that is a name it would be as well to remember ! "

It was indeed the young officer who had just entered the drawing-room. This time, the servant had not even dared to make her appearance, but after opening the front-door for the new-comer, she had hastily retreated to the kitchen, for fear of subjecting herself to further reproaches from Madame Tromblas. Gilbert, somewhat surprised at not hearing his name announced in a drawing-room which he was entering for the first time, advanced slowly, looking about him in search of some familiar face, but unable, at first, to see anything but the startling cap of the drum-major's widow. M. Hingant promptly came to his relief, however, and undertook the necessary introductions. François' and Charles's manner was rather cool, especially that of Charles, who already scented a favoured rival ; but Mathilde greeted the lieutenant with marked eagerness. She had always had a weakness for soldiers, and her face brightened at her first glance at a uniform. As for Madame Tromblas, she expressed her delight by standing straight up, like a sentinel presenting arms, and muttering : " A handsome soldier ! He would have done honour to the Twenty-ninth. "

The fact is, the lieutenant would have been considered a handsome officer anywhere. He no longer carried his arm in a sling, and his wound had left no trace but a slight pallor. His supple figure, regular features, expressive eyes, silky black moustache, and white teeth, made a deep impression upon Mademoiselle Pelchat, who was exceedingly susceptible to the personal charms of the sterner sex. Perhaps she showed this a little too plainly. Marthe, as usual, was reserved almost to coldness. She merely exchanged a look with Paul, and then quietly resumed her work. Lovers understand the language of the eyes, wonderfully well, and this single glance had sufficed for them to say to each other : " How disagreeable to be obliged to spend our evening with these people. "

" Do you expect anyone else, little one ? " the widow inquired addressing Mathilde.

" It seems to me everyone is here, now, excepting cousin Jacques, " said Mathilde, simpering.

" Le Planchais ! Oh, he won't come, " exclaimed François Dolley.

" The fact is, he is not particularly fond of tea, " sneered the handsome Dugenêt, who professed intense scorn for the low instincts of the absent heir.

"But I wrote to him that I wished to see him on important business," remarked Mademoiselle Pelchat.

"Yes, as you did to me," the schoolmaster replied, irouically; "but I fear that he has not received your letter, for he moves very often."

"Then it isn't worth while standing guard over the tea-urn any longer," remarked Madame Tromblas. "A little while ago I felt awfully empty, and now that I have eaten a tart, I feel as dry as touch-wood. Suppose we treat ourselves to a glass of rum grog? What do you say, lieutenant?"

Paul Gilbert bowed, and tried to smile, though he felt but little inclined to do so. Although not much accustomed to society, he had soon perceived that M. Hingant's friends were not people of good standing, and it annoyed him to see Mademoiselle Moulinier brought in contact with them. However, although he determined to avoid any possibility of a future meeting, this was not the time to show the repugnance with which they inspired him, for he could not bear the thought of wounding the old magistrate's feelings. The guests now seated themselves around the table, and in compliance with the importunities of the thirsty widow, Mathilde displayed all her graces in serving each guest with a cup of tea. She took advantage of the opportunity thus afforded her, to bestow one of her most gracious smiles upon Paul Gilbert, but the young officer did not even appear to notice her advances. He was furtively watching Marthe. It was evident, alas! too evident, that he was only thinking of her; and Mademoiselle Pelchat, vexed by his indifference, bit her lips until the blood came. This first touch of jealousy almost proved disastrous to the widow; for Mathilde, in her agitation, nearly spilt a cup of tea over the red dress. The fact is, the privateersman's niece had a very susceptible heart, and since setting aside the sceptre with which she had ruled the Café Militaire, she had been kept completely aloof from the charms of epaulets. Moreover, she had not renounced all hope of fascinating the hard-hearted soldier, for, on mentally comparing herself with Marthe Moulinier, she said to herself that M. Gilbert would show very poor taste in continuing to prefer her rival. How could a penniless girl, reduced to teach for a living, hope to compete with a wealthy beauty, who would bring her husband a dowry of two hundred thousand francs? While Mathilde was thus fostering a hope of winning the love of a decorated lieutenant, her cousin Charles was indulging in meditations of a similar character. His heart was still set upon the conquest of Marthe, with or without a dowry, and he was trying to think how he could oust the handsome officer from favour. As a beginning, he lavished upon Mademoiselle Moulinier a number of countrified attentions, which she entirely ignored, but which made Paul frown.

M. Hingant was not wanting in tact, in spite of his simplicity, and seeing that his friends were not pleased with the flirting turn which the conversation was taking, he hasteued to introduce a more general subject. "My friends," he remarked, collectively addressing the whole party, "I wish to interest you in a great project." Everybody looked at him, and Madame Tromblas, who was about to deposit a fourth lump of sugar in her tea-cup, paused to listen, with the sugar tongs in mid-air. "You like Paris," resumed the old magistrate. "I am aware of it, and I have nothing to say against the place, but I hope you have not all entirely renounced our dear province."

"The dear province is not particularly gay," sneered Charles.

"The ladies of Saint Malo are frightfully stuck up," added Mathilde, with a grimace.

" And I have business here," muttered Dolley.

" You, my dear François," continued Hingant, " will certainly have to be in Brittany by Michaelmas to settle your accounts with your tenants, for you are a sensible man. I suspect that Charles and Mathilde won't pay much attention to such matters ; but, perhaps, they will not object to a trip to Brittany, late in the summer, to rest a little after the pleasures of the capital ; so I hope to assemble all the relatives of my poor friend Léridan in my old home at Cancale, where I trust Mademoiselle Moulinier and Monsieur Gilbert will join us."

The invitation was received with smiles of condescension, rather than approbation ; and the drum-major's widow was the only one who made any direct response. " An excellent idea. I agree to it. The heat is suffocating in Paris, and the sea air will do me good," said she.

" As for our friend Jacques," resumed Hingant, without seeming to notice what little enthusiasm his proposal aroused, " I am sure I shall be able to persuade him to come. A seaman cannot stay on land long, and he will be delighted to meet our fishermen of La Houlle again."

" Humph ! I think you had better not rely upon him," growled the ex-schoolmaster.

" The fact is, he will not be any more likely to put himself out for Monsieur Jean-Marie than for me," remarked Mademoiselle Pelchat, rather bitterly.

" You must not be angry with him, my dear child," interrupted the peacemaker. " He lives a long way off. Besides, it is still early, and we shall, perhaps, see him this evening after all. But now I think of it, what is our friend Jacques doing in Paris ? How does he spend his time ? You must know, Dolley ; although I suppose he has not launched out into speculation like yourself."

" I ! " exclaimed Dolley. " I know nothing at all about him, and I beg of you to believe that I have not the slightest desire to know."

" What ! You think our friend Le Planchais—"

" I think he is leading a life that I don't at all approve of. But that is his business ; and providing he doesn't compromise me, I care nothing whatever about it."

" Nonsense, he isn't so bad as all that," said the widow. " I'd gladly pour him out a glass. Pass me the decanter of rum so that I may drink to the health of our dear Le Planchais."

" Here I am—Le Planchais ! Who wants to see Le Planchais ? " responded a thick voice at the end of the room.

Everyone turned, for the surprise was a strong one. Certainly Mademoiselle Pelchat's servant was not born to serve in fashionable society. She allowed persons to enter her mistress's drawing-room as one would enter a café. " We were just speaking of you, my dear Jacques," said Hingant, advancing towards the tardy guest.

" Better late than never. The more the merrier," said Madame Tromblas gravely.

" He's as drunk as a Pole. It'll be amusing," muttered Dugenêt.

" Salute, company ! " growled Le Planchais, approaching the ladies.

Then came a most astonishing climax. Marthe rose up, extended her hands, as if to ward off some terrible vision, and sunk fainting on the floor. At the same instant Le Planchais sprung back, and pushing M. Hingant, who endeavoured to detain him, roughly aside, darted from the room. The murderer and the daughter of his victim had recognized each other.

XVI.

ON the day following the family gathering which had begun so well and ended so badly, Mademoiselle Pelchat was engaged in animated conversation with her two cousins, Charles and François, in the same drawing-room where the sight of Le Planchais had caused such a scene. His abrupt disappearance and Mademoiselle Moulinier's swoon had been the signal for a general disbanding, and no one had thought of pursuing the assassin or even of asking for an explanation. M. Hingant, overcome with consternation, had only thought of his dear ward. Paul Gilbert, understanding nothing whatever of what had occurred, and exceedingly desirous, moreover, of escaping persons he disliked, had hurried out in search of a cab, and afterwards assisted the old magistrate in taking Marthe home ; so that the heirs of the privateersman were left to look at each other, scarcely knowing whether to laugh or grieve over the dramatic scene which Dolley alone was in a position to explain. Perhaps they would have exchanged opinions then and there ; for each of them, for very different reasons, felt the need of relieving his mind, but then the presence of the drum-major's widow interfered with anything like a confidential chat. Moreover, the worthy old woman on seeing Mademoiselle Moulinier swoon, had begun to utter frightful shrieks. Whether these were caused by emotion or by the jam tarts she had eaten, it is hard to say ; but she annoyed everyone so much by her groans that the party abruptly dispersed.

Mathilde, however, took care to appoint an interview with her cousins for the following morning, and at an hour when she had reason to suppose the worthy widow would still be sound asleep. Both cousins were punctual, for they were eager to discuss certain points of interest to each of them. The conversation began with some sharp reproaches which the ex-schoolmaster heaped upon Mathilde for having invited him at the same time as Le Planchais and M. Hingant. "It was a regular trap," he said testily, "and had I known I should meet that brute, Jacques, I would certainly not have come."

"It wasn't my fault," exclaimed Mademoiselle Pelchat, dolefully. "I am certainly sorry enough. It was Monsieur Jean-Marie who worried me until I consented to assemble all the family here, and we all have an interest in not quarrelling with him."

"True. But why didn't you warn me that I shouldn't be the only guest, and then I should have known what to do."

"But who could have suspected that the evening would end in such a tragical manner ? I certainly had no reason to think that Jacques had ever had any adventure with my music-teacher ; and even now, as truly as my name is Mathilde, I don't understand the meaning of all this fuss."

"Nor I," remarked Dugenêt ; "but I can't say that I care very much. It isn't Jacques that troubles me, but whether that little Moulinier will have any dowry or not."

"Indeed !" exclaimed François, ironically, "you fancy she fainted for nothing, and that our connection with Le Planchais won't injure us. And you, Mathilde, think you can invite the brute to your house without compromising yurself in the eyes of the police."

"The police ?" repeated Mademoiselle Pelchat, in alarm.

"What? what?" inquired Charles, almost as much dismayed as his cousin. "Has the wretch stolen anything?"

"No ; on the contrary, he is continually fleeced by the companions with whom he spends his time in wine-shops. He has something worse than a theft on his conscience, however. He has committed a murder."

"Good heavens!" groaned poor Mathilde.

"Impossible!" muttered Charles, sceptical as usual.

"It is a fact, my friends. On his arrival here, Jacques connected himself with some drunkards of his own stamp who enticed him into political clubs, and made him believe that he would enrich himself by dabbling in politics. They succeeded so well that when the June riots began, the fool took his gun and followed the others to the barricades. As he isn't very courageous, and didn't care to be the victim of a bullet, or a bayonet thrust, he bribed a doorkeeper, and concealed himself in a house near the Porte Saint-Denis. From there he could fire without running any risk, and he did not allow such a fine opportunity to escape him. With his first shot, he killed a captain who was marching at the head of a company of National Guards. The guards broke into the house in search of him, and he, rushing up to the floor above, entered the apartments of Mademoiselle Moulinier, the daughter of the captain whom he had just despatched to the other world."

"And she recognised him last evening at my house? I am ruined!" exclaimed Mademoiselle Pelchat.

"Ah, you are beginning to understand now."

"And I as well," said Dugenêt. "But why didn't she have him seized by her father's men while he was in her power."

"Because she knew nothing about the affair. He wasn't inclined to boast of what he had done, but presented himself as a poor wretch who had been forced into the rebel ranks against his will, and who was now trying to make his escape from a crowd of ferocious men who wanted to kill him. The girl believed his story, and opened a door by which he made his escape."

"This sounds like a romance," remarked Charles; "but she must have learned the truth afterwards, for a single glance at Jacques made her faint yesterday."

"Exactly ; and strange as it may appear, it was Monsieur Jean-Marie who told her everything. He was a sergeant in Moulinier's company ; and he saw him fall. There was but one thing he could not tell the girl, and that was the name of the murderer. Now he knows it."

"The deuce! This is serious, very serious. But how did you hear of it, Francois?"

"Well, I knew that Jacques had killed an officer on the Boulevard Bonne-Nouvelle, for the very good reason that he took refuge in my rooms, and told me about the whole affair. But I did not suspect that Jean-Marie was interested in the daughter of the deceased captain. However, by questioning the doorkeeper of the house on the Boulevard Bonne-Nouvelle, I learned some curious things."

"Is it true that the girl is poor?" inquired Dugenêt, who was particularly interested on this point.

"That, my boy, is another question which we will discuss by-and-bye. I will now return to Le Planchais, because I am anxious to convince you both that it is best to dispense with his society."

"Oh, there is no danger of my seeking it," muttered Mathilde.

"As you may very readily believe," continued Dolley ; "I didn't care to keep him in my rooms, especially as the affair had caused a good deal of talk, and the police were looking everywhere for the culprit ; so I took him to the honse of a friend, who consented to give him a room.   You think, perhaps, that he was glad to remain there quietly ?   Not at all.   He persisted in going out disguised as a workman, tippling in all the wine-shops, from which he generally returned too drunk to stand.   In short, he behaved himself in snch a manner that I begged my friend to get rid of him.   He was sent into the snburbs to live there till he wonld be got safely out of the country.   Judge of my alarm, however, when I learned last evening that he was expected here.   I cannot even understand how he received your letter," added Dolley, addressing Mathilde.

" I sent it to his lodgings ; the address he gave me on his arrival in Paris : ' Quai de Béthune, on the Ile Saint-Lonis.' "

" And it reached him—a proof that he still ventures back to his old quarters.   That was the only thing wanting.   We can now rely upon his immediate arrest, unless his meeting with Mademoiselle Moulinier makes him a little more prudent.   In any case, I have warned you, and now it is your own business to close your doors against him."

" You need have no fears on that score," exclaimed both cousins.

" Bnt what if Monsieur Hingant should report me to the police for having received him ? " added Mathilde.

" The poor dear man is incapable of that ; and, besides, I'll jnstify you to him if needs be.   But let ns now pass to a snbject that affects us almost as mnch as Jacqnes' rascality.   Yon, Charles, asked me if Mademoiselle Moulinier was really poor.   I will answer that qnestion when you explain your motive in asking it."

" Nothing.   Mere cnriosity," stammered the handsome Charles, rather at a loss for a lie once in a way.

" Very well, my boy, you can try to deceive me if yon like, bnt I warn yon that yon won't sncceed.   Do you suppose I have no eyes nor ears, and that I can't see your partiality for the girl as well as Mathilde's for the young officer ? "

" Indeed !   How can yon say that," stammered Mademoiselle Pelchat, blushing.

" And what if it were the case ? " asked Dngenêt.

" Why, if yon formally admitted it, I should have a proposal to make to yon."

" And what might your proposal be ? "

" A marriage between Monsienr Dugenêt, land owner, and Mademoiselle Monlinier," promptly answered Dolley.

" Come !   You are mad," said Charles.

" Not at all ; and to show yon that I mean exactly what I say, I will tell you what you are thinking, just as if I could peep into your heart.   Yon are very anxious to learn this yonng lady's real financial status, for the very good reason that yon find her to your taste, and would be very glad to marry her, providing she is rich ; if not—well, yon would, perhaps, still try to win her favours.   Yon are, however, very anxious that there should be no mistake about the matter, and as I am, perhaps, the only person who can give yon any reliable information on the snbject, yon had better apply to me.   Don't go to Jean-Marie ; he has other views for the girl, and would simply show yon the door."

" You, perhaps, have an idea of selling me the information yon possess ? " said Charles.

" Information of a mnch less valuable nature than this brings good prices every day : but as you are a relative, I shall charge you nothing. It is only right to do something for one's family, so I will instruct you gratis."

"That is your profession," sneered Dugenêt.

"True. I was a teacher once, and I am not ashamed of the fact; but I have not followed the profession since you resigned your clerkship. Profit by what it pleases me to do for you this morning. This evening, it will perhaps be too late."

"I am only waiting for you to finish your preamble."

"I have already finished. At the present time Mademoiselle Moulinier only possesses her beauty, her talents, and a nice little lot of furniture, worth perhaps some three thousand francs."

"A charming prospect for beginning housekeeping ! "

"Her father having only left debts behind him, she is absolutely without a fortune."

"I suspected as much from what I heard last evening, and if you have no other news to tell me—"

"She is absolutely without a fortune," continued Dolley, imperturbably ; "but she has, as folks say, expectations."

"What expectations ? "

"In the first place, one must be a fool not to see that Monsieur Hingant, having no heirs, and having great affection for the girl, intends to leave her all his property some day ; and very fine property it is ! "

"Very fine ; but I don't believe in waiting for dead men's shoes, and even if the old fellow has any idea of leaving the girl his property, he may live twenty years longer. I should have a chance of wearing out several pairs of shoes before I slipped on his."

"That's why I don't dwell much upon this side of the question, though it is well worthy of consideration. But I have something better to tell you."

"What ? An uncle in America? The grand prize in a lottery ? "

"You will never be serious, and it is a great mistake. Know, then, that Mademoiselle Moulinier may at any time come into possession of a large, very large, fortune to which she is entitled."

"What do you mean ? When will she receive it?"

"On the day she is in a position to produce a title, which will establish her rights ; and which, though not in her possession now, may be so to-morrow."

"To-morrow? If she were as sure of it as that, she wouldn't be giving lessons on the piano in the meantime."

"I don't mean to-morrow exactly. I merely intended to say, and I do say, that she is likely to find it at any moment."

"Then this title is lost, I presume ? "

"Lost or stolen—it matters little which, since it exists and may be recovered at any time."

"Perhaps the task of recovering it has been intrusted to you."

"Precisely ; and I will add that I am sure of recovering it as I know where it is."

"Does Jean-Marie know it as well."

"No, for it was he who requested me to interest myself in the matter."

"Does Mademoiselle Moulinier know ?"

"Not at all."

"Then why are you waiting to give them this agreeable surprise ?"

"I am only waiting until I am in a position to derive some benefit from my discovery."

"Hingant and the girl will pay you well."

"Not what the discovery is worth, and perhaps they won't pay me at all, for I am requested to interest myself in the matter as a friend, and it will not look well to ask anything for my services."

"The deuce! In that case you may have all your trouble for nothing."

"No, my dear fellow, for I rely on you to reward me for my pains."

"Well, that's cool I must say!"

"Not at all. Suppose that you succeed in marrying Mademoiselle Moulinier, when she has become a millionaire. You would at least enjoy her income, even if the capital were settled on her. Well, then, it seems to me that under such happy circumstances I should have a well-founded right to ask for a part of the wind-fall."

"And I should be very willing to give it to you; but first of all tell me, if you please, who is to run the risk? Am I to marry before you have enriched my wife, or will you bring her her fortune before I marry her? I should like to be enlightened on this point, for if I followed the first course, I should run the risk of finding myself victimized."

"Ah, ha! young man, you are sharper than I thought," said Dolley, laughing. "But you forget that there is a way to arrange all this. If you hand me your note, for a sum we agree upon, I will give you in exchange for it, on your marriage day, a document or documents which will establish your bride's claim to her fortune. In that way no one would incur any risk."

"Such a step demands reflection; still, if you could show me authentic and palpable proofs that the girl is rich, I wouldn't refuse to promise you a part of her dowry."

"That is all I ask of you. But while waiting for the conclusive hour to come, you will have plenty to occupy yourself with."

"What, pray?"

"You must win Mademoiselle Moulinier's love, and you have no time to lose."

"If you think that an easy matter—"

"It suffices that it is a possibility; and you are sufficiently interested in your success to win. I am too old to play the gallant, but, if I were in your place, I should not be at a loss."

"I should very much like to know how you would proceed."

"In the most natural manner in the world. I should manage to find a good opportunity to tell the young lady that you had not dared to declare your intentions, because you believed her rich; but that, finding her poor, and no longer fearing to be accused of mercenary motives, you have no reason for concealing your love. This is a rough sketch—I leave you to fill it up."

"Not such a bad idea; but—"

"Come. Put plenty of disinterestedness, passion, all the fine feelings to the fore. Girls are always hooked with them."

"Unfortunately the girl is evidently head over heels in love with that lieutenant."

"Is it that which troubles you? Well, cousin Mathilde, here, will lend you a helping hand. We have been boring her with our affairs for the last half hour, and it is quite time that we should pay a little attention to hers. Come, confess, my girl, that if you chose to take the trouble, you could soon make a conquest of the soldier."

"I haven't thought much about it," said Mathilde Pelchat, with affected carelessness ; " but the fact is, I flatter myself that I am quite as attractive as a skinny little school-girl, pale enough to frighten one."

" With your rosy cheeks and bright eyes, you could easily turn the heads of the entire garrison of Paris ; and I give this young man just one week's time to fall in love with you. Mademoiselle Moulinier will become frightfully jealous ; and jealousy may lead one a long way, when one has on hand a good-looking young suitor like cousin Charles. Everything would be arranged for the best ; both weddings could come off at the same time, and you may be sure, Mathilde, that we shouldn't be ungrateful. I, for one, will promise to make a handsome addition to your dowry."

" And so will I ! " exclaimed Dugenêt.

" We will see—I don't say no," stammered Mathilde, much more interested in the matter than she cared to appear.

" That's right. There's nothing like coming to an understanding. So it is decided ; we will work together, and we shall succeed, never fear. In union there is strength, as I told you in Brittany on the evening we divided the property. That brute Jacques, wouldn't believe me ; so much the worse for him. And now I advise each of you to call upon Monsieur Hingant, without delay, and inquire how dear Mademoiselle Moulinier is to-day. If you should happen to meet her there, or if you should find Monsieur Paul Gilbert there, it will be all the better, for you will be able to begin the attack at once."

" Shall you be there ? "

" No ; I am not obliged to pay court to any one, and I have something else to run after," said the ex-schoolmaster.

" What, pray? " was Charles's query.

" Your wife's fortune, my boy," replied François as he took up his hat and hurried off.

XVII.

FRANÇOIS DOLLEY, through his father, had Norman blood in his veins, and his lack of success since his arrival in Paris was entirely due to the fact that previously, he had always resided in a country town. A man must have experience to navigate through the shoals and quicksands of a capital city, and that is why the ex-schoolmaster's *début* in the part of a speculator had not been very fortunate. In allowing himself to be imposed upon by Billebaude, he had acted the part of a genuine provincial who has not yet learned to judge either things or people. However, he was one of those persons who quickly profit by experience, and it did not take him three weeks to form a just estimate of his partners. He was now perfectly well aware that these two respectable gentlemen were capable of anything, which means they possessed every aptitude except that of acting rightly. An honest man, under such circumstances, would have had no other thought than that of rescuing from their clutches the capital which he had so imprudently trusted to them, and he would have attempted this, if only to prevent himself from being some day implicated in transactions which were likely to end in a criminal court. But François Dolley reasoned in an entirely different manner. Not that he could quietly contemplate the possibility of losing his hundred thousand francs ; on the contrary, that would have been a hard blow for him ; but he decided to watch his accomplices so closely that they would be unable to play any tricks with him, and he said to himself that in their hands his money would no doubt yield him a high rate of interest so long as they had no motive to try and get rid of him. As a kind of bait they had already given him one thousand francs, and to continue drawing handsome profits he had only to make himself necessary to them ; in other words, to secure some valuable secret which would place them at his mercy. These gentlemen black-mailed their clients —Dolley was unacquainted with the word, but he fully understood its meaning—and he wished to retaliate by black-mailing them in their turn. Now the secret he had been longing to procure had just been revealed to him by the merest chance. His conversation with M. Hingant had afforded him a ray of light, and intense delight followed upon his previous anxiety.

Reassured in regard to his uncle's property, François now saw a new horizon stretching before him. He had mentally placed Jean-Marie's words side by side with certain things he already knew. He had often seen the old Jew, who kept the second-hand clothes shop in the Rue des Canettes, and it had already occurred to his mind that the old fellow was a secret accomplice of Billebaude & Co. To make sure on this point, as soon as he left Mathilde's, after Marthe's fainting fit, he repaired to the café which Billebaude patronised every evening, and there, between a couple of glasses of beer and a game of dominoes, he easily obtained precious information from his partner. He naturally turned the conversation on the old-clothes shop, and Billebaude, while refraining from stating that Mardochée was Galmard's agent and spy, nevertheless complained bitterly of the old Jew, who was a great nuisance, as his shop attracted prying loungers. "And besides," he added, "old Mardochée often stares at our clients, who don't want to be remarked."

Billebaude had scarcely mentioned this name of Mardochée, than Dolley divined the truth. He felt convinced that all these scoundrels were plotting something against M. Hingant. What it was he did not know ; but rising the next morning betimes, he went to the Boulevard Bonne-Nouvelle, where the doorkeeper told him everything he knew about the Mouliniers and M. Hingant's intervention in Marthe's favour. Dolley then repaired to Jean-Marie's residence, found the old magistrate just out of bed, and learnt the story of the auction. This greatly enlightened him. Mardochée had evidently acted in obedience to the orders of Galmard or Billebaude, and the book upon which M. Hingant set such value must be in the possession of one of the two partners. The rascals evidently intended to sell the secret of the Moulinier inheritance to Marthe and her protector for a large amount, and defraud him, Dolley, of his share in the profits. He, therefore, resolved to tear it from them, or rather to derive the benefit in their stead, by securing possession of the mysterious volume. Moreover, the idea of deriving a twofold benefit occurred to the wily ex-schoolmaster, and we have seen how, without losing a moment, he persuaded the susceptible Mathilde and his ambitious cousin Charles to enter into his scheme. After his conference with them, he was anxious to begin operations, for he was not a man to rest after a first success. The fight had begun, and he knew how to conduct it in a way to serve the many interests he had at stake. There was but one thing that still embarrassed him : Which of his partners should he attack ? In other words, was the book concealed at Billebaude's in the Rue des Canettes, or at Galmard's in the Rue de Cléry. Everything seemed to favour the latter supposition. In the first place, Galmard was the real head of the firm, and in a matter of such a serious nature, he would undoubtedly act himself. Moreover, his presence at the auction was a conclusive proof. Jean-Marie had told Dolley of the deplorable incident which had cost him the precious volume, and this was enough to satisfy the ex-schoolmaster that the scene had been preconcerted by the lawyer and the Jew. Besides, François was the more inclined to commence with Galmard, from the fact that he had an excellent excuse for paying him a visit.

It was necessary to inform him of Le Planchais' latest escapade, and to ask him to rid him of this dangerous relative for good, and so he hastened with a light step towards the lawyer's residence. It should be added that Dolley had not yet altogether decided upon the exact course he would follow, in order to attain his end. He relied considerably upon his innate tact, and a little on chance, for he was not fool enough to think of making any allusion to the book purchased by Mardochée. Had he done so, it would have been necessary to speak of his personal acquaintance with M. Hingant, and he determined to refrain from such imprudence. It was the first time, moreover, that he had gone to the office in the Rue de Cléry, for although Galmard had condescended to admit him into the firm as a third partner, he had only communicated with him through Billebaude, and had kept him personally at a distance. As a natural consequence, Galmard was a little surprised when his old servant informed him that M. Dolley wished to see him on urgent business. It was merely about ten o'clock in the morning, for François had made the most of his time, and the lawyer stood breakfasting off a smoked herring and a bit of Gruyère cheese, which he was washing down with water. His modest suite of apartments did not boast of a dining-room, and he partook of his frugal repast on a corner of his office-table. However, he was quite willing to allow Dolley to contemplate him in the exercise of his predominant virtue, frugality ; and the ex-schoolmaster was instantly admitted. "What good wind blows you here, my dear sir ?" inquired Galmard, without ceasing to fence with the herring bones. "Have you made some unexpected discovery? Are you on the track of Marie Bréhal ?"

"Alas, no !" answered Dolley. "I have no good news to tell you, and I only venture to disturb you at your breakfast-hour because—"

"You don't disturb me, and it is I who ought to apologise for compelling you to witness a repast which certainly does not remind one of the banquets of Lucullus. But I am not ashamed of the simplicity of my habits ; I only care for business, which is the one great matter in life. What is it you wish to see me about ?"

"About that good-for-nothing relative of mine whom you so kindly offered to get out of Paris. The rascal is still here, however, committing imprudence upon imprudence. Would you believe it, yesterday evening he had the audacity to present himself at a house where I was paying a visit."

"The deuce ! that must have been very disagreeable as well as compromising for you."

"It was the more disagreeable as he was drunk, as usual ; and the more compromising as there were some persons there who had heard of his conduct during the June riots."

"Well, how did it all end ?"

"Less disastrously than I feared. He perceived he had made a blunder, and hurried off ; but his visit caused a bad effect, and, as he may be guilty of another similar indiscretion at any time—"

"So you have come to ask me to get him out of the way as soon as possible."

" Yes ; as soon as possible," exclaimed Dolley, earnestly.

" Very well, I will think about it ; but, in the first place, I should like to know a little more about him. Is he rich ? "

Dolley was about to reply to this unexpected question, when his attention was attracted by an object which had so far escaped his notice. The manner in which Galmard's old servant had spread her master's table was as simple as the dishes she had served. The herring and the cheese were side by side on the same cracked plate, and a bunch of bread of inferior quality, a tumbler, a pinch of salt in a scrap of paper, such were the accessories of the feast, completed by a horn-handled knife, which Galmard, prudent man, always carried in his pocket. However, it was not the strange sight of a member of the Paris bar regaling himself after this primitive fashion that astonished François Dolley to such a degree as to prevent him from replying. Nor were his own tastes sufficiently refined for him to be shocked by this infraction of professional decorum ; but his eyes had chanced to light upon the end of the table, and he noticed that the plate stood upon a sort of pedestal formed by various large books, Galmard having no doubt wished to save himself the trouble of stooping to dissect his fish, an operation which he performed with his fingers. Books ! That sufficed, and more than sufficed, to attract the schoolmaster's attention, for he was eager to lay his hands on the volume of which M. Hingant had been defrauded, and so he looked eagerly at the works composing this novel pedestal, trying to read their titles.

The books were three in number. The two underneath had paper covers, upon the backs of which one could read this title, "Compendium of Jurisprudence," with the name of the great jurist Dalloz ; while the third and topmost one was an octavo volume, substantially bound in calf. Only the red edges of the leaves were visible to Dolley ; but the volume answered the description given by Marthe's protector so closely, that François was desirous of getting a nearer view of it. Unfortunately, the position of the octavo book was such that it was impossible to see its title, so he remained with outstretched neck and intent eyes, absorbed to such a degree by the discovery he thought he had made, that the lawyer was obliged to repeat his question. " I asked you if your relative was rich ? " he again inquired, raising his voice.

François gazed at him with a bewildered air, as if he did not understand.

" Why, my dear partner, what is the matter with you ? " continued Galmard, in a tone of raillery. " Only a moment ago you were talking as sensibly as possible—as you always do, by the way—and yet now you appear to be in the clouds."

" Excuse me ; I—I was dreaming of something else," stammered Dolley.

" When I say in the clouds, it is only a figure of speech, for your organs of vision are, on the contrary, directed on my plate with a persistence that puzzles me. Good heavens, can it be you are hungry? I never once thought of asking you if you had breakfasted."

" No, no, it isn't that, I assure you."

" Don't hesitate to say so, if such be the case. There are butchers and grocers near at hand, and my servant will fetch anything you wish."

"Many thanks, but I always breakfast early, and never take anything between my meals."

" Well, will you take the trouble to enlighten me in regard to your relative's financial position ? " laughingly asked Galmard, who seemed to be in a facetious mood that morning.

" Le Planchais is rich, if you like."

"If I like ! what do you mean by that? Explain yourself a little more clearly, please."

" I mean that he is well off—very well off ; however, owing to the life he is leading, he must have already made a big bite into his capital."

" A man always has a perfect right to ruin himself if he likes, and it wouldn't be worth while to live under a republic, if one was to be deprived of this valuable liberty."

" I do believe that the republic has had something to do with his folly, for he has been enticed into a number of secret societies, in which he is fleeced."

" How much is he worth ? Is his property in stocks or shares or in land or houses ? "

" He has two valuable farms in his native province, which is also mine," said François, surprised by the persistence with which the lawyer inquired into these particulars, " but I don't understand what connection there can be—"

"Between his financial position, and the project of getting him out of Paris ? The idea seems to astonish you, eh ? Well, all the same it is very simple. But one more question before I explain myself. Are you really interested in this fellow ? "

" I would like to see him—at the end of the world, and I care nothing at all about his interests, but I am afraid of him."

" Very well. Then you won't be offended, if I make him pay a good price for getting him out of harm's way."

" On the contrary, I should be delighted. It will teach him not to worry his family."

" And you will profit by the transaction as well as myself, for I shall act in the interests of the firm."

" I don't understand you very well."

" In other words, I shall draw from the common fund a sum, which I will lend him at a heavy interest, fifty per cent, for instance, taking in exchange a mortgage on the two farms you speak of."

"Ah, ha, that isn't a bad idea," exclaimed Dolley, stroking his chin. And he continued, half soliloquising : "Jacques must be in need of money, and, when he is drunk, he will sign anything you like. As soon as he reaches foreign parts he will finish ruining himself, and he won't return to trouble us again. In that case, too, we should always have the resource of denouncing him to the authorities, and having him arrested. In a year from now, we shall, perhaps, come into possession of the remnants of his property."

" That is admirable reasoning, my dear partner ; and, in my opinion, we ought to lose no time in taking up the matter."

"I ask no better, only I shouldn't like him to know that I am his creditor, for, you understand, it would place me, as a relative, in a rather bad light."

"Is that what troubles you ? I will lend him the money in my own name then, and merely employ you in helping me to persuade him."

" In that case I am ready."

" Very well, then ; as I don't like delay, we will start as soon as I have finished this bit of cheese, and pay Monsieur Le Planchais a visit."

" Gladly ; but if you know where to find him you are wiser than I am."

" Oh ! don't be uneasy on that score. I know his habits, and at this hour, he is at a place to which I could conduct you with my eyes closed. Give me time to swallow this last mouthful and we'll start."

As Galmard spoke, he worked his jaw with extraordinary activity. It was evident that he was enjoying his cheese, but Dolley, who was not eating, took advantage of the opportunity to reflect on other matters. The proposal which the advocate had just made to him, in regard to Jacques, pleased him fairly well; for he detested his cousin, and asked nothing better than to defraud him of his uncle's property. However, this scheme, satisfactory as it appeared, did not make him lose sight of his plan concerning the Moulinier property. The book in which he suspected the secret was concealed, lay there under his very eyes, within reach of his hand; and though he was not naturally generous, he would have given a handsome sum to examine it, and, above all, to take it away with him. But how could he manage to do so? The plate out of which Galmard was eating, still covered the volume, and such a thing as diverting the lawyer's attention, to secure possession of it, was out of the question; moreover, to make any inquiry on the subject, would at once arouse his suspicions.

François could only rely upon some lucky opportunity, and he tried hard to bring one about. He rose up as if he were tired of sitting still, and began walking about the room, taking care to direct his steps towards the window, whence he hoped he would be able to read the title printed upon the back of the volume; but the table formed a sort of rampart, and the distance proved too great to enable him to make out the name. "You seem restless, my dear friend," Galmard suddenly exclaimed. "Have a little patience. You will have plenty of exercise presently." François could only return crestfallen to his seat, although his eyes were still fixed on the precious book. "There, I have finished," said the advocate, as he prepared to wipe his mouth with his handkerchief instead of a napkin. As he did so, he chanced to knock his elbow against the pile of books which fell to the floor, carrying with them the unfortunate plate, which was broken into a dozen pieces. "Zounds! my set is spoilt," growled Galmard. "Never mind, though, your relative shall pay the damage."

However, instead of laughing at this would-be joke, Dolley flung himself on his knees to pick up the volume which he had been eyeing for more than half an hour. Maître Galmard probably attached equal importance to the fate of his books, for he also sprang forward to pick them up. The result of this impulsive movement on the part of both partners was that their heads came into violent collision, and Galmard won a large bump on his forehead. Dolley being a native of Brittany had a harder skull, and the shock did not even cause him to drop the volume he had seized hold of.

"Don't give yourself so much trouble," cried Galmard, who had only partially recovered from the collision, and, at the same time, he tried to take the precious book in his own hands. But the schoolmaster had already risen, and had found plenty of time to read the title printed in gilt letters upon the back of the work. He asked nothing more, and he now laid the octavo on the table, saying, with great calmness: "The corners were not damaged by the fall; that's fortunate. It would have been a pity to injure such a capital work."

"A capital work! You can call it so if you like," growled Maître Galmard, "but I only use it as a cushion or letterpress, and you needn't have knocked me so hard in your efforts to pick it up."

"Excuse me. I fancied— Indeed it seemed to me that this accident might damage your library."

"My library is in my brain, and I don't attach much importance to a musty old book that came into my possession I don't know how. We are losing time here, and time, as you are no doubt aware, is money—let us be off."

Dolley took up his hat, without making the slightest objection. He had seen what he wished to see, and he repeated mentally, "Encyclopedia, Volume IX." He would have been glad to have been able to carry his investigation further, and examine the first page, in order to learn the publisher's name and the date of the edition, but to do that it would have been necessary to open the book, and such persistence might have betrayed him.

True wisdom consists in being content with what one has, and François had gained a very valuable bit of information ; indeed, had he entertained any doubts of the importance of his discovery, Galmard's manner would have dispelled them. He noticed, too, that Galmard, before going out, carefully locked up this book for which he pretended to care so little. This was very significant, like the lawyer's evident embarrassment and eagerness to leave the place. "I am satisfied," Dolley said to himself, as he descended the stairs ; "and now that I have learned the secret, I will lose no time in making use of it. I must make haste, or my partners will get the start of me."

"Can this country bumpkin have got wind of anything?" Galmard was asking himself, and then he mentally answered his query with : "No, he is too stupid."

"Where are you going, my dear sir ?" inquired François, when the two rogues found themselves in the Rue de Cléry.

"Near the Hôtel Dieu, my friend."

The reply was laconical, but this was not a moment for offering objections. Dolley had decided to obey the advocate implicitly during the excursion they were about to make, for he had a great desire to get rid of his cousin Le Planchais. However he was anxious to conclude the business as soon as possible, as he had every reason to return and see M. Hingant. "That is a long distance from here," he said, timidly. "Would it not be as well to take a cab ? "

"Impossible ! The place where we are going isn't one of those to which a man can drive up in a cab. Half an hour's walk won't kill you."

"No, certainly not ; but—"

"But what ? "

"Is our expedition attended with any danger ? "

"What makes you suppose that ? "

"What you have just said. A place where a man can only go on foot must be situated in a decidedly disreputable street. If the place is some den, and knowing my relative's habits, that wouldn't surprise me I confess—"

"That you wouldn't care to risk your life there. I understand your scruples and have no more desire than yourself to expose myself to being murdered. But don't be alarmed. We are only going to the corner of the Rue du Petit Pont and the Rue Saint-Jacques, to a wine-shop kept by a man, who at my request consented to give shelter to your relative ; however, as this shop is frequented by all sorts of people I don't think it advisable to take a cab."

"Yes, it would be better to avoid attracting attention, for the police, who are on the look-out for that brute Jacques, may be tracking him, and watching the place."

"There is no danger of that. My friend, who keeps the wine-shop, is very well known in that part of the city, and the police would never think of troubling him ; but all kinds of people go to drink there, and I don't wish to attract attention."

"Nor do I. I would rather walk six leagues."

"Let us proceed, then, and quicken our pace."

Having arrived at this conclusion, the two partners walked on side by side towards the Seine ; but there was little or no conversation during the remainder of their walk. Galmard was thinking over a new scheme which he had just devised. Dolley was also meditating, his thoughts dwelling upon the new turn that his affairs were taking|; however, in spite of all the lawyer's assurances, he was not altogether reassured concerning the result of this adventure. In the first place, he was afraid of Le Planchais who was apt to resort to violence, and secondly, he had noticed serious discrepancies in Galmard's various assertions.

For instance the lawyer had originally pretended that Jacques was in the suburbs, and now it turned out that he was in the heart of Paris. However, it was too late to turn back ; so Dolley resolved to make the best of the matter. On reaching the Quai Saint-Michel, Galmard pointed out to him a narrow street leading towards the so-called Latin Quarter of Paris. "There it is, the sixth house on the left," he said, laconically.

Dolley had never before visited this part of Paris, and he was struck by the desolate appearance of the buildings that stood at the corners of the streets. One of them especially seemed to have been the scene of a determined encounter, for the walls pierced by cannon balls scarcely stood erect. The men who were moving about were clad in blouses—at least the majority of them, and it was easy to see from their faces that if they had taken part in the late struggle, it was certainly not in the ranks of the loyal National Guards. The schoolmaster could not help thinking that this was a singular place to conceal a rebel, for such a street must certainly be under the special surveillance of the police. "We are approaching," said the lawyer. "I will walk on in advance. Follow me closely and do exactly what you see me do."

Dolley complied, and they had not advanced thirty paces when he saw Galmard stop for an instant in front of a wine-shop, then proceed a few steps further and walk into an alley ; Dolley advanced in his turn, and also entered. In passing he had glanced into the wine-shop where there were four or five men drinking at the counter, but he did not perceive Le Planchais among the party.

"This is the place," muttered Galmard, after conducting his companion to the end of the alley. "Did any one appear to notice us ?"

"No ; at least I didn't see anyone."

"I ask you this because I fancied I saw a suspicious-looking man standing on the pavement opposite, but I might be mistaken ; besides, I will send the potman out on a reconnoitring expedition by-and-bye."

"Suppose we go ourselves. Wouldn't it be more prudent ?" stammered Dolley, who felt very ill at ease.

"You must be jesting. I haven't come for nothing; I certainly sha'n't go back now without seeing Le Planchais !" As the advocate spoke he rapped three times upon the wall in a peculiar manner.

The signal elicited a prompt response. A door of which there was no visible trace, unless perhaps to a practised eye, opened noiselessly, and a human face peered out. We say a human face, but the fact is, its possessor was uncommonly like a ferret. A retreating forehead, pointed nose, receding chin, and small twinkling eyes made up an *ensemble*, which was more grotesque than repulsive. The man who possessed this absurd physiognomy seemed in no haste to admit his visitors. The passage was dark, however, and he had probably not recognized them. ¸"It is I, you old sinner," said Galmard.

"Oh, excuse me, I couldn't see you," exclaimed the ugly man gliding into the passage ; "besides, I wasn't expecting you, you come here so seldom."

"If I come now it is only because I have some business to attend to," said the advocate drily.

"Is this gentleman with you?"

"This gentleman is one of my friends, and we wish to speak with your lodger?"

"With Jacquot? Hum ! that is not a very easy matter, just now," said the landlord.

"Has he gone out?"

"No ; he is drunk."

"What of that? He always is according to what you told me."

"Always, or nearly always ; but this morning he began early, and so he's laid up."

"We will make him get up then. Take us to his garret."

"He isn't there, but in the back room, under the table I think. Some of his friends came to take some absinthe, and they particularly wanted him to join them ; but he was unconscious, and couldn't even give a reply to their invitation."

"His friends ! You allow him to drink with everybody, it seems. If this is the way you obey my injunctions, Fil-en-Quatre, we shall end by quarrelling."

The landlord scratched his ear and replied, with an air of embarrassment : "It isn't my fault, sir. Jacquot, as we call him, isn't a bad fellow, but he is hard to manage, and allows no interference on my part. Yesterday he went to his former lodgings in the broad daylight, and in the evening he dressed himself in a new frock-coat, and went out again in spite of all I could say to him. He will certainly be nabbed at last, and get me into trouble, too."

"Don't be alarmed. I have come to relieve you of him. But have you perceived any one watching you?"

"Some one is always watching, detectives I know, but for a week past I have seen some persons who are strangers to me, hanging about the street."

"The deuce ! You ought to have warned me. I shouldn't like to be found here if the police make a raid on your establishment."

"We had better go, I think," muttered Dolley, who was still disposed to beat a retreat.

"Oh, my good sir," said Fil-en-Quatre, taking the schoolmaster's measure, "you have nothing to fear. If the police enter the shop while you are talking with Jacquot in the back room, you will still have plenty of time to make your escape through a passage I'll show you, and which communicates with the next house."

"All right," interrupted Galmard, "where's your back room?"

"At the end of the alley there. The door which is usually used opens into the shop, behind my counter, as you know, but there is another one further on. Oh, my house is admirably planned ; one can get out of each room without passing through another." As Fil-en-Quatre spoke he moved cautiously on, and the two partners followed him. "There it is," he whispered, pausing before a glass door. "You have only to push it open.

Jacquot is in there, and no one will interrupt your conversation, if you can succeed in making him talk. In case you hear any disturbance in the shop, it won't take you a second to reach the passage there, and you will have only to go straight down it to reach a narrow street where not even a cat ever passes."

"All right, only your passage is very dark."

"Oh! my cellar door's there; I go twenty times a day there without mishap. But if you have no further need of me now, I will return to the shop, for I have customers waiting for me."

"Very well," said Galmard, "don't let your customers disturb us, and if I wish to speak to you before leaving, I will knock at the little door."

Thereupon the obliging landlord went off on tip-toe.

"Now, my friend, we will proceed to business," said the advocate; "and I think it would be as well for you to allow me to do the talking."

"I am quite willing; but if Jacques is dead drunk, you will find it diffi-cult to get anything out of him."

"We will see," said Galmard, opening the glass door.

He entered, and Dolley followed, though regretting more and more that he had come. The room in which they found themselves was dimly lighted by one window facing an inner court, and while the visitors tried to accus-tom themselves to the kind of twilight which pervaded the apartment, a strong smell of alcohol revealed Le Planchais' presence. They finally per-ceived him seated beside a table with his head resting on his arms, and his heavy breathing testified that he was in a drunken sleep. Before arousing him, Maître Galmard went round the room, and perceived that it was separated from the shop by a partition of the thinnest kind, so that loud talking was not prudent, if one wished to avoid being overheard by the customers standing in front of the bar; however, the communicating door had a bolt, which the lawyer took care to push, as a precaution against any intrusion. This done he returned to the sleeper, and struck him roughly on the shoulder. A loud growl was the first response he received. "Jacques, Jacques, it is I," said Dolley, in his cousin's ear.

The sound of a familiar voice finally aroused Le Planchais, who raised his head and gazed with startled eyes at the visitors who had disturbed him. As soon as he recognised his cousin, he growled : "What do you want with me, you rascal?"

"We have come to get you out of your trouble, my good fellow," said Galmard, persuasively.

"Ah! so there's the old fellow," murmured the drunken man, talking to himself.

"Don't be alarmed, Jacques, it was for your own good we came," replied the schoolmaster.

"Thunder!" suddenly exclaimed Le Planchais, trying to rise up. "I recollect now; that girl recognised me last evening, and you have come to arrest me, you scoundrels." He fell back heavily upon the bench despite his efforts, still he had strength enough left to seize hold of an empty bottle by the neck and brandish it like a club.

Dolley sprang back, but the lawyer did not flinch. "Arrest you, my friend!" he said in a wheedling tone. "You do very wrong to threaten us when our only thought is to defend and save you, for the police are looking for you."

"That is true; the police are looking for me," repeated the drunkard.

"Yesterday a man followed me to the door of Fil-en-Quatre's shop," and partially pacified, Jacques placed the bottle on the table again.

"You see then, my dear fellow, that you need our help, and that it is time, high time, you left this house."

"Where could I go, then?"

"Why, you ought to leave Paris; leave France, even, if necessary."

"What are you jabbering?" interrupted Le Planchais. "I leave France, my lovely country! Never! Besides, I like Fil-en-Quatre. He's a good fellow; he lets me drink as much as I like. He isn't like that old miser in the Rue des Canettes, who put a jug of water by the side of my bed. I'm comfortable in Fil-en-Quatre's house, and so I intend to remain there."

"Very well," said the lawyer, coldly, "but I warn you that you won't remain here as long as you think, for if you persist in refusing my advice, you will spend this very night in prison."

The word prison produced a magical effect on Le Planchais. He leant back, passed his hand over his forehead two or three times, as if striving to clear his ideas, drew a long breath, and suddenly turned a more intelligent face upon his visitors. Aroused from his drunken torpor by the lawyer's words, in two minutes he became the Jacques of ordinary times—that is to say, a vicious creature, but perfectly conscious of his actions. "Good, good, I understand you now, my lambs," he exclaimed. "You, Mr. Lawyer, are afraid I may get you into trouble; but never mind, I bear you no ill will, for you did me a kindness all the same in sending me to Fil-en-Quatre's house. But with you, cousin, it is quite a different matter. You set a trap for me last night, and as I wasn't fool enough to fall into it, this morning you have come here to catch me. You won't make much by the operation, I assure you, for if you have me arrested, I shall denounce you also. You can depend upon that as surely as upon high tides in September."

"You are mad, Jacques," exclaimed Dolley, greatly alarmed. "I wasn't the cause of your being invited to Mathilde's house; besides, I didn't know that the girl from the Boulevard Bonne Nouvelle would be there. We have come here solely out of interest for your welfare, and, as for denouncing me to the authorities, as I have nothing to reproach myself with—"

"Nothing, but having urged me to join those friends who erected the barricades, because you were too much of a coward to risk your own skin. When I tell the police about it, and they learn that you concealed me after the affair, you will go to prison as well as myself. And the old fellow there will perhaps go as well."

"Excuse me, my friend," said Galmard, coolly, "this is evading the question. Distrust and accuse us much as you please, but take the necessary steps to save yourself, or us, if you like, from the clutches of the police. They are looking for you; they have seen you, as you yourself admitted a moment ago, and as I have learned from reliable sources. If you refuse to protect yourself, your relative and myself may have cause to regret our generosity towards you; but, believe me, we shall get off with a few days' imprisonment, while you—"

"Well! I sha'n't be hanged for it."

"No, you will be shot!"

"Shot! Bah!"

"Unless you are guillotined; that will depend on your judges. But don't delude yourself with false ideas; your situation is critical. You won't be treated as a rebel, but as a murderer. The story of that shot from the window is well known."

"If I thought that—"

"What would you do, pray?"

"I should try to make my escape, of course."

"Very good; we shall come to an understanding, I see. Well, when a man has made a good resolution he oughtn't to lose time in carrying it into execution, so I advise you to start this evening."

"Start for where, old fellow?"

"For England, my friend."

"Thanks; that's too far, and the notice is too short. I couldn't even say good-bye to my friends."

"You will soon meet them over there, never fear. Paris doesn't agree with their health, and they too will soon make arrangements to cross the channel."

"After all," muttered the drunkard, "there's plenty of gin to be had in England. What a pity it's so far; ah! if it were only to Jersey or Guernsey, now—"

"Go to Jersey, if you like; providing that you are out of the country, that is all that is necessary."

"Jersey is a little too near," said Dolley, who had made a grimace on hearing the Channel Isles mentioned. He had not forgotten the privateers-man's missing treasure, and he did not care to see his cousin located near the island where the gold was supposed to be hidden.

"Why should you object to our friend's choice of a residence?" exclaimed Galmard. "Come, it is decided, Le Planchais. You leave this evening?"

"Leave this evening! You are in too much of a hurry," growled Jacques. "How could I leave? I have neither a passport nor any money."

There was a gleam of joy in the lawyer's eyes as he hastily replied: "I will bring you all you need in an hour's time."

"Oh, yes, I know you. You are quite capable of manufacturing a passport, but how about the money? What do you call enough? A thousand or five thousand francs probably. You might as well offer me one hundred pence. Do you imagine that I will consent to start for England without knowing when I shall return, and without money enough to quench my thirst in that land of fogs. You forget that I have property worth two hundred thousand francs."

"Will fifty thousand francs satisfy you?" asked Galmard coldly.

"What! you would bring me fifty thousand francs—you?"

"In gold, or in bank-notes, or in drafts upon London, as you please."

"I prefer gold; but, pray tell me, it isn't in exchange for my word that you will lend me this, is it?"

"No, I regret to say; I have every confidence in you; but, as you know, I am not enough of a capitalist to have such a sum at my disposal."

"You don't look much like a man of money, what with your seedy coat and six sous cravat—that's a fact."

"However, one of my friends will lend the money to you on my recommendation, strengthened by that of your relative, Monsieur Dolley, and by your signature."

"Impossible!"

"You shall see."

"Well, old fellow, while you are about it, couldn't you induce your friend to make the sum one hundred thousand?"

"One hundred thousand, if you like. You are worth double that amount Monsieur Dolley tells me."

"Then I will accept. When will you have the money ready?"

"By three o'clock. I only need the time to take the notes which you will give me to my friend and return with the money."

"What, the notes! But I sha'n't sign anything until I receive my money."

"Then we may as well let the matter drop. You must understand that the capitalist in question won't think of giving me the money without receiving some equivalent, or of coming here to give you money in exchange for your bond. He isn't in the habit of transacting business at wine-shops."

"But why couldn't I go to him with you?"

"It is more than likely that you would be arrested in the street, and I should not like to be mixed up in such an affair. Besides, you distrust me; so we will say no more about it."

"One hundred thousand francs!" repeated the drunkard, mentally computing how many hogsheads of brandy, gin and absinthe could be purchased with such an amount.

"Now," continued Galmard coldly, "nothing remains for us but to take leave of you. We have warned you, and it is your business to get out of the dilemma as best you can."

"But how can you expect me to sign the notes here? I have no stamped paper in my pocket."

"I have some," said the lawyer, drawing out a well-worn pocket-book. "But I repeat that I haven't the slightest desire to influence you, and if you doubt my integrity—"

"I do," growled Le Planchais; "but if you deceived me, I should still have time to wring your neck before I was arrested. Where's the paper?"

Maître Galmard was always prepared for any emergency, and he spread before the privateersman's heir all the necessary writing materials to enable him to ruin himself, a number of bill stamps, a pocket penholder and a horn inkstand.

"And I shall have the money by three o'clock?" asked Jacques Le Planchais.

"By three o'clock at the very latest. Now let me draw up the notes; you are too nervous; you shall simply sign them. We will make them each for ten thousand francs payable in six month's time—my friend won't mind giving that amount of time—and he will only charge you ten per cent interest as you have good security to give."

"Very well, fill in what you say and hand the papers here to sign," exclaimed Le Planchais. The lawyer did as suggested, pushing each sheet over to Le Planchais who appended his name with an unsteady hand, after which the lawyer replaced the notes in his pocket.

François Dolley had not said a single word for a quarter of an hour; but he watched the scene with very natural eagerness, for he confidently expected his share of the booty, and he scarcely knew which to admire most—Galmard's audacity, or Le Planchais' folly; for though he coveted his cousin's money as intensely as the lawyer, he would never have dared to propose to Jacques such a step, as signing notes for the amount of one hundred thousand francs without receiving any equivalent. "I have so far never paid sufficient attention to the effects of absinthe," he said to himself, sorrowfully. "It is evidently a beverage from which one can

derive great benefit in business transactions." François was delighted in
his secret heart, and he had reason to be so. At least he fancied it,
although, had he been better acquainted with Galmard's craftiness, he
might have come to a different conclusion.

However, Le Planchais, after completing his task, laid down his pen like
a man wearied by an unusual effort, and looking Galmard straight in the
eyes, said : "If you are not here at three o'clock precisely, it will be the
worse for you."

"What part of the amount do you wish in gold?" inquired Galmard,
without deigning any response to the threat.

"I should like all I can carry on my person, say twenty pounds weight,
and the rest in a draft on London."

"Fifteen hundred francs weigh one pound, exactly ; and twenty pounds
is a heavy load about one's waist."

"Bring it all the same, old fellow. I'm strong, much stronger than you;
so no nonsense, or I will snap you in two as I would a match. As for you,
my dear François—"

"Hush!" whispered the advocate at this moment. "It seems to me I
hear a row in the shop."

Dolley pricked up his ears, and listened attentively, but Le Planchais
showed no signs of alarm, being used to the boisterous habits of his landlord's
customers. Nevertheless, the uproar which was going on the other side of
the partition seemed to be of an unusual nature. There was shouting,
swearing, and stamping of feet especially ; in short, it was the kind of
uproar that accompanies a quarrel between several persons assembled in a
small space. "One might swear our friend and his customers were being
nabbed," muttered Galmard.

"What if it should be the police?" said the schoolmaster, rising in
alarm.

"Pay no attention to it. Some friends are having an explanation, that's
all," sneered Jacques.

The lawyer had already placed his hand on the knob of the glass door
leading into the passage. "You may be right, my friend," he remarked
in perfect calmness, "for you know the house better than I do, but if you
are mistaken, your money and your liberty will be imperilled. That is
why I advise you to prepare for flight."

Jacques shrugged his shoulders, still he decided to rise from the bench
upon which he had been seated, and to approach the door.

"You are familiar with the passage which communicates with the next
house, I suppose?" Galmard asked.

"Yes; it also leads to the cellar, where the landlord stores his liquor.
I have hung about the trap-door often enough, but the rascal always takes
care to close it."

"Good! then we will make our escape that way. You go first, as you
know the way."

"And I'll follow," Dolley hastened to add.

"Very well. I will remain until the last, like the captain of a ship-
wrecked vessel," said the lawyer, opening the door and standing aside to
let his companions pass.

They had no sooner begun their retreat than a formidable blow resounded
on the partition separating the room from the shop. "The police! fly!"
cried Fil-en-Quatre's sonorous voice, which sounded in their ears like the
trumpet of the day of Judgment.

There was a general scattering. Dolley darted out first despite previous arrangements and rushed down the passage indicated, while Le Plauchais hurried after him, as fast as his legs would allow. As for Galmard, however, he had either suddenly lost his senses, or he had no confidence in the mode of escape which he had pointed out to the others ; for, instead of following them, he turned abruptly in the opposite direction, and hastened down the alley by which he had entered the house.

It was well for him that he did so, for the flight of his companions was not of long duration and it terminated most disastrously. Before they had gone ten paces in the dark beyond the glass door, the floor suddenly gave way beneath their weight, and they were precipitated into unknown subterranean depths. Their fall was so sudden that they had not the time to utter a cry, and so severe that they remained for several moments motionless and almost unconscious, extended on a rough soil. Le Planchais, who had solid bones, was the first to give signs of life by uttering frightful oaths. Dolley only replied at first, by profound sighs. "That fool, Fil-en-Quatre, forgot to close his trap-door," growled Jacques.

"Then we are in his cellar," muttered François.

"Where else did you suppose we were, you ass ? "

"Then we shall, perhaps, succeed in getting out, though I feel terribly shaken and hurt."

"I'm not such a fool as to make any attempt at present, for we should only be collared by the police agents up there. But, look here, the other fellow didn't fall with us or we should hear him moaning. They must have caught him up there."

"Unless this is a trick he has played upon us."

"A thousand thunderbolts ! if I thought that—"

"Let us first try to see where we are. Fortunately, I have a box of matches in my pocket."

This was fortunate, and by the flickering of a match they were enabled to gain a knowledge of their real situation. Moreover, Dolley soon discovered a box of tallow dips hard by and proceeded, without the slightest scruple, to provide himself with a more durable light. "How many casks ! What a number of bottles ! " This was the first exclamation that escaped Le Planchais' lips as he looked around him.

"We are at least ten feet from up above and there isn't any ladder," groaned Dolley. "We shall never be able to get out."

"And why are you so anxious to get out, you simpleton ? Are you so eager to spend the night in prison that you don't care to stay here ? "

"And how do you know that we sha'n't be obliged to spend the night in prison ? Do you imagine that the police who are hunting for you will go away without searching the house from garret to cellar ? "

"They may search, but they will never find the cellar. Fil-en-Quatre has told me twenty times that he alone was acquainted with the secret of the trap-door."

"Then that's why it has closed again," exclaimed Dolley, raising his candle high in the air to examine the ceiling. No aperture was visible, and plainly enough the trap they had stepped on, after revolving, had closed again.

The mechanism was certainly ingenious, and the fact of the trap-door having closed gave François abundant cause for uneasiness. He thought all this looked very like treachery, and he asked himself in alarm how the adventure was likely to end. "We are caught," he said, in a voice husky with terror. "We shall be left here, and we shall perish of hunger."

"No, not of hunger or thirst, my boy. Don't you see this pile of hams?
It will take us six months to eat them: and as for liquor, why, just look
at me," cried Le Planchais, seizing a bottle and breaking off the neck. "I
am going to try this vintage. Ah! It's rum—and excellent rum," he
added, pausing to breathe. "Here, taste it."

Dolley roughly pushed back his cousin's outstretched hand, exclaiming
in a despairing tone: "You wretch, have you sworn we shall die here?"

"You don't like it? It's capital, however, but there is certainly no
accounting for tastes," growled Le Planchais, at once returning to his
favourite occupation.

"But don't you see that I need you as a ladder?" said Dolley. "To get
out of here I ought to climb on your shoulders. However if you go on in
this way, you will be dead drunk in less than five minutes?"

"And what of that? It isn't such a bad thing to be drunk. I shall at
least escape the sight of your face!"

"But how about the notes you signed and gave to Galmard, and your
money?"

"My notes? The old fellow has them, and he will bring me my money."

The rum was already beginning to take effect, and Jacques' eyes were
rolling heavily, while his tongue gave utterance to some incoherent words
which were all that his heavy brain could originate. He swayed first on
one side, then on that, in an idiotic fashion, and finally fell backwards, drop-
ping the bottle as he did so upon the damp floor of the cellar. "He will
perish here like a dog, and I—I am lost!" murmured François Dolley in
despair.

XVIII.

MADEMOISELLE PELCHAT'S *soirée* effected great changes in Marthe's life. In
the first place, she fell ill from the shock she had experienced on seeing her
father's murderer suddenly appear before her, and at least a week of careful nursing and absolute rest was needed to restore her; even then she was
still afflicted with great weakness and a kind of nervous irritability that required infinite consideration. The slightest physical effort or strain of mind
threw her into a state of profound despondency, while the slightest worry
brought tears to her eyes—so that M. Hingant took the greatest care not to
oppose her whims. The first resolution she expressed was that she would
never again set foot in the house of her pupil in the Rue d'Amsterdam, and
to this her adoptive father made no objection. One naturally feels a repugnance to revisiting a house in which one has experienced such a shock, and
what did it matter to good Jean-Marie whether Mademoiselle Moulinier
carned a few crowns more or less when he had decided to ensure her a little
fortune.

However, Mathilde, on her very first visit, declared she could easily understand the young teacher's aversion to coming to her house; and added
that she did not intend to give up her music lessons on that account, but
would call every day at the Rue Bergère to continue studying under Mademoiselle Moulinier's tuition. Hingant thanked her heartily for her kind intentions, and saw no reason for declining her offer; but when he acquainted
Marthe with this new scheme, he experienced some little disappointment.
Even prior to Mademoiselle Pelchat's entertainment, the young girl had
found her pupil's society extremely irksome; and now, she felt an un-

conquerable aversion to all the cousins. She looked upon Mademoiselle Pelchat herself as a simpleton, upon Charles as a conceited fop, and upon François as a low schemer. As to the Widow Tromblas, that vulgar lady simply inspired the young girl with horror, and really the drum-major's relict had anything but attractive manners or mind. Marthe made no attempt to conceal these very natural antipathies from her adoptive father, who found himself in an extremely embarrassing position. In his artlessness he had dreamed of reconciling his affection for Mademoiselle Moulinier with the interest he felt in his old friend Léridan's nephews. And here all his plans were shattered at a single blow.

To learn so suddenly that one of those whom he had befriended at Cancale was a scoundrel of the deepest dye ; to discover a cowardly murderer in the person of a young man he had always looked upon as a simpleminded seaman, rather rough and too fond of strong drink, but honest at heart, these were surprises for which the old magistrate was little prepared. Still, he had no desire to pursue the scoundrel and deliver him up to justice, and on this point he came at once to an understanding with the daughter of the victim. Marthe was not one of those persons who wish for revenge at any cost, and she realized that she would break M. Hingant's heart by insisting upon his ensuring the punishment of Le Planchais ; so she only required an assurance that she should not again be exposed to the danger of meeting him, and Jean-Marie willingly promised to spare her this misery by taking measures for getting Jacques out of the country in the shortest possible time; Marthe, relying upon this promise, thereupon consented to continue giving music lessons to Mademoiselle Pelchat. She even agreed, also, that her protector should from time to time receive the two nephews who had not the sin of murder upon their consciences.

That of the old magistrate was none the less troubled by these events. At first he had felt a strong desire to use the privateersman's will to punish the whole set of heirs to which such a monster belonged. Then he had said to himself that the iniquity of one should not be visited upon the other three, and that by striking the guilty he would make the innocent suffer.

Dolley was still in his eyes only a worthy Breton, spoilt somewhat by bad company ; Dugenêt, a mere lad, beguiled by the pleasures of the capital, and Mathilde a thoughtless young woman whose head had been turned by compliments. To Jean-Marie—Jacques Le Planchais was still the only member of Mériadec Léridan's family who had really gone astray.

If the nephews had listened to him they would never have come to Paris; but unfortunately, they were there, exposed to all the dangers of life, and it was a question whether he, Hingant, ought not to try and persuade them to return to Brittany, and live quietly like honest country people. To achieve this result, Hingant decided to let nothing remain untried. He still kept the will which enriched Marie Bréhal in his pocket-book ; and after a little reflection he came to the conclusion that to promote harmony among the heirs he had better begin by marrying Charles to his cousin Mathilde. They were of about the same age, and apparently congenial in their tastes. A union of their fortunes would insure them a very handsome income, and they could satisfy their vanity by returning to dazzle their former associates, whereas in Paris they could only vegetate in obscurity. It was necessary to convince them on this last point ; and, to succeed in the attempt, Hingant resolved to bring them together at his house, as often as he could, without shocking Marthe. It would not, perhaps, be equally easy to lead Francois Dolley back into the right path. A countryman cannot accumu late money rapidly and easily with impunity ; and when he has acquired a taste for speculation it is not easy to make him satisfied with investments in land, which yield only two and a half per cent. However, since Hingant had become aware of the schoolmaster's connection with Billebaude, he relied on finding a powerful auxiliary in the person of his friend, Galmard, for he still possessed sufficient confidence in the lawyer's integrity to believe that he would assist him in making Dolley understand that "private diplomacy" was not a suitable profession for a person who knew nothing at all about Parisian life. As for the restitution of the hundred thousand francs, Hingant, in his innocence, did not doubt for a moment but what this could be easily arranged ; and, to induce François to return to Brittany he held in reserve a powerful argument based upon the possibility of marrying a certain young lady of Dol, who was as liberally endowed by her parents as by nature, and who resided only a short distance from the estates that Dolley had inherited from the privateersman.

Alas ! it was in the plans concerning François that the old ex-magistrate's misfortunes began. He went to Dolley's rooms on the day after Mathilde's entertainment, and learnt, with surprise, that François had not returned there since the evening before. He called again two days afterwards, and again at the end of the week, but François was still absent—nothing had been heard of him.

M. Jean-Marie then went to make some inquiries of Galmard, and Galmard told him things which surprised him very much. In the first place, the advocate formally denied that Dolley had ever intrusted any money to Billebaude's keeping, and he added that he had strong reasons to suspect the ex-schoolmaster of complicity with a vile scoundrel, for whom he had begged and obtained an asylum in the house in the Rue des Canettes. It was more than probable, Galmard declared, that the two rascals were concealing themselves somewhere to escape from the police who were on their track, and who would be sure to capture them, sooner or later. The lawyer furthermore affirmed that if he had suspected that his friend Hingant was at all interested in these fellows, he would long since have warned him of their conduct, but that now it was too late, as he had not the least idea what had become of them, any more than of the old Jew and the precious book; he, Galmard, had been fruitlessly seeking for the latter, for more than a fortnight already.

Hingant, greatly disheartened, thereupon returned home, saying softly to himself : " So there's another one gone astray."

Mathilde and Charles remained, however, and against them Hingant had no serious grievance, so that the reasons which had prevented him from producing the will still existed. By depositing that vexatious scrap of paper, rescued from the ashes, in the hands of the judge of the Saint-Malo court, Jean-Marie would ruin Dugenêt and Mathilde, as well as the other two cousins, who so richly deserved punishment. Certainly the unknown legatee had not yet been discovered, and perhaps she never would be ; but the property would not escape a more or less prolonged sequestration, and this would plunge two innocent young people into ruin. What would become of them if they were abruptly cast back into their former humble condition, having lost their industrious habits, and acquired a taste for luxury ? Hingant dared not even think of this contingency, and he repelled, with all his strength, the idea of assuming such responsibility. On the other hand, the responsibility he had assumed by keeping Mériadec's will, weighed upon him none the less heavily ; and he began to ask himself if he had not been most imprudent in thus usurping the power of Providence, which alone distributes rewards and punishments to the human race.

The old magistrate had unquestionably obeyed a generous impulse in thus striving to atone for what he considered to be an act of injustice ; but what was there to prove that he had not made a mistake, and that Méria-dec Léridan had not been correct in his estimate of the relatives, whom he had always refused to ackowledge? So far as the elder two were concerned, Hingant was obliged to admit that the privateersman had done right in closing his doors against them. And then he realised that money does not improve men, and that it is not always well to change the distribution of wealth in this wicked world. What had this family gained by the lucky chance, which had raised them two or three rungs on the social ladder? Nothing good, certainly. Their wants had increased in proportion with, and even beyond, their resources ; and they had entirely ceased to practise patience, humility, perseverance—all the virtues that sustain the humble, and gradually enable them to raise themselves to a better position. Instead of feeling the hope that consoles and strengthens, the cousins partook of the fictitious pleasures of idleness—pleasures which enervate and degrade.

However, when worthy Jean-Marie, as happened at times, was assailed by these very sensible, though rather tardy reflections, he quickly consoled himself by the thought of repairing all this by taking, at least, two happy persons back to their native province. His plan of marrying Charles to his cousin, had become a fixed idea ; and as the worthy man was equally determined upon uniting Paul Gilbert and Marthe Moulinier, he found himself principally occupied with matrimonial affairs. This was passing strange for a confirmed old bachelor, who had lived sixty years without thinking of taking a wife, and old Brigitte, who had charge of the house at Cancale, in her master's absence, would have been greatly astonished had she known the manner in which M. Jean-Marie was employing his time in Paris. Hingant applied himself to his self-allotted task, with the youthful ardour that he brought to bear upon everything, and he never missed an opportunity of alluding to Mathilde's virtues and personal charms before young Dugenêt, any more than to praise Charles's somewhat problematical good qualities in Mademoiselle Pelchat's presence. Nor did he neglect any opportunity for bringing them together at his house ; and though he had not the satisfaction of perceiving any great increase in their mutual affection, he was more and more determined to broach the great question at the earliest possible day. The season was advancing, and he said to himself that his pears must be getting ripe. Paris was fast becoming odious to him, and he wished to have the two weddings celebrated before autumn had set in, for he relied upon taking the newly married couples back to Brittany with him—Charles and Mathilde to remain there permanently, and Paul Gilbert and Marthe, for at least a month. Consequently, he was eager to have everything settled : but although the love affairs of Mademoiselle Moulinier and the lieutenant were progressing favourably, those of the two cousins only existed, as yet, in the old magistrate's imagination.

They met often, however—much oftener; indeed, than Jean-Marie suspected. Dugenêt was a frequent visitor at the coquettish apartments in the Rue d'Amsterdam, where he had never once set foot during the earlier part of his sojourn in Paris ; and Mathilde did not disdain to take a cab and traverse the distance that separated the fashionable quarter in which she resided, from the distant solitude of the Rue des Feuillantines. Such freedom is permissible between cousins ; besides, they did not spend their time at these interviews in saying sweet things to one another. If Hingant had been present, he would long since have become aware of their real intentions. On a certain evening in August, for instance, if he had taken a fancy to stroll under the tall chestnuts in the garden of the Luxembourg, he might have witnessed a scene which would have destroyed his last illusions in regard to the Mériadec family. The palace clock had just struck seven, and the paths round about the orangery were thronged with promenaders. The people residing in the quiet neighbourhood of the Odéon dine early, and then like to come out of doors and take a breath of fresh air, so that in place of the students, who were only seen in limited numbers on account of the summer vacation, a number of quiet couples were strolling along the terrace. Tennis players were disporting themselves under the trees, troopers ogled nursemaids, and young folks stood watching the swans on the ornamental water. At the corner of the quincunx, near the Rue de Vaugirard, a handsomely dressed young lady and a foppish young swell were seated upon a bench talking earnestly together. It was easy to see, from their stylish attire, that they did not reside in this quiet neighbourhood, and that they had merely appointed a meeting here to avoid interruption, for the spot was lonely, and admirably adapted for a conversation between lovers. No love talk, however, was going on between Charles and Mathilde, who were the two persons we allude to, although their converse was very animated. Nearly half-an-hour had elapsed since their meeting, and it certainly was not chance that had brought them together. "Do you know that what we are doing isn't quite proper?" Dugenêt was saying.

"I don't care for that," answered Mathilde, "so long as it proves successful."

"But anonymous letters are not countenanced in fashionable society, and if anyone knew—"

"What difference does that make to you, so long as you didn't write them ?"

"I shouldn't like to be compromised in such an affair."

"Bah ! you coward !"

"Coward, eh ? Ah ! it is all very well for you to talk ; you are only a woman ; but it would not be very pleasant for me if Lieutenant Gilbert should take it into his head to challenge me."

"Have no fears on that score. I will prevent any duel," replied Mademoiselle Mathilde.

"Besides, I have very little to gain," said Charles. "If the girl was really likely to be worth a million, as François tried to make me believe, a man might risk his life for a chance of marrying her. But that was only a joke which the schoolmaster wanted to play on me, for he hasn't shown himself since the morning after your famous tea-party ; and now, if I assist you in carrying out your new scheme, I shall safely get myself into hot water with Monsieur Hingant."

"And do you suppose he will forgive me for disturbing these young people ?"

"But you are dreaming of capturing an officer—which would be a very fine thing for you. You might become the wife of a colonel some day. That prospect makes it well worth your while to incur a slight risk."

Mademoiselle Pelchat could not help blushing with delight at the mere thought of a future, of which she had never even dared to dream, when she sat enthroned behind her desk at the Café Militaire. However, she replied rather drily: "I see no reason why you should be dissatisfied. The girl is attractive enough for you to be pleased with your conquest, even if you don't care to marry her." Women of Mathilde's stamp are pitiless when a rival is in question.

"That's true," replied Dugenêt: "but let us try to avoid any blunders. Tell me again exactly what you have done?"

"I wrote to Monsieur Gilbert—that is to say, Madame Tromblas penned the letter, for I was afraid the lieutenant might show it to old Hingant, who knows my hand-writing."

"A fine production it must have been," growled Dugenêt·

"Hold your tongue. You don't know what you are talking about. Madame Tromblas received a very good education. She wrote to Monsieur Gilbert that the lady he was to marry was deceiving him, and that if he desired proof of it, he had only to look about him near the orangery in the garden of the Luxembourg this evening at half-past seven o'clock. Madame Tromblas likewise wrote to Mademoiselle Moulinier, that if she wished to see her lover promenading with a lady, she had only to enter the garden by the gate facing the Rue de Vaugirard, at a quarter to eight o'clock."

"What! You expect me to approach the young lady, and offer her my arm? I have an idea that she will refuse it."

"She won't refuse it if she sees me leaning on the lieutenant's."

"Supposing he consents to offer it to you?"

"If he doesn't, he will be very ill-bred."

"But it seems to me that there is one possibility you have not foreseen."

"What's that?"

"Why, if the officer is a little late, or the girl a little early, they may both arrive at the same time."

"I thought of that," said Mathilde; "but, really, I fancy there is very little probability of Monsieur Gilbert keeping us waiting."

"One can never tell. He is so sweet upon the girl that he may, perhaps, regard the warning as a piece of slander. In such a case what do you propose doing?"

"We won't wait for that to happen; in fact, we must set to work at once. I will go and walk about slowly in front of the orangery, and you will stroll backwards and forwards near the gate facing the Rue de Vaugirard. The important thing is that we shouldn't be seen together."

"But what the dickens shall I say to the girl?"

"Anything that comes into your head, providing you detain her long enough for her to see me on the arm of her lover, though you must be sure to make her think that you are here by chance."

"Of course I sha'n't be fool enough to allude to Madame Tromblas' letter. I am positive, however, that I sha'n't be very well received."

"You must be used to such treatment by this time."

"You talk very coolly, upon my word! For more than a fortnight I have been doing everything I could think of to please the girl, and without the slightest success. She scarcely condescends to look at me. Still," continued Charles, with a sneer, "I don't think your love affairs are any more prosperous than mine are. The handsome officer does not seem to appreciate your charms as they deserve."

"That is my business," said Mademoiselle Pelchat, drily. "First of
all, I must open his eyes in regard to his Marthe."
    "And you hope that out of spite he'll give you his heart. However,
even if everything takes place in accordance with your programme, and
they are content to watch each other from a distance, what am I to do with
the young lady afterwards?"
    "Whatever you like; but to your post. The hour is approaching, and
it is useless to waste time talking here."
    As Mademoiselle Pelchat spoke, she rose up, smoothed her dress, which
had been slightly crumpled by her prolonged sojourn on the bench, and
walked deliberately toward the orangery. There is no telling the ravages
which love and ambition may produce in the heart of a susceptible queen
of the counter. This Machiavelian scheme was the invention of the gentle
Mathilde, and the idea that she was guilty of really atrocious conduct had
never once entered her brain. Her cousin Charles, less determined but
equally unscrupulous, went to his post without the slightest remorse, and
prepared himself for action by adjusting the bow of his cravat—a wonderful bow, which he had studied for a long time before his looking-glass.
He walked on slowly, turning from time to time to watch his accomplice,
who swept majestically along swinging her parasol, and the sight gave him
fresh courage, just as the sight of a veteran marching unflinchingly to a
cannon's mouth revives the faltering courage of a recruit. It must be admitted that he was excusable for a want of enthusiasm in the present
instance, for he recollected his first adventure in the Res des Feuillantines;
however, on this occasion old Hingant would not turn up to interrupt the
business, and besides, his cousin's theories on the effects of jealousy were
beginning to bear fruit. Charles now stationed himself near the railing
skirting the Rue de Vaugirard, and as the officer would arrive the first,
according to his cousin's calculation, he looked towards the garden in hopes
of perceiving him. Mathilde was walking about among the children and
nurses, who were beginning to gather up their traps, for the closing hour
was near at hand. She had just taken a third turn up and down the walk
when Lieutenant Gilbert approached under the trees. He was in undress uniform, and advanced rather hesitatingly, pausing at every step,
and looking anxiously around him. One might have supposed that he
regretted having come, and that he had half a mind to retrace his steps.
"Now let us see how she will manage to detain him," soliloquised Charles,
watching his cousin, who was cautiously approaching the lieutenant,
manœuvring in such a way as to conceal herself for a time behind the
chestnut trees, and finally turning so as to find herself face to face with
Paul Gilbert, who seemed absorbed in disagreeable reflections. Charles
saw her make the gesture of a person surprised at an unexpected meeting, and could almost hear her little cry of surprise and stammered
apology.
    Paul Gilbert, disturbed in his thoughts, took a step or two backwards,
and almost cut the charming Mathilde. Then, doubtless recollecting that
he was in the presence of a lady, he raised his hat and apparently made
some commonplace remark. This was the critical moment, for the game
would he lost if Mademoiselle Pelchat allowed the lieutenant to go off.
But she took good care to prevent such a contingency, beginning a discourse so arranged that the officer could not leave without listening to the
end. Mathilde spoke with great volubility, punctuating her prattle with
gracious smiles and timid gestures. Her unhappy listener moved restlessly

about, glancing first on one side then on the other, and evidently looking for some one who had not made his appearance.

Charles was too far off to hear what Mathilde said, but he could guess its substance. "I will wager any amount," he said to himself, "that she is telling him some story she has just invented. For instance, how she came here with the Widow Tromblas, and lost her on the way, and now finding herself here alone so far from home, she has expressed her delight at meeting an acquaintance who will at least protect her until she can find a cab."

Were these conjectures correct? The result of the colloquy certainly indicated that such was the case. Dugenêt had the satisfaction of seeing Mathilde accept the arm which Paul Gilbert somewhat reluctantly offered her, and she leaned heavily on it as if she had a right to its support. "What assurance!" thought Charles. "I shall certainly be a simpleton if I can't manage the girl."

But the most difficult part of the business had yet to come. Mademoiselle Pelchat had captured her man, but it was necessary to detain him there until Marthe appeared. To her cousin's infinite amusement, Mathilde leaned in a delightfully confiding manner upon Paul's arm, and led him towards a group of little girls, who were constructing a miniature sand castle. She paused to contemplate this pretty tableau with all the interest of a young woman who dreams of having children of her own ; and although Paul twisted and turned uneasily, he did not succeed in hurrying her away. "I wish the girl would come; this is the right moment," muttered Charles. And almost in the same breath he added: "Ah! I believe I see her coming."

It was indeed Marthe who advanced slowly, occasionally casting a furtive glance around her. Her air of embarrassment betrayed her anxiety and it was evident that she had dressed hastily under the influence of great emotion. Her bonnet strings were scarcely tied, and her mantle had been carelessly thrown over her shoulders. Charles, who watched her, was so placed that she did not perceive him at first ; besides, he took good care to keep out of sight, in order to choose his own time for approaching her. She unconsciously directed her steps straight towards the spot where Mademoiselle Mathilde Pelchat was parading on the lieutenant's arm. Dugenêt had only to allow her to pursue her course unmolested for her to meet the pair face to face, and for a second he was tempted not to interfere. But he suddenly recollected that such a course would endanger the success of his cousin's plans, for it was of the utmost importance to Mathilde that the lieutenant should be convinced of his betrothed's unfaithfulness ; moreover, Charles's natural conceit urged him on. He was again inclined to hope that the finish of the adventure would be most flattering to himself.

The daylight had been fading for more than a quarter of an hour, and the promenaders were beginning to make their way towards the garden gates. Children were running in all directions pursued by their nurses, and the stir and confusion that prevailed were well calculated to blind a much calmer observer than Marthe. Everything therefore favoured the designs of the two accomplices, that is providing they did not lose any time; for if they allowed their victims a chance for reflection, the scheme might prove a complete failure. Charles now walked on for a short distance, keeping close to the side of the path, so that Mathilde, who had not lost sight of him, might understand the meaning of his manœuvre ; then, suddenly turning and retracing his steps, he so managed as to find himself face to face with Marthe. She recognised him, uttered a cry of surprise and

F

anger, stopped short, and seemed about to turn back ; but Dugenêt was not the man to allow her to escape him. "Good heavens! mademoiselle; are you here at such au hour?" he said, bowing with every appearance of profound respect.

"Leave me, sir," faltered the girl, still trying to retreat.

But he had placed himself in such a way as to prevent her passing, and he continued gently: "Mademoiselle, pray forgive me if I venture to give you a bit of advice ; but the Luxembourg garden is frequented by any number of disreputable persons, especially at twilight, and you will be exposed to serious annoyance if you venture in alone."

"Leave me, I tell you."

"Monsieur Hingant would never forgive me for not having offered you my escort," continued the rascal, with unblushing impudence. And, as Marthe gave him a contemptuous glance, he exclaimed, like a man who suddenly recollects something : "Ah, I understand ; and really I was wrong to think of offering myself as your escort, when Lieutenant Gilbert is waiting for you. A thousand apologies, mademoiselle, for my thoughtlessness. I will—"

"Monsieur Gilbert, did you say? He is here then?" murmured Mademoiselle Moulinier.

"Certainly. Were you not aware of it? Why, I met him only a moment ago, over there under the trees. He is strolling about with a lady, one of your friends I suppose." Marthe tottered and turned pale. "What! didn't you know it?" exclaimed Dugenêt, in a tone of the most perfect sincerity, and at the same time, he sprang forward to support the young girl, who seemed about to faint.

"I wish to see him. Show me the way," she said, breathlessly catching hold of his arm.

This time Charles needed no urging. His ruse had succeeded, and so hastily leading Marthe towards the chestnut trees, "They were standing there a moment ago," he remarked, "and perhaps they are there still," he added, quickening his pace.

Then suddenly pausing, he pretended to be looking for the couple whom he knew perfectly well where to find. "There they are!" he exclaimed, after a moment. "Look, near that group of children. The lady wears a pink dress and a blue bonnet."

Mademoiselle Pelchat was plainly visible, for her bright clothes made her conspicuous a hundred paces off, and as for Paul Gilbert, his uniform made it an easy matter to recognise him at a distance. "It is he!" said Mademoiselle Moulinier, almost in a whisper.

"Oh, yes, it is certainly he!" replied Dugenêt. "But—and it is very strange, he doesn't see us. No doubt the lady is telling him something of great interest, for he is listening very attentively, and seems only to have eyes for her."

"It is infamous!" murmured the young girl.

"And who can this charming lady be? One would think—but don't you recognise her, mademoiselle?"

"No, and I wish to know."

"Ah, wait a bit. I spoke too fast the lieutenant is looking this way now. He sees us ; a soldier, you know, has good eyes, and besides, when one loves a person—"

It was true. Paul Gilbert was gazing intently at Mademoiselle Moulinier on Charles's arm, but Mathilde did not let go her hold on the officer, and if one could judge correctly in the twilight under the trees, she was leaning upon his arm in a most affectionate manner. Marthe and Dugenêt, who were standing in an open space, were much more distinctly visible, but the privateersman's prudent nephew had taken care to place himself in such a position that his face could not be seen by the officer. He did not care to be obliged to take up the lieutenant's challenge later on, in case the scheme should prove a failure. Mademoiselle Moulinier, on the contrary, faced her betrothed, and the distance was not great enough for him to be mis-taken as to her identity. "He sees me," she said in a husky voice; "he sees me, and he does not leave that woman."

At the same time she made a movement as if to dart towards him, but Charles detained her, and immediately began to talk to her with great vol-ubility, his gestures and attitude being such as would lead an observer to suppose that he and his companion were a pair of lovers engaged in tender conversation. "No, mademoiselle," he said warmly, "no, I will not allow you to compromise yourself like that. I do not know what is passing in your heart, but I can guess. Ah, Monsieur Gilbert is extremely guilty. How can he deceive you for a person like that? It is outrageous, outrageous! and if I were in your place, I should only reply to such an in-sult by disdain. I would leave Monsieur Gilbert to his amours and go off."

But Marthe did not hear him. She was standing motionless, with her eyes fixed upon the couple in front of her, and her emotion was so great that she leant somewhat heavily upon the supporting arm that Charles had treacherously offered her. A similar scene was taking place between Paul, who stood horrified, and Mathilde, who was leaning lovingly on his arm, and whispering in his ear. She was evidently telling M. Gilbert much the same as Charles was telling Marthe.

The passing crowd did not notice the scene, as everyone was hastening out of the garden. The hour for closing had arrived, and the roll of a drum warned promenaders that it was time to return home, while keepers were here and there urging the people on towards the gates. When Marthe, at last determined upon risking everything, attempted to spring forward to have an explanation with her betrothed, it was too late. She only escaped Dugenêt's arm to find herself almost in the embrace of a gigantic veteran, who stopped her, saying politely: "Where are you going, my little lady? No passing allowed here. Don't you see they are closing the gates?"

Marthe cast a last glance in the direction of the chestnuts, and saw her rival and Paul moving off, driven away, like herself, by one of the keepers, but in an opposite direction. The regulations of the Luxembourg garden had effected what Charles Dugenêt's exhortations had failed to bring about, and Mademoiselle Moulinier, overcome with emotion, allowed him to lead her into the Rue de Vaugirard.

XIX.

NIGHT was fast approaching, and it was already quite dark in the Rue de Vaugirard, for the street lamps had not been lighted, and there are but few shops there. The majority of the promenaders, after being turned out of the garden, proceeded towards the Odéon, or the Place Saint-Sulpice. Marthe, however, yielding to the natural instinct which impelled her to seek darkness and solitude in order to conceal her emotion, turned in an opposite direction and hastened towards the outer boulevards. She hastily dropped Dugenêt's arm after passing through the gateway, and walked straight on, troubling herself no more about her companion than if he had not existed. She was no longer able to reason; her heart throbbed almost to suffocation; indignation and sorrow had dispelled the calmness she had maintained during the whole of that frightful ordeal in the Luxembourg grounds. She looked at the tall houses without seeing them, and she allowed herself to be jostled by the careless passers-by without even perceiving them, as she hastened blindly on like a leaf carried away by the autumnal wind. She did not love her betrothed with the common-place affection in which most young girls indulge on leaving their convents. She loved him, because she believed him worthy of love, and not solely because he possessed those personal good looks which turn the heads of young school-girls; and the pain caused her by his treachery was all the greater as she had so far placed the most implicit confidence in him. Too proud to be jealous of a rival, she suffered intensely from the present knowledge that her love had been ill-bestowed; indeed, her grief was not so much due to the fact that her dearest hopes had been blighted. And even in this suffering of hers there was still love, for it was for Paul's unworthiness that she blushed; it was his degradation that she bemoaned, and not her vanished illusions.

Had Charles Dugenêt been able to read his victim's heart, he would certainly have failed to understand the emotions that overwhelmed her; they were of too delicate a nature for him to comprehend them; however, he had other business at hand than a study of the effects of disappointed love. Delighted with his success, he now only thought of profiting by his victory. He realized that the plan he had at first formed of immediately offering his arm and himself to Marthe had not the slightest chance of success. Such a course might have been pursued with favourable results with a *grisette*; but Dugenêt, who prided himself on his knowledge of the fair sex, wisely concluded that he must employ more delicate means with Mademoiselle Moulinier. So he at first merely kept close to her, without attempting to utter a single word. He said to himself, however, that Marthe would soon have to stop and rest if she hurried on at this rate, that her mental and physical strength would speedily become exhausted.

Anger still sustained her for the time being; but feminine anger is generally too violent to last very long, and it generally ends in a paroxysm of tears followed by complete nervous prostration. This was the moment for which the crafty young swain was eagerly waiting, and he held his consolation in reserve for the occasion when there would be some chance of its being accepted, the moment when Marthe's grief-stricken heart would give way. Dugenêt relied, moreover, upon the state of bewilderment in which she would find herself after her reckless flight, and he knew very well what he was doing when he allowed her to hasten blindly on through this strange neighbourhood. It was now dark, and pedestrians were becoming scanty. Sooner or later, Mademoiselle Monlinier would emerge from her hallucination, and perceive that she was a long distance from home. To whom then would she turn to in her embarrassment if not to the respectful young man who was silently following her? This opinion was fully verified, and even sooner than Charles thought probable. After twenty minutes' rapid walking, the girl paused and began to look around her. She stood at the corner of a badly paved and ill-lighted street, with a high wall on one side and on the other a long row of houses which seemed unoccupied, so gloomy and deserted did they look.

Charles hesitated no longer, but advancing towards the young girl, he said in an insinuating voice : "Pray, mademoiselle, don't go any further, I beg of you. This is a very dangerous part of Paris at such an hour, and some misfortune will surely happen to you. I am here to protect you, it is true ; but what can one man do against a band of scoundrels? "

"Who gave you permission to follow me?" asked Mademoiselle Moulinier, drily.

"Have I done wrong to watch over you in the agitated condition you have been in since that unfortunate meeting?" persisted Dugenêt, who had profited by the opportunity thus afforded, to draw a little nearer to his companion.

"I need no one, and I only ask you to tell me which way to take to reach home."

"We are a long distance from your residence, and you are certainly in no condition to walk, mademoiselle. If I am not mistaken there is a cab-stand at the end of the street. Will you accept my arm until we can find a cab? I deem it a pleasure as well as a duty to see you safely home."

"I thank you, but I prefer to go alone," replied Mademoiselle Moulinier, as she began to walk in the direction Charles had indicated.

However, young Dugenêt was not a man to be easily repulsed, and he followed her closely, repeating and accentuating his offers of service. "Do you know that you are really too hard upon me," he murmured, "when all I desire is to please you? I can readily understand your annoyance, but confess that it is no fault of mine if Monsieur Gilbert behaves badly. Come, mademoiselle, be reasonable, and, instead of visiting this gentleman's infidelity upon me, allow me to take his place in your affections."

Charles speedily realised that he was going too fast and too far, for Marthe silenced him with a look and a gesture of scorn, and then hastened on without deigning to give him any other response. Dugenêt now lost patience, and all his fine projects of strategy ended in smoke. "This is too much this time," he muttered, angrily. "We will see." And as Marthe began to run, he did the same.

This trial of speed could not fail to end disastrously for the girl, who perceived her imprudence only too soon, for she was scarcely half-way down the street when her breath failed her, and she soon drew up exhausted ; however, she had the presence of mind to dart under a gateway, intending to ring, in the hope of finding a refuge in the house it led to, or at least to bring someone to her assistance. But before she could grasp the bell-knob Charles seized hold of her arm. "No folly, if you please," he said, with all his natural coarseness of manner. "It isn't worth while making a scene in the street. You will be no better off if you succeed in having us both taken to the station-house."

"Scoundrel ! "

"Come, come ; I know your high and mighty airs. But take my advice, keep them for your lieutenant when he comes to ask your forgiveness, and let us two make peace."

Charles followed up this pleasant proposal with an attempt which was promptly put a stop to by a defender who providentially appeared upon the scene. Just as young Dugenêt was trying to slip his arm round Mademoiselle Moulinier's waist, he received a terrible blow on the nape of the neck which sent him rolling on the pavement.

Marthe, freed from his loathsome embrace, had scarcely time to glance at her preserver, for he hurried her unresistingly to the other end of the street.

She felt that she could trust this stranger, and that the first thing to be done was to escape from the scoundrel who now lay prostrate in the gutter, stunned by that terrible blow. "Where do you wish to go, madame?" inquired Dugenêt's conqueror, when they had reached the cab-stand.

Then, and for the first time, Mademoiselle Moulinier turned to look at the man upon whose arm she was leaning. He was of medium height, but of robust appearance, although his grey hair and bent shoulders denoted advanced age. His angular face, sunburnt skin, and rather heavy gait, were not particularly prepossessing; but his eyes were gentle, and though his features were wanting in distinction, they denoted honesty and kindness. His garb was that of a well-to-do mechanic. All Marthe's confidence instantly returned to her. "I should like to return home to the house of my adoptive father, in the Rue Bergère," she murmured, trying to regain breath.

"The Rue Bergère is a long distance from here," said the man, "and it will be better for us to go in a cab, especially as that rascal may take it into his head to pursue you."

"Yes, yes! I am particularly anxious to avoid him; but I also wish to thank you, sir."

"Get in, get in, madame," said the stranger, brusquely. "It seems to me that I see him coming now, and if he overtakes us I shall be obliged to pummel him, and it would be better to avoid scandal."

It was no time for hesitation, and Marthe hastily sprung into an open victoria. Her preserver seated himself beside her, and gave the address to the driver, who started off his horse at once. "I greatly regret giving you so much trouble," said Mademoiselle Moulinier, "but your kindness in accompanying me home at least gives me an opportunity to express my gratitude—"

"You don't owe me any. I only did what anyone would have done in my place."

"But for you I should have been lost."

"No danger of that. The scamp wouldn't have got off so easily if I had not been desirous of avoiding a scandal on your account, but if he ever comes in my way again—" And this protector of outraged innocence added, in a milder tone: "It is true that I should have considerable difficulty in recognising him, for it was so dark in that wretched street that I couldn't see his face."

"You had followed us then?"

"No; I was just coming out of my house two doors further on, and I had no sooner set foot in the street than I overheard your conversation. Ah! I arrived just in time."

"Ah, sir," said Marthe, warmly, "you have just done me a service which I shall never forget, and which my father will certainly reward."

"Let us say no more about that. I'm pleased, however, to know that you are going to your parents? Seeing you with a fellow who looked like a student, I half fancied at first that it was a mere lover's quarrel."

Marthe blushed, and reflected that after all love certainly had something to do with the adventure. Her protector's coarse frankness somewhat disconcerted her, so that she made no reply, and as he showed no inclination to ply her with questions, the conversation ceased, not another word being exchanged until the vehicle drew up in front of the house where Jean-Marie resided. By a lucky chance, Jean-Marie was standing on the threshold, engaged in drawing on his gloves. Marthe, delighted to see him again, sprang out, and threw herself into his arms. But before she had time to introduce him to her defender, an exclamation of surprise from behind suddenly checked her, and Hingant hastily pushed her aside to get a look at the person who had given vent to it. "Mathurin !" exclaimed the magistrate, as soon as he saw the features of his ward's companion.

"Monsieur Jean-Marie !" murmured the other.

"What ! is it really you," cried M. Hingant, "you, whom I supposed dead, or at least gone off, never to return ? "

"You see that I am alive, Monsieur Jean-Marie, but—"

"Do you know that you acted very badly after poor Léridan's death ? To sail off in your boat without even bidding me good-bye."

"It was not you that I fled from. It was from those rascally heirs."

"A fine reason for abandoning your native land, and hiding yourself like a criminal. What have you been doing during the six months that have elapsed since you disappeared ? "

"He has saved me," said Marthe, quietly, extending her hand to the old sailor.

She did not know him—nor did she understand the meaning of this conversation, in which the stranger was questioned respecting facts she was ignorant of, but her heart told her that the misdemeanours of her generous defender could not be very grave.

"Saved you, and from what ? " repeated M. Hingant. "When ?—where ? What has occurred ? "

Mathurin Callec looked down, and made no reply ; in the first place, because he was not naturally boastful, but above all, because he feared to make some misappropriate remark. The situation seemed to him rather delicate, for he had never seen this young girl before, and did not know how she stood in regard to M. Hingant. So it was Marthe who explained the matter. "He came to my assistance," she said, in a firm voice, "at a moment when I was exposed to the insults of a man I hate and despise, Monsieur Charles Dugenêt."

"What ! he dared," sighed Jean-Marie, in consternation.

"Charles Dugenêt !" cried Mathurin, "my captain's nephew !"

"The same, my friend," said Jean-Marie, "but—"

"Ah, if I had only known it ! Instead of stunning him, I would have strangled him. The scoundrel !—the blackguard !—the rascal !"

Such forcible exclamations would eventually draw a crowd, for this scene was taking place in the Rue Bergère, so that M. Hingant exclaimed : "Let us go in-doors."

No urging was required to induce compliance. Marthe could scarcely stand, and Mathurin Callec was anxious to have a private talk with his old master's friend, so he paid and dismissed the driver, who had been watching the party with a sneer on his face. Two minutes later the three were seated in the magistrate's little drawing-room—Marthe silent and despondent, Hingant all in a flutter, and Mathurin most exasperated. "Ah, Monsieur Jean-Marie," he exclaimed, "I always told you that those fellows were good for nothing, and that the captain did right to turn them out of his house. I thought I was well rid of them, and yet here I find one of them engaged in a piece of rascality, to say nothing of the others, who are doing, no doubt, even worse."

"Alas ! you are too much in the right, and I confess—"

"I don't know whether this young lady is a relative of yours, but—"

"She is the daughter of a friend who is dead, and I love her as if she were my own child."

"Then it was fortunate that I decided to go out and smoke my pipe in the open air."

"Well, what has happened."

Mathurin was about to describe the adventure, but Mademoiselle Moulinier checked him by a gesture. "I beg that you will leave me the task of informing my adoptive father of what happened this evening," she said hastily. "I will do so later on; for just now I need quiet, and so I will retire to the next room to rest a little."

These words were accompanied by a glance addressed to M. Hingant, who saw that it was useless to insist, and the young girl left the room unhindered. "I am awfully puzzled about all this—my head's in a whirl," murmured the ex-magistrate, "and if you don't assist me in solving the mystery, Mathurin, I really think I shall go mad."

"This isn't the time for that, Monsieur Jean-Marie, for I am greatly in need of your help, and our meeting in Paris is certainly providential."

"But what, in Heaven's name, brought you to Paris?" asked M. Hingant.

"I came to find the captain's true heiress, Monsieur Jean-Marie."

"What do you say? What heiress?" exclaimed M. Hingant, more and more surprised.

"Ah, that's true. I forgot that you didn't know; that the captain didn't tell you of his intentions."

"Well, he often told me that he did not intend to leave his property to his nephews, and I even tried to make him change his mind on the subject."

"Very wrongly, Monsieur Jean-Marie, for his idea was a good one, but I'm afraid he followed your advice."

"Explain yourself, Mathurin, for I don't exactly understand what you are driving at. Can Léridan have really requested you to find the person he desired to make his legatee, to the detriment of his family?"

"Quite so. He requested me to do so, at least a dozen times, and if you have a moment to spare, I will tell you all about it."

"Go on, pray, and omit nothing."

"You know, of course, Monsieur Jean-Marie, that my poor master had full confidence in me."

"And he was quite right."

"I don't say the contrary, for I would have thrown myself into the fire for him, and he knew it. That is why he gave me orders concerning what was to be done after his death, and he knew I would obey them as implicitly as I had obeyed all his instructions when we were aboard the *Goëland*. 'Mathurin,' said he to me, 'when I expire, my rascally nephews will come aboard ship and rummage about everywhere. Keep as close by as you can, in order to get ahead of them if possible. My will is in the drawer of the Chinese cabinet which I captured near Ferrol, in 1809, on a vessel belonging to the English East India Company.'"

"I recollect the cabinet well," muttered Hingant, "it was in the room where he kept his spy-glasses and sextants."

"That was it," replied Mathurin. "Well, the captain told me to open it, as soon as he breathed his last, to take the will and keep it until I could place it in the hands of his heiress."

"Then, he left his property to a woman?" inquired the old magistrate, in great emotion.

"Yes, to a woman."

"Did she belong to Cancale?"

"No: but let me finish. As you may well suppose, on the day the accident happened, I lost no time in going to the house and looking for the will in the cabinet. But the document wasn't there. The rascally nephews had been ahead of me, and had secured it."

M. Hingant knew what to think on this point, and he did not blame the heirs for a theft for which he alone was responsible; but he could not understand how the paper upon which the privateersman had traced his last wishes, had fallen into the fire-place, unless, indeed, Léridan had changed his mind at the last moment. This supposition consoled him a little, and he felt strongly inclined to adopt it; but he did not take time to reflect much upon the matter, for he wished to hear the remainder of Mathurin's story. "What, you think they dared to abstract it?" he asked, feigning astonishment.

"They would have felt no scruple about burning it, I assure you," said Mathurin.

"But under those circumstances, your duties were ended—you had nothing more to do."

"Oh, yes; I had to discover the captain's heiress."

"But what good would that do if the will was destroyed?"

Mathurin was evidently embarrassed, and he could only find an evasive response. "Such were my instructions," he said; "besides, I had an idea of my own."

"Very possibly; but all this does not explain why you came to Paris."

"To find the heiress, as I have already told you, Monsieur Jean-Marie."

"Then, you knew she was there?"

"I knew that as well as many other things. The captain told me all he knew," said Mathurin.

"And he bequeathed his entire fortune to a stranger? It seems inconceivable."

"No, not to a stranger; on the contrary, he knew her well, although more than thirty years had gone by since he had last seen her."

"But he must at least have heard from her?"

"Not once."

"Written to her, then?"

"No. You see, Monsieur Jean-Marie, it's quite a story. I am the only person acquainted with it, and I swore never to reveal it to any one; still, I am going to tell it you all the same."

"I thank you for your confidence in me," said M. Hingant, "and I promise you shall never have cause to repent it. Besides we might come to an understanding with the same object in view, and I might tell you various things you don't know."

"Well, Monsieur Jean-Marie," began Mathurin, "you have, perhaps, not forgotten that my master once made a journey to Paris."

"I recollect very well that Mériadec's journey was the talk of the neighbourhood. It took place during the Hundred Days, and Léridan returned to Cancale near the close of the summer of 1815. I always thought that he had gone to offer his services to Napoleon, in case of a maritime war with England. The old privateersman remembered his former deeds of prowess, and wished—"

"I thought so at first, myself," said Mathurin, "but later on I learned, or rather I guessed, the real reason. The captain was often gloomy, very gloomy ; so much so, in fact, that at times he forgot to smoke his pipe or swear about his sisters whose conduct wasn't to his liking. I said to myself : 'There must be some sentiment under all this.' He was still quite a young man then, and there was no reason why he shouldn't think of marrying. At last I recollected that he had often visited the other side of the bay—between Granville and Regenville, on the coast of Normandy. A man who had been mate on board the *Goëland* had settled in a village there, and a month seldom passed without he and the captain drinking a glass of grog together."

"Yes, I have a vague recollection of that ; but what connection did you see between these visits to an old comrade and—"

"Well, this : the mate of the *Goëland* had adopted an orphan. When I say an orphan, it's only a figure of speech ; for the child knew nothing at all about her parents as she had been found one morning in a ditch on the road to Coutances."

"How old was she in 1814 ? "

"Only sixteen or seventeen at the most, but as pretty as a picture, sweet-tempered, and well educated. It was the sister of our mate who found her and brought her up as her own child."

"And Mériadec fell in love with her ? "

"Yes ; I can swear to that, for he could neither eat nor drink for think-ing of her."

"But what prevented him from marrying her ? "

"What ? The fiend that turns the heads of all young girls, I suppose. She liked the captain, but, perhaps, she thought him too old. At all events, she decamped one day without giving any one the slightest warning, indeed merely leaving a letter in which she said that she was going to Paris."

"What, alone ? "

"Some folks said that she had followed a commercial traveller ; others, that she had gone to the capital through ambition to seek her fortune. No one ever knew the real truth of the matter however, but it broke the heart of our poor mate, for he died of grief less than three months afterwards."

"And how about Mériadec ? "

"The captain ? Ah, it troubled him in a different manner. He flew into a furious rage, and immediately started off for Paris."

"Where he found her ? "

"I won't say so as he never told me so, but I think that he did meet her there ; for he remained away for six months, and when he returned he was so changed that no one would have recognized him."

"But you told me a few moments ago that he had spoken to you about his will, and it is evident from you suppose it was made in this person's favour. It isn't at all likely then that during the thirty-three years that elapsed between his return and his death, he failed to make some allusion to this affair."

"Such confessions are all very well for soldiers, but when a man has commanded the *Goëland* he doesn't tell his heart troubles to an old sailor like me. All I know is that the captain intended to disinherit his nephews, and leave his whole property to a lady in Paris. It was for her that he put money by. I am sure of this for he said it to me a hundred times, and certainly one needn't be very shrewd to guess that this lady was his old sweetheart."

"That seems only too probable ; but, cautious as Mériadec was, still when he instructed you to search for this legatee, he must have given you some idea where you would be likely to find her."

"Yes, a short time before his death. He then told me I could ascertain what had become of her by applying to the porter of a house in which she had resided here in Paris, and that I should find her name in his will."

"And the will having disappeared, you fancy this name must be that of the mate's adopted daughter."

"Certainly."

"And what was that girl's name?" inquired M. Hingant in great emotion.

"Marie Bréhal," was Porpoise's prompt response.

M. Hingant turned pale on hearing the name which reminded him of the heavy responsibility he had assumed by retaining the will. Still, the information he had just received was somewhat reassuring. The young girl, who had probably fled from home like an adventuress, could certainly not have been worthy of the paternal affection of the seaman who had protected her, or of Mériadec's love. It therefore seemed that Jean-Marie would not have cause to repent having refused to despoil the natural heirs to enrich the mysterious legatee. However this was not a time to indulge in reflections, so the ex-magistrate eagerly resumed the examination to which he was subjecting old Porpoise. "Marie Bréhal," he repeated, thoughtfully. "How did the child bear this name?"

"She derived it from the town of Bréhal, a couple of leagues from Granville. She was found on the public highway, only a short distance from Bréhal, where the mate resided."

"Then I suppose it wouldn't be difficult to obtain information concerning her there?" said M. Hingant, thoughtfully.

"After thirty-three years! Oh, dear! no, Monsieur Jean-Marie. Every one who knew her there is dead and buried long ago. I went there expressly before coming here; but when I made inquiries no one even knew whom I was speaking of."

"Yes; the living soon forget the dead. But did you imagine you would be any more fortunate in Paris? I am surprised that you decided to undertake the search, especially without consulting me."

"Really, Monsieur Jean-Marie, I didn't reflect much on the matter. When I was on the *Goëland* and the captain said to me: 'Porpoise, head her south, southwest,' I never troubled myself to find out why he wanted it done, but simply obeyed orders. This is a similar case. Monsieur Léridan said to me: 'Go to Paris.' So I'm here."

"But in Heaven's name, my friend, how did you manage to make this long journey—you who had no resources? If you had applied to me I would willingly have helped you; besides, your long stay in a city like this, where living is so dear, must have cost a deal of money."

"I did not inform you of my plans, Monsieur Jean-Marie, because I knew you would try to dissuade me from carrying them into execution. Those rascally nephews had got you well under their thumbs—I mean no offence—and you would have been afraid of injuring or offending them." This time Hingant blushed, for he knew that Mathurin spoke the truth, and his own eyes were now open. "So that is why I decided to leave without saying anything to any one," resumed the old seaman. "I had not a penny, it is true; but I would rather have died of hunger than profit by the offer of that scoundrel, François, the schoolmaster. The *Goëland*, however, was mine, for the captain had really given her to me during his lifetime, and I could do what I liked with her ; so one evening I weighed anchor and sailed cautiously away, tacking round about Chausey, for I suspected that that rascal Le Planchais was watching me."

"It does seem to me that he was out at sea on the night of your departure, and that some accident happened to him."

"Ah ! if he had gone to the bottom of the sea and served as food for the crabs, it wouldn't have grieved me much. Indeed, it wasn't my fault—But enough. I will return to my story. I had a fair wind and a good sea and on the third day I reached Plymouth. I knew the place, for I had once spent six months there as a prisoner on the hulks, from which I was released at the time of the peace of Amiens, and I also knew that the English were always ready to profit by a good bargain. I found a man who did a bit of smuggling and who wasn't inclined to be too particular, and I sold him the *Goëland* for half its value. I didn't like letting her go, for I prized her highly as she was a present from the captain—"

"Finish your story, my friend," interrupted M. Hingant, who was eager to avoid digressions and learn what Porpoise had been doing in Paris.

"Oh ! I sha'n't he long. I went to Southampton, where I took the boat for Hâvre, and from Hâvre I came straight here."

"Did you go to the address Mériadec had given you ? "

"Oh ! I lost no time in doing that."

"Where was the house which Marie Bréhal had lived in ? "

"In the Rue du Mouton near the Place de Grève."

"Well, what were you told there ? "

"I couldn't find either the house or the street."

"Why was that ? "

"Everything had been pulled down to enlarge the Place. Paris has changed considerably since 1815, as you can readily understand. The captain hadn't thought of that."

"And no one could give you any information ? "

"I questioned the neighbours, but they only laughed at me. I went to the Préfecture of Police, but everyone took me for a fool ; and for a time I feared the police were going to arrest me, to teach me not to meddle with matters that didn't concern me, so they said. They pretended there were politics in the matter."

"So you renounced the search then, I suppose ? "

"By no means. I took a furnished room and fed at a cheap eating-house, for I wished to make my money last as long as possible, as I still hoped that some day or other I should hear of Marie Bréhal."

"That was pure folly."

"Perhaps so ; but what else could I do ? I couldn't go back to Cancale and see those scoundrels in possession of the captain's property. The sight would have killed me, or rather I believe I should have finished by killing them. I preferred to remain here where no one knew me ; and you see I was right in doing so, as I have found you, Monsieur Jean-Marie."

"I am very glad of it, my friend, and yet—"

"It is true that I have also found one of the rascals that Monsieur Léridan detested so much, but the thought of the blow I gave that scamp Dugenêt consoles me a little. So the fellow has come to play the beau in Paris ? "

"Alas ! yes," sighed M. Hingant.

"And the others, Mathilde and Dolley, the schoolmaster, and that villain, Le Planchais ? "

"They have all established themselves here; and they have made a great mistake in doing so."

"Well, I say so much the better; for if I chance to meet them, I will say a few words to them."

"Do you dislike them so much then?"

"Do I dislike them so much! Ah! I would willingly give all the money that remains from the sale of the *Goëland* to wring their necks—the neck of one of them in particular."

"Which one, and why?"

"Jacques! Because he murdered the captain."

"Mathurin, pray, pray be careful what you say. Jacques is capable of very wicked deeds, as I know only too well; but it is too much to impute his uncle's death to him, when every one knows that my unfortunate friend perished by accident!"

"I know what I say. Jacques sawed the beams that supported the platform, and I have proof of it, for I found some of them the next morning among the rocks."

Hingant was about to protest, but the recollection of M. Moulinier's murder suddenly occurred to him, and he did not insist on the point. "Listen, Mathurin," he remarked, after a little reflection, "I think, with you, now, that perhaps poor Léridan would have done as well to bequeath his property to others than his lawful heirs, for wealth has ruined them. But he must certainly have changed his intentions towards the close of life, for the will had disappeared. Have you no reason to think that he changed his mind?"

"No; that is three days before his death, he told me that he intended to draw up another will, and intrust it to you to keep. But it was not to enrich his relatives; on the contrary, he spoke of including in it complete information concerning Marie Bréhal, and of bequeathing a legacy to me and another to you."

"Ah, I understand now!" exclaimed the old magistrate, "Mériadec began by throwing the first will into the ashes on the hearth, and didn't have time to write a second one."

"The ashes—on the hearth! What do you mean by that?"

"Nothing, my friend, nothing," stammered M. Hingant, regretting the remark he had unwittingly made in a moment of intense excitement. Then, to divert his companion's attention, he added: "But as the will is lost, why do you continue your search for Marie Bréhal? Even if you succeeded in finding her, you could not place her in possession of the captain's property."

"Not of the land, unfortunately, nor of his home either, but of the rest of the property."

Hingant was about to ask Mathurin what he meant by these words, when, to his very great surprise, the door of the drawing-room was thrown violently open.

XX.

Hingant and Mathurin both turned round and beheld a person whom they little expected to see. The visitor who had entered so abruptly was none other than François Dolley. Old Porpoise no sooner perceived him than he sprang up and rushed towards him with clenched fists and inflamed face,

peaceable Jean-Marie barely having time to fling himself between the seaman and the ex-schoolmaster. Ten seconds later, Dolley would have
measured his length upon the floor, as his cousin Charles had measured his
upon the pavement an hour before. "No violence under my roof," said
Hingant, firmly.

Mathurin stepped back, growling like a dog prevented by his master
from springing on a stranger. As for François, he sank upon a chair trembling with fright. Marthe's protector was in no laughing mood, and yet he
could scarcely refrain from smiling, as he beheld Dolley's pitiful plight. The
latter's face was haggard, his coat torn and covered with dust—in short,
he looked very much like a man who has just escaped from prison, or some
asylum. Moreover, one of the glasses was missing from his gold spectacles,
so that his near-sighted eyes had a most peculiar expression. "Where do
you come from in such a state as this, François?" inquired Jean-Marie.
François' only reply was a groan. "I have been to your house a dozen
times during the past fortnight," continued Hingant, "and no one could
tell me what had become of you. I thought that you had, perhaps, decided
to return to Cancale."

"Cancale!" muttered the former schoolmaster; "ah! Monsieur Jean-
Marie, no one will, perhaps, ever see me there again."

"Why not, my friend? It seems to me that you would be much better off in
Brittany than in Paris."

"But what should I do in Brittany, now that I am ruined?" moaned
Dolley, in a piteous tone.

"Ruined! What do you mean? What has happened to you? But
first of all, tell me where you have come from."

"Out of a cellar, Monsieur Jean-Marie."

"What is this joke?"

"I am not joking, unfortunately; but I have only my deserts for
meddling with the affairs of that rascal, Jacques."

"Jacques!" roared Mathurin Callec. "Where is he? so that I may
strangle him."

Hingant silenced the seaman with a gesture, and then said gently:
"Explain yourself, my dear François, for you really frighten me."

"It was in trying to do you a service that my misfortunes befel me,"
moaned Dolley. "After the scene I witnessed at Mathilde's, I wished to
relieve you of Le Planchais—to get him out of Paris—so I went to the
house where he was hiding; and I had persuaded him to leave the city that
same evening, when the police arrived to arrest him. We fled, and, in
doing so, fell into a cellar through a trap-door, which the landlord had
forgotten to close."

"Good heavens! How fortunate that you were not injured seriously.
But you did not remain in this cellar for a fortnight?"

"I was only taken from it this morning."

"But this story is absurd. You would have died of starvation before
now."

"There were some provisions in the cellar. I ate and Jacques drank."

"And who restored you to liberty?"

"The police, who decided rather late in the day that they ought to make
a more complete search through the house."

"Then Le Planchais is in prison?" asked Jean-Marie.

"He is dead," was Dolley's reply.

"Dead drunk?"

" No ; dead."

" So much the worse. I only wish he had died by my hand," cried old Porpoise.

" How terrible ! " said Hingant, although in his secret heart he could not feel much regret on hearing of the richly-deserved punishment of M. Moulinier's assassin. " But you, François, are at least safe ; and, if you will allow me to give you a little advice—"

" Ah, Monsieur Jean-Marie, the best advice won't enable me to recover what those rascals have stolen from me," rejoined the ex-schoolmaster, in a whining voice.

" What rascals ? "

" Messrs. Galmard and Billebaude. They have fled with the money I confided to them."

" What ! Galmard, my old schoolfellow ! What is this you are telling me ?—some joke, no doubt."

" My only hope is in you now, Monsieur Jean-Marie," rejoined Dolley, dolefully.

" I certainly won't abandon you, but—"

" You promised me a large sum if I succeeded in finding a certain book which contained information that would enable that young lady to recover her father's property."

" I have no very distinct recollection of such a promise," said Hingant, who was greatly excited ; " still I am certainly willing to pay a good price for the volume. But tell me, if you please, what you are aiming at ? "

" I mean to say that I know where your book is," replied François, with wonderful assurance.

" You knew where the book was, and you did not tell me ! " exclaimed Hingant, in a somewhat indignant tone of voice.

" I have come here now for that express purpose," replied Dolley, quite unabashed.

" Then speak ; speak quickly, my dear François," said Jean-Marie, quivering with agitation. " Ah, my friend, you restore me to life ; for I was really beginning to despair of ever being able to learn the secret upon which depends the happiness of a young girl whom I love like my own child."

" Her happiness and her fortune, eh, Monsieur Jean-Marie ? That is why I hope you will acknowledge the service I render you, and assist me in escaping from the unfortunate position in which I find myself."

" Nothing would please me better ; but what can I do for you ? " asked M. Hingant.

" Repay the money which that rascal Galmard has stolen from me," was Dolley's answer.

" But I am not rich. I think you told me that the amount was one hundred thousand francs. That is a very large sum—"

" Which would not be missed from the young lady's fortune," insinuated the ex-schoolmaster.

" Don't promise, Monsieur Jean-Marie," cried Mathurin. " Dolley is ruined. I see it. It is only what he deserves, and if you set him on his feet again—"

Again Hingant silenced the seaman with a gesture ; and then, turning to Dolley, he said in a tone which admitted of no reply : " It is impossible for me to make any such promise without consulting Mademoiselle Moulinier, and especially without knowing the value of her father's estate ; still, I think I can safely say to you that her gratitude will be in proportion to the amount of the fortune she receives, thanks to your exertions. However, you ought not to set a price on a good action."

François reflected for a moment, and the vile feelings which rent his mercenary soul could be plainly read upon his face. "I should have preferred a stipulated amount," he stammered ; "but I can trust you. I am sure you would not deceive a poor devil like me."

"I have never deceived any one," said M. Hingant, peremptorily.

"That is more than you can say, low cur that you are!" growled Porpoise.

"Well, I will risk it," continued François.

"Then where is the book?" asked M. Hingant, coldly. Dolley's avarice had fairly disgusted him.

"Ah ! I had a deal of trouble in finding it ; and, as for getting it from Galmard—"

"What ! from Galmard? Did he have it?"

"Yes, and he has it still. The old Jew who purchased it at the auction-room only acted in compliance with your old schoolfellow's orders."

"The scoundrel ! "

"Ah ! you may well call him a scoundrel ! He has stolen my hundred thousand francs, to say nothing of the money he got out of that brute, Jacques."

"So he fleeced him, too. That is good !" muttered the old sailor, rubbing his hands.

"But as for the trick he intended to play on you, Monsieur Jean-Marie, and the young lady," continued Dolley, "that won't succeed ; I could not obtain possession of the book, but I managed to read the title."

"And what was it?" the magistrate asked, with nervous impatience.

"The Encyclopedia, volume IX."

"Wait for a moment and let me run to the National Library in the Rue de Richelieu," exclaimed Hingant, springing to his feet, in great excitement.

"It is closed at this hour; besides, you need not take the trouble, for I never do anything by halves when I wish to oblige a friend," said Dolley, almost pompously.

"What do you mean ?" asked the ex-magistrate.

"I mean," replied Dolley, "that I have not been wasting my time since the morning, as you yourself may judge. It was fully ten o'clock when the police released me from my cellar prison ; and, as you will readily understand, it was necessary for me to satisfy them that I was in no way implicated in the shooting affair on the Boulevard Bonne-Nouvelle. By noon, I had learned that my misfortune was complete, for I went to the Rue des Canettes, after calling at the Rue de Cléry, and I ascertained that both the lawyer and his partner had disappeared. Any one else would have hastened home to weep over his fate ; but I thought of a worthy man to whom I could render a great service, and, without losing a moment, I hastened out in pursuit of volume IX. of the Encyclopedia."

"Did you find it?" asked M. Hingant, eagerly.

"It wasn't an easy matter. The public libraries would not consent to lend it to me, so I was obliged to apply at various book shops, which I did."

"You are a good fellow, François," said M. Hingant, in his emotion.

"Well, even at the shops, I met with a great deal of trouble. Some did not have the work ; others asked prices that I was unable to pay. Finally,

I found a bookseller who, on receiving a deposit of one hundred francs—all I had about me—consented to lend me volume IX. until to-morrow."

"Where is it, in Heaven's name?"

"Here," replied the schoolmaster, unbuttoning his overcoat.

Neither Hingant nor Mathurin had noticed the strange corpulence which Dolley had acquired; his captivity seemed to have fattened him. However, his obesity was only fictitious, for it vanished as soon as he had drawn the precious volume IX. from his bosom. By concealing it in this way, between his shirt and his waistcoat, he had contemplated producing a grand effect, and the fact is, his premeditated surprise proved a success. Placid Jean-Marie, suddenly forsaking his accustomed calmness, rushed up to François and snatched the book out of his hands.

"You will not forget your promise," cried Dolley, as the old magistrate hastened with his prize to a table at the further end of the room. As soon as he was installed there, Hingant drew from his pocket-book the paper which the late M. Moulinier had covered with figures, and began to turn over the pages of the encyclopedia with feverish eagerness.

The old seaman, who understood nothing whatever of this scene, watched the movements of his captain's friend with wondering eyes, and began to think that he had lost his senses. Jean-Marie had seized hold of a pen and a blank sheet of paper, upon which he noted down the words as he found them in the book. It is useless to add that he employed the method which his ex-friend Gaimard had indicated to him. The operation was not extraordinary in itself, but the further M. Hingant proceeded with his task the more excited he became. Mathurin saw him throw up his hands and heard him ejaculate strangely over each new discovery. The fact that his face gradually became more and more radiant reassured the old sailor a little; but, after asking himself over and over again what it all meant, he at last began to think that the schoolmaster was trying to play another of his tricks. So he took him by the arm, dragged him near the window, and then whispered grimly in his ear : "Beware, if you are trying to fool us, my boy !"

"I trying to fool you, Monsieur Callec? Such a thing as that is very far indeed from my thoughts," sighed Dolley.

"Well," rejoined Porpoise, "I don't know what's in the book which you have just sold to Monsieur Hingant ; but if it is anything in it that will injure him or the young lady, I warn you that you will only leave this house with your ribs broken."

"I swear to you, Monsieur Callec—"

"Don't swear, but remember Chausey. That night I could have sent you and your scoundrel of a cousin to the bottom of the sea with a single stroke of an oar. It seems that that dirty dog, Jacques, has met with his deserts ; but I am still here to give you yours, if you don't walk straight."

"Good heavens ! do you really hate us so much ?"

"Dare you ask such a question ?"

"I need not, for I see that you do only too well ; but, really, I don't know why."

"Because the captain left you only his curse, because you have stolen his property, because you are all scoundrels."

"The others may be, Monsieur Callec, but I'm not. Ah, I loved my poor dear uncle well," said Dolley hypocritically.

"Restore his property, if you loved him so well—the property he would have left to the town-poor had he imagined you would have claimed it."

"Alas! my good Monsieur Calleo, we are the ones who will soon be paupers. My farms are mortgaged now for more than half their value; Charles is terribly in debt, I know; Mathilde is spending all her money in fine clothes, and won't have a penny by the end of the year. As for Le Planchais' property, we shall derive no benefit from that, for he has signed it all away with blank promissory notes. God knows what Galmard will have done with them."

"Ah! so you have already squandered the property the captain saved for the person we are now looking for," cried old Porpoise, frantic with rage. "And you think you'll get off scot free?"

He was already lifting the same ponderous fist which had well-nigh crushed Dugenêt, and cousin François was in imminent peril, when M. Hingant intervened, exclaiming as he brandished the paper on which he had noted down his translation. "I have found it, my friends; I have found it!"

"Found what?" exclaimed Mathurin, forgetting to strike, so great was his stupefaction.

"The property! the estate! The secret is now in that dear child's hands." And opening the door of the adjoining room, he called: "Marthe, Marthe, come quickly. We are saved!"

Some seconds elapsed before his adopted daughter responded to his call. Dolley turned pale, and Mathurin was still as bewildered as ever. Finally, the orphan appeared upon the threshold. She seemed to be greatly agitated, and it was evident that she had been weeping; but, on perceiving Dolley, she instantly assumed the cold grave expression habitual to her when she found herself in the presence of an enemy. "Did you call me, sir?" she asked, addressing M. Hingant.

"Ah, my child, we are on the track at last. It is a miracle—a true miracle; and it is to our dear François that we owe it," said good Jean-Marie, quite losing his head in his delight.

"I don't know to what miracle you allude, but I expect no favours from that gentleman," said the girl rather scornfully.

"But I expect a handsome reward from you, mademoiselle," Dolley retorted with rare impudence.

"Explain this enigma, if you please," said Mademoiselle Moulinier turning to the old magistrate.

"I ought to have begun by doing so, I confess," said Hingant, "but I was so delighted. Think of it; I have just found your father's will; here, in this big book, is an explanation of the paper written in cipher, which we found in the secret drawer on the day we visited the apartments on the Boulevard Bonne-Nouvelle."

"Is it possible?" muttered Marthe, who had become very pale.

"It's certain. I have just deciphered it myself. Read," said Hingant, handing her the sheet upon which he had just jotted down the words in the order they occurred.

The orphan took the paper with a trembling hand, and her cheeks became still paler as she read the contents. It was only natural that the impression should be one of pain on reading the singular instructions which M. Moulinier had couched in such dry, and almost insulting terms. Jean-Marie became conscious, though not until it was too late, that it would perhaps have been better to spare her this sorrow, and he exclaimed: "The concluding sentences, my dear child; read the concluding sentences aloud."

Marthe hesitated for a moment, and then she began to slowly read the words which had so excited Galmard, when he deciphered them : " · Having said this, I will now pass to a subject which affects you more particularly, and I am willing to point out to you the means of establishing your claim to the very large inheritance to which you may some day become entitled.' "

" The very large inheritance ! " repeated Dolley in ecstasy. " Do you hear that, gentlemen, it is very large ; that is to say, it amounts to one or more millions. I'm sure of it, and it is to me, mademoiselle, that you will owe it ; I sincerely hope you will reward my services as they deserve."

"Silence !" said M. Hingant, severely. "Go on, if you please, Marthe." While the schoolmaster was indulging in this rather premature outburst of enthusiasm, Mademoiselle Moulinier finished her perusal of the passage. " Well," resumed Jean-Marie, " you see that your father says : ' The figures which follow correspond with those in a book with which you are familiar. It is the one I gave your daughter on the day of her first communion.' And now, my child, try to recollect what that book is, and where it is. If it is no longer in your possession all will be lost."

" All, even my reward," muttered Dolley, in consternation.

" The book he refers to," said Mademoiselle Moulinier, " is this prayer-book, which I have kept constantly with me ever since, as it is the only thing I possess which came directly from my father." As she spoke, she drew from her pocket a small and elegantly bound volume.

" Give it to me," cried the old magistrate, eagerly. And, seizing hold of the book, he ran to the table, and resumed his task of deciphering the late Moulinier's hieroglyphics. " Good heavens !" he exclaimed, " I did not notice this. The same number is repeated twenty, yes, fifty times : 219, 219, 219. This has no sense. However, let us look at page 219. It is one of the last in the prayer-book. Ah, this time, we shall have to give it up. Monsieur Moulinier made a mistake. The page contains nothing but Latin." And Hingant returned with a dejected face to show his beloved ward the sad discovery he had just made.

"But you are mistaken," replied Marthe, leaning over the book. "See, the page is number 217, and—this is very strange—the one which follows is page 220."

" Ah ! there are two leaves pasted together," exclaimed Jean-Marie. "Yes ! the paper seems thicker to the touch."

He took a pen-knife, introduced the point into the gilded edge, and with great dexterity divided the two pages which had seemed to be only one. The next moment a cry of exultation escaped him. " Ah, we have the secret now ! "

François Dolley heaved a sigh of relief. He had feared for a moment that all his hopes of remuneration would end in smoke ; but M. Hingant's exclamation told him that the clue was found again.

" I understand now why Monsieur Moulinier fastened these pages together," said the old magistrate. " Here he has abandoned the use of figures, and has written his last wishes in very legible characters. See ! " And he showed Marthe a scrap of very thin paper which had been placed over the print on the aforesaid page of the prayer-book. This paper was entirely covered with close lines of very fine, but perfectly legible hand-writing.

The orphan made a movement to take the book from her protector's hands, but changing her mind she said, in an agitated voice: "Read it, sir; read it aloud."

Jean-Marie did not wait for her to repeat the request, but immediately began to read this paper which in a different manner was to prove of interest to all who chanced to hear it : "'Marie, I think I have taken such precautions as will insure that what I say to you will be known to you alone. I am weary of life, and I hope to die before you do. When I am no more, you will remember the last conversation we had together—on the day your daughter left school—and in the secret drawer of my writing-table you will be able to find the paper, written in cipher, which contains such directions as you will need. I can now, for the first time, perhaps, after thirty-three years of life together, speak to you with open heart. Don't be alarmed. I have no desire to refer to the past; I shall not remind you that I loved you, and that you loved me. I freely pardon all the offences for which I reproached you ; I confess mine and indeed, it is to atone for them that I write this. The time when fatality brought us to-gether, is now long since past ; but I am sure that all the circumstances of the sad story are still fresh in your memory. There is one incident, however, which you were never acquainted with, and which I feel bound to reveal to you before leaving this world. It occurred many years ago ; indeed prior to the birth of your daughter, and even before our marriage. It took place, during the first part of our connection, just when you had left the worthy people who had brought you up, in order to follow me to Paris. We were happy then ; but our happiness was short-lived—so short, indeed, that it now seems to me like a dream. But it is not neces-sary to refer here to what jealousy has caused me to suffer, or to the sus-picions which have poisoned my life, and which still disturb me. I have even less desire to refer to my reverses of fortune. If the unhappy passion which devoured me, if the anxiety which you gave me, led me to neglect my business, and contributed to my ruin, I forgive you, for you have been obliged to endure privations as well as myself, and you have done so cheer-fully and courageously.'"

As Hingant proceeded with his perusal, he regretted more and more having begun aloud. He hesitated, and gave Marthe a furtive glance, for he disliked to wound the young girl's feelings by thus revealing the un-happiness which had marred her parents' domestic life. There had, perhaps, been just grounds for Moulinier's dissatisfaction, and Hingant began to fear that he would mention these grounds more clearly. The orphan, doubtless, perceived her protector's embarrassment, for she said in a firm tone : "I know that my mother was unjustly accused, and I entreat you to continue."

So Hingant resumed his reading with increasing emotion. "Conse-quently, Marie, I will now reveal what I have always concealed from you, but what it is my duty to disclose; for, though I have kept silent while living, I have no right to leave you in ignorance of the truth after my death. One day a man called on me—a man I had never before seen, but of whom I had often heard you speak. He came to tell me that he loved you ; that he knew everything. That he had decided to marry you, and that to win you from me he was ready to stake his life against mine. We fought : I wounded him severely ; and I never saw him again ; but, a few days after the duel, I received a letter, in which my adversary told me that he no longer felt any ill will on the matter, that he had realised it was impossible for you to love him, but that, as he could not tear his affecting for you from his heart, he had bequeathed you his entire fortune, which was immense ! "

"Immense ! Do you hear that ? " Dolley once more repeated, ecstatically.

"I thought, at first, that this man had died of his wound ; but I made inquiries, and learned that he was still alive, and that he had returned to his native province. I was told, subsequently, that he led a very secluded life there ; that he refused to see his relatives, and that he was supposed to have bequeathed his property to other persons than his own nephews. Everything, therefore, seems to indicate that you will be his legatee, and, our circumstances being so reduced, I wish you to be in a position to assert your rights when you become a widow. The man referred to, was Captain Mériadec Léridan, who resides at Cancale, in Brittany. You know him well, for you were to have become his wife when you were still Marie Bréhal."

There was a general exclamation of surprise. Hingant and Mathurin were delighted. Marthe, who had never previously heard of anyone called Mériadec Léridan, and who had not even known that her mother had ever been named Marie Bréhal, looked at them with anxious eyes as if asking for an explanation of the mystery. As for Dolley, he had actually turned green, and trembled like a leaf. Yet he was the first to recover the power of speech. Cupidity sometimes works miracles, and the thought of losing both his inheritance and his expected reward speedily loosened his tongue. "Upon my word ! " he exclaimed, with pretended carelessness, "this is a good joke. The gentleman really makes very free with my uncle's property."

"You are mistaken, François," said M. Hingant, gravely; "nothing could be more serious."

"Bah ! This is a fine story ; but even supposing that Monsieur Moulinier did not invent it, you know as well as I do that the captain left no will."

" Are you quite sure of that ? " asked Jean-Marie, rendered indignant by Dolley's unseemly manner.

" Why ! it seems to me you searched carefully enough in all the drawers when you came to remove the seals. If the old man had scrawled only three lines on a scrap of paper you would certainly have found them."

" I did indeed find them, and I assure you that you and your cousins are absolutely disinherited."

" For the benefit of this—"

" For the benefit of Mademoiselle Marie Bréhal, who by marriage became Madame Moulinier, the mother of the young lady here present."

" Impossible ! You are only trying to frighten me, eh ? It is not kind of you to make fun of a poor fellow like me."

" I have no desire to do so : but I repeat that I discovered your uncle's will, which has never been out of my possession since, and that I have now only to place it in the hands of the judge of the court, at Saint Malo, for Mademoiselle Moulinier's claim to the property to be immediately recognised."

" It isn't true ! " cried François, losing all self-control. " If it had been in your possession, you would have produced it long ago."

" I did not produce it for the reason that I had not succeeded in discovering my friend's legatee. Now that I have found her, or rather her child, nothing shall prevent me from fulfilling my duty."

"It was through me that you did discover her," bellowed Dolley: "and to think that I was fool enough to start out in search of this book, and that, but for me, you would have known nothing whatever about the matter ! This is abominable. It is a trap you have set for me, for if you have told me the truth—"

"I did tell you the truth, for I declared that I was searching for Mademoiselle Moulinier's fortune, and nothing could have been more true," said Jean-Marie.

"No, no," cried the ex-schoolmaster, "it is a piece of treachery, and matters won't end like this."

"Come, come ; shut up, or I'll silence you," said Porpoise, with a threatening gesture.

But Hingant once more interposed, and François, although he had momentarily recoiled in terror, continued his recriminations. "In the first place, the will cannot be valid," said he.

"On the contrary, it is, for it was written, dated, and signed, by the hand of the testator."

"Then, if it exists and is genuine, you had no right to keep it in your pocket, and I shall sue you for damages."

"Oh ! you won't get any," cried Porpoise.

"At all events, everyone in our part shall know that our justice of the peace suppressed a will, and he will be disgraced."

"Hold your tongue, you cur ! cried Mathurin, frantic with rage.

"Calm yourself, Mathurin," said the old magistrate, coolly. "François is right."

"How's that."

"Yes, he is right ; he accuses me of exceeding my powers, and he has a right to do so ; he can with justice reproach me also for having violated a law, which no one should be allowed to disregard. I thought, however, that I was repairing an act of injustice, by concealing this will, and I committed one by retarding the execution of a friend's last wishes. I tried to take the place of Providence, which is punishing me for doing so, and I am ready to accept all the consequences of my error. But François Dolley, personally, has no right to reproach me ; for, if I erred, it was only in placing too much confidence in him. I took an interest in Léridan's relatives, and I hoped that wealth would make them honest and good. It has depraved them, however. God is just, and He is punishing them to-day."

"Preach your sermon in court, you old fool," yelled Dolley, darting towards the door. "For, as truly as I should like to see you all in perdition, I shall sue you, and I shall gain my suit."

Mathurin rushed towards him with his fist raised but the ex-schoolmaster darted from the room with the rapidity of a hunted hare. "Good riddance, you blackguard !" cried Mathurin, as Dolley crossed the threshold and disappeared in the hall outside.

"Let the poor fellow go, and think no more about him," said M. Hingant. "His sin has brought its own punishment, for his avarice has ruined him. Had it not been for him and the mercenary spirit which actuated him, we should never have found the slightest trace of Monsieur Moulinier's will, and François would have continued enjoying a fortune which his uncle did not intend for him. Really, the intervention of Providence may be discerned throughout the whole of this affair."

"Upon my word ! Monsieur Jean-Marie, your setting your hand on the captain's will was a very happy thought indeed. Had it fallen into the clutches of these rascally nephews they would certainly have destroyed it."

"Again, you have chance, or, rather, Providence, to thank. I found the will among the ashes on the hearth while looking for a bit of paper to light my pipe."

"That is the reason, then, why I did not find it in the drawer of the Chinese cabinet. The captain had thrown it into the fire, intending to write another and more complete one, but death surprised him before he had time to do so. I hope this one will stand, however, and that the schoolmaster will lose his suit if he decides to begin one."

" I don't think he will try such an issue, for Marthe's right to the property is too well established to be contested. You are now rich, my child," added M. Hingant, approaching the orphan, who had listened to the conversation without uttering a single word, and without the slightest expression of joy upon her face.

"What do I care for that?" she muttered, shaking her head despondently.

"Ah!" said Jean-Marie, "I know that you attach very little importance to money, my dear Marthe, and I am not at all inclined to blame you; but there are situations in life in which one really ought to desire a competence. You should not forget that this inheritance will insure your happiness and that of Monsieur Paul." The young girl's eyes drooped, but she made no reply. "We will refer to this subject again, presently," continued M. Hingant. "Now we must discuss business matters. I will see that the necessary formalities are carried out to-morrow, and I shall perhaps need your testimony as well as Mathurin's. You, my old friend, can testify that poor Léridan often mentioned his intentions to you, and that he had been a suitor for Marie Bréhal's hand in former years."

"Yes, and I can produce other witnesses, if necessary. There's still at Granville a retired pilot and his wife, who knew both the captain and the mate of the *Goëland*," said Porpoise.

"My dear Marthe," resumed M. Jean-Marie, "the magistrates will, perhaps, ask you how it was that your mother never spoke to you about the conversation to which your father refers—a conversation in which he certainly must have disclosed the place where he had concealed the paper written in cipher."

"My mother knew she was going to die," said Mademoiselle Moulinier, sadly, "and she undoubtedly wished to leave my father free to reveal his secret to me or keep it, as he chose."

"Yes, I understand. It would have been necessary for her to enter into explanations, and refer to the past. But why did your father neglect to warn you, after your mother's death?"

"I don't know, sir. I think, however, that he fully intended to make some provision for me, in case of his death; for, only the evening before that terrible day in June, he told me he should soon have a serious conversation with me, and he gave me to understand that the subjects on which he desired to speak to me were my marriage and dowry."

"And the next day he was murdered by that scoundrel!" exclaimed Jean-Marie. "That explains everything, my child, and we shall not encounter any difficulties in establishing your claim to the property. I shall send to Bréhal for the certificate of Madame Moulinier's birth. I can obtain here a copy of the record of her marriage and death. If I had begun by doing that, we should have been spared a vast amount of trouble ; but who could have suspected that Marie Bréhal and your mother were one and the same person.   Galmard and Billebaude might, perhaps, have made the discovery in following up the search with which they were charged ; but I am glad they did not learn the secret, as they would certainly have tried to take advantage of it."

"I say, Monsieur Jean-Marie," suddenly exclaimed old Porpoise, "does the young lady inherit the property in spite of the fact that her mother is no longer living ?"

" Unquestionably.   What led you to suppose—"

" Excuse me, Monsieur Jean-Marie, I know nothing about law."

" For Madame Moulinier to legally transmit her rights to her daughter, it was only necessary for her to survive Mériadec Léridan by a single day, even an hour.   Now, the poor captain died on the 13th of March, 1848."

"My mother died on the 12th," remarked Marthe.

" The 12th !   Then all is lost !" exclaimed M. Hingant.

" What do you mean by that !" inquired Mathurin, bewildered.

" Madame Moulinier died before Mériadec ; hence the will is null and void," M. Hingant sadly replied.   The old magistrate might just as well have responded in Hebrew.   That dead language would have been no less intelligible to Porpoise than a word borrowed from the civil code.   "That is to say," resumed Jean-Marie, who was anxious to make the matter clear to the old seaman, "that Mademoiselle Moulinier has no right whatever to the captain's estate, since her mother could not transmit to her property which she did not possess."

" That's absurd," said Porpoise with a contemptuous shrug of the shoulders.

" Absurd or not, it is the law ; and no one is exempt from it."

" Then because the poor lady happened to die twenty-four hours too soon, the last wishes of my captain are not to be carried out.   A thousand thunderbolts ! this is certainly a little too strong ! "

" Alas ! it is most unfortunate, but I see no help for it."

" And do you suppose, Monsieur Jean-Marie that I shall let that rascally François, and all the rest of them, remain in possession of property which doesn't belong to them ?"

"I can readily understand that it will be a great trial for you, but we can do nothing.   We can only submit to the will of God, as this young lady has done ; she is giving us an admirable example of resignation."

The praise was deserved, for Marthe had not even frowned on learning that she was condemned to remain poor.   She had seated herself near the table upon which the encyclopedia was still lying, and while M. Hingant was explaining the laws that regulate such cases, she had sunk into what seemed to be a profound reverie.   The old magistrate did not venture to disturb her, but addressed his consoling remarks to Mathurin Callec.   "There is one good thing about it, at all events," he continued, with feigned gaiety, " we must recollect that we shall escape a long and disagreeable lawsuit such as François might bring.   Besides, I must confess that I should have disliked to deprive these poor wretches of a fortune to which by my fault they believed themselves entitled."

" Oh ! what strange scruples, Monsieur Jean-Marie.   Upon my word, one would think that those scoundrelly Normans had bewitched you."

" After all, Mademoiselle Moulinier will lose nothing by it," rejoined the old magistrate : " I have no family, and I am at liberty to dispose of my property as I choose. She shall be my legatee, and in the meantime—"

"There will be no meantime, for she will be rich immediately," interrupted Porpoise.

"What do you mean?"

"I mean that your foolish law will not prevent me from executing the captain's orders."

"What orders?"

"His orders to pay Marie Bréhal the sum of one million francs in gold. Marie Bréhal is dead, but her daughter lives, and that is enough for me."

"A million?—in gold? Why, my poor friend, I believe you are losing your senses."

"You won't think so in a week from to-day," replied Porpoise, peremptorily. "That is the time it will take me to go to Chausey, and bring this young lady a barrel full of Spanish onzas and English guineas which I buried on the Island of Aneret."

"Mériadec's treasure? Good heavens! those reports were true, then?" said M. Hingant in amazement.

"Is it likely I should have gone there so often in the *Goéland* if the captain had not charged me with watching over his gold?"

"I know that such reports were circulated, but I never attached any importance to them."

"Ask that rascal Dolley, who followed me in his cousin's boat on the last night I was in the bay, ask him if he didn't believe them."

"Yes, I recollect now. An accident happened to them."

"Aye, and the fiend took care of his own. But they haven't profited by his help, as Jacques has drunk himself to death, and François is nearly ruined. But I must make haste now to dig up the barrel; I don't want to keep the young lady in suspense."

"But this gold is part of Léridan's estate," muttered honest Jean-Marie.

"I shall have no trouble in proving the contrary, although I haven't studied quibbling. But just look here; doesn't the money in my pocket belong to me?"

"Undoubtedly, but—"

"Well, it is just the same as if I had this gold in my pocket, for I alone know where it is, and the captain told me a hundred times that he depended upon me to deliver it to his heiress—the true one. Search through your code, and see if it says anywhere that I am wrong."

"The code says that, in case of furniture and personal property, possession gives ownership; only—"

"Ah! So the young lady can marry her sweetheart in a fortnight," exclaimed Porpoise, joyfully.

"I shall never marry," said Marthe, looking up.

In this heated discussion on French legislation, Hingant had almost forgotten his ward, but when he heard her make this unexpected announcement, he hastily turned to her, and said: "Why do you say that, my dear child?"

"Because I have decided to enter a convent," replied Marthe.

"What! You cannot seriously contemplate such a thing. I know someone who would be inconsolable if it were true."

"Monsieur Paul Gilbert, you mean I suppose," said Marthe coldly.

" Certainly, I do," was M. Hingant's reply.

" You are mistaken, sir. He would release me from my engagement as readily as I release him," rejoined the girl, somewhat bitterly.

" I do not understand you. Explain yourself, my dear girl, I beg of you."

" Paul is already consoled. Paul has deceived me." In making this avowal the young girl's voice trembled ; and it was with difficulty that she could refrain from bursting into tears.

" Impossible ! " exclaimed M. Hingant, earnestly. " I know Monsieur Gilbert, and I am sure he is incapable—"

" And I am equally sure of what I say. My eyes have seen," retorted Marthe.

" But what has he done ? "

" You wish to know it, you refuse to believe in such baseness. Ah, well, this evening, only two hours ago, I had proofs of his treachery. I saw him walking with a lady—"

" Where ? "

" In the garden of the Luxembourg. She was leaning on his arm and taking to him in a low tone."

" But, my child, there is nothing to prevent this lady from being one of his relatives," urged M. Hingant.

" You know that he has none," replied the girl, bitterly.

" Or, who can tell ? Possibly the wife of one of his comrades."

" One's heart cannot be deceived, and mine feels the wound. Monsieur Gilbert is guilty ; for he saw me, and if he had no cause for self-reproach, he would have come to me and explained everything for he must have known that I was suffering."

Jean-Marie remained silent. All his arguments were exhausted, and he was beginning to believe that the lieutenant might have failed in his obligations to his betrothed, although, in his secret heart, he did not censure the delinquent so severely for this little escapade, as did Mademoiselle Moulinier, for the recollection of his own youth made him charitable in such matters. However, he realized that faults which an old man might readily excuse, would seem unpardonable to an artless and loving girl. So, despairing of persuading Marthe to accept an excuse, at least at that moment, Hingant decided to say no more, trusting to time to calm his ward's anger, and intending to have a serious explanation with the young officer. " I will insist no further," he remarked, with an air of resignation, " though in spite of what you say, my dear child, I still hope and believe that all this is only a misunderstanding. But—and I trust you will pardon my curiosity—by what chance did you happen to be in the Luxembourg grounds at the very time when Monsieur Gilbert was there ? "

The girl hesitated for a moment before replying, but finally she said : " It was not chance that sent me there. I had been warned of what was going to happen."

" Warned, and how ? "

" By a letter."

" Signed by whom ? "

" It was an anonymous letter."

" And it is upon the strength of an anonymous accusation that you condemn Monsieur Paul ! " cried the old ex-magistrate.

" The accusation proved true, and I do not regret my step."

M. Hingant, in his turn, began to reflect before continuing his questions.

Some strange suspicions in regard to the identity of this unknown corres-
pondent had occurred to him. " Well the harm's done ; but how did this
unfortunate meeting end ? Did you speak to Monsieur Gilbert ? "

" Do you imagine that I lowered myself to contend with another woman
for his affection ? " asked Mademoiselle Moulinier, bitterly.

"No, no. Only you might, perhaps, have had an explanation. But I
don't understand what occurred afterwards, or how Charles Dugenêt became mixed up in the affair ? "

" I met him at the entrance of the garden," replied Marthe, "just as I
caught sight of Monsieur Gilbert. It was he who called my attention to
the fact that Paul was not alone."

" That is a strange coincidence. But afterwards ? "

" I left the garden, walking straight on and not knowing where I was
going. Monsieur Dugenêt followed me, and when we reached a deserted
street—"

"The scoundrel ! " exclaimed M. Hingant. " I understand everything
now. It was he who—"

But the old magistrate did not complete the sentence he had on his lips,
for the door abruptly opened, and Paul Gilbert entered the room. He was
very pale ; and an invincible determination gleamed in his eyes. He advanced slowly, looking around him, and started on perceiving Marthe, who,
as he entered, had retired to the further end of the room. " I expected to
find you alone, sir," he said, turning to M. Hingant.

"Mademoiselle Moulinier has just returned—she took refuge here,"
stammered the old ex-magistrate, greatly disconcerted. "As for Mathurin
Callec, whom you see there, he was my friend Léridan's faithful servant.
I think I have spoken of him to you before."

"It is of no consequence," replied the lieutenant, coldly. "What I have
to say to you, sir, will be short, and it will be better for mademoiselle to
hear it."

The young girl stood silent and motionless. but her face wore an expression of haughty, disdainful indifference. " My dear Paul," began M. Hingant, anxious to have the first say. " I can guess what you are going to
tell me, but I know what occurred at the Luxembourg, and I can assure
you—"

" What ! she has dared to confess to you that—"

"Marthe has told me that she had the sorrow of meeting you with a lady
on your arm, and I ventured to declare that you had been guilty of nothing
really wrong."

" Mademoiselle Moulinier neglected to inform you that I detected her in
familiar conversation with a stranger," said the officer, bitterly. " As for
the charge she makes against me, I could easily justify myself, but I scorn
to do so, and I come here only to break the engagement which must now
be as irksome to her as to myself."

" You are right, sir," replied Marthe. " It is irksome, and from this
moment everything is ended between us."

" My child ! Paul ! Think a moment, "cried M. Hingant, in dismay.
"All this is childish—an unfortunate error which can have no serious consequences. Besides, it's my opinion that you have both fallen into a trap
which was intentionally set for you."

" I thank you sincerely, sir, for your excellent intentions, but it is useless
to insist. All the explanations in the world can avail nothing against evi-
dence, and it is not worth while to prolong a painful scene."

"Painful, indeed," murmured M. Hingant, "but allow me to ask a single question. Was your meeting with Mademoiselle Moulinier the result of chance?"

"Why should I tell a falsehood?" exclaimed the lieutenant, not without some embarrassment. "I went to the Luxembourg because I had received a letter which stated that I should see Mademoiselle Moulinier keeping an appointment with a young man in front of the orangery"

"I was sure of it!" exclaimed the old magistrate. "And now, one question more. It will be the last; and I beg of you to believe that it is not impertinent curiosity which prompts it. You were strolling about with a lady—"

"Who forced her company upon me, and from whom I could not escape for the simple reason that you introduced me to her in her own house a few days ago. It was Mademoiselle Pelchat," said the young officer, scornfully.

"Mathilde!" cried M. Hingant. "Ah, now, everything is explained, and I would wager any amount that she called your attention to Mademoiselle Moulinier and her companion."

"In fact, sir, I did not perceive Mademoiselle Moulinier at first, but I was soon sufficiently edified by Mademoiselle Pelchat."

"Did you recognize the person with her?"

"I could not see his face, and he went away with Mademoiselle Moulinier before I had time to approach him and tell him—"

"Ah, well, this man was Charles Dugenêt, the cousin of the shameless creature who undoubtedly concocted this conspiracy. Do you understand now?"

"Scarcely," stammered Paul, "and yet—"

"What! you don't understand that the pair of them planned brewing dissension between you and this dear child—that both anonymous letters came from the same source."

"Both letters! Did Mademoiselle Moulinier also receive one?"

"Here it is," said Marthe, suddenly stepping forward.

Paul Gilbert took the letter she held out, glanced at it, and instantly exclaimed: "It is the same hand-writing!"

He hastily perused the infamous composition which had so nearly condemned them to life-long misery, and then, yielding to the promptings of his heart, fell on his knees at the girl's feet. Marthe's resentment was not proof against this demonstration of repentance. She made her betrothed rise, and worthy M. Hingaut had no difficulty in effecting a speedy and complete reconciliation. The cousin's plot was so crude, that it was only necessary to seize hold of the slightest clue to discern its object. All the manœuvring became apparent as soon as one noted that both anonymous letters were in the same hand-writing; the two appointments could not have been made for the same time and place without the most perfidious intentions. Mathurin Callec eagerly availed himself of this opportunity to call the old magistrate's attention to the depravity of the privateersman's relatives. "Ah, well, Monsieur Jean-Marie," he said, with a meaning wink, "do you consider yourself still bound to protect the interests of those people after such rascality as this?"

"I own that they don't deserve the friendship I have shown them," replied Hingant, sadly, "and, to tell the truth, my last scruples have nearly vanished."

"I never had any scruples at all, for I knew them better than you did; and to-morrow, at the latest, I shall start for Chausey. 1 have still enough money left to buy a boat on the coast and accomplish the business alone."

"You are free my friend, I have no right to interfere, and yet I don't know whether one can conscientiously dispose of poor Léridan's savings in this way."

"Bah! the rascals certainly have no right to complain. They will still retain the land, and that is more than they deserve."

"And what will Dolley say when he sees that I don't produce the will, as I threatened to do?"

"He will think you only intended to frighten him, and that will be the end of it. Don't be alarmed; he won't come to you for any explanation, for he will be only too well pleased that you let him alone."

"Well," said M. Hingant after a pause, "I am not sorry to be spared the necessity of appearing in court, although I should not have hesitated to do so had it been necessary to protect the interests of this dear child. But I hardly like the rather irregular course you have resolved to pursue. What else could you expect? A man cannot be a justice of the peace for thirty years without remaining more or less of one."

"But I assure you, Monsieur Jean-Marie," replied old Porpoise, "that no one could find anything to say against my plan. The million belongs to me, and I have a right to give it to whom I choose, and I choose to give it to the young lady."

"And I refuse it," said the orphan, quietly.

"You refuse it?" exclaimed Mathurin. "Then, do you want to compel me to throw myself into the sea? What would you have me do with the captain's money? Am I fit to be a millionaire?"

"What is the matter?" inquired Paul Gilbert, who, since he and Marthe had become reconciled, thought himself authorised to interfere, and he was not mistaken.

"Ah, my friend," exclaimed M. Hingant, "it means that, by something little short of a miracle, we have at last recovered Marthe's fortune, or rather this worthy man is going to restore it to her. He is the custodian of an immense sum of money, intrusted to him by that poor Léridan, of whom I have sometimes spoken to you, with instructions to pay it over to Madame Moulinier, whom the captain was anxious to marry many years ago."

"And the mother being dead, I pay it to the daughter," added Mathurin.

If the old seaman expected the lieutenant to help him in persuading Marthe to accept the privateersman's legacy, he was greatly mistaken. Paul listened with knitted brows to some brief explanations given by the old magistrate. "I don't know that I fully understand the situation," he said, in a firm voice, "but it seems to me that Marthe does right to refuse."

The girl looked at her betrothed. One could read in her eyes that she was proud of him. "Have you reflected?" whispered M. Hingant to Paul. "Recollect that if Mademoiselle Moulinier deprives herself of this property she will be compelled to renounce her dearest hope. Your marriage becomes an impossibility."

"On the contrary, it will soon be accomplished," said Marthe, who had overheard these words, and she held out her hand to her lover with a smile, "Yes, accomplished, for I accept the dowry you offered me," she continued, turning to her benefactor. "From yon, who have taken the place of my father, I can surely accept a gift. Paul will not tender his resignation. We shall be poor, but we shall be happy."

"And so shall I," echoed M. Hingant, with tears in his eyes.

Old Porpoise listened to these words with bowed head, and when he realised that his million was flatly refused, he sprang up with a despairing gesture, and fled from the house like one demented.

＊　　　＊　　　＊　　　＊　　　＊　　　＊

It will be readily understood that M. Hingant felt no desire to prolong his stay in Paris. He was anxious that the young people's nuptials should be solemnized in the parish church at Cancale, and his wishes were gratified, for the wedding was celebrated late in October, in the presence of a large assemblage of old friends, who were delighted to see the ex-magistrate again, and to learn that he had no intention of again forsaking the province. The young couple also came in for their share of good wishes. Marthe was really lovely to behold beneath her bridal veil, and the young officer's good looks left a lasting impression in the hearts of many a Breton damsel. It is not necessary to add that the privateersman's relatives did not mar the festivities by their presence. François Dolley had paid a short visit to Saint Malo, a few days before, to sell his land, already heavily encumbered by a mortgage for the hundred thousand francs, carried off by Galmard and Billebaude, who had fled no one knew where. François had also come to Brittany in the hope of obtaining a share of his cousin Jacques' estate; but he was too late. The advocate had lost no time in having the notes which he had extorted from drunken Jacques discounted by a banker at Rennes, so that both farms had passed into other hands, and the schoolmaster could only return to Paris, where he probably intended trying his fortune anew.

Neither Charles or Mathilde felt any desire to attend the wedding of Paul and Marthe. They were too busy amusing themselves in Paris, and too much vexed by the failure of their machinations. They continued leading the same life on the banks of the Seine, mortgaging their property so as to defray their expenses. No one in Brittany regretted them, M. Hingant least of all, for he had now learned to know them as they really were. On the other hand, he and the bridal pair were greatly grieved by Mathurin Callec's absence. After that final explanation, which had led to the marriage being decided upon, Porpoise had disappeared again, and all efforts to find him had proved unavailing. All that could be ascertained was that he had left Paris without stating his destination, so that his presence had to be dispensed with at the nuptial ceremony. M. Jean-Marie had all the more trouble in consoling himself for this sudden departure, as the conduct of Mériadec's nephews had made him mistrustful, and he began to suspect Mathurin of having turned the captain's million to his own use. He suffered in silence, however, and religiously kept the secret of the treasure concealed on the isle of Aneret.

Eleven years passed by, eleven years of happiness for M. and Madame Gilbert and their old friend Hingant, whom they visited as often as garrison life allowed. Paul had become a captain in Kabylia, a major in the Crimea, and a lieutenant-colonel on the battlefield of Solferino. One day a few months after the Italian campaign, Colonel Gilbert and his wife, then sojourning at Cancale, received a letter from a Concarneau notary, who was quite unknown to them. This letter contained a copy of a will couched in the following terms : " I, Mathurin Callec, shipowner, engaged in the sardine fisheries, being of sound mind, and wishing to repay a debt of gratitude, bequeath my entire property to Mademoiselle Marthe Moulinier, now the lawful wife of Monsieur Paul Gilbert, an officer in the French army."

The sensation caused by this unexpected legacy may be readily imagined. M. Hingant was naturally consulted, and by his advice Marthe accepted the bequest. It had been written that Mériadec Léridan's gold should revert one day to her, and this was only right. However, in lieu of there being one million there were two, for Porpoise had turned the Chausey treasure to profit, and the ex-boatswain of the *Goëland* had died one of the wealthiest shippers in the department of Finistère.

Paul Gilbert, as a general of division, reaped glory during the German invasion of France, and there is nothing wanting to complete his happiness, for Marthe has given him two sons, who went through the campaign of 1870 under his orders. The destiny of the privateersman's heirs has been less brilliant. They long since finished spending their inheritance. Dolley has become a scrivener, Dugenêt is a commercial traveller, and Mademoiselle Pelchat is a suttler woman in the army. As for worthy Jean-Marie, he died full of years, and tenderly loved by his adopted children. His last words were : " God has his plans ; never try to substitute yours for His."

THE END.

VIZETELLY'S ONE-VOLUME NOVELS.

By English and Foreign Authors of Repute.

"The idea of publishing one-volume novels is a good one, and we wish the series every success."—*Saturday Review*.

CRIME AND PUNISHMENT
BY FEDOR DOSTOIEFFSKY.
Pronounced by the *Athenæum* to be "the most moving of all modern novels."

THE TRIALS OF JETTA MALAUBRET (Noirs et Rouges).
By VICTOR CHERBULIEZ, of the French Academy.
Translated by the Countess GASTON DE LA ROCHEFOUCAULD.

ROLAND; or, The Expiation of a Sin.
By ARY ECILAW.
" A novel entitled 'Roland' is creating an immense sensation in Paris. The first, second, and third editions were swept away in as many days. The work is charmingly written."—*The World*.

PRINCE ZILAH.
By JULES CLARETIE.
"M. Jules Claretie has of late taken a conspicuous place as a novelist."—*Times*.

THE IRONMASTER; or, Love and Pride.
By GEORGES OHNET. From the 146th French Edition. Sixth Edition.

A MUMMER'S WIFE.
By GEORGE MOORE. Author of "A Modern Lover." Sixth Edition.

MR. BUTLER'S WARD.
By F. MABEL ROBINSON. Third Edition.

NUMA ROUMESTAN; or, Joy Abroad and Grief at Home.
By ALPHONSE DAUDET. Third Edition.

COUNTESS SARAH.
By GEORGES OHNET. Author of "The Ironmaster." From the 110th French Edition

THE CORSARS; or, Love and Lucre.
By JOHN HILL, Author of "The Waters of Marah." Second Edition.

THE THREATENING EYE.
By E. F. KNIGHT. Author of "The Cruise of the Falcon."

BETWEEN MIDNIGHT AND DAWN.
By INA L. CASSILIS. Author of "Society's Queen.'

PRINCE SERGE PANINE.
By GEORGES OHNET. Author of "The Ironmaster." From the 110th French Edition

THE FORKED TONGUE.
By R. LANGSTAFF DE HAVILLAND, M.A. Author of " Enslaved."

A MODERN LOVER.
By GEORGE MOORE. Author of "A Mummer's Wife." Second Edition.

In double volumes, bound in scarlet cloth, price 2s. 6d. each.

NEW EDITIONS OF THE

GABORIAU AND DU BOISGOBEY
SENSATIONAL NOVELS.

NOW READY

1.—THE MYSTERY OF ORCIVAL, AND THE GILDED CLIQUE.
2.—THE LEROUGE CASE, AND OTHER PEOPLE'S MONEY.
3.—LECOQ, THE DETECTIVE.   4.—THE SLAVES OF PARIS.
5.—IN PERIL OF HIS LIFE, AND INTRIGUES OF A POISONER.
6.—DOSSIER NO. 113, AND THE LITTLE OLD MAN OF BATI-
GNOLLES.   7.—THE COUNT'S MILLIONS.
8.—THE OLD AGE OF LECOQ, THE DETECTIVE.
9.—THE CATASTROPHE.   10.—THE DAY OF RECKONING.
11.—THE SEVERED HAND, AND IN THE SERPENTS' COILS.
12.—BERTHA'S SECRET, AND WHO DIED LAST?
13.—THE CRIME OF THE OPERA HOUSE.
14.—THE MATAPAN AFFAIR, AND A FIGHT FOR A FORTUNE.
15.—THE GOLDEN PIG, OR THE IDOL OF MODERN PARIS.
16.—THE THUMB STROKE, AND THE NAMELESS MAN.
17.—THE CORAL PIN.   18.—HIS GREAT REVENGE.

In small post 8vo, ornamental covers, 1s. each ; in cloth, 1s. 6d.

VIZETELLY'S POPULAR FRENCH NOVELS.

TRANSLATIONS OF THE BEST EXAMPLES OF RECENT FRENCH
FICTION OF AN UNOBJECTIONABLE CHARACTER.

"*They are books that may be safely left lying about where the ladies of the family can pick them up and read them. The interest they create is happily not of the vicious sort at all.*"
SHEFFIELD INDEPENDENT.

FROMONT THE YOUNGER & RISLER THE ELDER. By A. DAUDET.

"The series starts well with M. Alphonse Daudet's masterpiece."—*Athenæum.*
"A terrible story, powerful after a sledge-hammer fashion in some parts, and wonderfully tender, touching, and pathetic in others, the extraordinary popularity whereof
may be inferred from the fact that this English version is said to be ' translated from the
fiftieth French edition.'"—*Illustrated London News.*

SAMUEL BROHL AND PARTNER. By V CHERBULIEZ.

"Those who have read this singular story in the original need not be reminded of that
supremely dramatic study of the man who lived two lives at once, even within himself.
The reader's discovery of his double nature is one of the most cleverly managed of surprises, and Samuel Brohl's final dissolution of partnership with himself is a remarkable
stroke of almost pathetic comedy."—*The Graphic.*

THE DRAMA OF THE RUE DE LA PAIX. By A. BELOT.

"A highly ingenious plot is developed in 'The Drama of the Rue de la Paix,' in
which a decidedly interesting and thrilling narrative is told with great force and
passion, relieved by sprightliness and tenderness."—*Illustrated London News.*

MAUGARS JUNIOR. By A. THEURIET.

"One of the most charming novelettes we have read for a long time."—*Literary World.*

WAYWARD DOSIA, & THE GENEROUS DIPLOMATIST.
By HENRY GRÉVILLE.

"As epigrammatic as anything Lord Beaconsfield has ever written."—*Hampshire Telegraph.*

A NEW LEASE OF LIFE, & SAVING A DAUGHTER'S DOWRY. By E. ABOUT.

"'A New Lease of Life' is an absorbing story, the interest of which is kept up to the very end."—*Dublin Evening Mail.*
"The story, as a flight of brilliant and eccentric imagination, is unequalled in its peculiar way."—*The Graphic.*

COLOMBA, & CARMEN. By P. MÉRIMÉE.

"The freshness and raciness of 'Colomba is quite cheering after the stereotyped three-volume novels with which our circulating libraries are crammed."—*Halifax Times.*
"'Carmen' will be welcomed by the lovers of the sprightly and tuneful opera the heroine of which Minnie Hauk made so popular. It is a bright and vivacious story."—*Life.*

A WOMAN'S DIARY, & THE LITTLE COUNTESS. By O. FEUILLET.

"Is wrought out with masterly skill and affords reading, which although of a slightly sensational kind, cannot be said to be hurtful either mentally or morally."—*Dumbarton Herald.*

BLUE-EYED META HOLDENIS, & A STROKE OF DIPLO-MACY. By V. CHERBULIEZ.

"'Blue-eyed Meta Holdenis' is a delightful tale."—*Civil Service Gazette.*
"'A Stroke of Diplomacy' is a bright vivacious story pleasantly told."—*Hampshire Advertiser.*

THE GODSON OF A MARQUIS. By A. THEURIET.

"The rustic personages, the rural scenery and life in the forest country of Argonne, are painted with the hand of a master. From the beginning to the close the interest of the story never flags."—*Life.*

THE TOWER OF PERCEMONT & MARIANNE. By GEORGE SAND.

"George Sand has a great name, and the 'Tower of Percemont' is not unworthy of it."—*Illustrated London News.*

THE LOW-BORN LOVER'S REVENGE. By V. CHERBULIEZ.

"'The Low-born Lover's Revenge' is one of M. Cherbuliez's many exquisitely written productions. The studies of human nature under various influences, especially in the cases of the unhappy heroine and her low-born lover, are wonderfully effective."—*Illustrated London News.*

THE NOTARY'S NOSE, AND OTHER AMUSING STORIES. By E. ABOUT.

"Crisp and bright, full of movement and interest."—*Brighton Herald.*

DOCTOR CLAUDE; OR, LOVE RENDERED DESPERATE. By H. MALOT. Two vols.

"We have to appeal to our very first flight of novelists to find anything so artistic in English romance as these books."—*Dublin Evening Mail.*

THE THREE RED KNIGHTS; OR, THE BROTHERS' VENGEANCE. By P. FÉVAL.

"The one thing that strikes us in these stories is the marvellous dramatic skill of the writers."—*Sheffield Independent.*

www.ingramcontent.com/pod-product-compliance
Lightning Source LLC
Chambersburg PA
CBHW030544040726
47497CB00008B/2576